In a Heartbeat

"Contemporary romance with an intriguing twist. A pleasure for fans of romantic suspense."
—*New York Times* bestselling author Deborah Smith

"IN A HEARTBEAT augments [Wainscott's] growing reputation for some of the finest off-beat tales on the market today . . . Anyone who wants to read a believable enactment of the unbelievable needs to peruse a Wainscott novel because she makes the impossible possible."
—Harriet Klausner, *Painted Rock Reviews*

"Tina Wainscott has her finger firmly on the pulse of the romance genre, and with IN A HEARTBEAT she catapults to the top of her peers. . . . A unique plot complements characters of depth and perception that fold in and around a story as fresh and exhilarating as a spring breeze. Run, don't walk, to the nearest bookstore to buy this novel, which could possibly be the best contemporary of the year."
—Kathee S. Card, *Under the Covers Book Reviews*

Second Time Around

"Ms. Wainscott has a talent for making unusual situations believable . . . Bravo!"
—*Rendezvous*

"A fabulous romantic suspense drama that melts readers' hearts. . . SECOND TIME AROUND is worth reading the first time around, the second time around, and the nth time around."
—*Affaire de Coeur*

"Make plans to add it to your library!"
—*Old Book Barn Gazette*

"This highly satisfying paranormal romance is a must read . . . SECOND TIME AROUND is a well-written, romantic, feel-good story."
—*Gothic Journal*

Back in Baby's Arms

Tina Wainscott

St. Martin's Paperbacks

BACK IN BABY'S ARMS

ISBN: 0-312-97688-7

Printed in the United States of America

St. Martin's Paperbacks edition / January 2001

St. Martin's Paperbacks are published by St. Martin's Press, 175 Fifth Avenue, New York, N.Y. 10010.

10 9 8 7 6 5 4 3 2 1

⟨⟩ ACKNOWLEDGMENTS

MY SINCEREST APPRECIATION to Pattie Steele-Perkins for her help with all matters sailing. And thank you for many years of friendship and guidance. May your journey always be smooth sailing.

Jackie Bielowicz who has given me much medical input over these past few years and who has been an invaluable help.

My appreciation to the following people who took time out of their busy lives to help someone they didn't even know:

Vincent Checa for sharing *Shakila,* his wonderful sense of humor, and all his funny sailing stories.

Mary Anne Frounfelker for her help on childhood illnesses, and the folks on the NINC Link for all their input.

Joe, a good cop who didn't arrest me for playing loose and fast with the law (fictionally speaking, of course). His information on police matters was greatly helpful.

Johnie Greenwell for Coast Guard protocol.

(However, I claim responsibility for any errors found herein.)

I also want to thank all the people who help get my books into the hands of readers, from my editor and her assistant, to my publicists, sales reps and book binders, the distributors and booksellers. And finally, thank you to my readers, whose letters I cherish and enthusiasm I treasure.

CHAPTER I

"THIS BABY IS going to kick some serious butt." Wayne Schaeffer scrambled from the engine to the cockpit of the sleek red boat with the fancy name Maddie had forgotten.

"I thought I was your baby." She kicked one of the pilings, then winced at both the pain in her big toe and the whine in her voice.

He gave her the smile that had captured her heart in high school and hadn't let go, even after six years of marriage. "You're *the* Baby. This is a generic 'baby.' Come for a test-drive with me. The guy I bought it from says it roars like a lion."

She cursed her fine, shoulder-length hair that whipped into her face for the gazillionth time. It didn't have the decency to be blond or brown, so it hovered somewhere between.

She said, "Too choppy out there today."

Wayne's thick, black hair danced in the warm breeze blowing off Sugar Bay. The Sugar Bay Marina hugged the curve of the half-moon bay. Three rows of docks snaked out into the cove where a maze of sandbars and oyster beds lurked. Her uncle Barnie said someday those dangers would chew up a boat and its passengers, that it was just a matter of time.

Wayne made another adjustment. "How could I have married a girl who gets seasick?"

"I don't get seasick, just queasy."

"I keep telling you, that *is* seasickness."

She didn't much like going fast either, but she kept that to herself. It was Wayne who loved careening through the black night on the Gulf of Mexico, hugging her against his chest as she squeezed her eyes shut.

"Should I go faster?" he'd ask. She wanted to say no, but always said yes because she didn't want to be a fuddy-duddy.

What *she* enjoyed was taking out the dinghy—the *Dinky* Wayne called it—and skirting the little islands looking for shells and driftwood. She also knew it bored him to death, going slow and leisurely. She did not want to bore Wayne.

He came from money, if there was such a thing in Sugar Bay. The real distinction was whether you lived on the water, had a pool, and owned the place you worked at. Back in the thirties, Wayne's family bought up acres of land on the water and built the marina that had recently been bequeathed to Wayne. The Schaeffers envisioned Sugar Bay as a resort town for the northern coast of Florida.

Unfortunately, they forgot one tiny requirement for resort towns: beaches. Oh, they'd tried to bring in the beach. They'd dredged and pumped and trucked it in and dumped it onto the rocks. Mother Nature laughed in their faces and washed it all away.

The sudden roar of the boat's engine made Maddie jump. The green piling she brushed against sent a sliver of wood into her thumb. Wayne cut the engine and hopped onto the dock.

"What's a'matter, Baby?"

"Splinter," she muttered, thumb jammed against her teeth as she tried to extract it.

"Here, let me see." He squeezed it out and kissed the pad of her thumb. "Okay?"

She nodded. Everything was okay since Wayne had rescued her from terminal wallflowerdom all those years ago.

The rest of the boys in town saw her as the scrawny girl who was sick through most of her school years. Besides all of them picking up her family's nickname for her, "Baby," the boys said those dreaded words whenever she even thought about kissing them: *You're just like a sister to me.*

Well, heck, she could have told them having a sister wasn't all it was cracked up to be. But she didn't, because she was quiet, nice Maddie Danbury who didn't cause any trouble, no how, no way.

Then Wayne's dad, God bless him, had moved back to Sugar Bay. He took over the old marina and turned it into something new and full of life. And Wayne walked into her English class and did the same for her.

"You gonna come for a ride, or what?"

"Well . . ."

"Come on, you never say no to the one who loves you. Besides, this is your place, too. It's your duty to get a feel for the boats we sell." He kissed her on the forehead, and before she could even kiss him back, hopped onto the boat. "Selling used speedboats is much more exciting than just taking care of other people's boats. There isn't anything sexier than a Scarab. This baby'll go so fast, you'll pee your pants."

Her face lit up. "Ooh yeah, that convinces me." A twinge lit her stomach when she felt herself giving in like she always did. "Not today, okay, Wayne? Besides, it's my day to walk the dogs at the society."

"You'd put dogs before your own husband?"

She wrapped her arms over her stomach and nodded.

"Really?"

"Those dogs are homeless and you're not, so today I would."

"All right, I won't twist your arm. Maybe we'll take the *Dinky* out tonight and catch the sunset."

She didn't miss his disappointment and tried to make up

for it with her enthusiasm. "Kewl! I'll grab some subs and a six-pack from Homer's. Did you fix the gas gauge yet?"

"Nah. Got to be some excitement on that thing, never knowing if we'll be stranded out there." She must have let her apprehension show, because he said, "You know I wouldn't let anything happen to you, don't you?"

She smiled. "Nobody takes care of me like you do."

" 'Sides, it'd be romantic, alone on the *Dinky* at night, no one knowing where we are."

He did look right at home on that snazzy boat, moving deftly around, yet taking a moment to touch the fiberglass curves like it was some woman. A sexy woman. Wayne didn't even like sexy women. If he did, he sure wouldn't have married her skinny, flat-chested self. When he started that blasted motor again, she stopped breathing for a minute. The hari-kari look flickered in his blue eyes. That fire made her heart beat faster and sent a trill of fear through her. He got the look when he was skirting the edges of oyster beds or sending a boat into full throttle.

The engine churned the green water as he maneuvered out of the navigational challenge of Sugar Bay. No one had removed the pilings from the original marina. They had disintegrated into spiky talons over the years. Wayne thought they added atmosphere and had dredged the pass to go right by them. As long as boaters made the passage warily, they'd be fine.

But Wayne was showing off. She couldn't complain too much, since he was showing off for her. He'd threaded through the maze a gazillion times, even on moonless nights with a couple of beers in his belly.

He gunned the engine as soon as he cleared the docks and the one boat coming in. She knew exactly what he was going to do: head straight for the warning sign on the mound of oysters, then feint to the right at the last possible second. She leaned against the piling, mindful of splinters and powdery white pelican poop. Yep, he was going to give her a scare.

A seagull squawked from above. Wavelets sloshed around the pilings and sent a tiny brown crab scurrying out of the water's reach.

Wayne glanced back at her and grinned. She smiled back because he expected it.

"Someday that boy's gonna get himself hurt fooling round like that," Barnie said from his docked sailboat, just like he always said when he saw Wayne pulling his stunts. Barnie was her dad's uncle, her great-uncle, but she just called him Barnie.

"Not Wayne."

Wayne tugged on the wheel, but the boat wasn't turning to the right.

She forced a laugh, but it sounded brittle. "Always fooling, isn't he?"

He wasn't fooling. His motions turned frantic as he jerked the wheel. She wanted to yell, "Jump!" but she couldn't even breathe. Time slowed to a halt as she stood helpless on the dock, hoping it was a joke after all, hoping the boat wasn't actually going to hit the piling.

The boat hit with a deafening thud that shuddered through her entire body and loosened the hold of shock and fear that paralyzed her. Wayne was thrown free, and his arms and legs pummeled the air. His scream rivaled the warped sound of the boat's engine as it rocked sideways and hit the oyster beds.

Signs didn't have to warn what the eye could see: jagged edges clawing out of the green depths. Wayne sailed through the air, hit a sign, and dropped into the water.

She started to run, but stumbled. Her rubbery legs weren't cooperating.

"Calling for help," Barnie yelled and took off in the other direction.

She never took her eyes off the place where Wayne had disappeared.

The two men on the nearby boat turned around. Maddie reached the corner and ran down the narrow dock. Someone's senseless wails penetrated her brain. Who was screaming like that? she wondered, then realized the screams were coming from her.

The men reached Wayne first. She heard them say, "Oh, my God," and "Let's get him out of there," but she refused to hear the resignation in their voices. Wayne was all right. He'd be bruised, sure, maybe even break a bone.

The two men lifted him gingerly out of the water. They wouldn't have done that if there was no hope, so he must be all right, and the blood, just superficial cuts, that was all.

She climbed to the stern of one of the docked boats, then tumbled into the water. "I'm his wife, I'm his wife," she heard herself say as they helped her aboard.

"It don't look good. Let's get him to the dock," one of the men said.

Wayne was curled in on himself. One arm was pressed over his stomach where the torn fabric of his shirt was soaked in blood. *Superficial, just a scratch.* The tiny cuts on his face wouldn't even scar probably.

She knelt beside him. "Wayne, you're going to be all right, you hear me. Help's on the way."

She bent to kiss him, but the kiss was warm and sticky. A trickle of blood seeped from the corner of his mouth.

"I'm sorry, Baby." He sounded like he was gargling.

"You have nothing to be sorry about. You're going to be fine," she said firmly, in case anyone dared doubt her.

He swallowed, then winced. "I don't . . . think so, Baby."

She stared into his eyes, willing him to believe her words. "You're fine."

His eyes were glassy and filled with tears. "I'm sorry . . ." He coughed, and more blood trickled out. She quickly wiped it away. He'd probably bitten his tongue.

"You promised you wouldn't break my heart." Her voice was a stretched whisper. "You *promised*."

"I know . . ."

He took a wheezy breath. More coughing, more blood. She wiped it away again.

"I won't break your heart. I'll . . ." He squeezed his eyes shut and swallowed like he had a sore throat. When he opened his eyes, he was looking beyond her. His expression changed from pained to peaceful. "An angel."

"What?"

"Look, Baby."

She didn't want to take her eyes off him, but she looked anyway. Through the waves of her tears, she saw two rainbows. She blinked to clear her eyes, but there were still two of them, one above the other. That had to be a good sign, a sign of hope.

"I'll send you an angel, okay?" he said. "To heal your broken heart."

She looked back at Wayne and was startled by the gray pallor of his face. "My heart's not broken, because you are not dying. Do you hear me?"

He closed his eyes again. "Baby, are you going to listen to me, or what?"

"Or what. Look, we're docking, and I hear the ambulance coming. Don't move—"

He reached out with a shaking hand and took hers. "I love you, Baby. I always will."

"I love you, too," she said on a choked breath.

But he was already gone.

Whenever you feel alone,
look for the end of the rainbow, and I'll be there.

CHAPTER 2

MADDIE MADE THE morning transfer from her bedroom to the couch. She couldn't muster enough energy to change, so she stayed in her oversized pajamas. She snuggled into the faded comforter with the pink flowers and stared at the television while the morning routine went on around her. It was comforting, that routine, even if she wasn't part of it. Dad came in wearing his blue uniform with the grease smudges on it even though Mom had washed it a gazillion times. He said he didn't mind the stains; he was an auto mechanic and proud of it. Even if he did work for the Schaeffers.

Everything about being back home was comforting. Nothing had changed since she was a kid, except that Mom had turned PTA bake sales into something of a career. By six in the morning she'd already baked and delivered her goodies.

And just like when Maddie was a kid, Mom's clowns watched her. They didn't jibe with the country charm décor (farmhouse clutter, Dad called it), but Mom didn't care. Clowns were nestled between cow and pig figurines, were sitting on top of the pinecones in a bucket, and were tucked into nearly every basket in sight.

Maddie didn't mind the rustic furniture or the cast-iron

duck she stubbed her toe on regularly. But she hated clowns.

Her sister Colleen walked in the front door, looked at her, and rolled her eyes. Just like she had every single morning for the last few months. She was born mean-looking and hadn't changed much since then. "Wow, big surprise: Baby's sitting on the couch, still wearing her PJs, and dirty hair to boot."

Through the magic of maternal instinct, Mom sailed into the room with the brush and planted herself beside Maddie. "Just like when you were a little girl," she said, running the brush through Maddie's hair. Mom's strawberry curls billowed around her hairband. "You were too sick to do it yourself sometimes, but you loved having your hair brushed."

"Oh, gawd, she's not a little girl anymore," Colleen said. "She outgrew the asthma when she was fourteen."

Mom pushed her big glasses down her nose. "She has gone through hell in a hand basket, and don't you forget it."

"How could I? She's never going to get over it if ya'll keep babying her—"

Mom shoved her glasses back up to the bridge of her nose. "Colleen Anne Danbury Sewell, I swear you don't have a heart at all. What if your Bobby left suddenly? Wouldn't you want your family to rally around you, try to ease your pain? That's all we're doing, and"—this was where Mom's voice got shrill from impending tears—"if you can't understand that's what family is all about, I . . . I have failed as a mother."

Colleen opened her mouth to say something, but let out a sigh instead. "You didn't fail, Mom. It's just that Baby's been getting this kind of attention since the day she was born, and I don't think you're helping by doing every little thing for her."

"I am helping, by giving her time to heal without having to sweat the details. She can stay here as long as she likes, forever even. And you can't blame your sister for being born with asthma. We almost lost her three times."

"I know, I know," Colleen said.

"You almost didn't have a little sister."

"I know."

Mom's shrill voice returned. "It was only by the goodness and mercy of the Lord God that she lived to be here today."

Maddie always faded off whenever they started talking about her as though she weren't there. She stared through the picture window to the pink house across the street. That was where Colleen lived with her husband and her son, who was standing by the mailbox waiting for the bus.

Maddie had moved farther away when she had gotten married. Wayne's grandparents had given them a little cottage on the Gulf, and Wayne had added a pool. But living there alone . . . heck, living alone period was beyond comprehension. Her family and friends had closed up the house and moved Maddie back home. She hadn't been back since, not there or to the marina. It hurt too much.

It hurt that life went on. After Wayne died, the sun came up bright and clear, people went to work, and the marina kept operating. Maddie's life screeched to a halt, but everyone else kept on living. It hurt to see her family look at her the way they used to when she was sick. This time she wasn't sure she could get better, and she felt like she was letting them down. It even hurt when her dad kissed her on the forehead every morning and said, "Bye, pumpkin. You try and have a good day, hear?," like he really wanted her to, but knew she couldn't.

Mom grabbed Maddie's chin and asked, "You okay, Sugar Baby?"

Maddie had heard this question all through her growing-up years. For every cough, every sniffle. During the last year she always answered, "Okay," but couldn't help the one-shouldered shrug that said, *Not okay*.

"My poor Baby, you just let your mom make it all right." When the kitchen timer went off, she asked, "Would you like a banana pecan muffin?"

"No, thanks," Maddie answered as Mom went into the kitchen to bring one anyway. Maddie would pick at it until it kind of looked like she'd eaten some of it.

Mom sailed out of the kitchen bearing the muffin and a mug of coffee for Colleen. "Chocolate raspberry this week," she said to Colleen before heading back to the kitchen.

Mom changed the flavor of coffee every week to add excitement to the old routine. Dad complained every morning, but she swore he'd come to like it. She'd been doing it for three years. Maddie happened to know that he dumped out his coffee in the front yard (which was why the gardenias were all brown out by the clown mailbox).

Colleen kept running her fingers through her hair as she stared out the window. She had the hair Maddie didn't, loads of it that fell just past her shoulders. It was, however, the same drab shade of blond Maddie had. Colleen denied to the moon that she highlighted it, but they all knew she did. It was all Maddie could do to muster the energy to wash her hair, which she just had, thank you very much, Colleen. She just hadn't brushed it since her shower last night.

Colleen took after Mom, with slanted eyes and a sharp nose. Maddie wasn't sure who she'd taken after. She got her square face from Dad, but her small frame? The doctor had once told them asthma could postpone the onset of puberty; he'd never mentioned that puberty might never catch up.

Colleen was still looking out the window.

"Bobby go to work early again?" Maddie asked.

"Yep. Hardworking man, he is." There wasn't any real pride in those words. "He's been going in at six for the last few months. Then he gets off early and goes out to the workshop and makes furniture till late."

"He still talking about quitting Schaeffer Cabinets and starting his own business?"

"He wants to. I told him our finances are just the way we want, down to the dime. In three more years we might be able to afford the down payment on a pool, unless I win the Publisher's Sweepstakes this year." She opened the front door. "Have a good day at school, Quigley!"

He waved, rather sullenly Maddie thought, and got on the bus as though his feet weighed ten pounds apiece.

"He wants to be called 'Q,' " Maddie said after Colleen closed the door.

"What?"

When the bus dropped Quigley off, he came over and baby-sat Maddie, though it was portrayed the other way around. "He wants to be called 'Q.' He says it's cooler. And the kids are starting to tease him, calling him Quiggles and Quig Pig."

"That's ridiculous. Six-year-olds aren't cool."

Just like when they were kids, Colleen gave her the vulture look: her hair pulled back, shoulders hunched and face thrust forward. "Playing Nintendo with him for a few hours a day doesn't qualify you to tell me how to raise my son."

Maddie crossed her arms over her chest. "We do more than play Nintendo. We play Scrabble sometimes, too."

"Don't put thoughts in Quigley's head, all right? It's just a phase. And unlike you, he'll get over it. Unlike you, he's not waiting for some stupid angel to fix his problems."

That again. Every day Colleen managed to bring it up with some dig. Maddie pulled the comforter up to her chin. Colleen didn't know anything about getting over things.

She'd never lost one of the most important people in her life. And she'd never had to wait day after day for a promise to be fulfilled.

"Someday I'd like to sit you down and tell you what you look like, moping like a rag doll," Colleen said. "But you'd go running to Mom."

As Colleen headed to the door, Maddie said, "Q hates the trolls at your house, too."

Colleen's shoulders stiffened. "What?"

"They creep him out."

The quaint exterior of Colleen's house belied a cavelike interior filled with trolls. She had Bobby build a wall unit that looked like a tree, with little caves and even a working waterfall. Their furniture was made of lacquered cypress, the walls were covered in dark paneling, and the sculptured carpet was moss green.

Colleen narrowed her eyes. "My home is the only place where I don't have to defer to your wishes. All my life it was no, you can't have a dog, or you can't do this or that, because it'll make Baby sick, or give in just this once because Baby had a rough night. Between Mom and a husband who spoiled you rotten, no one has ever let you grow up. I'm sorry he died, Baby, I really am. I'm sorry he left, I mean," she added, because no one was supposed to say the D-word around Maddie. "But just because you're miserable doesn't mean everyone else is miserable, too. Just once I'd like to see some evidence that you're growing up and moving on with your life."

Colleen waited for a response. Maddie could have come up with some biting reply if she'd had the motivation. Instead she stuck out her tongue.

Mom had turned her big, square kitchen into a bit of country heaven over the years. The floor was covered in a flat, flowery carpet. Dad had scavenged the heavy oak table at a barn sale in Georgia. Bobby had built two open cabinets that were now crammed with plates and pitchers and hanging teacups and all the things that reminded Mom of the farmhouse she'd grown up in.

Ever since Bobby started working late, Colleen and Q ate dinner with the rest of the Danburys. Q's mouth was in a pout and his blue eyes were downcast as he picked through his mashed tators for the lumps. Lumps were his favorite. His curls were the color of the copper gelatin molds on the brick wall behind him. His skin was pale as cream except for the spray of copper freckles, just like his daddy.

"How come Dad don't eat with us no more?" Q asked.

"He's working hard so we can have a pool someday."

Q traded a look with Maddie, then went back to spearing lumps. She noticed the flush on her sister's face. Something wasn't right. She wasn't meeting anyone's eyes. *Is everything all right?* The words hung in Maddie's throat. Of course it was. At least Colleen had a husband to spoon with at night.

Maddie picked at her drumstick, but her appetite disintegrated when she took in the two empty chairs in the dining area. Bobby's at the table . . . and Wayne's, which had been set by the phone, like she wasn't supposed to notice. If he were there, he'd be tipping his chair way back and making Mom nervous. He'd be telling some joke he'd heard and laughing harder than anyone else at the punch line.

"Oh, Maddie," Colleen said in a taunting voice. "Ran into Wendy today. Darcy told her about a guy who came to town in response to Barnie's ad. Darcy checked him out, of course. He's in his late twenties maybe, dark hair. He's going to be working on that sailboat Barnie started before hurting himself."

"He crushed his nuts," Q said. "*Nuts* isn't a bad word," he added at Colleen's lifted eyebrow.

"I swear he's proud of it. Anyway, the guy doesn't even have enough money to stay at Marylou's, so Barnie's letting him sleep on his sailboat."

That's how Maddie figured the angel would make her, or his, appearance, a stranger wandering into town. Some of the strangers who stayed at Marylou's bed-and-breakfast (Maddie checked every week) were nice enough, but they usually had earthly ties like spouses or children. She was sure one older lady was her angel until she stole Marylou's jewelry and even the quarters in her coffee tin.

Maddie leaned forward, then realized she'd dipped her elbows in her gravy. "What else?"

"Oh, come on, Maddie. An angel's supposed to be . . . I don't know. Angelic. This guy sounds too good-looking to be angelic."

"Nicholas Cage played an angel in that movie, and he's good-looking," Maddie said.

"He is not."

"What about John Travolta then? He played a cool angel. A cool, good-looking angel."

"That was a movie, made up, fantasy. Then again, so is your whole angel infatuation."

Maddie wiped the gravy off her elbow. "There was so an angel in my hospital room that night I almost died."

"It was a visiting doctor," Colleen said.

"Then why couldn't anyone say who she was?"

Mom pursed her mouth. "If Maddie wants to believe there was an angel in her room, let her believe it."

"Tell me more about the guy," Maddie asked.

"Darcy said he had a tattoo on his arm. No angel is going to have a tattoo."

Excitement surged through Maddie. "An angel can be disguised as anyone. Most of the stories I've read—"

"We know," Colleen said. "We've heard them all."

"If it makes her happy to believe in angels, then let her," Mom said, then turned to Dad. "Isn't that right, dear?"

"I don't think she should—"

"You're right, she shouldn't be thwarted by someone else's cynicism," Mom said.

Colleen buttered a roll with jerky movements. "But she's not happy. She hardly ever leaves the house, doesn't help at the Humane Society, doesn't go to the marina, or anywhere."

"She's as happy as she can be having lost the love of her life," Mom said, that shrill tone creeping in. "She tried going back to the Humane Society, but the thought of those dogs and cats being put down was just too much to bear. And how can she go to the place where that awful thing happened?"

"She owns it! The Schaeffers have taken it over just like they've taken over everything in this town."

Maddie slid into her own thoughts, but this time those thoughts weren't never-ending bleak days that rolled one to another without joy. This time she thought about the stranger. It was too late to see him tonight. Her throat tightened at the mere thought of going to the marina.

Mom said, "I haven't seen that much life in her eyes since . . . well, since the last time she thought a transient was her angel."

Dad said, "I don't think—"

"Of course you don't think there's anything wrong with her looking for that angel," Mom cut in. "What kind of father would you be if you did?"

"Tell me more about him," Maddie asked Colleen. "What kind of tattoo does he have?"

"I was kidding about him being your angel, Baby!"

Maddie leaned forward, mindful of the gravy. "Tell me anyway."

Colleen rolled her eyes. "It's a tattoo of . . . a naked woman. When he flexes his muscle, she dances. And he has long hair. And he has . . . an eye patch. He's missing some teeth. And he walks with a limp."

"I thought you said he was good-looking."

"Well, you know Darcy. Anything male is good-looking to her."

Maddie tried to put the items together in the picture of her mind: John Travolta with a tattoo, eye patch, missing teeth, and a limp. "I don't care what he looks like. I'm going to go check him out tomorrow."

CHAPTER 3

COLLEEN WALKED INTO the house and stopped. "Oh my gawd, I can't believe it. The lump on the couch isn't there." Baby wasn't sitting there swaddled in blankets and her too-large PJs staring at the television with those enormous doe eyes. She wasn't there at all.

Saturday mornings were for family breakfasts, and Mom's bacon filled the air with the promise of crisp edges and too many fat grams to contemplate. Colleen should have been home making pancakes and bacon for her own family, but Bobby was already in his workshop.

Mom moved effortlessly in the kitchen as she put breakfast together.

"Morning, Mom." She snatched a piece of bacon off the platter instead of going for the bowl of cherries.

"Having breakfast with us?"

"Quigley and I had cereal."

"Doesn't Bobby eat with you anymore?"

"He had to get working on Marylou's bookcase. Said if he could make furniture full-time he'd be able to spend more time at home."

"Your father went through that, too, wanting to open his own shop. I told him he didn't really want to, it was just a phase. We've got to keep our men in line. Maddie's the only one who let her husband run wild, and look what happened. Bobby'll get over it just like your dad did."

Colleen's mouth dropped open. Mom had taken her side

over Maddie's. She had the strangest urge to curl up against her and cry. She wanted to tell Mom how alone she felt in her own house and how long it had been since she and Bobby had kissed, much less made love. She swallowed back the thickness in her throat and asked, "Where's Maddie?," instead.

"Upstairs getting ready to see if this guy is her angel."

"I wish I hadn't said anything."

Several strands of Mom's strawberry hair escaped her ponytail. She looked young and carefree. "She would have found out anyway. It's making her happy for a few hours, and that's all that counts."

"Mom, does she know yet? About you and—"

"Shh!" Mom looked at the doorway. "We just keep on keeping on for Maddie."

"You can't—"

Mom shushed her again.

There was no point in arguing. The world had revolved around Maddie since the day she was born and always would.

Maddie sat in Wayne's Sunbird convertible in the marina's parking lot. Just like she'd been doing for almost two hours. Why did the guy have to be staying at the marina? Marylou's was easy to infiltrate with an offering of Mom's muffins.

She couldn't breathe every time she started to open the car door, making her wonder if her asthma was returning. The last time she'd been in that parking lot, she'd been about to see Wayne's new toy. Even the prospect of finally meeting her angel couldn't quite nudge her out of the car. She was a ten on the anxiety meter.

Rain drizzled out of a gray sky and made everything wavy through the glass. Not much had changed over the last year. The row of shops still had the old fisherman's village look, with weathered blue walls and a welcoming front porch. The marina was in back facing Sugar Bay. Where all the boats sat bobbing in their slips. Where Wayne had left.

Her thumb brushed over the rubber disk on the key fob and covered the words *World's Greatest Husband!* She squeezed her eyes shut, and a tear rolled down her cheek and splashed on her wedding band. Maybe her heart was too shattered for even an angel to heal. She envisioned herself as an old lady still sleeping with a picture of Wayne every night. Mom and Dad would be down the hall, Colleen would still live across the street, and Q would be married with kids of his own. She wondered if they'd still call her Baby.

She looked across the main drag and thought about going to the 7-Eleven to get a hot cocoa. Most of Sugar Bay's businesses were clustered along that strip that ran between the coastline and the rest of the small town. Beyond the businesses was the network of streets where most of Sugar Bay's population lived, including her parents.

She jumped out of the car and slammed the door shut before she could have second thoughts. A hundred-pound rock settled in her chest as she faced the marina.

"You can do this."

She nearly chickened out at the entrance. To make matters worse, Mr. Barber walked out and said, "Why, Baby, it's good to see you out again. Surprised to see you here, though."

"Me, too." She forced a smile she knew was as phony as any clown's smile before slipping inside the marina's store.

"Hey, Baby," Dave Trumbel said from behind the long counter. "Good seeing you again."

"Hey." Her smile was a little less tense. "Where's Barnie keep his boat nowadays?"

"At the end of the new dock on the north side of the bay."

She nodded like she knew what he was talking about. That's right, she'd signed papers the Schaeffers brought over to make the bad place go away. The old pilings had been removed and a new dock had been added.

She looked out the steamy, rain-drizzled glass and prepared herself for the sight of the docks. Her throat tightened, and her legs felt as rubbery as they had that horrible day. Maybe this was a test to see if she was worthy of the angel's help. She took a breath and stepped out into the damp air.

Before looking at the bad place, she focused on what was different. A huge boat-storage facility hogged the south shore of the half-moon bay. The center of the bay had been dredged with a straight, safe channel to the Gulf. The new dock, tucked against the northern curve, had been added for boats coming into Sugar's Eats, the restaurant at the north end of the building. To encourage business, Alma had added an octagon deck out back where people could sit beneath umbrellas, sip drinks, and look out over the area where Wayne had . . . left.

Maddie started down the walkway that curved along the shoreline, passing Cuppa Joe's coffee shop, the nautical gift store, and then Sugar's. Thunder rumbling in the distance drew her gaze to the sky. Her feet skidded to a stop and so did her heart. The miracle of it stole her breath away. Hanging above and to the west of an endless sheet of gray metal sky was one incredible, spellbinding, miraculous thing: a double rainbow. The second rainbow wasn't as vivid, but it was there, so it counted.

And at the end of the rainbow was Barnie's boat.

It was the first time she'd really smiled in a year. Her muscles felt tight, but it was wonderful to smile again. "Wayne, you came through. You came through." Her eyes watered. "You sent me a tattooed, one-eyed, gap-toothed angel."

She was pretty sure she floated down the rest of the pathway. Up ahead was the big metal building that used to be the marina. Now it was just a warehouse where Barnie built his boats and where he was living while his broken leg and other injured parts healed.

She skirted the deck outside Sugar's where tables were empty and chairs were stacked under an awning. She searched for the rainbow again before stepping onto the dock. It didn't end above Barnie's boat at this angle, but it was still there in all its double glory.

She shifted her mint-green gauzy shirt when she felt a cool raindrop on her shoulder, but her shirt slid off her other shoulder. She untwisted the straps on her flowered overalls and hoped she looked presentable. With a deep intake of breath, she walked to the end of the dock.

The Barnacle was a stately old sailboat that, like Barnie himself, was in need of some repairs. She remembered going down into the cabin the first time and being enraptured by the novelty of him living on that boat. She missed listening to Barnie's tales while she waited for Wayne to return from fishing with his buddies. She remembered how it felt when she first spotted his boat. He said he loved finding her at the dock waiting for him. She missed his smile, missed him right down to the center of her soul. She didn't want to stop missing him; she just wanted the tearing ache to go away.

The boats squeaked against white rubber bumpers as she made her way to the end of the dock. An old Rolling Stones tune floated over the damp air. Wayne's favorite song was coming from *The Barnacle*. Appropriately enough, it was "Miss You." She clutched at her throat. The boat rocked slightly from movement on the other side of the cabin trunk. All she could see of the stranger was his back since he was kneeling down.

He hadn't seen her, and that was all right because she couldn't breathe, which made talking rather difficult. He wore a faded black T-shirt with the words *Sagres, a nossa seleção* on the back in white letters. Colleen hadn't said anything about him being foreign. His jean shorts were frayed at the edges and almost faded to white. They contrasted with legs tanned a honey brown. The sleeves of his shirt were cut off, and his muscles moved as he used a screwdriver to pry loose the frame of a cabin porthole. No naked woman adorned his left arm. Must be on the other one.

She thought stepping aboard would get his attention, but with the small waves already rocking the boat, he didn't notice.

His hair wasn't that long really, just to his collar. When he turned slightly, she caught his profile. The eye patch must be on the other side, too.

She would have been more comfortable with someone who looked like the ceramic angel on her dresser, a beautiful blond woman with a serene expression, or perhaps a Moses-like man. This man was . . . well, too much of a *man*. He had a lean, muscular build. She didn't want to notice the blend of male sweat and deodorant or the line of muscling down his legs. She didn't want to be this aware of him on a physical level.

She was about to step closer and initiate a conversation when he stood so fast, it knocked her off balance. He looked startled, too, but he instinctively reached for her hands. Just as quickly, he let them go.

"Jeez, you always sneak up on people?" he said, surprise turning to annoyance. Well, at least he spoke English.

What did one say to an angel? "You don't have an eye

patch" wasn't on the top of her list of witty openers, but that's what came out.

"No," he answered, drawing the word out. "I don't."

There was something exotic about his looks. If he were a regular person, he might have Hawaiian in his background. He had a long face, a small nose, and a hint of shadow on his jaws and upper lip. And he had gorgeous eyes, two of them, as brown as coffee.

Her gaze went to the arm she couldn't see before. No tattoo, though she kept that observation to herself. And she could see no gaps in his white teeth. That darn Colleen.

"Can I help you?" he asked in a voice that captivated her with its deep richness as though he were telling her something personal and intimate.

"Of course you can. Took you long enough to get here."

He had nice eyebrows, and he arched one of them. "It only took a day."

"Time must sure be different where you're from. Well, you can start right now. Doing what you're here to do, I mean."

"I start tomorrow. He said I could take today off to settle in and fix up the boat."

He. Wow, a direct line to God. "You talk to Him a lot?"

"No, just once before I headed over, and then when I got here."

"Oh. You're new at this, then?"

His shoulders stiffened. "I know enough to get by."

The drizzle started up again, the cool, fresh breeze washing away the smells of fuel. "How much did He tell you about what you're doing here?"

He picked up a rag and ran it along the edge of the cockpit, though his gaze never left her. "Not much. He's going to give me instructions as I go along."

"Oh. Well, that's okay, I guess. I never gave up, you know. But it's been so long. I've been patient, well, most of the time." Now all the words were spilling out. "I don't know how this works," she said, gesturing to him and her. "This is my first time. What do we do, exactly?"

He stopped wiping with the rag and asked, "What, exactly, are you talking about?"

She laughed, though it died down to something like a gargle in her throat as she stared into his eyes. "You know. You're supposed to . . ." She tilted her head. "Don't you?"

His eyes searched hers. "Do you know me?"

"Not by name. I just knew you were coming. Wayne told me."

"Who's Wayne?"

"My husband. He used to own this place, and he . . . went away and asked you to come. Didn't he?"

The wind shifted, ruffling his hair. At least Colleen had gotten the dark hair right. And the good-looking part. She pushed her own hair aside as it blew across her face.

She'd expected her angel to waltz in, announce her—or his—intention, and go about fixing her heart. She'd never considered how he would do it, except for vague fantasies about a wave of a hand and quoted Scripture. Or like in *Touched by an Angel,* her angel would appear as a gentle soul who stepped in to help. Then again, she hadn't thought it would take a year for him to arrive, either. God always had a plan, isn't that what the Reverend Hislope said whenever something happened to test one's faith? Like when Wayne was taken away. The Reverend said healing wouldn't be a dramatic event like the appearance of an angel. It would be a gradual process of small triumphs. Maddie was too impatient for small triumphs.

When she moved closer, he backed up. "Why are you making this so hard?" she asked. "I've been waiting all this time for you to come and do whatever it is you're going to do to me, and you're not even a woman or old or anything like I expected, and you don't seem to know what's going on. Hasn't your Boss told you what your job is?"

He put the large wheel between them, taking her in with a wary look. "My boss said he needed to get some supplies before we could begin our work. I get my instructions tomorrow."

So maybe he didn't know his mission yet. "What kind of supplies?"

"C-Flex, fiberglass, and resin."

"You are kidding . . . aren't you?" She put her hand over her chest. No way was he using resin to mend her broken heart! "What do you intend to do with that?"

She saw a mixture of annoyance and curiosity on his expression. "This might sound crazy, to you anyway, but I'm going to build a boat. I work for Barnie Danbury." He seemed to brace himself. "What are *you* talking about?"

"Barnie . . . Barnie is the boss you mentioned?"

"For the new few weeks anyway."

"Oh, boy." A warm flush of embarrassment washed over her face. "So you really don't know who I am?"

"Look, you've obviously mistaken me for someone else. I need to reseal this porthole before the rain kicks in."

She glanced up at the rainbow. Maybe this guy didn't *know* he was her angel. Maybe what scraps of faith she had left were to be tested further. She laughed that nervous laugh she hated because it sounded so obvious. "Sorry." He didn't smile, which made it worse. She cleared her throat and held out her hand. "I'm Maddie Schaeffer. Barnie's my uncle," she added as though that would lend some credibility. Then, picturing her scruffy great-uncle, decided maybe not.

He nodded and said absolutely nothing. Worse, he eyed her hand speculatively before reluctantly taking it in his. She shouldn't have to work this hard at being healed!

His palms were rough and warm. She wondered how they'd come to be so work-worn, then realized she was rubbing her thumb against his palm as she contemplated. She jerked her hand back. "So . . . where are you from?"

"Here and there."

Well, what had she expected? He couldn't just come out and say *Heaven,* could he?

"What's your name?" she asked.

"Chase."

"I'm Maddie." And then that awful nervous laugh again. "I already said that, didn't I?"

The first drop of real rain hit her nose. Not a big drop, but a portent of more to come. He pushed his dark hair back from his face in a useless gesture since the breeze blew it right back. "Listen, I know I'm some kind of oddity, being a stranger and all, and maybe you local girls need a . . . diversion. But like I told the blonde earlier, I'm not here to romance anyone. So could you pass the word, which seems pretty easy here, that I'm not interested?"

More raindrops hit her, but she was too busy putting his words together to notice them much. He thought she was hitting on him! That came first, and then the blonde, well, that had to be Darcy, and boy, couldn't she see Darcy coming out in her tightest jeans flaunting a real chest and not the miniature version Maddie had. She laughed then, a laugh worse than her nervous one, because this one sounded like the bleating of sheep. "I'm not hitting on you! Oh, my gosh, if you knew . . ." He should know. But he didn't. Maybe he had sins to atone for, and that atonement meant having to figure out what he had to fix. Apparently he thought it was Barnie's boat.

She squinted in the rain, crossing her arms, then uncrossing them. "I'll tell them."

He was covering the porthole with a piece of tarp, working as though she weren't standing there, as though the rain weren't sprinkling his shirt with dots. She wondered if rudeness was one of his sins.

"Okay, bye then," she said.

She thought he nodded in response, but couldn't be sure. If rudeness wasn't a sin, it ought to be. "I'm . . . going now." She spun around and started walking.

Go, go, go, you've made a big enough fool of yourself for the day.

Chase watched Maddie Schaeffer pick her way across the wet boards as rain pelted her from a sideways angle. He shouldn't be watching her at all, shouldn't be tensing when her feet skidded across that slick spot near the ramp. Certainly shouldn't spend an ounce of energy noticing how cute her skinny little butt was, because he was fairly certain he didn't even *like* skinny anything. And when that little butt was connected with a woman clearly on the edge of nuttiness, even more reason not to notice that her blond hair was plastered to her head, and that it made her ears stick out, and somehow even that was cute.

What he didn't need was another complication in his life. Just the one was plenty.

He was crouched on the deck in the pouring rain trying to make sense of their conversation. Had she thought he was a gigolo or her handyman?

He grabbed up his tools and stepped into the cabin. It smelled musty even though he'd scrubbed it down. Barnie wasn't exactly picky on cleaning details. Still, he was grateful for a space of his own. It was better than most of the places he'd been sleeping. Chase hung up the tools before settling on the tiny couch with a can of Dr. Pepper. He pulled out an old copy of *Moby Dick* he'd taken from a Laundromat after leaving his last read, *Lord of the Flies*, in its place. He knew they were considered classics, but couldn't remember if he'd read them before. The patter of rain was comforting as it echoed throughout the cabin. And familiar. He studied it, searching for clues. As usual, nothing came.

The book was open to the place he'd marked with a napkin, but he was staring out the window. *So what the heck was that all about?*

Maddie had slipped back into his mind again, pushing Ahab out of the way. She reminded him of Ally McBeal, or at least the one episode of the television series he'd seen. Eyes and mouth too big for her face, a long, graceful neck. Cute, in an odd-duck sort of way. He could still hear Maddie's nervous laugh and the way she cleared her throat when she couldn't think of anything to say. Was it normal to remember so many details of a woman you'd only talked to for a few minutes?

Then again, was it normal for a man to forget who he was?

It was an odd feeling, knowing you were someone, yet not knowing who that someone was. Not even your own name. Chase was a possibility. He'd been wearing an expensive watch with the inscription on back: *Chase, well done. Dad.* So he could be Chase. Or he could be some guy who either bought the watch or stole it from Chase.

An innate sense of boating and that name was all he had left of who he was. He traveled from marina to marina searching for something familiar, something that would set off a bell or produce some kind of emotional response. Only sailing did that, looking at sailboats, watching one come into a harbor. His heart would start beating faster, and his mouth would go dry. An ache to be on that boat burned in his stomach. Being on a boat was part of his former life, that much he knew. It wasn't a hard conclusion to come to, especially since he'd been found in the waters of the Bermuda Triangle.

The ship that had fished him from the sea had saved his life. It was only by the grace of God that they'd spotted him clinging to a broken, abandoned Cuban refugee raft. He had few memories of even that time, however many hours or days it had been, floating under the raging sun like so much other ocean debris.

That the ship was Portuguese, that hardly any of the people aboard spoke English, well, that was just one of those tricks of fate. He could remember those first few hours, when they'd revived him. They stared at him as though he were some strange specimen, and asked him questions in another language. Five men had had to hold him down when he'd tried to bolt in manic fear.

The guy that loosely passed for the ship doctor explained as best he could that Chase had sustained a nasty bump on the head, perhaps from the accident that sent him overboard. He'd been conscious enough to latch onto the piece of raft. During those days he'd been at sea, he'd lost his identity.

When his health returned, he merged into their routines, communicating in a mixture of gestures and sounds. Those first few days were the worst. The whole world was a black hole. Gradually some knowledge returned. Not in dramatic bursts, but the way water seeps into fabric. He knew things about life, that he was, for instance, American, that up was up, down was down, what peas and potatoes were, and that standing on the deck during a thunderstorm wasn't a great idea. He even knew a sort of comfort at being on the ocean, felt a vague familiarity. And a gnawing feeling of loss. These things he knew; what he didn't know, even when they finally arrived in Lisbon, was who he was.

The ship hadn't radioed the Coast Guard because, as one of the crewmates obliquely implied, they were carrying cargo they didn't want to bring anyone's attention to. Which meant they couldn't alert the authorities when they arrived in Lisbon, either. He was a virtual prisoner on the ship, though he could hardly object too loudly. They had saved his life, after all.

When the ship left with a new load of their mysterious cargo two weeks later, Chase faced the problem of getting into the country without papers. He didn't ask them how they knew about sneaking a man into the United States when they came up with a plan.

Even through the language barriers, he'd forged tentative bonds of friendship with some of the men on the ship. Frederico had found books at the library on amnesia, then translated them as best he could. Others had donated faded uniforms, blue jeans, and T-shirts. Another crewmate had given him a backpack and stashed some bags of chips and slices of bread inside. They committed their meager American dollars to his cause. And in the dark of the night, they put everything he had in plastic bags sealed with duct tape and sent him over the side of the ship to swim to Block Island near Rhode Island.

Another two months had passed while he'd traveled down the eastern coast searching for something to spark a memory. His watch had netted him enough money to live on for a while, but that was running out. He'd intended to continue southward, sure that his home was somewhere on the East Coast. He still wasn't sure why he'd ended up in Sugar Bay, Florida, a small bit of a town on the *west coast* of the state. He knew *how* it had happened: he'd been reading a maritime publication, looking for another odd job on his next stop.

A guy walked up and said, "I know a job if you're looking."

"Sure."

"Barnie Danbury needs someone to help him finish building a twenty-six-foot one-off sailboat. It's on the other coast, Sugar Bay."

"That's out of my way, but thanks anyway."

The guy gave him a confident smile. "It's a good place to find yourself. Besides, Barnie's a nice guy, and he's stuck." And he'd rattled off a phone number.

Chase had been stuck on the finding yourself part, but he'd written down the number anyway. "Thanks . . ." When he'd looked up, the guy was already heading down to the docks.

He was on the phone before he could even question whether the job was worth going out of his way for. But it was a job, which meant luxuries like eating and hopefully having a warm, safe place to sleep. Better yet, Barnie, who had broken a leg and was obviously in desperate need of help, would pay in cash. Chase bluffed about his qualifications like he bluffed about all questions regarding his background. It wasn't that hard, actually. While he couldn't think of one recent memory, couldn't remember if he had a woman he loved (no wedding ring anyway), he knew boats. For the past few months, he'd been swabbing decks and doing maintenance for yachts along the coast. The prospect of building one was the first thing that breathed life into the blank morass of his life.

The second was Maddie. And he wasn't going to do one damn thing about it.

⌒ CHAPTER 4

MADDIE WALKED INTO the cavernous metal warehouse where Barnie was staying in the office in the back. The scent of sawdust filled the air. Fiberglass panels let in some light, but on a dim day, the interior was barely visible. She wasn't sure if he was awake or not. With Barnie, you never knew. He slept in four-hour increments throughout the day. Unless you kept a chart, who could keep up with his schedule?

She tapped on the door, and a few minutes later Barnie answered. He was in a wheelchair with his cast-covered leg sticking out in front of him. He'd brought his plate to the door.

"Hey, Maddie. What's up?"

Barnie might have been a distinguished-looking man if he'd put any thought to it. His thick hair, graying at the temples, was always in need of a brush. He cut his hair once a year, an event that had become like the Northern tradition of seeing if the groundhog saw his shadow. He was tall, though his shoulders had stooped over the years. He liked old, faded clothing because they were worn in and comfortable.

"If you're eating, I can—"

He held up a finger, closed the door, and a minute later, reopened it. The pieces of steak and pile of mashed potatoes were gone. "Come in."

Barnie had a thing about people watching him eat. During the holidays he took his plate into the bathroom.

Maddie walked into the office-turned-apartment. It was as cluttered as his sailboat had been. Yellowed, wrinkled charts adorned the walls and were etched with scribblings of journeys past. A portable TV blared from the old desk Barnie obviously used as a dining table.

"How are you doing?" she asked

"Nuts are crushed, how do you think?"

Barnie had taken a misstep on the deck of his boat. One leg went down the companionway, and one stayed up on deck, which left those vulnerable male parts to take the brunt of the fall.

How did one diplomatically ask about crushed nuts? "Are . . . they all right?" She wondered if they'd put those in a cast, too.

"Hurts to walk, hurts to sit, hurts to piss—"

"Forget I asked. I wanted to find out about the guy you hired to finish the boat."

"Chase?"

"Yeah. Where'd he come from?"

"The other coast."

"Of Florida?"

"Yep."

"Is that where he was living?"

"Didn't say." Barnie wasn't exactly a conversationalist unless he was talking about something that interested him.

She perched on the edge of the desk. "How did he hear about your job?"

"Said a guy told him."

"What guy on the other coast would tell him about your job?"

"Don't know."

"Aren't you curious? Did you advertise over there?"

Without giving it any thought, he answered, "Nope. And nope."

"Don't you think it's weird that he found out about the job in such a vague way?"

"Didn't care when he said he knew about the drywall screws."

"Huh?"

"First he knew about using a heat lamp to make the foam pliable. Then he knew about using drywall screws which don't need a pilot hole and don't split the wood."

"Oh, right." Maddie had no idea what he was talking about. Besides, asking Barnie if he thought something was weird was rather ineffective. "I'll see you tomorrow."

Just as she was ducking out the door, Barnie said, "Maddie? Good to see you again."

She returned his smile. "You, too, Barnie."

Whoever managed the guardian angels wanted to drive Maddie crazy for sure. For one thing, her angel wouldn't ignore her or be busy working on a sailboat. And he wouldn't be talking to Darcy, who was leaning against one of the sawhorses in the warehouse, wearing her usual too-tight white pants and low-cut tropical blouse and looking too pretty in the muted morning light.

Darcy was an early bloomer, getting perky breasts when she was thirteen that, by the time she was fourteen, earned her the nickname, "Darcy the Bod." Not that Maddie was jealous, mind you, she just didn't think anyone should get that much bod. Maddie had impatiently waited for her own breasts to grow in, and they finally did when she was seventeen. Then development stalled completely after filling out an A cup. Darcy's curves always reminded Maddie how boyish her figure was. Her only retribution was that while Darcy had been interested in Wayne, for whatever reason, he'd been more interested in Maddie.

Maddie crossed her arms over her chest before approaching the boat. The good thing about Darcy's appearance, if there was a good thing, was that Chase wasn't paying all that much attention to her. He was balanced on scaffolding that looked like it was about to collapse, continuing to work while Darcy talked to him.

The upside-down hull was positioned near the big opening to take advantage of the breeze blowing off the Gulf. Maddie stepped over the orange extension cords snaking over the floor and skirted a wooden ladder. Between the sawdust all over the floor and the discarded pieces of wood, it looked like a party of beavers had just left. When she accidentally kicked a stray piece of wood, the sound drew their attention.

"Well, well, if it isn't our Baby," Darcy said, not even bothering to smile. "I haven't seen you in forever and an age. You met Baby yet?"

Chase's eyebrow quirked as he took her in. "Baby?"

"She's the baby of Sugar Bay, everyone's darling. Ain't that right, Baby?"

"Hey, Darcy. I met Chase yesterday—"

"And here you are again," she finished, glancing at Chase. "So, this is what it takes to get you out of that house of yours." To Chase, she added, "Her husband died in a boating accident a year ago." Maddie cringed at the D-word. "The man positively adored her, so I can understand her being torn up and hiding away at her folks' house. Guess I would too if I'd lost a man that treated me so good. Ain't that many around here, that's for sure. Though I wouldn't have put up with the way he licked you like he was a dog."

"It was just something he did, teasing like." Maddie would never admit she'd hated it, too.

Darcy glanced at her watch, then pushed away from the sawhorse. "Better get back to the shop or Maribelle will be hollering. Some of us gotta make a living. See you later."

Maddie watched Darcy sashay out of the warehouse,

then turned and readied herself to catch Chase doing the same. Which is why she was surprised to find him looking at her with his head tilted.

"Why do you let her talk to you like that?" He hopped down from the scaffolding and grabbed a Dr. Pepper out of a cooler, then offered her one.

She accepted, grateful for the gesture and the chill of the can against her skin. "Like what?"

"She talks down to you, condescending. And all that 'baby' stuff." He rubbed the icy can over his forehead and cheeks, then down his neck before popping the top. Drops of water slid down his temple and jawline as he drank. She watched the muscles in his neck move with every gulp, the drops of water sliding into the hollow of his throat. He wiped his arm over his mouth and looked at her, and she realized he'd asked her a question, and she'd gotten distracted.

"That's just the way she is, I guess. And Baby . . . that's what people call me, always have. I had asthma when I was a kid and everyone kinda took care of me. That's how we are in Sugar Bay. Isn't it like that where you're from?"

He nodded to the skeleton of the hull. "Look, I gotta get back to work."

"Are you sure that's why you're here? To build that boat?"

He picked up a hammer. "Why else would I be here?"

He didn't know. Or he was great at bluffing. She wished she could come out and ask him, but if he wasn't saying, maybe she couldn't, either. He was poised with the hammer, but just stayed there motionless for a moment. Then he asked, "She said your husband died in a boating accident? What happened?"

She swallowed hard. No one made her talk about it. But maybe this was part of the process, her telling him. So she did, without any of the details, and without the angel promise part.

He absorbed her story for a few moments after she'd pushed out the last painful word, then went back to work.

"That's it? Aren't you going to say something?" she asked at last.

"I'm sorry," he said, hammering a nail into one of the wood strips.

"That's all?"

He stopped and looked at her. "What do you want me to say? Seems like you've been getting plenty of pity, you hardly need mine, too."

He was exasperating. "Have you ever lost someone you loved?" she asked.

"I don't know. I mean, no."

His vagueness further convinced her he was sent from Heaven. That and his indifference to Darcy. No guy in Sugar Bay was indifferent to Darcy the Bod, not even Wayne. She'd caught him a few times admiring her behind, which Darcy flashed with frequency. Only an angel would be immune to that.

She watched him hammer several strips of wood to the hull. He had great legs, lean and muscular. Then she realized she was admiring his physique and stopped. She wasn't even the kind of woman who admired men's bodies. Except for Wayne's, of course. Wayne was built like a runner, too, but he was much more compact. Short, Colleen called him, when she was being spiteful.

She cleared her throat, but Chase kept his attention on the wood strips. Wayne had never ignored her. He would have let her chatter on. He would have gotten her a chair so she could watch him work. The pain was still as fresh as it had been a year ago. Three weeks ago, on the anniversary of Wayne's leaving, Maddie had gone to his grave. Instead of flowers, she'd brought toy cars and boats.

When she sniffled, Chase looked at her. "You still miss him?"

She rubbed the back of her hand across her nose. "Yeah."

"But it's been a year."

"When you love someone, you never stop loving them. Especially when they go away suddenly."

His eyebrows furrowed, as though he were putting together a puzzle. "What if your husband had been lost? Like at sea. What if you didn't know whether he was alive or not but everyone else thought he was dead?"

She found herself walking closer in response to the depth of his voice. "I'd never give up looking for him. Why?"

She felt something move inside her as he studied her. Then he broke the gaze. "No reason. Just curious."

"I'd never give up," she repeated, thinking now of the angel she'd been waiting for. She walked close enough to reach out and touch the sleeve of his black shirt if she'd been brave enough.

He wasn't looking at her, but he wasn't working, either. He was taking in every word she said, which was much better than being ignored.

"How did you hear about Barnie's boat?" she asked.

"Guy saw me reading the Help Wanted section and told me about it."

Maddie's heart did a little hip-hop. "What did he look like?"

Chase shrugged, though he seemed caught up in the memory. "Kind of short with dark, curly hair."

She sucked in a quick breath and nearly choked on it. *Wayne!*

"You all right?"

She nodded, but her face was flaming hot. "Did he say what his name was?"

"No. Look, I've got to get back to work."

"Can I help?"

His gaze scanned her lace crop top, pink shorts, and flip-flops. "I doubt it."

He sank into his work, and she became invisible. Well, of course he had to work, if that was what he thought his job was. Still, when she should have left, she stayed and watched him. He was precise in his movements, but every now and then she caught his gaze slide toward her.

He nailed another strip of wood to the frame and hopped down to the floor. She watched him walk over to something that looked like a sawhorse with a rolling pin on top. He positioned more strips of wood on top of that and started up the bench saw. As he moved the pieces of wood toward the grinding blade, she grimaced, imagining his fingers going into the blades. She did that a lot since Wayne's death, imagined the worst. Whenever she saw someone crossing the road, she imagined a car coming around the corner and hitting them. Whenever anyone left her house, she wondered if they'd come back.

She felt her whole body cringe every time the blade cut through the wood.

"What's wrong with you?" he asked when he cut the engine. "You looked like you were pitying the wood as it was being cut."

"Don't be silly. I was imagining you cutting your fingers off." This time he grimaced, and she added, "I mean, I was worrying about it."

He waved his hands and wiggled his fingers. "All here." Then he went back to work nailing more of those strips to the mold.

"Well, guess I'll go now," she said at last. Not that it mattered since she might as well have already left.

He paused long enough to say, "See you," in that velvety voice.

Just before she walked through the large opening, she glanced back and caught him watching her. For the first time in longer than she could remember, she felt a speck of warmth start to melt her heart.

Colleen walked toward the warehouse in the mid-afternoon heat and told herself she was doing this for Maddie's own good. Mom had told her Maddie was more convinced than ever that this stranger was her angel. The farce had to stop here. It wasn't healthy to believe in angels healing broken hearts, and it wasn't safe considering Baby had picked some stranger who may well be a homicidal maniac. So she was going to do something big-sisterly. She searched her motives and found nothing self-serving.

Sometimes Mom mentioned how sad it was that Colleen and Maddie weren't close. They had their share of disagreements, but they didn't have their share of confidences, laughter, and guidance. Colleen had never shown Maddie how to do her hair or makeup (the lack of which had always been evident), and she'd never given advice on dating. 'Course, Maddie hadn't dated much, and when Wayne had shown interest, she'd glommed onto him and that was that. The truth was, Colleen couldn't much see through her resentment of Maddie's babying to offer her much of anything.

Her throat started tightening as she walked toward the big entrance that faced the bay. She felt a layer of perspiration spring out of her skin. She hoped Barnie wouldn't be around. Not only would that make it harder to say what she had to say, but she didn't like the man, even if he was family.

When she spotted the stranger, her throat went even tighter. He was crouched on scaffolding nailing strips of wood to the hull of a boat. And he was gorgeous. Not that she was interested since she had a husband, but it was hard not to notice when this guy had his shirt off and was glistening with sweat. Specks of sawdust stuck to his skin and dusted the hair of his muscular legs. It had definitely been too long since Bobby had touched her.

"Hi," she said, walking up to the edge of the scaffolding and trying not to notice his ratty tennis shoes.

She could have sworn he looked annoyed. "Look, I really don't have time to sit and chat," he said.

She told herself it didn't matter that he hadn't even noticed her as a woman, especially since no one had noticed her as a woman in a long time.

"I've come to talk to you about my sister, Baby. Maddie." It did bother her that her sister's name got his attention.

He walked along the six-inch board that passed for scaffolding. "What about her?"

"Her husband died last year."

"In a boating accident," he said.

"She told you about that?" When he nodded, she said, "Wow, she never talks about it."

"It wasn't easy."

Colleen tried not to get bothered by the flash of compassion in his eyes. "When her husband was dying, he promised to send an angel to heal her broken heart. You have to understand that this was a man who'd do anything for her. She's been looking for this angel ever since."

His expression hardened. "And she thinks I'm it?"

"Yep."

"Why me?"

"I have no idea," she said, taking in a physique that looked anything but angelic. "I mean, she thinks it's you because there was a double rainbow in the sky yesterday, the same as there was the day Wayne died."

"So that's why she keeps coming around."

"Yep, and she's going to keep coming around until she's

convinced you're not this angel. What she really needs is to grow up, but that *will* take a miracle. The best thing you can do is dispel her theory that you're her angel. I'm sure the last thing you need is her hanging around."

"You got that right. Thanks for the info."

"Believe me, it'll save us all a lot of grief."

He went back to work, and Colleen walked out into the hot sun. Maybe that would be the last they'd hear about this angel business.

~ CHAPTER 5

CHASE WASN'T SURE why he was disappointed about Maddie's real reason for coming around. He didn't want any woman hanging around, especially the town's little darling who was hung up on her dead husband and believed in angels healing her broken heart.

"Baby," he said with a laugh and shake of his head.

Maddie might need an angel, but he sure wasn't it.

As he thought over their conversation the day before, it made sense. She'd obviously thought he was someone else, and she'd thought Wayne had sent him. This would be easy. The next time she came around, he'd assure her he wasn't her angel, and that would be the end of her.

"Taking lunch today?" Barnie asked as he wheeled into the work area.

"Nah. I've had a few distractions this morning and I'm running behind. I'm hoping to lay down the C-Flex tomorrow."

"You're going to need help with that, aren't you?"

"I'll handle it."

"Good. *Barnacle* working all right?"

"Yes, sir. Appreciate it. Notice you haven't taken her out in a few years."

"Nearly capsized her and realized with the vicious cruelty of old-age wisdom that this guy's too old to handle her alone. Hell, crushed the nuts just walking on the deck while it was docked." The alarm went off on his watch. "Two minutes to bedtime. Gotta go."

Chase immersed himself in letting the strip into the mold. He turned the battered radio to a country station, always searching for a clue to his past. Did he like country and wear boots? Or was he a rocker? Maybe a dance fanatic who tore up the clubs on Saturday nights.

He wondered if he were a bit eccentric like Barnie. He'd met a lot of boat-oriented people. Some were crusty old salts, some were egotistical about their boats. Some were helpful, others suspicious and ill-tempered.

It drove him crazy wondering what he was like. He hoped he was a good guy, though he knew he sometimes had a short temper. He wondered if he had a woman like Maddie who hadn't given up on him. Did anyone love him that much? The fierce look in her eyes sent an ache spiraling through him. Had he loved anyone that passionately?

He ran his hand through his hair and pulled it tight in frustration. The secrets of his life were locked away in his mind. He just couldn't reach them.

Near the end of the day, he'd completed the hull form. He was starting to get hungry, and thinking of the canned mac and cheese on the sailboat wasn't doing much to pique his interest.

"Hello?" a woman's voice called out.

Oh, no, not again. Five women had come by on one pretense or another to check him out. Well, except for Maddie, who had only baffled him until her sister had cleared it up.

The woman who stood smiling up at him was in her fifties, he'd guess. She had strawberry blond curls that fell to her shoulders and wore big glasses that magnified her eyes.

She smiled. "You must be Chase. I'm Marion Danbury. Baby's mom."

Another family member telling him to dispel Maddie's fantasies?

She studied him for a moment, then gave him a shy smile. "Baby thinks you're an angel."

He decided to play dumb. "She does?"

Marion nodded. "You're not an angel, are you?"

"No." He climbed down from the scaffolding and wiped his hands on his shorts. Then, out of respect, he pulled his shirt back on. "Definitely not."

"Baby's been through a lot this last year. Losing her husband so suddenly shattered her like a piece of glass, and she hasn't been the same since. Wayne—that's her husband, was her husband—he made this promise that he'd send an angel to heal her broken heart so she could go on with her life. She's convinced you're it."

"I know what you're going to say, and I'll take care of it."

"You will?" She clasped her hands together as though he'd granted her some wish. "All I'm asking is that you just play along with her, maybe say a few words of wisdom. What'll it hurt?"

"Wait a minute. You want me to play along? Pretend I'm this angel?"

"Yes!" she said, obviously delighted.

"I can't do it. For one thing, I don't know how an angel's supposed to act."

Marion waved her hand. "Neither does she. She almost died when she was a child, and she thought she saw an angel in the hospital. We thought it was probably a visiting doctor checking in on her, but we didn't see any harm in letting her believe it was an angel. And there's no harm in letting her believe you're one, either. It's wonderful of you to do this. She's my sugar baby, you know, and she needs to be happy again. You can do that for her. Thank you." And then she left.

Great. He'd agreed to be Maddie's angel.

*   *   *

Chase had thought about Maddie all night. His thoughts drifted to what she'd gone through losing her husband right in front of her, holding him while he died. She was obviously well loved, though if her nickname were any indication, maybe too much.

It was probably pretty easy to overlove Maddie. She was small and fragile-looking. Cute. Maybe he could do her one favor and help her to stop believing in all this stuff.

He set his small cooler on the deck, then climbed out of the cabin. Stocked with a day's supply of Dr. Pepper, he was ready to tackle the C-Flex. Another thing that mystified him was that he knew C-Flex was reinforced fiberglass sheeting. When Barnie had asked if he'd worked with it before, Chase had instinctively answered yes, and could picture the striped, flexible material.

Dew had settled over everything, though the early morning sun was already warming the air. He stepped over the slippery spot on the ramp and headed to the warehouse. The large doors were open and the boat was waiting for him.

So was Maddie.

He was surprised at the lack of annoyance he felt; he was more surprised at the thrum of anticipation surging through him. Especially considering that, if he had anything to do with it, he wouldn't see her hanging around anymore.

Barnie was sitting next to the hull form sipping a cup of coffee. Chase wondered if the man owned a brush; his wavy hair sprung out in all directions. Yet the hair, even the scruffy look, suited him somehow.

"Morning," Chase said, training his eyes away from Maddie, who looked like a waif wearing a pastel jumpsuit, leather boat shoes, and a wide grin. She was sitting on one of the sawhorses, knees pulled up.

Barnie raised his coffee cup in greeting. "Maddie here's going to help you with the C-Flex."

"Thanks, but I don't need any help."

"Stuff can be a pain handling it by yourself. Take the help. Going to the marina to see about instrumentation. Then got to talk to Maddie's father about a knock in the truck's engine. Holler if you need anything."

They watched Barnie maneuver down the pathway by the docks.

"I was surprised he was up," Maddie said, jumping to her feet. "You never know with him."

"He says he alternates four hours of sleep and being awake all day," Chase said.

"Yep, for years. And don't ask him to eat with you. He's got a thing about people seeing him eat. He's always been a private person."

"I notice he never refers to himself."

"That's my uncle. So, what do you need me to do?"

Her enthusiasm almost made him smile, but he quelled the urge. "You ever work on a boat before?"

"No, but I'm a fast learner."

"What do you do? For a living, I mean."

She shrugged, lifting one shoulder higher than the other. "I used to help Wayne out at the marina, and help out at the society—the Humane Society. Sometimes I'd help at the nursery around the corner."

Chase set his cooler down. "You're just the little helper, aren't you? Didn't you have a real job?"

"No. I couldn't figure out what I wanted to do, and after I married Wayne, I liked being able to help him whenever he needed me."

"Didn't he want you to get a real job?"

Her smile was bittersweet. "He liked me with him. Not that he told me what to do. He just said he liked me around, so I . . . stayed around."

"Didn't you ever want to be a responsible adult?"

She gave him the lopsided shrug again. "Not really."

She was so naïve, he almost wanted to play along and be her angel. He wanted to make her smile and heal her broken heart. But then the sensible side took over and shook sense into him.

"Look, Maddie, I'm not an angel. Your husband didn't send me. I'm an ordinary guy here to build a boat, and then I'm gone."

Her mouth dropped open. "Who told you?"

"It doesn't mat—"

"Colleen." She stomped her foot and sent sawdust spiraling upward. "Damn her." Her face was red when she met his gaze again. "You might not know it, but you are my angel."

Those words curled through him in a strange way. Had he ever wanted to be someone's angel? "Because of some double rainbow."

Outrage played over her expression again, but she regained control. "The day Wayne died, he looked beyond me and saw an angel. I saw a double rainbow. For a year there hasn't been a double rainbow, and Friday when I came out here, there it was, and it ended at you."

"And if you would have been standing over there, it would have ended over the Dumpster. It was a coincidence. Here's what I think, Maddie. All your life you were babied and coddled, and then you married a guy who took over where everyone else left off." He hated the way the hopeful expression on her face faded to a sober one. "Wayne might have been a great guy, but he didn't do you any favors promising you some angel. You can't go around relying on other people, including your family, to come save you."

She had shored up her shoulders, and that luscious mouth of hers thinned into a firm line. "My family has stood by me through the toughest of times. Sometimes they were the only reason I hung on. That's what family is for, to hold you up when you can't stand on your own."

For a moment he was distracted by thoughts of his own family, whoever they were. "What have you done for yourself to move on?"

She crossed her arms over her chest. "I've waited patiently for my angel."

"Depended on someone else to fix your problems. I don't know you that well, but I can guess that after your husband died, you moved back home and buried yourself in your family's bosom. I'll bet your mom does every little thing for you, and nobody makes you do anything you don't want to do, including grow up. Let me tell you something: When it comes down to it, you only have yourself to depend on." He exhaled softly. "And even then, you get let down."

"This isn't the way it's supposed to work."

He moved close enough to smell her sweet perfume. Close enough to make her look up at him. "If I were your angel, what would you want me to do? Say, poor baby, how awful that this has happened to you, it isn't fair, and we're going to make everything all right? Should I tell you that we promise nothing bad will ever happen again? Should I kiss you and make it all better?"

She stiffened with every word. Her big, hazel eyes filled with pain, and then she wrenched away from him. He steeled himself against the way the shine in her eyes stabbed his insides. She took a deep breath, and when he thought she might tell him off, she turned and walked away. And still he felt the overwhelming urge to call her back and apologize, even when this was what he wanted. It was for the best. Especially considering he'd wanted to follow through on that threat to kiss her.

He consoled himself with thoughts about doing the right thing as he wrestled with the coil of C-Flex. Had he ever felt this particular kind of remorse? This softness for a woman? It seemed even more unfamiliar than the concept of family and home.

Lucky for him, Maddie was a runner. If she'd been a fighter, well, he'd be done for. As easy as it had been for him to abstain from any kind of attachment, Maddie had gotten to him.

When he changed the station on the radio, Don Henley was singing about coming back to the land of the living. Most of the songs he heard sounded familiar, but they brought back no sliver of memory. Not even of whether he'd liked it or not. He stripped off his shirt and flung it over one of the sawhorses. He was tired of feeling disconnected from the world.

Chase worked with the unwieldy material and the box of ice picks for an hour, stopping only to sip on his Dr. Pepper or slide a handful of ice over his skin. If he wasn't thinking about that look on Maddie's face just before she'd walked away, he was thinking about the kind of person who might harshly tell a woman to get over her husband's death when he didn't even know her.

"I want to know who you think you are to talk to me like that," a familiar voice demanded from behind him.

He was sure he couldn't actually be glad she'd come back. He turned to find her standing there, arms defiantly crossed. And as wordy as he'd been earlier, all he could think to say in response was, "Pardon?"

She pushed her hair back from her face and stepped closer. "Who do you think you are to tell me how I should live my life?"

"I don't know who I am." It had just come out, and the way he'd said it in a near whisper, with a sober look on his face, he knew he couldn't take it back or make it sound like a smart-assed response.

Maddie looked at him, her mouth going silent for a moment. She knew that he'd meant it, but she couldn't quite understand what his words meant, so she took a moment to digest it. He tried to turn his attention back to work, but he couldn't ignore her, standing there beside him, figuring him out.

"You don't know who you are," she said, not a question really, yet colored with disbelief just the same.

"Of course I do." He'd intended to make it a strong statement, but his voice had given out at the end. He repeated it just to make it sound more true, but again, those last words faltered. An ache throbbed in the center of his chest as he stared at the wood and felt her hand on his arm. He'd kept his secret and his distance for so long, he thought he was invincible. The ache said otherwise, said he needed to tell her, only her, but he didn't know why.

"Chase . . . who are you?"

He still didn't look at her, instead focusing on his hand braced against the hull of the boat. "I don't know." She tugged on his arm, forcing him to look at her. He didn't like the hopeful look on her face, the shine in her eyes. "I'm not your angel."

"But you don't *know* for sure."

"They found me floating in the ocean, clinging to part of a refugee raft. When they threw me a life preserver, I didn't even respond, though they said I was awake. They had to send a guy in after me. I don't remember any of that." The ache lessened with each word he spoke, though he hadn't intended to tell her much. "What I remember is waking up to find all these people staring down at me talking in a language I didn't understand. I thought they'd stolen my mind." He wasn't looking at Maddie directly, but at her shoulder. "It took a few days to remember things about life, what things were called, and that I believed in God. But that's where it ended."

She put her arms over her stomach and shivered. "That must have been terrifying."

He didn't want to remember how terrifying it had been. "When we docked in Portugal, I couldn't leave the ship because I had no papers. I read about amnesia and memory, and I think I was in a . . ."—he looked up, trying to remember the terms—"massive dissociative state when they pulled me out of the ocean. Maybe the trauma of being knocked out of a boat, drifting for days, and believing I was going to die caused me to dissociate. That's supposed to be a sideways slippage from consciousness. I lost my episodic memory. One of the five types of memory," he added at her blank look. "I lost the story of my life; all the events that shaped me. I know things, but they have no relevance."

She still had her hand on his arm, and she'd been squeezing slightly as he'd talked. That's why he'd spilled so much, he realized. Her touch was soft and warm, compassionate.

"How did you get back here?" she asked.

"I was part of a shipment to New York."

"How'd you get back in? Or did you turn yourself in to the authorities?"

Those were the questions he'd grappled with during the seventeen-day journey back to the United States. "I decided not to go to the authorities. If they couldn't determine who I was, I wasn't sure what they'd do with me. I didn't want them to hold me against my will." Or put him in a psychiatric ward. "And I didn't want to get into how I'd ended up where I was. I figured I'd come from the East Coast, and if I traveled long enough, someplace would trigger my memories." At least she was asking normal questions now. Nothing about angels.

"How do you know your name is Chase?"

"I wore a watch with the name engraved on back."

When she looked at the cheap plastic watch he wore, he added, "I had to sell it."

She looked at the hull beside them, at the ice pick he held in his hand. "But you know boats."

He knew his smile was tainted with frustration. "That's the annoying thing about memory. I know things, like how to build a boat. I can read navigational charts, and I feel more comfortable on a boat than off it. I know I like rice covered with hot sauce and relish"—Maddie wrinkled her nose at that one—"and I like Dr. Pepper. But not one thing that'll help me remember who I am." He found himself wanting a drink, too. Like that ache that foretold the need to share his story with someone, that was the ache he felt for a drink. But he couldn't afford to waste precious money on liquor, so he didn't. "Look, I'd better get back to work. I told you that because . . . I want you to understand I'm not who you want me to be." He started unrolling another section of C-Flex.

"If you think you're from the East Coast, why are you here?"

"I needed the money."

He didn't like the look on her face. It was that irrational look. "The guy who saw you reading the Help Wanted section. Did he look like this?" She pulled a picture out of her pocket and held it up.

He studied the picture, more curious about the man who had claimed Maddie's heart so completely than to compare. "I didn't get a good look at the guy." Those doe eyes glistened, and her face flushed pink. "Maddie, it wasn't him. This guy was flesh and blood, just like us."

He wasn't even going to mention that after the guy continued down the docks, Chase looked back at the paper and realized he hadn't had the Help Wanted section open. He was sure there was a logical explanation.

"Don't you see? It's perfect! You don't know who you

are, you were found in the ocean as though dropped from the heavens, you believe in God, and Wayne sent you to me."

"I never said anything about being dropped from the heavens." And he wished he hadn't mentioned believing in God. Maddie had a way of making a man talk too much.

She still had that glowing look, and worse, she was grinning at him.

"I'm not an angel."

"Maybe you don't *know* you're an angel."

He spread his arms out. "Do I look like an angel to you?"

Her gaze drifted down his neck, over his bare chest and jeans that were uncomfortably tight. "Angels can look sexy—" Her eyes widened. "I didn't mean sexy like that kind of sexy. I meant . . . they can look like anyone. Even you."

He let out an exasperated sigh, despite the compliment. Before he could think twice about it, he did something he hoped would dispel the notion for good. He kissed her.

It wasn't dramatic, no tongues were involved, but he ran his mouth over hers for a long minute. Her surprised squeak echoed in his head, but he was mostly focused on the way her mouth felt beneath his. She was incredibly soft and tasted sweet.

Her hands had pushed against his shoulders when he'd taken her by surprise, and then stilled against him. Now she pushed again and backed away. Her eyes were wide, and she put her hand over her mouth and said, "Wha . . . how . . . you're not supposed to do that! You're supposed to listen to me, tell me everything's going to be all right, and make it happen."

"If I were an angel, I wouldn't want to kiss you."

"And you sh—" She tilted her head. "You wanted to kiss me?"

"Against my better judgment. I'm a man, Maddie. Nothing more, nothing less."

Her gaze took him in again, but she still didn't look convinced.

And definitely against his better judgment, he said, "Still offering to help? I could use a hand."

The boat was beginning to look like an acupuncture patient. The C-Flex was held in place by dozens of ice picks. Maddie held the material, and Chase stuck in the pick. It was hot, and sometimes their skin brushed.

Working on a boat wasn't on the list of ways to mend a broken heart, but there she was. She'd come up with the idea during the long hours of the night. He couldn't use work as an excuse to push her away if she were helping him. She'd gotten up earlier than anyone else, left a note, and headed to the marina. This time when she'd pulled into the parking lot, she hadn't dreaded the bad place. She'd concentrated on getting Chase to admit or see that he was her angel.

Barnie had already been up and looking over the form in the warehouse. "He's doing a good job."

"On the boat, anyway," she'd muttered, but Barnie hadn't asked what she'd meant, and she didn't explain. Sometimes his lack of curiosity was a good thing.

When Chase had said all those mean things, combined with the fact that her sister had sold her out, Maddie couldn't stand it. She'd gone home to her bedroom, pulled the covers up to her chin, and sunk into her comfortable hole. Nine on the sad meter.

Then she realized something: since Chase had come into her life, she'd edged to four or even three. The double rainbow, and the way she felt when she looked at him, had sent her back into the light. If she gave up on him being her angel, she might have to give up on the angel altogether. That thought had sent her even deeper into her darkness looking at a future that held no color. She decided that he must be her angel. He just didn't know it.

Telling him off had given her a different kind of feeling, a feeling of strength she'd never felt before. She'd held it under control until he'd kissed her. That had thrown everything off. He wasn't supposed to kiss like that, with a hot, soft mouth armed with an electrical charge. And she wasn't supposed to react like that, not when she still loved Wayne and didn't want to love anyone else again.

"You all right?" he asked, bringing her out of her reverie. "You were just kind of staring off. I don't want you to fall off the scaffolding."

"If you lost your memory, how can you remember how to kiss . . . like that?"

He blinked at her question, then got a chagrined look. "Forget I kissed you. And don't spread it around that I don't know who I am," he added. "It's not something I go around telling everyone."

She tilted her head and smiled. "Who else have you told?"

He seemed to weigh his answer, then said, "Just you. Now forget about it."

Yeah, right.

A lone fan washed warm air over them and made her hair stick to her neck. She pulled her hair up and closed her eyes for a moment. When she opened them, he was watching her.

He averted his gaze. "Ready to break for lunch?"

She wanted to ask him if she'd really seen the burn of hunger in his eyes, but pushed out the word "Yes" instead.

"You don't have to do this, you know."

"Aren't I helping?"

He took in her expression and smiled. "Yeah, you're helping. But you're obviously not used to working."

"No, but you know what? It feels good to be doing something again."

Chase climbed down from the scaffolding and held out his hands to help her down. She leaned into them, feeling them tighten around her waist as he set her down in front of him. He seemed to notice that his hands remained on her waist even after her feet had touched down and let go.

"Jeez, you weigh almost nothing," he said.

"Don't tell me I'm skinny."

"Don't women like to hear that?"

"Not this woman. All my life I've been called skinny and string bean, and people are always saying, 'Baby, are you losing weight?,' and I'm sick of it. I don't like being skinny, but I am and there's nothing I can do about it. Ever since Wayne left, my family pays more attention than ever to my weight."

He was studying her, one eye narrowed. "You can't even say it, can you?"

"Sure I can. See . . . skinny."

"No, died."

She shook her head. "No one's supposed to say that word around me. *Left* is better."

He grabbed up a battered cooler and walked out to the old picnic table that overlooked the bay. "Maddie, you're a case."

She grabbed her cooler and followed him, trying not to look at the bad place even though it looked different now. "A case of what?"

He sat down. "Denial, for starters. It's been a year since your husband died. Isn't it time to accept that and move on?"

She sank to the bench on the other side of the table. "I don't want to move on. He was the only man I'll ever love, and the only man who will ever love me. I don't want to lose what I feel for him or replace it with something else."

She felt her mouth tighten along with her chest. "I just want the pain to go away."

His expression softened, but he focused on opening his cooler. "You're never going to date anyone? Marry again? Have kids? I'm assuming you don't have kids."

She shook her head to all of his questions. "I'll never love anyone the way I loved Wayne. I know that, so it's useless to even think about it. And as you've no doubt guessed, there isn't exactly an overabundance of eligible men in town. The ones who are in town . . . well, they aren't interested in me."

"Why not?"

He was serious.

"Come on, look at me."

He did, sweeping his gaze over her face and down as far as he could see of her. "And?"

She laughed, but couldn't help feeling a little warm inside that he still had to question. "Besides being plain and . . . skinny, nobody here is ever going to see me as anything more than 'Baby,' the scrawny, sickly kid they grew up with. But it doesn't matter, because, like I said, I'm not going there."

"Ah-huh." He pulled out what looked like a peanut butter and jelly sandwich, and a sloppy one at that.

"I brought lunch for both of us." She opened her own cooler and pulled out leftover chicken and potato salad.

"You didn't have to do that." But his hungry eyes gave him away.

He watched her put out the paper plates and spoon a heap of salad onto his plate and a smaller one onto hers. Then she doled out the fried chicken, two thighs for him and a wing for herself.

"Is that all you're eating?" he asked.

"I don't eat much. And no, I'm not anorexic. Food just doesn't appeal to me anymore."

"Since Wayne died."

"Left."

He shook his head. "Maddie, you're not just a case; you're a truckload."

⟶ CHAPTER 6

"I NEVER THOUGHT about how these things were actually made." Maddie stepped back to survey the work they'd completed by mid-afternoon.

Sweat glistened on her collarbone and neck, and she was sprinkled with flecks of sawdust. The fan blew her blond hair away from her face. Her skin was flushed with heat and exertion, and Chase refocused his thoughts. He could think about her later, when he was gone and she couldn't tempt him.

"You like going out on boats?" he asked.

She looked out the big open door to the choppy water beyond. "Yeah. Wayne and I went out at least three times a week. I liked going out on the *Dinky*—that's what he called it. It's just a little boat we took out to watch the sunset and go shelling. He liked to go fast, whether it was on a boat or in a car." She got a wan smile on her face. "He used to get this hari-kari look, and I knew he was up to something. Sometimes I could feel it. Like when we'd go out at night, and he'd open the throttle all the way."

"In the dark?"

He had been listening to her talk about Wayne since lunch. He didn't know whether to like the guy or hate him. He seemed too perfect, too wonderful.

"That's what made it exciting, going into that black void full tilt."

Ah, perhaps he'd found the crack in Wayne's silver armor. "What if you'd hit something?"

She waved that away. "He knew where everything was. Besides, out in the Gulf, it's pretty much open."

"Except for buoys. And other boats, debris, traps."

"Boats would have lights on."

"Not always."

She turned to him, her admiration for Wayne still intact. "But nothing ever did. He knew what he was doing. He wouldn't let anything happen to me."

Chase let out a *hmph* sound, deciding not to mention that something did happen, though luckily Wayne was alone. Things *could* happen out there, especially in the dark. Something had happened to him, too. And hadn't he found part of a raft floating out there?

"Wayne was like that," she continued. "He brought adventure into my dull life. He liked taking chances. Did I tell you he got me scuba diving?"

Let's see, she'd talked about meeting him in high school, their wedding, their honeymoon in the Caribbean, but no, not scuba diving.

"He was certified, and he taught me how to dive."

In the oddity that was his life, Chase knew nothing about himself, but knew diving without being certified was wrong. "You didn't go through the course?"

"Nah. He knew everything about diving, so why go through the formalities? He opened up a whole new world to me down there. He used to feed barracudas by putting a hot dog in his mouth. They'd come right up to him and take it. And he rode a shark once. He said it was a nurse shark so it wouldn't attack. It was amazing."

Behind Maddie's excitement, he detected a hint of the worry she'd felt then. She tucked her arms around herself, bunching up her now-dusty jumpsuit.

"He lived on the edge, didn't he?" he asked.

She walked up to the fan and spread her arms like a cormorant drying its wings. "He made life worth living. You know, it's nice to talk about him like this. My family is very supportive of me, but whenever I try to bring up Wayne, they change the subject. I'm probably boring you to death, but I appreciate you letting me talk about him."

"He sounds like a jerk." The words weren't exactly what he'd intended to say, but they'd slipped out anyway.

She spun around. "What?" The fan blew her hair into her face.

It was too late to take it back now. "Your prince charming had a serious character flaw. He took dumb chances, and worse, he took them with you. It's one thing to be reckless with your own life, but it's a whole different matter to endanger someone else's life. Especially someone you love."

He didn't love Maddie, of course, and wasn't sure he'd loved anyone. But he knew he'd never take those kinds of risks with her. He hated putting that defensive hurt on her face.

"Don't say that about him. He took good care of me. He paid the bills, made me happy, always made sure I had a coat and something to drink. He was careful."

And she believed it. "I know you loved him, and I'm sure he loved you. But don't make him out to be some saint, because he wasn't. You shouldn't have been diving if you weren't trained, and it's plain stupid to play with a shark, any shark. It's real easy to lose your bearings out there on the ocean in the dark. Unless you have the right instrumentation, you don't know what could be out there. Think about what he was doing the day he died."

"Don't say that word!"

Before he could think better of it, he'd taken hold of her shoulders.

"Maddie, he died. It's an ugly word, but that's what

happened." He squeezed her shoulders. Jeez, they were small. "He died because he was playing games. Luckily he didn't take that chance with you on the boat . . . that time. But regardless, he took a chance and he lost."

Her eyes darkened, and she turned away from him. "He knew what he was doing. It was the boat that failed."

He took her chin and made her look at him. "If you're not familiar with a boat, you don't take chances. He was stupid to play games like that, especially in front of you."

"But he was doing it for me."

The sound of someone stepping on a board drew their attention to the opening. A little boy stood there. He looked like a miniature Howdy Doody with bright red curls and freckles.

Maddie quickly wiped at her eyes, and Chase realized he'd made her cry. The thought twisted his gut as he watched her walk to the boy.

"I had the bus drop my nephew off here," she said, steering him closer.

Chase crouched down to the boy's level. "Hi, there."

"What's your name?" the boy asked, his head tilted, looking at Chase the way everybody in town did.

"Chase. What's yours?"

"Q."

"That's a funny name."

Oops. Wrong thing to say. The kid's face sagged, though his little shoulders stiffened.

Chase added, "Sounds like a sci-fi kinda name. Yeah. There's a guy on *Star Trek* with that name. A cool bad guy."

The usual annoyance set in: how could he remember details like that and not a thing about his life?

Q beamed. "I want to be a kewl bad guy." He tilted his head again. "Are you Uncle Maddie's angel?"

"*Uncle* Maddie?"

She shrugged. "He's always called me that." She nodded to Q. "So, you going to answer him?" she asked Chase.

Sure, put me on the spot. "No, I'm not her angel. I'm just a regular guy, like you."

"Are you a bad guy?"

"I hope not."

Q looked at Maddie for confirmation. She only shrugged. "Why were you having a . . . a . . . discussion like Mom and Dad do?"

Damn, he must have heard part of their conversation. "I was just telling your . . . uncle Maddie that she shouldn't be sad anymore."

Q brightened at that. "I always ask her where she is on the sad meter." He looked over at her. "She looks like a nine."

She knelt down and whispered, "That's our secret, remember?"

Chase asked, "Where is she usually on the sad meter?"

"Seven or eight. Except when I hug her." He demonstrated, wrapping his little arms around Maddie's neck. She closed her eyes and hugged him back, a gesture that tugged at something deep inside Chase.

"Now what are you?" Q asked after the hug.

She forced a smile. "Only a three."

Q looked at Chase. "Give her a hug and see where she is."

Maddie gave a nervous laugh. "Now, Q, I'm not a carnival game where everyone gets a try."

It was a bad idea to hug Maddie, but he kept thinking about the hurt he'd put on her face, and maybe a hug would make up for it a little. Just one hug.

She didn't protest when he slid his arms around her and pulled her close. They were both hot and sticky and covered in sawdust, but all that didn't matter once their bodies met, and her cheek pressed against his shoulder. She fit so perfectly there, he felt a sense of homecoming he was sure had to be his imagination. He heard her sigh as her body relaxed, and that made him involuntarily squeeze her closer. When he discovered he'd closed his eyes in the process, he figured he'd better end this here and now. He set her apart from him so suddenly, she blinked in confusion and had to gain her balance.

"Uncle Maddie, you had a funny look on your face."

She brushed sawdust off herself and gave Q an odd smile. "That's 'cause he's all sweaty."

"No, it was a good funny look," Q said. "Where are you on the sad meter now?"

She cleared her throat and avoided Chase's eyes. "The same. You're the only one who can lower my sad meter."

Q was clearly tickled by those words, and a little embarrassed, too. He focused on the boat hull. "Wow, what's this?"

"We're making a boat," she said. "See, we put this on today. Doesn't it look like a whale having acupuncture?"

Chase couldn't help but laugh at the analogy.

"What's acu . . . acu . . . whatever?" Q touched one of the ice picks. "Can I help?"

"We're done for the day," Chase said. "I've got to get everything ready for the messy part tomorrow."

Q's eyes widened. "I like messy parts!"

"Q, you get to help your daddy in his workshop."

"No I don't. He gives me kiddy tools and makes me sit in the corner."

Maddie frowned at that. "Well, I guess we'll go if there's nothing more for me to do."

Chase forced himself to shake his head, even as his mind searched for things she could do. "Thanks for your help today. So, what am I going to pay you?"

"You don't have to pay me."

"You worked hard, you should be paid."

She waved the idea away. "You keep the money, I don't need it. I live with my parents, and the marina pays my expenses and mortgage."

"You own a house?"

She stiffened. "The one Wayne and I lived in. I can't sell it, but I can't live there, either. And don't lecture me about it. It's silly for me to live all by myself when I can be surrounded by my family." She gave Q another affectionate squeeze. "I've never lived by myself and I don't think I'd like it much."

He'd obviously been too hard on her, though he couldn't help thinking it was for her own good. Instead he said, "You're lucky to have family."

She let out a long breath. "Yeah, I am." She glanced down at her dusty shoes, then back at him. "When should I be here in the morning?"

"Maddie, you don't have to help me tomorrow. It's going to be messy. I'm wetting out the C-Flex with resin, then working with fiberglass."

Her shoulders drooped. "Don't you want my help?"

He thought it curious that Maddie would fight him over Wayne's integrity, but back down on something she obviously wanted to do. He felt himself backing down even though he knew the best thing was not to see her again. "You really want to mess with all that sticky stuff?"

"Yes." She looked at the hull. "Today's the first day in a year that I've had some kind of purpose. I like it."

"All right."

Her smile was worth giving in when he knew better. "I'll even bring lunch."

Maddie was going to be a problem. He was already looking forward to seeing her tomorrow. And it had nothing to do with lunch.

*   *   *

"Can we go out on your boat?" Q asked as he and Maddie walked away from the warehouse.

"No, we can't."

"Don't you have the *Dinky* no more?"

"I imagine it's somewhere around here. Going out there"—she nodded toward the bay glittering in the late afternoon sun—"makes me a ten on the sad meter."

Going out on the *Dinky* without Wayne was unimaginable. But she had to admit she missed the sunsets and the shelling. What surprised her most was how much she missed being held by a man. Sure, Dad gave her a hug once in a while, though he wasn't too comfortable showing affection. But being held by Chase was different. She'd felt her body melt against his, and her blood thicken to the consistency of hot fudge. Her mind had shut down and let her body take over for a minute. She'd been afraid to do more than put her hands on his hips. If she'd slid them all the way around him, she might not have been able to let go.

"Baby, what in heaven's name are you doing here?" a female voice said, rocking her out of her thoughts.

Carol Schaeffer, her mother-in-law, was coming toward her on the walkway. She was an attractive woman with bright blond hair and a made-up face that always seemed a little overdone. She was not impressed by Maddie's bedraggled appearance, but then again, that was the look she'd always given her. "Dick said he saw you here this morning, but I told him surely he was mistaken. But here you are, and what have you been doing?"

"I've been helping work on Barnie's boat."

That got a raised eyebrow, a finely tuned one at that. "With that strange man?"

Maddie watched Q wander to the docks and peer down into the water. "He's not strange. He needs help, and it's nice to be working again."

Carol gave her the laugh that wasn't really a laugh. "Baby, you've never worked a day in your life. Why start now? You've got it made, with us running the marina and you just sitting back collecting the revenues. It works out well, don't you think? Don't push yourself. It's been a hard year on all of us, but especially you. Everyone knows how much you loved Wayne, and they all understand that you need to take your time to get over him being gone."

"I appreciate that, and all that you've done to this place and handling the day-to-day duties. But maybe I should come back and—"

"No need for you to face this place and all its terrible memories. Dick and I don't mind in the least making sure everything's running smoothly." Her forehead wrinkled. "You do think we're doing a good job, don't you?"

"Of course, but I—"

"Then you just sit back and let us keep handling it. It's good seeing you again, Baby."

Carol headed onward to Sugar's, probably getting a mid-afternoon mocha like she used to do. Something bothered Maddie about the conversation, probably that the Schaeffers were doing all the work at the marina. But Carol seemed happy to keep running the place, so she let the feeling go.

Q was spitting into the water and watching to see if the fish were interested. She walked over, afraid he'd fall in and hit his head and drown.

"Think fish like boogers?" he asked when she joined him.

"Ew, yuck! Don't say that word."

"But it's not a bad word. It's a funny word."

"It might be a funny word, but it has an unfunny meaning. Come on, let's get home."

"And you can just butt out of my life," Maddie told Colleen as they were getting dinner ready that night.

Colleen's eyes widened. "Baby, you can't seriously still think this guy is your angel."

"You went to see the guy?" Mom asked Colleen.

"It was for Baby's own good. I mean, the guy could be a serial killer for all we know."

Maddie wrinkled her nose. "Well, if he is, it won't matter none because he can't remember who he is. I spent the whole day with him and he didn't try to kill me once."

Colleen hunched her shoulders and gave her the vulture look. "He's probably sizing you up, waiting for the right opportunity."

"Sheesh, and you call *me* fatalistic!"

Mom set the green bean casserole on the counter with a thud. "Wait a minute. Colleen, you told Chase that Maddie thinks he's her angel?"

"Fine, shoot me, I did. I'm worried about Maddie's safety. And my son tells me he met her down at the warehouse, so now I'm worried about his safety, too."

"What did Chase say to you?" Mom asked Maddie.

"He said he wasn't my angel and he kissed me to prove it."

"Kissed you!" Colleen yelled. "He's a rapist. I knew it!"

"He's not a rapist. He was trying to prove a point."

"Yeah, that he's a rapist!"

Mom frowned. "Mm, he wasn't supposed to do that."

"What do you mean?" Maddie asked, setting a platter of roast pork on the table. "Don't tell me you talked to him, too?"

"Well. . . ."

Colleen smirked. "Let me guess. You asked him to go along with it."

"I didn't think it would hurt anything. And what do you mean, he doesn't remember who he is?" Mom asked as she rolled the new potatoes around in a bowl of melted butter.

"Just that. He has no memory of who he is. A Portuguese ship found him on the ocean hanging on to a Cuban refugee raft. He was in some kind of mass something state and he lost his some-kind-of-memory. Anyway, he can remember things about life in general, but not his identity. Which just goes to prove that—"

"Maybe it's not a good idea, you seeing him," Mom said. "I have to agree with Colleen on this."

Colleen dropped the tub of butter she was setting on the table. "You do? You agree with me?"

"Baby," Mom said, taking her hands in her own. "You know I'd go to the ends of the earth to make you happy. But Colleen's right—"

"I can't believe she keeps saying that," Colleen muttered as Dad and Q walked into the kitchen. "I mean, I know I'm right, but no one ever sees it."

"Whether he knows who he is or not, *we* don't know who he is. I was hoping he'd say a few things to you, maybe tell you you're healed or whatever, and that'd be that. But you spending the day with him, and him kissing you . . . it's just not good."

Maddie wished she'd left out the kissing part. She definitely wasn't going to mention the hug.

"He hugged her, too," Q offered. "But he didn't make her any less sad on the sad meter."

"He hugged you?" Mom looked more horrified than she had over the kiss. "That's it. You're not seeing him again. This guy is no angel, sure as shootin'." Mom looked over at Dad. "Tell her what a not good idea this is."

"I never thought the whole angel business—"

"Would go this far, I know," Mom finished for him. She clasped her hands together. "I know you want to find your angel. But it's not this Chase person. Discussion closed, let's eat."

"Discussion not closed," Maddie said. Everyone stopped

in mid-movement and looked at her. "Maybe . . . okay, maybe Chase isn't an angel. Maybe—"

"There, now you see the light," Mom said. "Let's eat."

"Wait a minute!" Maddie looked at her father, who had an understanding expression on his face. Mom had never cut her off before, but now she realized how it felt. "Chase may not be an angel, I'll give you that. But Wayne sent him to me just the same. How else can you explain how he ended up here when he's searching for his identity on the other coast of Florida? How else can you explain that a man who looked like Wayne told him about the job when Barnie hadn't advertised or told anyone over there?"

Maddie couldn't quite bear to tell them what Chase had been saying to her all day. She felt as though she were betraying Wayne's memory just thinking about it.

"Quigley," Colleen said. "Sit nice and eat. No playing with your food."

"Baby, you know we love you, and we want you to be happy as a lark," Mom said. "But there are limits, and you hanging around some stranger passes those limits. Now please cooperate and give up the idea of this man having anything to do with Wayne. Sit nice and eat."

Everyone started piling food on their plates. She traded a look with Q, feeling as though she were six, too. She couldn't remember a time when she had gone against her mother's wishes, but the thought of not seeing Chase again made her stomach ache. Besides, she'd promised him she'd help, and Barnie sure couldn't do it.

"Mom, don't you think that Wayne's spirit could have—"

"Baby, after all we've done for you, I don't understand how you can doubt my judgment on this. When everyone else tells me I'm sheltering you too much, I've told them that you need lots of extra love and attention during this trying time. I have gone out of my way to help you through this. Please don't repay my kindness by worrying me."

Colleen was smiling, and not trying awfully hard to hide it. Maddie sank her fork into a new potato and broke it in half. She was actually hungry for a change, owing no doubt to working. Her arm muscles ached in a good way. Mom started talking about the reception her apricot muffins had received this morning, and that was that.

She wasn't giving Chase up. Okay, maybe he talked to her like she was a kid, too, but when he'd kissed her, she'd felt like a woman. Forget the kiss, she told herself. She liked the way she felt when she was around him. Even if he was telling her things she didn't much want to hear. Being with him made her feel . . . special.

She caught Dad's gaze across the table. Mom told him what to do, too, and cut him off before he'd had a chance to say what he wanted. But he got around her in a most time-honored way. He sneaked around.

And so would Maddie.

CHAPTER 7

THE WHOLE CHASE discussion had been closed as far as Maddie's family was concerned. After dinner and cleanup, Dad went out to the garage to work on his car, Q sat on the couch playing Nintendo, and she, Colleen, and Mom sat around the coffee table and worked on a puzzle. Unfortunately it was a clown puzzle.

"Baby," Mom said. "Clowns are good things. They're happy, they make people laugh."

"I think it's a conspiracy. Expose your kids to it while they're young, infect their minds. All that face paint, all a lie with the phony smile."

"Someday I'm going to change your mind about clowns," Mom said.

Colleen put another piece in place. "Let her hate them. Why does everything about Baby have to be a campaign? Every sniffle, every upset."

Instead of phasing out, Maddie felt . . . annoyed. It had never bothered her before when they talked about her as though she weren't there. She found a piece of the puzzle that didn't have a part of the clown in it and put it in a group of the same color.

"I want to start working at the marina again," she announced.

Both women looked at her. As if in punctuation, one of the Nintendo creatures died with a whirling sound.

"I realized I've dumped everything on the Schaeffers,

and besides, I'm getting restless." Being at the marina would give her a good excuse to see Chase. And was much more entertaining than the "trash talk shows" she watched when no one was around.

Mom looked as though Maddie had announced she had a fatal disease. "Baby, are you sure you're ready? Being at the place where Wayne went away? The Schaeffers don't mind running things, you know.".

Colleen snorted. "They were horrified when they found out the marina was going to you. And more than happy to take it back."

Maddie didn't remember her own reaction to the news, much less theirs. All she could remember was that everything looked gray and bleak, and there was no hope of ever seeing colors again. Until that rainbow. "I saw Carol yesterday. She acted weird, like seeing me there was not a good thing. She assured me that she was happy to continue overseeing everything. But I'd like to get back into the groove again."

Mom had her concerned look, one she'd honed to perfection over the years. "I think it's too sudden."

"Mom, she's been moping around for a year! It's time—"

An explosion sounded from the vicinity of the garage. "Daddy!" Maddie screamed, bolting to her feet and running toward the door.

"The car just backfired," Mom said. "Nothing to get into a lather over."

Maddie couldn't help but imagine the car in flames, her father trapped beneath it.

The old Buick was grinding away, not a flame in sight. Her dad was under the hood cranking on something.

"You all right?" she asked, though she could see he was.

"Just backfired. Scared the piss out of me." But he didn't look scared. He looked happy, even more so when the engine smoothed out to a hum. "Ah, there she goes."

"You really like working on cars, don't you?"

"Yep."

"Do you still want to open your own garage? I heard Mr. Baker once say he'd take his car to you anytime if you had your own place."

Dad shrugged. "I thought about it, but it really isn't feasible. We'd lose our benefits and taking a vacation would be hard." That warm, happy look had faded from his face as he recited things she'd heard Mom say over the years.

"But you want to, don't you?"

"Wanting something and it being the best thing aren't always the same."

She thought of Bobby's dream of opening his own cabinetry shop.

Dad turned off the car's engine and leaned against the side. "You okay, pumpkin?" He was a big man with a pocked complexion. The kids used to be afraid of him until they got to know him. He'd dwarfed Wayne.

"Thinking about going back to work at the marina."

"It *is* yours."

"I don't want to run it or anything. Just . . . be there."

"But your mom doesn't think it's a good idea," he said.

"You got it. What do you think?"

"When you're ready, you're ready."

Another of Dad's nonanswers.

"Thanks, Dad." She gave him a kiss on his grease-smeared cheek and pushed away from the car.

Bobby had helped a friend build a boat once. Maybe he had an extra pair of gloves or other tools she could borrow to impress Chase with. She walked across the street, breathing in the warm jasmine-scented air and discovering herself enjoying life for a moment.

All because of Chase.

Which made her think of that kiss again, and how long

it had been since she'd been kissed, and how nice it felt. There was a strange stirring in her stomach, or maybe it was lower than her stomach.

For the first time in a year, she thought about sex.

It jolted her. When Wayne left, she swore she'd never think about sex again, would never want it. Sometimes she dreamed about making love with Wayne, so that didn't count. But the thought of making love with another man was preposterous. Wanting another man was unthinkable.

But for that moment, she had wanted another man.

She pushed onward, erecting a wall of guilt between her and those thoughts. If Wayne had sent this man to her, and she was sure he had, she couldn't have those kinds of feelings for him.

In the distance she could hear kids splashing in a pool next door and music coming from Bobby's workshop in their backyard. She started to knock, then realized between the music and whatever tools he was probably using, he'd never hear her. So she opened the door—and found a bare, freckled butt bobbing up and down.

Bobby and Wendy, Wayne's sister, were going at it on a towel behind the bench saw.

Her gasp of surprise startled them into a frenzy of yelps and arms and legs tangling and untangling. Maddie was rooted to the floor for a moment, unable to comprehend what she was seeing. Had she conjured this up with her own thoughts of sex? Her heart squeezed as she realized this wasn't her imagination.

Bobby was shoving his long legs into a pair of jeans, and Wendy was struggling to get into a T-shirt. Maddie turned and fled.

"Baby, wait!" Bobby yelled.

She couldn't outrun him. He swooped up from behind her and lifted her into the air. Before she could make sense of it, he'd set her down again and faced her. "It isn't what it looked like."

"You were . . . and she was . . . naked!"

He kept one hand on her shoulder, probably to keep her from running, and rubbed the bridge of his nose. He at least had the decency to look embarrassed. "All right, it is what it looked like."

Her face felt hot with both anger and embarrassment. "How . . . how long has this been going on?"

"Just a couple of times. I built a dresser for her, and we got to talking, and before I knew it, we were kissing."

Her face flushed again at the memory of how easily that could happen. "But she's married. *You're* married!"

"It was a mistake. It won't happen again."

"What are you going to tell Colleen?"

"Nothing. And neither are you. Can you imagine how hard it would be for either of us to tell her this? And I know how fragile you are. Your whole world would tilt again, with Colleen getting all of Mom's attention, and nothing would be the same among all of us. You've got to promise me you won't say anything."

She imagined how hurt Colleen would be. She liked her world to be just so, with her gnomes and Bobby's income. And the pool she was drooling over.

"You'll break it off?" she asked.

He drooped with relief. "Yes, I promise!"

"But . . ." Her gaze went to the workshop door where Wendy was slinking through the darkness to wherever she'd parked her car. "Why?"

He fidgeted for a moment. "When I'm with her, I feel like a man. You probably wouldn't understand that, being a woman and all. And Wayne, well, you let him do pretty much what he wanted. Colleen keeps me on a short leash, like a dog. That's what I feel like with her. She tells me what to do, yells at me for leaving my socks on the floor or wearing the same pair of underwear two days in a row. I'm tired of living in that cave with those creepy gnomes."

"Why don't you tell her all this?"

"She won't listen. It's because of you. She says she had to live a certain way all her life because of you being sick. Now she wants to live her own way. She won't let me quit and start my own business, either."

Because of her. The reason she kept those gnomes around, because she hadn't been allowed to do much else.

"I'm doing what I can to make myself happy," he said.

"And that includes doing Wendy?"

"Well . . . she makes me happy. I feel in control, like a man." He raised his large hand in a pledge. "But I'll call it off."

She turned and walked slowly back to the house. She couldn't look at him anymore, not without feeling her stomach turn. Now the sweet jasmine smelled nauseating.

"Baby," Mom called when she finally had enough nerve to walk inside. "Aren't you going to help us finish this puzzle?"

She could only shake her head and go to her room.

"She's just mad about this whole thing," Colleen said, sounding self-righteous as usual. "You know how she can be."

Sometimes Maddie didn't like her sister, but she loved her too much to let on the real reason she couldn't look at them. She sank onto her bed, only dimly aware that Mom had rearranged her room again. She stared up at the three plastic angels hanging from the ceiling as they swayed in the air from the air-conditioning vent. Her world had already tilted without her telling a soul.

Maddie woke as soon as the sun came up, though she felt as though she hadn't slept at all. Mom was on the phone. "An extra order of the blueberry muffins? Got it."

"Good morning, Mom," Maddie said, kissing her on the cheek after Mom hung up.

"Good morning? Are you all right?"

"Yeah, why?"

"You haven't said that in a year."

"Is that a bad thing, me saying it this morning?"

"No. Well, of course not. But when you change, it worries me. Here, have a muffin."

Maddie piled the leftover pork and green beans into a Tupperware container while Mom was occupied with packing muffins on the delivery trays.

"Are you still going down to the marina?" Mom asked.

"Yep. I'm going to talk to Carol and see if there's anything I can help with." That much was true.

Mom slid her a sideways glance. "Colleen thinks you're going to meet that guy again, but I told her you wouldn't lie about it, so I'm not even going to ask you."

Maddie swallowed hard. If she didn't answer, she wasn't lying. She kissed her mom on the cheek. "Bye. Be careful driving around. I'll be home in time to meet Q's bus."

Just because Maddie felt her heart step up a beat as she approached the warehouse didn't mean anything. Naturally she was drawn to Chase because Wayne had sent him. But not drawn in *that* way.

And she maintained that, even though the first sight of him sent a surge of heat through her, and there was no way she could keep the smile from her face.

It felt good to smile. Maybe that was the only reason Chase was sent to her, so she could learn to smile again.

He was mixing something in a large bucket, and his biceps flexed with every movement. "You're a glutton for punishment, aren't you?"

She held up the cooler. "And I brought lunch."

"I haven't become your charity case, I hope."

"Being the resident charity case, I can say no. I just don't want you to feel bad watching me eat these wonderful left-overs." She pointed to the T-shirt with the foreign expression on it that stretched tight across his chest. "You wore this the first day I met you."

He gave it a tug. "One of the guys on the ship donated it to me."

"Do you know what it means?"

"Sagres is a local beer. *Nossa selecção* literally means 'our selection,' as in 'our choice.' It's their slogan."

He pulled a large container of something that sloshed nearer to the hull.

"Did they teach you any dirty words?" she asked.

"I picked up a few phrases. Nothing I'd use around you, even if you didn't understand."

She tilted her head. "Tell me one."

He grinned. "Forget it. Those guys would pin up naked pictures of their girlfriends or centerfolds and talk about them. You want to know what they'd call you?"

She wrinkled her nose. "Maybe. What's the word for skinny and gawky?"

When he slid his gaze down her body, she swore she could feel it. "You're not gawky. You'd be a *miuda gira.*"

"What's that?"

This time his grin had a teasing quality. "I'll tell you later."

It couldn't be too bad by the warmth in his smile. And he had a gorgeous smile, though it faded too fast. He had already laid out the tools, including, she noticed, two of a few things.

"We're going to wet out the C-Flex with the resin first."

She watched him apply a coat of resin and followed suit. "I'm not supposed to be seeing you."

"Oh, yeah?"

"My mom and sister think you might be dangerous. They don't think I should be hanging around with you."

"They're probably right."

She met his gaze on that one. "You agree with them?"

"Well, you don't know me. And you've led a pretty sheltered life. All I can tell you is that as of now, I'm not harboring any tendencies to do you bodily harm."

She thought of that kiss again, and the tender way he'd held her just because Q had asked him to. "Let me know if you do. Until then, no one is supposed to know I'm here, okay?"

"How old are you, anyway?"

She followed his gaze to her faded Pooh bear tank top, then folded her arm over it. "Twenty-six."

"I'll bet you always do what your parents tell you."

"Maybe."

"Why go against their wishes now?"

"I don't know." She couldn't even explain it to herself.

"You still think your husband sent me?"

"Yes. Though I'm not so sure about the angel part anymore."

He chuckled. "The kiss convinced you, didn't it?"

She had to stop thinking about that kiss, because whenever she did, she found herself looking at his mouth. He had a fuller mouth than Wayne, who'd hardly had any mouth at all, just a thin line. But he could kiss pretty well, and he used to say that Maddie had enough mouth for both of them. Chase's kiss had felt different, intriguing.

She forced her attention back to the dripping resin in front of her. "You think I'm immature, don't you?"

"Mostly I think you're naïve as hell. I mean, come on, everyone in town calls you Baby. And you don't even mind."

"That's the way it's always been. I can't change it now."

He moved toward the bow of the boat. "Why not? You've just gone against their wishes about seeing me."

"But that's different. I want to see you."

He'd stopped brushing on the resin, and she replayed her words and realized she'd admitted she wanted to be with him.

"But you only want to be with me because you think your husband sent me." He continued working, avoiding her gaze.

"No. Yes. I don't know. I've never felt like this before. Since I met you, I feel alive." Her voice went lower. "And I'm not ready for that feeling to go away yet."

He'd stopped moving again, and his gaze locked to hers. "Maddie, don't feel that way about me, okay?"

"Why not?"

She could see the muscles flexing in his arm as he braced it against the side of the hull. He let out a soft breath. "I'm only going to be around for a few weeks."

"You don't want me getting attached to you?"

"Maybe I don't want to get attached to you."

He was lying, of course. Who would get attached to her? Especially a guy like Chase.

"Baby?" a woman's voice asked.

Maddie turned to find Wendy standing there. Looking a bit more dignified than she had last night anyway, though her face was pink with shame. She'd always been a little on the heavy side and was one of the people who nagged Maddie about being too skinny.

"Can I talk with you for a moment? Colleen just called me."

The whole ugly affair rushed back just when she'd managed to push it out of her mind, including the bobbing white butt. Had Bobby admitted his affair to Colleen? He was right: Maddie would rather the whole thing go away than have it blow up in their faces. She set down her brush and walked out into the fresh air.

"Colleen wanted me to check on you. She thinks—well,

she knows you're out here with that guy. She's worried about you."

"Will you tell her I'm helping Carol?"

Wendy nodded eagerly. As if she had a choice in covering for Maddie's tiny lie. "All right then," she said. "I'll tell her."

She started walking back to the marina without saying a word about the night before. Wasn't that how everything was in Maddie's life? Nobody *talked*. Nobody confronted. But this bothered her too much to let go.

"Wendy, aren't you going to say anything at all about last night?"

Wendy spun around and walked back to Maddie. "You're not going to tell anyone, are you? Bobby said you wouldn't, but I wasn't sure. It'd kill your sister, and Donnie would be devastated, too."

"Why weren't you thinking about Colleen and your husband last night?"

"Baby, you don't understand, bless you. You and Wayne were happy together. At least you have good memories of being with him. He would have never cheated on you. But Donnie has. I know every time he makes a run to Tallahassee for parts, he's seeing her. You wouldn't understand what that does to a woman, but I do. And when Bobby kissed me, I lost my head. Colleen's stifling him. They haven't had sex in months. What harm does it do if we have a little fun once in a while?"

"What about Q? Bobby's son, you remember him? A little boy who needs his family to stay together and be happy. And that's not going to happen if you keep seeing Bobby. Colleen'll find out, kick him out, they'll get divorced, he'll slack on child support, and we'll see his picture on the *Duds for Dads* program. The next time you get the hots for Bobby, think of Q."

"Huh?"

"I mean, think of him needing his parents together and a dad he can look up to. Bobby promised he'd break it off if I didn't tell Colleen."

"Baby, I didn't realize how mean you can be."

"I won't let anything bad happen to Q. And I'll be as mean as a snake if it does."

Maddie stalked back to the warehouse and found Chase leaning against the exterior wall. He had a surprised expression on his face.

"You heard everything?"

He shrugged. "Sounded like you might need some help, but you handled it just fine."

She rubbed her temples. "I don't know what to do. Last night I walked in on my brother-in-law bopping her."

"Bopping?"

"You know . . . doing it. And he asked me not to tell Colleen because he knew I didn't want my world upset. But it's Q I'm worried about."

"Maddie, you're something else, you know that?" He headed back to the boat shaking his head.

"That never means anything good."

He ran his fingers through his hair and turned back to her. "You let everyone talk down to you and probably walk all over you. But when it comes to protecting someone else, you're a spitfire."

"Spitfire. Is that good or bad?"

"It's good, Maddie." He wasn't quite smiling, and yet, there was a gleam in his dark eyes. "Maybe too good."

"And what's that supposed to mean?"

He leaned against a sawhorse and let out a sigh. "I'll tell you later."

CHAPTER 8

DURING LUNCH THE next day, Chase watched Maddie stare out to the Gulf. She'd drawn her knees up, her arms encircling them. The breeze toyed with her fine hair, but she was too lost in her thoughts to notice. Now that he could see more of her in her blue shorts and tank top, she was even smaller than he'd thought. He was sure he could circle her upper arm with his thumb and forefinger. Her stomach was flat, and he could just see the outline of her ribs.

In some ways, the role of mourning widow fit her. She had big, haunted eyes, and now her full mouth curved downward. He could understand why she'd slid into her child role, complete with her Pooh shirt. As small and fragile as she was, who could resist enfolding her in their arms and trying to make things better? No one.

Including him.

Which was a bad idea. He hadn't intended to admit he might get too attached to her. Maybe he was only kidding. Or maybe not.

He was a loner. Isn't that what the strange dream had told him the night before? He'd been on a boat by himself, on the leading edge of morning, and on the edge of the world. For as far as he could see in the gray morning light, there was no sign of humanity. Icebergs floated nearby like frozen polar bears, groaning as they brushed up against each other. He'd felt a soul-deep peace at being alone, though he was nagged by a vague sense of responsibility. There was someone he should have called, someone waiting at home for him. But he didn't want to break the solitude to hear another human's voice.

The boat's motor brought him back to the present. A small boat wended into the bay, and its motor whined like a mosquito. Maddie watched it with eyes the hue of burnt honey. She'd hardly touched her lunch, and he'd felt like something of a pig for nearly inhaling his portion.

He leaned across the weathered table and asked, "So, where are you on your sad meter today?"

The question startled her, probably because it came from him. It even got a twitch out of the corner of her mouth. "For a few minutes, I was an eight."

"Thinking about Wayne?"

"Seeing that little boat reminded me of the *Dinky*."

"I heard Q asking to go out on it the other day."

She shook her head, sending her hair flying in the breeze. "It'd be too hard." She hugged her legs tighter. The boat coming toward the docks held her gaze. "Maybe he was a little too adventurous, but he was so good to me. Nobody will ever love me like that again."

"How can you say that?"

She rested her cheek against her knee. "Because I'm Baby. Because all through high school not one boy gave me a second look. And those boys are now the men who live here. But I don't want to think about loving again. It makes me shiver every time someone says, 'You'll fall in love and get married again someday. I know it seems impossible now, that you'll get over Wayne, but you will.' I don't want to move on because I don't want to let him go."

Chase was at once annoyed with her devotion and sad for her loss. Somehow he knew he'd never loved anyone with that kind of intensity. He wasn't sure he could. He had the insane desire to be the one who could love her enough that she'd let Wayne go. Bad idea. Really bad idea. Without knowing who he was, he had no right to get involved with anyone. He shouldn't even want to get involved, but Maddie touched him in ways he couldn't explain. Every time he decided to sever their friendship, she showed up all bright and smiling, and he handed her a brush instead of a pink slip.

"We had fun," she said, looking out to sea again. "We laughed together all the time. I never worried about things back then. I never worried about hitting anything out there at night or running out of gas on the *Dinky*, because I knew he'd take care of me. I never thought about people dying. Now every time someone leaves, I worry that something terrible will happen to them, and I'll never see them again. I imagine things happening, like the lift giving way and crushing my dad, or the oven blowing up and killing Mom. I can't help it, the images come. Sometimes I even imagine the funeral. I go through it in my mind, maybe to prepare myself. Am I morbid?"

He shrugged. "Probably comes with having someone you love suddenly taken away."

"When people avoid answering a question, it means they don't want to say the truth. I've noticed that lately."

He rubbed his nose and said, "You're not morbid."

"You're itching your nose. You're lying to make me feel better."

He looked at his hand and wondered if she was right. "Okay, you're morbid. But I still think it comes with losing someone suddenly."

She faced him, her hands clasped together. "Have you ever wanted to relive a moment so bad, you concentrated on it until you almost believed you'd turned back time?"

"Maddie, he's gone. He'll never come back, nobody is going to come and magically take away the pain, and if you're as tough as I think you are, you'll survive anyway."

She blinked. "Me tough? Nobody's ever called me that before."

He gathered up the trash from lunch and stood. "You're tough for others. Someday you'll learn to be tough for yourself."

How could you hate what someone said to you and like them at the same time? Maddie wondered as they had worked on the boat after lunch. She ran the water in the utility sink, but her gaze was on Chase. An hour before he'd stripped off his shirt, wiped his face, and tossed it aside. She'd had trouble concentrating ever since. It was just curiosity that made her keep sneaking a peek at him. It had been a long time since she'd seen a half-naked man, especially one who looked as delicious as Chase. He was a study in concentration as he worked the resin across the hull, smoothing it with precision. Every now and then he'd look up and catch her and she'd fumble with her brush and pretend she hadn't been watching.

It was still curiosity that made her watch him even though water splattered into the big plastic sink. His back was to her, his muscles glistening with sweat, drops of which slid down the indent of his spine, and had she really thought he looked *delicious,* jeez, that wasn't a word she'd ever used to describe a man, even Wayne.

She wasn't supposed to notice these things or feel this hunger deep inside. She was still in love with her husband and always would be. She certainly wasn't supposed to be letting her gaze drift past the waistband of his jeans shorts to where the pockets molded his behind.

The ache spread as she imagined walking up behind him, sliding her hands down his slick back. She turned to the sink and splashed water on her face. This was crazy thinking. Sex had been fun, lighthearted play. Even the cool water didn't keep her thoughts from drifting back to Chase, to kissing him again, but this time really kissing him. It sprang to mind too easily, him holding her, kissing her, sliding his tongue inside her mouth. Her heart was thrumming, and she was only fantasizing! She felt a throbbing sensation between her legs, and she pressed them together and tried more water. It dripped down her collarbone and into her bra. She kept splashing, driving her thoughts back to Wayne, to lovemaking that had never made her feel this intense.

"Stop it," she whispered, turning off the water and towel-drying her face. Her hair dripped down her shoulders and left damp patches on her shirt. Her nipples strained against the fabric the way they did when she jumped into the pool in cooler months. Wayne would tease her and make her feel self-conscious. Chase wouldn't have to say a word—she already felt that way.

"Thought you were taking a bath over there," he said as she approached, giving her a smile.

She tucked her arms around her, covering her chest. "The water felt good," she muttered, then realized the words and her tone of voice didn't match. She forced a smile she knew was phony.

"What's wrong?"

"I gotta go. I'll see you tomorrow."

"If your folks don't find out about your being here," he said.

She shrugged and headed out into the fresh air. If her mom did find out, there'd be a fight. Maddie didn't do fights well. Especially when her mom had been right. It *was* dangerous to hang around Chase. He wasn't even doing anything wrong, other than stripping half-naked, and she could hardly blame him in this heat.

She pushed her hair back from her face. She was the one who was letting her imagination take her places it shouldn't. He'd only kissed her to prove a point, and hugged her because Q had asked him to. No way could he be interested in her skinny, flat-chested self. No way could she be interested in him, either, because she loved Wayne. But her body, that was a different story. Maybe she should remind it that she wasn't a sexual person.

The cool air inside the marina raised goose bumps on her damp skin. She waved at Dave behind the counter and headed to the office. It was a big room divided into four sections. Wayne used to take the back desk, and Maddie used the one in front of him when she helped out.

Carol now sat at Wayne's old desk. She'd transformed it from the male décor to her own feminine décor. Carol could do feminine well, along with looking professional and put-together. She had a vase of flowers in the corner, and country charm items she'd picked up at the annual craft fair.

Maddie didn't have any style. Carol had tried to make Maddie into someone with more class. The perm had been disastrous, frizzing her fine hair and making her look like an alien in a sci-fi movie. Every Christmas and birthday Carol bought her color-coordinated, accessorized outfits. But instead of feeling more like Carol in them, Maddie felt like an imposter. Wayne wouldn't commit one way or the other on which style he liked better.

Carol looked up from her paperwork and gave her one of the usual smiles that never quite looked real. "Baby, what a surprise."

Maddie clasped her hands together and sank into the metal chair. "I know."

Even that phony smile disappeared. "You want to come back to work at the marina." It wasn't a question.

"How did you know?"

"If Colleen hadn't mentioned it to Wendy this morning, I would have still heard it from your mother. She's concerned, that's all. A stranger comes into town, you're actually leaving the house, and now you're lying."

"She asked if I'd come to see you about working," Maddie surmised. "And then she asked if I was at the warehouse."

Carol nodded. "I saw you working on Barnie's boat with him. Maddie, people are starting to talk."

"Starting? They've probably been talking. Probably everyone in town knows." At Carol's confirming expression, Maddie added, "Wayne sent him to me."

"Baby, I miss Wayne, too. Not a day goes by that I don't think about him. But he's gone, and if he were going to send you an angel, he would have done it before now."

"Maybe time is different up there."

Carol shook her head, as though she were the authority on Heaven. "Chase is a transient. Is that what Wayne would send to you?"

"He's not just a transient."

"He doesn't know who he is."

"But how—Mom told you." Oh, brother.

"He's probably making that up. My gosh, he's probably a criminal wanted for some hideous crime. What easier way to avoid charges than to pretend you don't remember who you are."

"He's not lying."

"Baby, you're a sweet girl, but you're too trusting. And that's fine as long as you're surrounded by people who care about you. Go home and let your family take care of you."

Maddie started to get up, but something strange happened. She could see Chase's pride at the way she'd fought for Q's happiness. *You're tough for others. Someday you'll learn to be tough for yourself.*

She sank back down again. "I want to come back to work, at least part-time."

"Your mother doesn't think you're ready, and neither do I. Besides, we've got everything under control."

Maddie's fingers curled over the square arms of the chair. She hadn't expected a fight, not here. "But it's . . . my marina."

Carol blinked and turned away, letting out a huff of breath as she took in Wayne's picture above her on the shelf. "This marina has been in our family for fifty years."

"And I've been part of your family for six years. And Wayne made this marina what it is. *We* made it what it is. Okay, mostly it was him. I'm not asking to take over. All I'm asking is to be part of it again."

Carol flexed her fingers, crunching up a piece of paper in the process. "That's how it starts. First you do some filing, then you want a little more responsibility. Then you ask for a formal position, like running the counter. Next you'll be asking to manage the place."

"I'm not even thinking that far in the future."

"But you will be," Carol said in a shrill voice. She cleared her throat.

"Carol, I do own this place. Wayne left it to me."

"By default. He never made a will."

"But he put my name on the deed."

"The Schaeffers have been working their tails off to make this marina healthy. In the last year, Dick and I have put everything into running this place while you sat around and did nothing. Did we ask anything of you? No. Did we complain? No. We did it because we love you and wanted you to be financially secure. Now we have a routine. Every piece of the puzzle is in place. I will not let you come in and try to rearrange things just because of a legal technicality. If you want to feel useful, go play with the dogs or help your mother build her little muffin business. Let us keep everything going here. After all we've done for you, the least you can do is let us continue on." The phone rang, and Carol lunged for it. "Cookie, I'm glad you called. Listen, I've got three shipments of anchors coming . . ."

Maddie knew the conversation was over. She pushed out of the chair and left. Carol was right in many ways. She and Dick and Wendy and Donnie had all pitched in and kept things going. If it weren't for them, the marina would have crumbled. Like Maddie had. Maybe it wasn't fair to barge in and demand a part of the puzzle.

She walked outside and headed to her car. Her feet felt leaden, as did her heart. Because Mom knew she'd been with Chase, and all hell was going to break loose. If she couldn't stand up to Carol, how could she think of standing up to Mom?

Chase turned up the radio once Maddie left, but music didn't make up for her absence. He actually missed her. Well, that was just great.

And he couldn't ignore the possibility that he could be dangerous. He had a temper, that much he knew, though it usually flared when his loss of memory frustrated him. Every time he thought about his whole identity being locked somewhere in his brain, being right there but inaccessible, he had an overwhelming desire to hit something. And he'd gotten into that fistfight at a truck stop once.

Some nematode was trying to get fresh with the woman trucker he'd hitched a ride with. She was no delicate flower like Maddie, but she was a woman who couldn't hold her own against a six-foot-two drunk. Chase had gone at the guy without giving it a thought, even though he was a few inches shorter and a lot of pounds lighter. The guy had nearly busted Chase's nose. They'd gone at it for a few minutes before a security guard broke them up.

It was only after he'd returned to her truck so she could tend to the cut on his forehead that he'd gotten the full story: she'd recently broken things off with the guy and hadn't done it nicely. Even though Chase was curled up in pain, she was so touched that he'd defended her honor, she'd kissed him. His body had reacted instinctively, but his mind had overruled. He'd lost his ride, but he'd kept his life neat. No entanglements until he knew where he was coming from and what responsibilities he had.

Now Maddie was messing with his mind big-time. She didn't even want sex. But it wasn't sex he necessarily wanted from her, and that's where the scary part came in. He found himself just . . . wanting her. He wanted silly things, like to make her smile and take care of her. He wanted her to fight him. He admitted to being harsh with her sometimes. He didn't know how to soft-talk anyone, and telling her things that weren't true was impossible.

It made him afraid to find out he was someone unworthy of Maddie. And that was plain silly, because once he found his identity, he would merge back into his life and never come back here. Once he found his familiar territory, everything would return, and the person he'd become during his journey would disappear. So would these strange feelings he had for Maddie.

The whining of an engine drew his attention to a small boat making its way out to the Gulf. She missed going out on that boat—the *Dinky,* she'd called it. He could see the melancholy in her face, and hear it in her voice. That's what she liked, watching sunsets, going slow. Wayne liked speed, and she went with him because she'd do anything for him.

He didn't like Wayne. Part of his dislike, he had to admit, was the fact that she was still so in love with him, and the other was that Wayne had risked her life.

Barnie wheeled through the open doorway and made Chase wonder again if the man owned a brush.

"Hey. Just taking a little break." Not good getting caught daydreaming on company time.

"Man's entitled to stop and think for a minute." He looked up at the hull, partially covered with the sandwich laminate. Another piece was sitting under the heat lamp where the foam interior would be pliable enough to stay in place against the curve of the boat. "Good job."

Chase wasn't sure why he warmed under the man's praise. "Thanks. Maddie's been a big help. I'm trying to pay her for her time."

Barnie shook his head. "She won't take it. Likes giving, always has. Used to volunteer at the Humane Society, play with the dogs and cats." He wheeled around to the far side of the hull and inspected it. "You're causing quite a stir, you know."

"Pardon?"

Barnie looked serious. "Well, you caused a stir all by yourself, being a stranger in town and all. But now that you've taken up with Maddie—"

"I haven't taken up with her. She's just helping." The last thing he wanted was Maddie catching hell because of him.

Barnie pointed to himself. "This guy knows that, and you know that. But people in town like to imagine all sorts of things when they lead boring lives. Talked to Marion again—that's Maddie's mom."

"Again?"

"She called couple of days ago, after Maddie first come around. Asked what this guy knew about you, which ain't much." He gave Chase a pointed look. "Could have said you lost your memory."

Great, now Barnie knew. Which probably meant everyone knew. "It's my business."

"Sure it is. But once you come here, you don't have any personal business. Ran into Marion this afternoon. She's all worried about Maddie hanging around you. In a tizzy, 'zat a word, *tizzy*? Seems as though Maddie told her she wasn't going to see you anymore, and here she was. Maddie don't lie. Even when she was little. So you can imagine what

Maddie's going to hear when she gets home tonight."

"I can talk to Marion, explain that nothing's going on."

"What about the kiss?"

Chase pressed the heel of his palm against his forehead. "Damn, she's got a big mouth." He couldn't help picturing that mouth.

"Both Marion and Carol are convinced you're a bad influence on Maddie."

"Who's Carol?"

"Maddie's former mother-in-law. See, Maddie went in to see her just a bit ago and asked for a job. Maddie owns the marina, got it when Wayne died. But his family took over, and of course, Maddie didn't say anything about it. Too busy mourning for her fella. You getting the picture? You come to town, she spends time with you, leaves the house for the first time in months, except for church, lies about being with you, and now is asking for a job."

Chase got the picture. Though he was glad Maddie was standing her ground, things didn't look good for his future in Sugar Bay. "So is Maddie going to be working at the marina, then?"

"Nope. Carol told her things were fine the way they were, and Maddie should just leave things be. The Schaeffers have owned this place for years; Carol's not about to give it up without a fight, even if Maddie has rights to it."

"And Maddie didn't fight." Chase heard the disappointment in his voice.

Barnie obviously did, too, because he gave him a funny look. "Suppose you'd tell her to fight for what's hers?"

"Yep." Which was probably the death knell for his job.

Barnie considered him for a moment, then said, "Carol and Marion said to let you go."

Chase nodded. "I just want you to know one thing. Maddie's not a little girl anymore. She's not a . . . baby. People here have to stop treating her like one."

"You are a troublemaker, aren't you?"

Chase started gathering up the tools he'd been using and headed to the sink to wash them. "Guess I am."

Barnie wheeled over to the sink. "Really don't remember who you are?"

"No, sir. But I'm trying to find out. Thanks for taking a chance on hiring me."

"Usually a pretty good judge of character."

Usually, but not this time. Chase suspected he felt as sad about not seeing Maddie again as he did about losing the income. Worse, he had no way of saying goodbye. "I'd appreciate it if I could stay another night on the boat and head out in the morning. We can settle up then."

"Settle up? What are you talking about?"

"I presume I'm fired."

He waved his hand. "Hell, no. This guy's a trouble-maker, too. Need the boat built, and you're doing a damn good job at it. Besides, haven't seen my niece out of the house in a year. And smiling. Kiss her all you want. It's worth the controversy." His watch alarm beeped, and before Chase could get any words out of his shocked mind, Barnie said, "Nap time. Read once a long time ago that the body works best on short increments of sleep. You know what? Keeps this guy young."

Chase couldn't find the words of gratitude, so he asked, "Why do you refer to yourself in the third person?"

"Spent some time in the Pacific islands in a village that believed referring to yourself is bad luck. Bad social manners, too. Kinda stuck. Last time the word"—he mouthed the word *me*—"came out of this mouth, fell down the companionway and ended up with crushed nuts. G'night."

"Hey, Barnie . . . thanks."

Barnie nodded, spun his wheelchair around, and headed to the office. At the door he paused. "Since you've already cleaned your tools, might as well head on out for the day.

Besides, you work too hard. Makes this guy feel guilty sitting around while you work into the night."

Chase couldn't help smiling, even though Barnie couldn't see it. He was beginning to like the guy who could talk about his crushed testicles with as much ease as the weather.

Chase closed down the two large doors and wandered to the sailboat. It was overcast with a nice breeze coming off the Gulf. He pulled a Dr. Pepper out of his cooler and sat on the deck. Clouds piled up on the horizon, promising a spectacular sunset.

Some of the good feeling about staying had dissipated. Once Maddie's parents put their foot down, she'd kowtow to them, and he'd never see her again. Which was a good thing, really. Then again, it wasn't. He liked watching her work, liked having her there with him even if they weren't talking. Liked watching her watch him from the corner of his eye. There was something about the way she looked at him with that mixture of delight and question. Then he'd look her way, and she'd pretend she hadn't been watching. They'd played the cat-and-mouse game all day.

He was much better at not getting caught watching her. She was definitely skinny with hardly a hint of a chest. Strands of her hair stuck to her long, graceful neck. He'd been tempted to push her hair back and caught himself nearly freeing one of those strands. At first he thought her mouth and eyes too large for her face, but now he couldn't imagine them any other way. Whatever her flaws, she was perfect.

Whenever she reached up to cover a higher area, her flat stomach peeked out beneath her top. He'd wanted to reach out and run his hand over her stomach. He could already imagine her expression, the same one she'd had when he'd kissed her: bewildered. Bedazzled. The tank top hadn't hidden much, but he still found himself imagining peeling away the top and seeing if small breasts did turn him on.

He leaned back against the wall of the cabin and closed his eyes. Sex wasn't part of his agenda, and he'd given it little thought with everything else going on in his life. Thinking about Maddie, however, was stirring his body. If sweet Maddie only knew what she was doing to him now. Wonder what she'd do if he told her he'd gotten hard just thinking about her?

He shook his head. Well, she wasn't going to find out. Most likely, she'd probably show up once more to tell him it wasn't a good idea, her hanging around with him, and she'd be right. He'd tell her how much he appreciated her help and that he'd enjoyed her company. He'd offer to give her money again, she'd probably refuse again. Then he'd watch her walk away, and he'd think that for a skinny woman, she really did have a nice butt.

And that would be that.

CHAPTER 9

EVEN WHILE MADDIE and Q killed each other playing *Psycho Boxing*, all Maddie could think about was Mom getting home. She felt like a kid, and then she wondered what it would feel like to *not* feel like a kid.

"Uncle Maddie, you're not playing right," Q whined after he'd killed her for the sixth time in a row.

"Sorry, Q, just got a lot on my mind."

He walked to the window. "I'm gonna see Dad in his workshop."

Again that disturbing image of Bobby's butt flashed in her mind. "Better not surprise him like that."

"Why not?"

"If he's sawing something, he could cut his finger off."

"Then maybe he wouldn't work so much."

"Q, that's terrible! Let me go first, and if I give you the okay sign, you can come over."

The door was cracked open when she got there, so she figured it was all right to knock and enter.

Bobby looked up. "Hey, Baby. What's up?"

"Your son wants to come see you."

He looked behind Maddie. "Well, where is he?"

"I figured I'd check to make sure you weren't otherwise occupied."

He held out his hands. "See, I'm not."

"Bobby, you can't just ignore what happened last night."

"I can if you can."

"I can't. We do that too much around here. Have you broken things off with Wendy yet?"

"I will." When she narrowed her eyes, he said, "What's got into you? Used to be you'd have slunk out of here and never said a thing."

She thought of Chase admiring the way she'd handled Wendy. "I'm tough when it comes to Q. You screw up your marriage, and that boy suffers."

"I'm just having fun. I'm not going to leave Colleen or anything."

"Life isn't about just having fun!"

"Whoa, this coming from the girl who did nothing *but* play?"

"But I played *with* my husband. There's a difference."

He ran his hand through his coppery curls. "You don't understand. Your marriage was fun. You let Wayne do what he wanted, you didn't worry about bills and saving money, you just lived. Colleen's on me about every penny I spend for myself. Can't even buy a six-pack without her muttering how that three bucks could have gone for the pool."

They'd had a good life, she and Wayne. They hadn't worried about money. Sometimes she'd put some aside to deposit into their savings account, but Wayne would suggest going away for the weekend, and it would be gone.

"I shoulda married you," Bobby said, startling her back to the present. "You probably even like sex."

She put her hands over her ears. "I don't want to hear this."

"Can't you talk to her about giving me some more slack?"

She remembered that sad look on Colleen's face the other night and how she'd wanted to say something. "I don't know how to talk to her."

He sighed. "Send my son over. I ain't meeting Wendy tonight."

"Or ever. And you're having dinner with us tonight, you hear?"

He started to protest, but said, "I'll be there."

Victory was bittersweet. She still had to deal with Mom.

Maddie had put her nervous energy to good use. She'd dusted all of the teapots, flowered plates, and dishes that lined the shelves of the cupboard. She'd even climbed up on a chair and shaken the dust out of the dried flowers twined around the drying rack. Now she leaned against the counter stirring the chili in the Crock-Pot. When Mom pulled into the driveway, dread knotted her stomach.

Mom had her betrayed look in place before she even walked into the kitchen. She shoved a bag at Maddie and walked to the counter. "I am so mad at you, I can't even see straight."

"I'm sorry, Mom."

"Sorry? Sorry? Everyone in town knows my daughter lied to me. The daughter I devoted my whole life to. Look at my face and remember what you've done to me." She removed her glasses and posed.

"Mom, I appreciate everything you've done for me. But I don't want to stop seeing Chase. I feel good when I'm around him."

"So you don't feel good when you're around me, is that what you're saying?"

"Of course I do, but it's a different kind of feeling good."

Mom sucked in her breath with a whining sound. "You are in love with that man!"

"I am not." She rubbed her nose, then thought it couldn't mean the same thing as when Chase rubbed his. "I will never love another man besides Wayne. But I like Chase. He listens to me."

"Oh, and I suppose I don't."

"Not really." At her shocked look, Maddie added, "No one listens to anyone around here. We only hear what we want to hear. Chase listens, and he tells me things I don't want to hear, but he's right. He challenges me. When I'm with him, I feel alive. And yes, I feel alive here, but . . . not as alive."

"Oh, I see. We give you everything you want, never challenge you or say things you don't want to hear, and we're wrong."

Maddie touched Mom's arm. "You're not wrong. Maybe I need to be challenged, though. Maybe I'm ready to live again."

Mom took her hand, and Maddie noticed her nails were stained with blueberries. "There's nothing wrong with living. I want you to live. But you're in a fragile emotional state, and I don't want you hurt." She smoothed Maddie's hair back from her face, just like she'd always done. "Take things slow. Mom knows best, remember? If you push yourself too fast, you might slip and fall. Go visit the dogs. Take baby steps."

Maddie nodded, because that's what she was expected to do.

"Good girl," Mom said, kissing her on the forehead. "Let's get dinner ready."

Peace reigned in the kitchen again while they warmed up corn bread muffins and made lemonade. But Maddie didn't feel peaceful. She'd survived her first big lie to her mother, yet she didn't feel victorious. And not once had Mom mentioned her not seeing Chase again. She found out why when she and Colleen were washing the dishes.

"Did Mom give it to you when you got home?" Colleen asked without the least bit of sympathy.

"A little. And neither of you have the right to check up on me. I'm an adult."

"Yeah, right," Colleen said with a snort. "How can you be considered an adult when everyone calls you Baby?"

Chase didn't call her Baby. She liked the way her name sounded when he said it. And she'd certainly *felt* like an adult when she'd been fantasizing about him. "Maybe I'll tell everyone to stop calling me Baby."

"Yeah, right. You'll always be Baby."

It was a grim thought. Yet, until she'd met Chase, she'd never thought about asking people to call her Maddie. "And thanks for telling everyone about Chase not knowing who he is. And that he kissed me."

Colleen shrugged. "We're just worried about you. You're falling for this guy, and even if he isn't a serial killer, he's going to leave town and you're going to be crushed again."

"I am not in love with him," she said, accentuating each word.

"Well, it won't be a problem anymore." Colleen hung up the towel covered in ducks.

Maddie grabbed her arm. "Why not?"

"Barnie's going to fire him."

Maddie nearly knocked Colleen over as she dashed out of the kitchen. She didn't even feel the pain when she stubbed her toe on the cast-iron duck in the living room. Mom was working on her clown puzzle.

"You told Barnie to fire Chase?"

"Yes. So did Carol. We don't like the influence he has on you. He's going to be leaving soon anyway, so what does it matter? Maddie, where are you going?"

She was already on the way out to her car.

It was dark, though two lights lit some of the dock. Just beyond the dock, the warehouse was closed up for the night. Sugar's Eats already had their deck furniture stacked up, and Maddie could only see a few tables with people inside. Creatures scurried out of the way as she walked down the dock, and she didn't even want to know what they were. Her heart felt squeezed in her chest. She imagined the boat dark and silent, Chase gone. The breeze washed her hair in her face and made the waves slap against the dock pilings.

She couldn't believe her relief when she saw the dim light inside the boat. Now she could admit how that thought hurt, that Chase would leave and she'd never see him again. He couldn't leave. He hadn't done whatever it was he was supposed to do.

"Chase?" she said after searching the deck of the boat.

She heard splashing in the distance. Her gaze slid past the dock to where the shoreline curved back toward the open water. Between the warehouse and the Gulf was the picnic table she and Chase had lunch on. When the moon peeked out from beneath the clouds, she saw something moving in the water straight out from the table. Dolphins often played near the bay, and sometimes a manatee would swim in and everyone had to be careful not to hit him.

"Chase?"

"Maddie?" she heard a distant voice answer.

She looked toward the dolphin. "Is that you?"

"It was hot, so I took a swim."

She walked over to the side of the bay where Chase was swimming. Light played off the ripples in the water, highlighting his silhouette. She could barely see his features.

"Aren't you afraid of what's down there at night?"

"Same as what's down there during the day, I'd guess."

Maybe she shouldn't mention the jellyfish that you could see during the day, but not at night. She sat down on the bank and hugged her knees. "Is the water cool?"

"It's about body temperature. Come in."

Those two words teased her sensibilities, which told her that she should definitely *not* get in the water with him. "I don't think that's a good idea. For one thing, I don't have a bathing suit on."

"Neither do I."

Her throat went dry. "You're . . . naked?"

"I'm wearing briefs." He swam sideways, and the splashing noises tickled down her spine. "Come in in your bra and underwear. Or leave your clothes on. I'm not going to try anything."

"You're not?" Was she relieved? Of course she was.

"You're like a sister to me."

She shot to her feet. "A sister?"

"Yeah, just like a sister. I don't know if I have one, but if I do, I'd feel about her the same as I do about you."

She didn't want Chase to, well, have those kinds of feelings for her. Despite her little spike on the sex meter that day, she wasn't in the least bit interested in making love with anyone. This wasn't about his being a man and her being a woman who'd been fantasizing about this man.

"Like a sister, huh?" she said, kicking off her shoes.

"Yep. You're perfectly safe with me."

He didn't get it. She flung off her shirt and tossed it aside. She didn't want to be anybody's sister. Then she shimmied out of her shorts. Before she could give it a second thought, which she knew she should, she jumped into the water.

"Jeez, Maddie, you just about drowned me."

She could see him better now, though his features were shadows and curves, his eyes dark. He was wiping water off his face.

"Sorry," she said, not sounding sorry in the least. And in fact, she splashed him again.

He splashed her back, but she was the champion of

splash fights, or at least she had been when she and Wayne had fought in the pool.

"I give!" he sputtered a minute later, but she couldn't get that sister comment out of her head so she kept splashing until he grabbed her wrists and held them up. And that action pulled her right up against him.

He hovered over her, dripping on her face. "Stop it. I'm sorry I invited you in."

She was breathing heavily, but she wasn't sure if it was because of her efforts in splashing or how close he was and the way his fingers felt closed around her wrists.

"You are?" she asked.

"No, I'm not. But I didn't really think you'd come in."

"You thought I was too chicken."

"Yep."

"You're too honest, you know that?"

"Yep."

Then he was probably being honest about the sister comment. She told herself to be relieved and ignored the disappointment.

But he hadn't let her go.

She could see his mouth glistening in the dim moonlight, and as though he sensed she was looking at it, he ran his tongue over his lips. She did the same. He was looking at her, that much she could tell. She wondered if it was in a brotherly way.

"Can you stand up here?" he asked.

"Yes."

"Good."

And then he fell backward, pulling her with him and dunking both of them under the water. He held her in place with his arms around her waist. As startled as she was that he'd dunked her, she was more startled at the feel of a man's arms around her bare skin. They were only underwater for a moment, and then he pushed them to the surface.

"What'd you do that for?" she sputtered through water-logged lips.

"Same reason you splashed me."

So she splashed him again. They tangled in the inky black water until he subdued her by wrapping himself around her.

"Are you going to stop it?" he asked.

Pressed up along the length of him, she could feel every inch of him. And that included every inch of . . . *him.* Not only did her face flush, her whole body flushed. She nodded quickly, and he set her on her feet. She had to cover her mouth to contain the squeal of surprise that she'd made him come to attention. Sister, her foot.

She wasn't sure if he knew that she knew, which made her feel awkward on top of everything else. Just that brief feel of him, not just that part, but all of him, brought swiftly back her earlier hunger. She shivered from the assault of desire that felt foreign and right at the same time.

"You all right?" he asked. "Cold?"

"Fine," she answered too quickly and in a too high pitch of voice.

"Maddie . . ."

She didn't know if he was going to address the, ahem, issue, but she didn't want to talk about it. What could he have said, really? *Maddie, sorry about the hard-on. Oh, no problem, it just reminded me how long it's been since I've touched a man and how much I want to touch a man, and not just any man, but you.*

"Did Barnie fire you?" she asked.

He ran his fingers back through his dark hair. "Not really."

"How can you not really be fired?"

He chuckled, and the sound tickled through her. "He

said your mother and the woman who runs the marina wanted me fired, but he wasn't going to do it."

She couldn't help the grin that erupted over her face. "Kewl."

"Is that why you came out here?"

"I didn't want you to leave . . . without saying goodbye. You won't do that, will you? Just disappear one day?"

"I won't leave without saying goodbye," he said in a soft voice that sounded delicious in the dark.

She took a ragged breath. "And how am I going to explain to my family that I came out here to talk to you and got wet?"

"You could say I threw you in."

"They already don't want me hanging around you."

His hand brushed hers as he moved it around in the water. "But here you are."

"See, you *are* a bad influence on me."

This time his hands slid down hers, fingers tickling her skin. "And you're a bad influence on me."

"Me, a bad influence?" She would have laughed, but his hands settled on her waist and took her breath away. She felt as though a fist were softly pushing in at the center of her body.

He spread his fingers, and his thumbs grazed her stomach. In the distance she could hear the soft clang of a buoy's bell.

"Yep, 'cause I want to kiss you, and kissing you is a bad idea."

"K-kissing. . . . why?"

"Because I don't know who I am, and you're still in love with your husband."

Her heart was pounding so loud, she was sure he could hear it. "And you're going to be leaving soon."

"Yep."

"Wait a minute. I thought you only thought of me as a sister."

He pulled her just a little closer. "I lied."

"Did you rub your nose when you were saying it?"

"Maybe."

As bad an idea as it was, she wanted him to kiss her. The wanting filled her body with heat and made her light-headed, and that's why she leaned forward. Their mouths brushed together, and she tasted salt.

They moved together instinctively, her legs gliding around his waist, his arms going around her and pulling her close. She ran her fingers up into his wet hair, and he tilted her head and deepened the kiss.

When his tongue slid into her mouth, her eyes rolled shut, and she gave in to it. She'd forgotten how wonderful French kissing was, and yet, this seemed different, slower, more sensual. Their tongues brushed together as he languidly explored her mouth. He ran his tongue along the edge of her teeth, then tickled the roof of her mouth.

She felt as liquid as the water around her. He tasted like the Dr. Pepper he liked to drink, sweet and intoxicating. She loved the way he felt, all of him, surrounding her. The water was one hundred degrees, at least, and if they stayed there much longer, she could easily imagine it boiling.

"Maddie," he whispered, pulling down on the strands of her hair. She thought his eyes were closed, and just the sound of her name on his lips, sounding breathy and dreamy, made her think she was in heaven.

She whispered his name, because she wanted him to know how wonderful it felt to hear it. His hands moved higher on her waist, and then his thumbs were brushing her nipples outside her bra, just barely, whisper-light touches that sent a jolt of fire through her. She kissed him again, feeling the evidence of desire and relishing that she was the cause of it. A growling sound came from his throat, and his kiss became more ardent.

There were only two thin pieces of fabric separating them. One of his hands slid down her back beneath the waistband of her panties, and then the other, and he cupped her behind and pulled her flush against his body. She wanted to grind against him and soothe this burning ache she'd never felt before.

Her heart jumped into her throat when his thumbs traced around her sides and tickled at the edge of her intimate hair. How far would this go, and did she want to stop it even though it was wrong, it had to be wrong, didn't it?

Yes, it was wrong, because she loved Wayne. Because this scared her, she'd never felt quite like this before, never wanted anyone's hands on her the way she wanted Chase's hands on her, and anyone meant Wayne, the love of her life, the only man she would ever want . . .

When she opened her eyes, she saw that the warehouse lights were on. Then she heard a familiar voice that reminded her of being a teenager again, of sneaking kisses and more on the back porch and being alert of her parents coming out at any time.

Mom!

She wriggled out of Chase's hold, feeling disappointed and embarrassed and ashamed all at once. "My mom's here!"

Chase groaned, but was already helping her toward the shore. "Get your clothes on and tell them you fell in."

Definite flashbacks of doing what she shouldn't be with Wayne and nearly getting caught. Her heart was pounding for a different reason as she scrambled toward shore and fumbled with her clothes.

"She shot out of the house like a pistol when she found out I asked you to fire Chase. I thought she was coming to see you," Mom was saying to Barnie. "She must be talking to *him*."

Maddie jerked up her pants and called out, "Mom?," as she headed toward the dock. She knew her smile was as phony as no-fat cream cheese, and her laugh that sheep-bleating kind. "I fell in the water."

Her mom, still wearing her pink housecoat and slippers, squinted at Maddie. "What?"

"When I got here, I saw dolphins swimming over there." Well, sort of the truth. "I lost my footing and fell in."

She expected fear and concern over her well-being, but all she got was Mom's narrow-eyed look. "You've got that same guilty look on your face as you had when you were doing something you shouldn't have been with Wayne." She looked toward *The Barnacle*. "I'm going to talk to that man." She pulled Maddie along as though she were a child.

Just minutes ago she definitely had not felt like a child. For the first time she'd felt like a woman.

Colleen's words came back to her. *You'll always be Baby.*

How could she explain that she'd been in the water in the dark with Chase? Betraying her husband's memory with the man he'd sent to help her?

"Excuse me! Hello!" Mom called out in a much-too-loud voice.

Several long minutes dragged by. It was going to look suspicious when he didn't make an appearance. Just when Mom turned to Maddie with an accusatory expression, Chase climbed out the companionway looking puzzled and delicious—that word again—wearing only a towel. He was drying his hair.

"Sorry, I didn't hear you. I was in the shower." He took in her mother, then glanced at Maddie, keeping his expression perfectly bland. "Hey, Maddie. What's wrong?"

Mom clearly didn't know what to make of it. She drew

a breath and puffed up her shoulders. "Didn't you hear Maddie fall into the bay a few minutes earlier?"

"Sorry, I didn't." He looked at her again and rubbed his nose. "You all right?"

She tried not to smile at the giveaway that he was lying. "Fine. Loose rocks down there."

He glanced over the dark water. "Aren't you afraid of what's down there at night?"

She really had to squelch her smile. "Same as what's down there during the day, I'd guess."

"Chase, she's gone through hard times this past year, and she doesn't need anything to send her off balance. She's got her family, and that's all she needs. Thank you."

With Maddie in tow, she headed back down the dock. Maddie tried hard not to look back at Chase.

"Mom, I hate when you do that."

"What? Straighten out your messes?"

"No, talk about me as though I weren't there." Once she'd said the words, she realized how true it was. Her long-held irritation bombarded her.

"Look at you, you're soaking wet. Let's see if Barnie has a towel you can borrow so you don't get your upholstery wet."

"Mom, please listen to me."

They had approached the warehouse where Barnie, wearing striped pajamas and a robe, was sitting in his wheelchair. Maddie started to put her thoughts together, but Mom cut her off.

"Baby, I love you, you know that?" Maddie nodded, and Mom tightened her hold. "And your mother knows best. That man is nothing but trouble. I never objected to you being with Wayne, because we knew his family. He was a good man who took care of you."

Chase's words about his recklessness filtered through her mind. She pushed them away. "I'm not in love with Chase."

She hoped the words didn't sound as empty as she thought they did.

"Maybe not, but you're infatuated with him, or with this idea that Wayne sent him. Don't turn to a stranger to heal your broken heart, Baby. That's what your family is for."

When Mom went into the warehouse to get a towel, Maddie looked toward the sailboat. She couldn't see Chase, which was probably a good thing. She wrapped her arms around herself, feeling chilled for the first time since getting into the water.

Maybe Colleen was right. Maybe she couldn't change the way things were.

CHAPTER 10

ONCE MADDIE ARRIVED home, her mom sat on the couch and focused on the television. Dad sat in his easy chair. He nodded at her when she plopped down on the other end of the couch, but didn't say anything. As though she always tore out of the house like that.

"Well, aren't you going to say something?" she asked at last, unable to bear the silence.

Mom didn't take her gaze from the television, even though there was only a commercial on. She just twirled one red curl over and over. "There's nothing to talk about, hon. If you lied, I have nothing to say to you. If you didn't, well, there's still nothing to talk about."

Nothing changed around there. She wondered what they'd say if she told them she nearly made love to that gorgeous stranger they wanted her to have nothing to do with. Bet Mom would say something then.

Maddie wisely held her tongue and said, "I'm going to go to sleep. G'night."

Mom had cleaned and rearranged her room again. Everything on the dresser was aligned, clothes put away. Maddie rearranged them back into their disarray, just because. She looked at her room, at the calico curtains and matching comforter, the angels hanging from the ceiling and sitting on every flat surface. Her room hadn't changed since she'd lived there before marrying Wayne. Mom had left it intact for the occasional relative who stopped into town for a visit.

She picked up the stuffed angel doll sitting against her pillows and plucked at the lace. The Reverend Hislope was right. God wasn't going to send an angel to heal her heart. She opened the bottom drawer of her dresser and set the angel doll inside. Then she took each of her porcelain figurines and set them in there, too. Lastly, she climbed up on her bed, took down the mobile of floating angels, and put them away.

Something broke loose inside her, and she felt awash in a bittersweet feeling of freedom.

When she faced her reflection above the dresser, she noticed a particular gleam in her eyes. Not guilt exactly. The corner of her mouth tilted up, a mouth that was a little pinker than when she'd left. It only took that thought to ignite memories of Chase's mouth. Following that came the feel of his hands on her body and the way his body felt plastered against hers.

"You're a sex fiend," she whispered, then let her forehead fall forward to hit the mirror. She'd never been kissed like that, though she hated to admit it. She'd never thought herself a sex fiend, either, even though she and Wayne had had a healthy love life.

And the one man who made her feel that way was off-limits. She already knew she'd have a fight on her hands if she returned to the marina tomorrow. And no one was going to believe that she was going anywhere else.

Giving in was the sensible choice, the one she was expected to make. And that's exactly what she was going to do.

The next morning Maddie put on the pajamas with the muffins and coffee cups print and went out to the living room. She hadn't brushed her hair since her shower last night.

The smell of strawberry muffins filled the room.

She found the pink comforter still folded at the end of the couch and pulled it around her. Then she turned on the television and stared at it without focusing.

Mom came out of the kitchen and stopped. Then smiled. "Baby." She disappeared for a moment and returned with a muffin on a plate. "Strawberry this morning." She went into the bathroom and returned with a brush. "Hope you didn't catch a cold from your little dip last night. You remember how easily you used to catch colds."

"Used to, Mom. Not anymore."

Every muscle in her body twitched to jump up and scream, but she held herself still while Mom brushed her hair.

"Isn't it nice to have everything back the way it was?" Mom said. "Eat your muffin, hon."

Nice to be back the way it was?

Colleen walked in, holding her mug ready to be filled with coffee. "Now, there's a sight I expect. Feeling back to normal?" Instead of giving Maddie a hard time about moping, Colleen was smiling.

Maddie's fingers tightened on the comforter as she came to a horrible realization: her family was dysfunctional! They liked her better when she was depressed and dependant.

Mom grabbed Colleen's mug and returned a minute later with fresh coffee. Dad walked in and said, "Morning, pumpkin. Morning, Colleen. Gotta go. Try and have a good day, hear?" He kissed her on the head, gave Colleen a squeeze on the shoulder and took the travel mug full of banana nut coffee and headed out. Even he looked happy to see her on the couch again!

She watched him pull out of the garage and dump his coffee on the flowers by the mailbox before driving off. This time Mom was watching, too.

"Doesn't it bother you, his dumping out the coffee every day?"

"Mm?" Mom blinked and looked at her. "Does what bother me? Eat your muffin, and if you want, we can bake some cookies later."

Colleen glanced out the window, then leaned out the door and yelled, "Bye, Quigley! Have a good day!"

Maddie shot up off the couch and got tangled in the comforter. "Q! Call him Q. And I don't want to be called Baby anymore. I want you to call me Maddie!" Finally she freed herself from the dratted thing and tossed it on the couch. "I'm going to work on Barnie's boat with Chase. Instead of worrying about me or being mad that I'm still seeing him, be happy that I'm not sitting there moping on the couch. Be happy for me." She looked at Colleen. "If you want me to watch Q this afternoon, ask the school to drop him off at the marina. Otherwise, take the afternoon off and spend some time with your son. Ask him how he feels about his given name and those trolls. Then send him over here and spend some time with your husband. Ask him how he feels, period."

"Quite a scene last night," Barnie said. He was still wearing faded blue pajamas, and he'd parked his wheelchair at the outer edge of the warehouse to catch the slash of dawn light coming around the side of the building.

Chase had been working on the boat for a half hour already. "Guess so."

"You didn't have anything to do with Maddie getting wet, did you?"

The old guy knew something, what with that gleam in his eyes. But Chase wasn't about to compromise her integrity. "I don't go around pushing women in the water."

Barnie harrumphed, but didn't press the subject. He

wheeled closer to the hull, moving his hand back and forth to check the layup. "Nice and smooth."

"Fair layup saves a lot of time later."

"Seems weird, you knowing about that and not who you are."

"Kind of frustrating, really."

He kept working as he talked with Barnie. He was nearly done with the second layer. Today he hoped he could finish the fiberglass outside skin. He didn't like talking about his memory loss. He felt like half a person when others knew. Except around Maddie.

"Doubt she's going to be coming around," Barnie said, as though reading his mind. Or face.

Chase wondered if his expression gave away the disappointment. "Me, too. Her mother made it pretty clear how she felt about Maddie hanging around me."

"Never been much of a rebel, especially where her mom's concerned." Barnie rolled his chair to the stern and ran his fingers along the edge. "She's a special gal."

Chase couldn't help the smile. "Yeah, that she is." And last night in his arms, she'd proven she was a special woman, too. A passionate woman. Damn all his good intentions about treating her like a sister.

"What are you going to do after you finish this boat?" Barnie asked.

"Got to move on." Chase kept his focus on smoothing out the area he was working on. "Now you know why."

"To find who you are."

"Right."

"What about Maddie?"

That question stopped him. He hadn't thought about his leaving being equated to leaving Maddie. He glanced out to the bay that caught the pink glow of the sky. "She's still in love with her dead husband. But she'll eventually get over him and move on, too. Find somebody here to fall in love with."

Barnie nodded, though it was obvious that wasn't the answer he'd been looking for. "If you ever come around to our town again, I'd be mighty pleased to give you a job."

Chase felt a surge of gratitude. "Thanks."

Barnie turned his wheelchair around. "Sail material came in late yesterday. Fortunately that's something this guy can do even in this blamed thing." He wheeled to the back of the warehouse to a heavy-duty sewing machine and a large swath of canvas. "You can be the first to test-drive this baby when it's ready. This guy sure as heck can't do it."

The prospect of sailing made his heart beat faster. He thought of something else that made his heart beat faster: Maddie. Every few minutes he caught himself glancing up to see if she was approaching. She'd surprised him last night. 'Course, he'd surprised himself. Everything had seemed so natural once she'd kissed him. They'd come together as though they'd been doing it forever. Strange considering that as far as Chase was concerned, he'd never made love to a woman before.

Physically he might have. He wasn't a bad-looking guy, and he figured he had to be about twenty-eight or so. Enough time to have had a woman or three. But mentally, emotionally . . . he'd never touched a woman. Naïve Maddie knew more about sex than he did.

Not that it mattered. He had no business getting involved with her on that level when he had a life waiting for him somewhere.

Not only had his body been charged since kissing Maddie, his brain's synapses had been charged, too. More memories had returned, pieces of a life he wasn't sure he liked.

"Hi," a familiar, heartwarming voice said beside him.

This was the kiss-off, the big goodbye. Then why was

he smiling even before he looked up to see her standing there in an old T-shirt cinched at the bottom and jean shorts?

Once their gazes met, he couldn't pull away. She swallowed and looked at the boat. "You've been busy."

"Yep." How could this waif steal away his words by just standing there? "Didn't think I'd see you today."

Her smile faded. "I think my family's happier when I'm not. Does that sound crazy?"

"No. They like taking care of you." He glanced around the corner of the boat to make sure Barnie wasn't within earshot. "Barnie asked if you were with me last night. I told him no."

"Good. No need to start any rumors."

"Maddie, about last night . . ."

"Let's . . . not talk about it, okay? It shouldn't have happened. Maybe it was just the allure of being in the water in the dark. Let's just stay . . . friends." She rubbed her hands together. "What can I do?"

She was staying, standing up for herself. And in a way, for him. So they'd stay friends. It was enough. It was perfect. He started her on the last section. He had no business wanting her when he had no past, and she had too much of one.

Once they'd dispensed with the subject of last night, they fell into their easy pace. She wandered over to see what Barnie was working on for a few minutes, and Chase caught himself glancing over at her. She still looked like that innocent waif, and it clashed with the memories of the woman he'd held in his arms.

She was growing up.

Maddie noticed that they kept their conversations on safe subjects, when they did talk. Truth was, every time she opened her mouth, she wanted to talk about what had happened the night before. Especially when she heard the distant clang of the buoy's bell. She needed to know he'd been aroused as much as she had. Not on the outside—she knew that. But on the inside. Just as she kept running the scene through her mind over and over, she wondered if he did. She wanted to know how he was feeling at every step, when she'd moved closer to him, when she kissed him, and when she'd really gone crazy and pushed up against his erection.

But then she was afraid to hear that he hadn't felt anything, other than the physical. Maybe he'd only felt that much because it had been a while. She couldn't deny that she did feel something for him, though she didn't want to explore too deeply what that was. She'd been devastated when Wayne had left. She didn't want to go through even a fifth of that feeling when Chase left. She'd shoot back to double digits on the sad meter. She looked up and caught him watching her.

He narrowed his eyes. "You look awfully serious over there, Maddie."

"I'm just wondering if Q is going to get dropped off here. Colleen didn't want him around . . . well, around you. I told her to spend some time with him. And with her husband tonight."

"The one who's cheating?"

"He'd better not still be cheating." She let out a long breath. "It's a terrible secret to keep, you know."

"I can imagine. You're probably not good at keeping secrets like that."

"I'd rather just forget I ever saw his big, white butt . . ." She shuddered at the memory. "But I can't make it go away. I just have to believe he's broken things off and will work it out with Colleen."

She could talk to him about anything. Well, almost anything. If Chase hadn't been around, who else could she have shared this with? Not Mom. She would have pretended not to have heard it.

Chase was wearing a faded, black button-down shirt. He'd left it open, probably not to drive her crazy with glimpses of his chest. His white pants were stained on one leg and too big. Which meant they settled low on his hips, below his tan line.

When she sensed he was about to look her way, she said, "I stopped by the garage where my dad works and asked him where the *Dinky* is. It's behind my house. He said he takes it out fishing once in a while, to keep the engine running. I never knew he even used it. Not that I mind. He didn't mention it because he didn't want me thinking about being on it with Wayne." She lifted one shoulder. "Too many memories. But . . ." *Push the words out, Maddie.* "I'd like to take it out and watch the sunset tonight."

"You going to take Q?"

"Maybe. That'll give Colleen and Bobby a chance to spend some time together." She was rather hoping, in some ways, that Chase would ask to go along, and then she'd feel obligated to say yes, he could come, because that was the polite thing to do.

He didn't.

But there was a solid reason for asking him to accompany her. She wasn't sure she could face that house alone.

"Come with us," she heard herself say, though she wasn't even looking at him. She blinked in surprise and met his gaze. "Please."

He only nodded, as though he understood, though she knew he couldn't. Her nervous little laugh sounded almost like relief. What could happen with Q there? Hopefully Q would be there.

Being alone with Chase who had no past was definitely not a good idea.

*   *   *

Later in the afternoon, Maddie had mixed feelings when Q arrived. That meant Colleen wasn't spending time with him. And it meant she wasn't spending time alone with Chase.

"Hi, Uncle Maddie," he said. "Wow, the boat's almost done."

"It's got a ways to go," Chase said, warming her with the words.

Because he'd be around for a little while longer.

"Guess what?" she said to Q. "We're taking the *Dinky* out."

She didn't quite share the enthusiasm her nephew displayed. She thought he was doing some kind of football end zone dance, but wasn't sure.

"We're going to leave from here. We'll get some subs from Homer's on the way."

"Kewl!" Q said.

Actually, Maddie didn't want to face Mom or Colleen about asking to take Q out. They would object, even if Chase wasn't going. So she was going to cheat and leave a message on Colleen's machine.

At just before five, she walked to the back where Barnie had taken up the sailing material after waking from his latest nap. "Is it okay if I steal your employee a little early?"

"He was here at daybreak, so can't complain if he knocks off early." He looked at her, really looked at her. "You're looking good, Maddie."

She was stunned by the compliment. Barnie rarely dispensed many words at all, particularly those kind. "Thanks." She couldn't help the involuntary glance at Chase.

"Remember, he's going to leave soon."

"I know," she said in a too-high, too-bright voice.

He went back to the sewing machine, and she returned to the boat. "Ready?"

"I am, I am!" Q ran over from where he'd been examining an anthill.

Chase gathered up the tools and cleaned them while she closed up the container of resin. The boat was coming along too fast. While she was helping him, she was also helping him to leave faster. But how else could she spend time with him?

They both washed up in the small locker rooms at the marina and headed to her car.

"Nice," he said as they approached the teal Sunbird. "I haven't driven . . . well, since I can remember."

She handed him the keys.

"I don't have a license." He handed them back.

She didn't take them. "So? We have two cops in Sugar Bay, and they never caught Wayne when he sped through town. You do remember how to drive, don't you?"

Resignation laced his voice. "Everything but who I am, it seems."

She pushed his hand back. "Drive."

The tiny smile he tried to hide was worth it. Though once he was in the driver's seat, she had the disconcerting thought that Wayne and perhaps her dad were the only males who had ever driven the car.

"You sure you want me to drive?" he asked, and she realized he was watching her.

"Yes. Let's go."

They picked up the subs, and he insisted on paying even though she knew he didn't have much money. It was strange, going into Homer's to get subs for a trip to watch the sunset . . . without Wayne. Danny had given her a strange look indeed when she'd walked in with Chase.

No doubt by the time she got home, her family would know all about it.

As they got nearer to her house, her throat tightened, and her heart slowed down. Q babbled on about the last time he'd played Merlin's Mini-Golf. He pointed out his friends' houses as they drove past the Gulf-side cottages. She heard her voice thicken as she directed Chase into the driveway of her dream house.

"You all right?" he asked.

She couldn't take her eyes off the front of that house, with its gingerbread accents and manicured little yard. It was a narrow house, with the garage on the right and a bay window on the other side of the foyer. "I haven't been here since . . . Wayne left. It looks different, yet so familiar, too."

"Mom and I come and swim in the pool," Q said, pushing against the seat even though they hadn't opened the doors yet.

"Looks like someone lives here," Chase said.

"John comes once a week to trim and mow." She started to look his way, but couldn't. "I'm a chicken not to have come here, I know. A baby. But this was our dream house. Wayne's grandparents gave us the house for our wedding present when they moved into a condo. We took some of the money he inherited from his great-grandfather and remodeled it."

The houses on either side were as old as hers, and just as quaint. The newer homes nearby were built higher due to new flood restrictions.

"It's nice," Chase said.

He waited until she opened her door first, giving her time. She loved him for that. Or rather, loved his understanding. She also knew he wouldn't let her back down, even though she was having thoughts of doing just that. She had another mission in mind, and that meant going inside.

Q ran around the back emitting something that sounded

like an Indian holler. Maddie walked up to the door. For a crazy moment, it seemed plausible that Wayne would be waiting inside, wondering where the heck she'd been for the last year.

Chase looked at the key fob, *World's Perfect Husband!*, before handing it back to her. She took a deep breath and shoved the key into the lock. As soon as the familiar smells of the house engulfed her, she wrapped her arms around herself and didn't move. The air was stale, though it was still scented with the dried eucalyptus in the flower arrangements. Gifts from her mom.

"It's too hard," she whispered. "It's like he's still here."

Chase's voice was just as soft. "He's not."

"I can smell him. I can feel him." She shivered. Everything was just the way they'd left it that terrible day. Wayne had gone to the marina earlier to oversee delivery of that damned boat. He'd called Maddie when he had it in the water.

"Baby, come down and see my new toy!" He was like a kid, so excited about everything. The way she used to be.

"I left to meet him at the marina," she said. "That was the last time I saw this place." She felt herself walking in, then realized Chase's hands were on her shoulders. They'd walked through the small entry area and into the dining room/great room combination. "We made love on that couch the night before."

He dropped his hands, and she wished she could take back the words. But they were out, and she was swept up in the memories of that last lovemaking as she touched the arm of the country charm couch. He'd pulled her down as she'd walked by. Just like every aspect of his life, Wayne was fast in that department, too. But he snuggled with her afterward to make up for it. He hated how fast he went, and that he wasn't big . . . down there. Maddie had told him countless times that she wasn't, either, they were a perfect match.

She sank down on the couch. "He used to play 'One little piggy went to market' with my toes." She hadn't realized that, just like old times, whenever she walked into the house, she had slipped out of her shoes. She pulled her legs up and touched her toes.

"He must have felt like he was seducing a child."

She jerked her head up, angry that he'd tugged her out of the memory. "He didn't have to seduce me."

Bull's-eye. He recoiled to the French doors to watch Q.

She tried to go back into the memory, but it was gone. She grabbed her toe and wiggled it, but now the ditty was only a child's game. She tried to imagine having breakfast in the nook that overlooked the Gulf, or making dinner with him, but they all eluded her.

Her gaze went to Chase, standing rigid at the doors in a white T-shirt and tight jeans. It was because of him that she couldn't remember.

"Let's go," he said, turning back to her. "Take me back to the marina and go home. You're not ready for this."

She pushed to her feet and walked to him. "I am."

He slid his thumb beneath her eye, then showed her the tears. "Maybe you'll never be ready. Maybe you should just sell this place and stay at home with your parents."

Q waved at them, oblivious of the fact that her heart was crushing even more than it had before. She waved back, but returned her gaze to the impassive expression on Chase's face.

"Why are you saying this?"

"Because it's true. Look at you. Maybe you did love him so much, you can't move on. Maybe you'll just grow old with your memories."

She rubbed away the tears, but more came. Not from

her memories, but his harsh words. "There's nothing wrong with that."

"Other than it being a waste. But if you want to waste your life and live in your parents' shadow, there's nothing I can do about it." He turned away from her as though he couldn't stand the sight of her. "In a few weeks I'll leave, and you can hide away from life again." His voice softened, but his gaze stayed on Q splashing in the pool. "And I won't be able to think about you, because I hate thinking of you living your life like this."

"Don't say that," she said through a fresh wave of tears. "Don't say you won't think about me." She blindly reached for his arm. "Because I won't be able to stop thinking about you."

His rigid stance collapsed, and he pulled her close. "Don't cry, Maddie." Hearing the compassion in his voice again made her cry even harder. He held her face in his hands, and when he gave up trying to wipe away her tears, he pressed his forehead to hers. "I'm sorry," he whispered.

She gripped his arms, afraid he'd change his mind and move away. But she couldn't talk, couldn't force any words through a throat tight with emotion. Heat emanated from her face, though the tears had stopped flowing. She wanted him to pull her close and hold her, but she was afraid that wouldn't be enough. She wanted to bury herself in him, in the smells of his soap and the faint scent of detergent on his clothing.

When she looked up at him, his eyes were squeezed shut. She'd admitted too much, more than she even knew. It was already too late. When he left, her heart was going to shatter.

He moved back, and she saw the pain as he took in her face, which must be a mess. "I'm sorry I made you cry, Maddie. I just don't want you to give up. When I leave . . .

when I think about you—and I will think about you—I
want to know you're okay."

She nodded. He was being tough on her, just like he'd
done before. But it wasn't his words that made her feel
alive. It was the way he was holding her, and talking to
her now.

"Maybe Wayne did send me to you," he said. "Maybe
he wanted me to bring you back to life."

His kiss made her feel more alive than anything. She
could taste the salt of her tears as he moved his mouth
against hers. His lips were soft, and she felt them part
slightly before he thought better of deepening the kiss and
stepped back.

"Ready to go for that boat ride?" he asked in a rough
voice.

She nodded again, then remembered why she'd come
inside to begin with. "Wait a minute." She turned to the
short hallway that led to the master bedroom. Then she
walked in, holding her breath and waiting for more memories to assail her when she saw the black lacquer bed in
the middle of the room. Nothing came. She was still too
raw from Chase's words, and still too ragged from his kiss.

She went to the closet and pulled down several shirts
and a few pairs of pants. She held them out as a peace
offering.

"I don't know if the pants will fit, but maybe the shirts
will. Mom got him these for Christmas, and they were too
big."

He looked inside the waistband of the pants and handed
them back to her. "I'm not a twenty-eight waist, but
thanks." Then he pulled his T-shirt off and slid into one of
the button-down shirts. It was a little tight, but it was new
and clean. "These'll work."

"Okay." She went to the kitchen sink and splashed water
on her face, then blew her nose with a paper towel. A

crystal angel caught the late afternoon rays coming through the window. "I'm ready."

And she meant those words in a new way. She just wasn't sure what it was yet.

CHAPTER II

"BABY IS OUT of control!" Colleen screamed.

Mom was peeling potatoes at the sink. "I don't think it's a good idea for her to go out on that boat either, but I'd hardly call it out of control."

"She kidnapped my son!"

Mom pushed her red hair out of her face. "I'm sure there's an explanation."

"Yes, she's gone crazy! She's with that man on a boat with my son. Danny told Marlene that they stopped for subs. I'm getting someone else to watch him after school. Mom, do something about her."

Mom poured two cups of coffee and pulled Colleen to the table. It was that awful banana nut coffee, but Colleen drank it anyway. She pulled her hair back from her face and looked at Mom.

"How can you be so calm?"

"Well, I don't believe she really kidnapped Quigley."

"I don't think she's going to keep him or anything. But she's gone against my wishes, and he's *my* son!" And she had the horrible suspicion that he liked his aunt better than his mother. "She left a message on my machine saying that she was taking Q—that's what she's been calling him—on the *Dinky* and for me and Bobby to spend some time alone. I will not let her rule my life anymore." She pushed to her feet. "I'm going to stop her."

Mom took hold of her hand. "Don't make a fuss. She'll

be back soon enough and then you can talk to her."

"I hardly ever caused you stress, yet you always stick up for her. Look what you've done for her, and this is how she thanks you. All you've sacrificed, putting your life on hold for her."

"We're not to talk about that. We just put all that ugliness on hold, don't even think about it." She pulled Colleen down to the chair. Colleen didn't want to sit down, but she complied. "Honey, Baby's going through a phase. This stranger gives her something we can't right now. So we're just going to have to wait it out. This morning she wanted to go back to being her regular self, but his influence overrode that. She'll come around, and everything will go back to the way it was."

Colleen didn't like it one bit, but she nodded and stood. "I hope you're right."

Mom lifted her chin. "Mothers are always right."

She glanced toward the kitchen window. "I'm going to talk to Bobby."

As she walked across the street, she realized she'd run to Mom before she'd even gone to her husband. She shivered. Despite her words to Mom about having had to put her life on hold for Baby, Colleen didn't want things to change. If Baby became Maddie and moved out, Mom and Dad would get divorced.

Mom had told Colleen first, to judge her reaction before breaking the news to Maddie. They no longer loved each other the way they should. Colleen had a family of her own, and Baby was settled into her life, so it shouldn't make any difference. Things would be amicable, they'd still spend holidays together.

Then Wayne had died, and Baby had fallen apart. They'd put the divorce on hold. As long as Baby lived at home with them, they would stay together. They'd do anything for Baby.

She could see Bobby's shadow moving around in the workshop. Since he'd installed air-conditioning, he kept the door closed. He'd taken most of their pool savings fund for this darn workshop, and she wouldn't let him forget the sacrifice she'd made. The only thing that made it better was that Bobby contributed what he made on his extra projects to the fund.

She felt the urge to knock first. Silly, it wasn't a house. She pushed open the door.

Bobby looked up from where he was about to push a board through the table saw. "What's up?"

He never smiled at her anymore. Had her own marriage gotten stale, too? It was too soon for that. "Maddie's kidnapped our son." She couldn't even manage indignation in her voice anymore.

"I heard the message."

"And you're not bothered? She's taking him out with that strange man from the marina."

"Baby's not going to let anything happen to our son, Colleen. Since Wayne's accident, she's the most careful person in the world."

"You would take her side."

Bobby, covered in a fine layer of sawdust, returned to his work without comment. He looked very manly, big and handsome . . . unavailable. Like before they'd started dating, when he was immersed in his work, and she'd marvel that she was attracted to a redhead.

"Want to get a bite? See a movie or something?" she asked.

"Can't," he said without even looking up. "I promised this bookcase would be done yesterday. 'Sides, I already grabbed a sub at Homer's on the way home from work."

She pulled her hair back and nodded, but couldn't get any words past the knot in her throat. Bobby's world seemed wrapped up in that workshop, and he spent more and more time there. She walked to the house and grabbed her car keys. If she'd lost control of everything else in her world, the least she could do was try to stop her son from going out on that boat with Baby.

Maddie hauled a gas can out of the storage area next to the pool. "The gas gauge doesn't work, so we always fill it up before we leave."

Chase took the can from her and walked to the little dock where the boat was tied. "You rode around in a boat with a faulty gas gauge?"

"Look, crabs!" Q said, pointing to the piling. He'd already climbed on the boat after Maddie had towel-dried him.

Her eyes still looked red, and it hadn't helped that Q had, upon seeing her, said, "Uncle Maddie, you're a ten on the sad meter!"

Chase already felt like a heel for making her cry, but he couldn't seem to stop himself from pushing her. Maybe he was a terrible person deep inside, a bully, or just cold and insensitive.

Everything went gray for a moment as a woman's voice echoed in his head. *Can you ever love me more than sailing? Tell me, Chase, are you capable of loving someone?*

He felt his stomach tighten at the tears in her voice, and the resignation that flowed through him. But before he could hear his answer, Maddie's voice pulled him back.

"Don't go on about Wayne not being careful and getting us stranded. He knew what he was doing. He wouldn't have let anything—What's wrong?"

"I'm . . . trying not to go on about Wayne not being careful." When she didn't buy that, he crouched down to take in the faded words on the side of the boat. "You even painted *Dinky* on it."

"Chase did that." Her eyes bugged open. "Wayne! Wayne did that."

. He stood, trying not to be annoyed that she'd called her dead husband Chase.

"I'm sorry," she said. "I don't have you two confused. Really. You're nothing like him."

"Grab the cooler and let's head out," he said instead of saying that he wasn't sure she could ever get over her husband. Sometimes she made progress, but other times, it seemed hopeless. Then again, what did he know about love? Maybe nothing at all.

He helped her down into the boat, but she paused in front of him and said, "I'm sorry," again.

"It's all right."

He didn't want to see that pained expression on her face anymore, so he squeezed her hand and smiled. She smiled, too, and he felt something in his chest shift. The same way he'd felt when he'd kissed her in the house. It wasn't a sexual kiss—that he could have handled. It was an I-want-to-take-away-all-your-pain-and-make-you-mine kiss, and that's what scared him. He could admit—to himself anyway—that he hated to see her wallowing in memories of making love with her dead husband. He might not know who he was, but he had enough of a male ego to hate when she thought about Wayne when she was with him. He'd lashed out at her because of that, and then when he'd made her cry . . . he'd felt like a sea slug.

Having her in his arms was the only thing that felt right in his life. When she'd admitted she couldn't stop thinking about him, it had nearly torn him apart.

"Looks like the gauge works now," he said, forcing his thoughts back to the matter at hand once he'd started the motor. His voice sounded thick and edgy.

"Dad must have fixed it."

Like a responsible man, he wanted to say, but held the

words inside. The Dinky was a little skiff with an engine made for puttering. The bottom was flat and covered with plastic turf. Maddie piled towels on the floor to make a comfortable place to sit as he steered away from the dock. Q was leaning over the bow watching the water.

The sun had at least another hour before setting, so Chase tooled around some of the small islands that bordered the shore. The Gulf was as smooth as ice with only an occasional roll. He sat on the bench by the motor, and she sat on the towels and looked at peace.

"Uncle Maddie, look at the fish!" Q said.

"Careful, don't fall in." She looked where he pointed and held on to him.

She was wearing white shorts and a long-sleeved, baggy shirt that danced in the breeze. Chase shifted his weight to the other side of the bench and watched her behind as she leaned over the side. She wasn't skinny; she was just little. She might not be curvy, but she was all woman. Even if she was giggling with Q. Chase didn't like what she was doing to him. Not just physically, but inside. She was making him want her. The trucker woman or even the sexy woman who'd offered him a ride and a place to stay for the night and had thrown him a condom . . . neither had sparked any interest. He'd headed on without regret.

Then there was Maddie.

She chose that moment to turn and look at him. He couldn't help but smile, and when she smiled back, he felt that shift again. Damn. Maybe it would have been better if Barnie had fired him. He would have left with a little cash and without this tangle inside. Even if he couldn't love, he could sure feel.

When the sun began to paint the sky orange and pink, he cut the engine and drifted. Q had spent the last hour looking at everything and scrambling all over the boat.

Once he'd come up to Chase and said, "Thanks for taking us out on the *Dinky*."

"It was your uncle Maddie's idea."

"Yeah, but she wouldn't go without you."

He'd scrubbed Q's red curls made even more vibrant by the dying sunlight. Now the boy was settled on the floor with his soda and sub.

There were a few other boats out, but none nearby. The only sounds were the buzz of distant engines and an occasional squawk from a seagull. He glanced back toward Sugar Bay's rocky shores. The marina and Maddie's house were farther south.

"Sit and eat," she said, patting the spot beside her. She laid out the food and cracked open the cans of soda.

As he settled in beside her, he realized this was the most peaceful he'd felt since . . . well, since he could remember. They ate in silence, absorbing the breeze and the sunset. The soft sigh she occasionally released penetrated to his very soul.

It was the first time he'd felt like he had a soul.

After they ate, Q snuggled in front of her, and she leaned back against Chase. He had the oddest sensation of being a family, which was a crazy thought, and one that kept him from saying anything to break the spell.

Once the sun had set, Chase noticed Q's slanted position. He'd fallen asleep. The last of the pink was being leached from the sky, which had turned a gray blue.

"Colleen accuses me of making everything into an issue about me. I was embarrassed to realize she was right. In our friendship . . ." Maddie turned to him, her shoulder rubbing against his chest. "This is a friendship, isn't it?"

He brushed a strand of hair from her cheek. "Sure it is."

She turned around again. "It seems that it's been about me. I mean, me and Wayne, me and my family. I want to know about you."

"There isn't much to know." His laugh came out soft instead of bitter. "There isn't much *I* know." He felt that strange ache again, knowing it was better if he didn't spill, but wanting to anyway. Wanting to tell her how empty the memory of the woman's voice made him feel.

"You don't remember anything about your life?"

"A few images of being a kid."

She turned around again. "Really?"

He shrugged. "They're almost like watching a movie. I don't feel anything, don't feel attached to them. But I'm pretty sure they're mine."

She turned sideways and rested against his leg. Q resettled against her, and she hugged him. "Like what?"

"I'm racing a small sailboat. I can see the markers and the other kids I'm racing against. It's a sunny day, windy. In another, I'm playing hide and seek. Or maybe just hiding. And . . ." He looked at her, but found his gaze going to her mouth. "Once I saw ice."

"Ice?"

He sank into the memory again. He could feel this one. "The sun hasn't quite come up yet. I'm alone. I mean, completely alone. I'm on a boat, but I can't really see it. There's a scraping sound, and when I turn to see what it is, I see . . . icebergs. It's beautiful and eerie at the same time. It's like I'm at the edge of the world. And it feels right being alone like that. Last night I saw myself on a boat during a race. I was calling maneuvers. I could feel my desire to win so clearly, I could taste it."

"Who do you think you are?" she asked, studying him as though she could find the answer.

"I think about it all the time. Every guy I meet, I wonder if I'm like him. And I've met all kinds, believe me. I think I liked to party. I used to want a drink really bad, but then I'd get a bad feeling about it and not have one." He ran his finger down her arm. "I don't know if I'll even like who I am."

"Then . . . you could come back here and be this Chase."

"The books said it might take one or more cues to bring back my memories. When I find out where I belong, and who I am, I'm going to become him again. That's the way it works in cases like mine. They call it . . ." It was something he didn't like to think about. "Psychogenic amnesia. In my head. It might be a combination of organic—brought on by injury—and psychogenic. That something traumatic happened, probably connected to falling off the boat. Combined with floating around in the ocean believing I was going to die, it was enough for my brain to lock away my identity. It'll come back; it has to come back. I can't go on living like a nobody."

"You're not going to be a bad person, Chase. I know, because of who you are now."

He ducked his head and rubbed the bridge of his nose. "Like making you cry."

"It hurt when you were saying those words, but it was worth your admitting that maybe Wayne did send you."

He met those beautiful hazel eyes that made her look both naïve and sexy at the same time. He'd never forget her impassioned words about not being able to stop thinking about him. "I won't forget you, either."

She smiled, though he caught a hint of embarrassment at her admission. "I wish you didn't have to leave." She ran her fingers down a lock of his hair. "I know you do." She dropped her hand. "Do you think you're married? Or involved with someone?"

"I didn't have a wedding ring or a tan line. If I sailed a lot, I may not have worn one." He glanced down at his left hand, thinking of the woman who wanted his love so badly. "Whoever is part of my life probably thinks I'm dead."

"Is that why you asked if I would miss him if he were lost at sea?"

Now he felt embarrassed.

She tilted her head, studying him. "It seems strange that you have a whole life you don't know about. You might have been madly in love with someone, living with her."

He felt that pang again, but forced out, "Maybe."

"You might have children." Her gaze took in his face. "I have to keep reminding myself of that. I think . . . I sometimes find myself thinking that you're mine, in a way."

The concept of belonging to Maddie sent a strange sensation curling through his body. But he wasn't, and couldn't. "I'm your friend, so in a way, you're right."

She smiled, but it lacked the sparkle of her previous smile. "But you'll leave, and I probably won't see you again. When you get your memory back, will you remember everything that's happened between then and the time you were plucked out of the ocean?"

"I think so." At the worry he saw in her face, he added, "I promised I wouldn't forget you. And what about you? When I leave, are you going to go back to moping around for your husband?"

She pressed her forehead to his chest. "Maybe I'll be moping around for you."

He threaded his hands through her hair and felt her shiver. If Q wasn't lying there like a little kewpie doll, Chase might have tilted Maddie's head back and kissed her. Good thing Q was there. He kissed the top of her head instead. "We'd better head back. It's getting dark."

He could hear it in his voice, could feel it deep inside. He was getting too close to her. Maybe it was already too late. She drew him with her honesty and sweet sensuality, and he was sure he'd never met anyone like her.

She cleared her throat and moved back, nudging Q to wakefulness. It was dark blue out, mere degrees from darkness. He started the engine and headed back to Maddie's house. She was still sitting on the bottom of the boat, Q snuggled into her embrace.

A jarring thud sent the boat sideways. Maddie stiffened. "What was that? Are we sinking?"

Chase kicked into reverse to see what they'd hit. A large chunk of wood floated in the dark water, nearly camouflaged. It made him think of the piece of raft he'd been found holding on to.

"What is it?" Q asked sleepily, watching Chase pull up a piece of it.

"Too big for a trap. Maybe part of an old boat. I'm going to steer it in toward land. Don't want anyone else hitting it."

The wood was slimy, but he got a hold on it as he steered the boat forward. Maddie was still staring at it.

"What's wrong?" He hoped she wasn't imagining boat wrecks.

"That was floating out there, where anyone could hit it."

"We did hit it."

"I know." Her voice sounded faint, and she still hadn't stopped looking at it. "What if we'd been going fast? What if we'd hit it then?"

Now he knew what she was talking about. Wayne flying through the dark in a speedboat. "You could do some damage. Maybe even send someone out of the boat."

She glanced at Q, then up to him. "Like when Wayne went fast out there. And he said there wasn't anything we could hit. He was wrong, wasn't he?"

He could go into a long dissertation on how wrong he'd been, but he only nodded.

"We were lucky."

"Yeah, you were lucky." That's all he was going to say. He'd already made her cry once, and she looked spooked as it was.

She wrapped her arms around herself and didn't say anything else until they reached the dock. They tied up the *Dinky*, and Q, revived from his nap, ran into the screened enclosure and jumped in the pool.

"Q, we've got to get you home," Maddie said, walking to the door. "Come on, I'm in enough trouble as it is." She gathered up the bag of clothes.

"They going to be mad at you?"

"Oh, yeah. I've been causing a bit of trouble lately. I hope Colleen and Bobby spent some time together. They've got to patch things up."

Chase squeezed her shoulders. "You becoming a troublemaker in your old age?"

She laughed, and for a moment, dipped her cheek to brush against his arm. "You're a good influence on me."

"Maddie, I don't want to cause any trouble with you and your family."

"I'd say it's about time someone did."

CHAPTER 12

MADDIE WATCHED CHASE walk around Sugar's Eats to the sailboat, wishing she could go with him. It had been worth seeing Q happy spending a beautiful evening watching the sunset. Now it was time to pay the piper. Or piperess, as the case would be.

"That was fun, huh, Uncle Maddie?"

"Sure was."

"Where are you on the sad meter?"

She leaned close to him and grinned. "I'm not."

He blinked. "You're not sad? At all?"

"Not right this moment."

"Kewl."

When that little boy smiled, her heart almost burst. At least someone in her family wanted her to be happy. She gave him a hug. "Thanks for coming."

"I wouldn't have missed it for the world!"

There had been moments when Maddie had wished she'd been alone with Chase. Those were the moments, in retrospect, she was grateful Q had been playing chaperone. Otherwise, she would have crawled into Chase's lap and stayed there for a long, long time.

She didn't want to think about that big chunk of wood they'd hit, or that Chase made a point of hauling it out of the water so no one else would hit it.

When she pulled up in front of the house, Q got out and ran to his father's workshop. She grabbed the cooler and towels out of the car, then thought to call Q back just in case. No, Bobby was past that.

Still, she followed him, because her first duty was to face Colleen. When Q walked back around the house, his expression was a worried pout.

"What's wrong?" she asked.

"The door was locked. Daddy was making weird noises."

Please let it be him and Colleen.

"Baby, you are in so much trouble, you have no idea!" Colleen's voice called from across the street.

So was Bobby. She looked down at Q. "Don't say anything about the noises, okay?"

"What'd you do, throw him in the Gulf?" Colleen said, stalking up to her. "Q, go in the house." He reluctantly complied, and Colleen waited until he'd closed the door. She had her vulture look, with her hair pulled back to emphasize her sharp nose. "What do you think you're doing?"

"You know, you've been harassing me for a year about moping around, and now you're still harassing me for not moping. What's the deal?"

Colleen took in the question, then shook her head. "Don't sidestep the issue, which is you kidnapping my son."

Maddie surreptitiously glanced toward the workshop in back. She hoped Bobby had heard the commotion, and if he was doing something bad, was getting rid of Wendy. "I did not kidnap Q. He's been dying to go out on the *Dinky* for months, so we went. No big deal. Like I said in my message, it was intended to free you up so you could spend time with Bobby."

Colleen's eyes shadowed for a moment, then her mouth tightened in anger. "His name is not Q. If you're going to have a nice thought, ask me first. But you weren't thinking of helping me out. As usual, you were thinking of yourself spending time with that . . . guy."

"I didn't need Q if I wanted to spend time with Chase." Well, she did, but Colleen didn't need to know that. "The fact was, I needed Chase to go out on the boat with Q. To help me face going to the house."

"You don't need to turn to some stranger, Baby. That's what family is for."

"No, family is for keeping me on the couch all day. You and Mom would have talked me out of going and don't deny it."

"You're just crazy, Baby. He's doing something to you. Look at yourself. Running out of the house at night, falling into the bay, kidnapping Quigley. Brainwashing him with that stupid nickname. He won't even answer me when I call him by his name. Well, I appreciate your watching him these past years, but your services won't be necessary anymore. Until you start acting normal, I'm having Beth watch him."

"Don't do that." Maddie couldn't keep the hurt from her face. "I love spending time with my nephew."

"You should have thought of that when you kidnapped him."

"I didn't kidnap him . . ."

Colleen was looking toward the workshop. Maddie was almost afraid to turn around and see what was putting that puzzled, hurt look in her eyes.

Wendy stepped out of the workshop. The slice of dim light made it all too clear that Bobby was giving her one last kiss before she slipped through the hedge. The door closed again, and in a minute, the sound of a drill pierced the air. He'd gone right back to work, screw and drill.

Colleen turned toward the house. Maddie grabbed her arm and pulled her back. "Colleen?"

"I have to put Quigley to bed," she said in a dull voice, pulling away.

Was Colleen going to ignore what she'd seen? Yes, entirely. Maddie jerked open the door to the workshop. Bobby gave her an innocent smile as he continued to drill screws into a cabinet.

She yanked the drill's cord out of the wall.

"Hey, Baby, what's the deal?"

"First of all, the deal is, I'm not Baby. I'm Maddie."

"Aw, man, you changing your name, too? First Quigley—"

"He hates that name."

"I know. I call him Q when Colleen's not around."

Maddie lowered her head. "Like you bop Wendy when she's not around?"

That stopped him for a moment. "You saw her leave?"

"So did Colleen."

He set the drill down with a thud. "Damn. I thought she was across the street."

"Yeah, too bad you're going to have to do something. Your son heard you in here. Good thing you locked the door this time."

"I learned my lesson with you."

"You didn't learn anything."

"Listen, Baby—Maddie, whatever. I know it's wrong, but if I don't have Wendy, I'll go crazy. I'm not happy with Colleen. We haven't had sex in months, and to tell you the truth, I don't even care. All she does is criticize me. I'm not even sure I love her anymore." He took a deep breath, looking down at his big hands. "If I don't have Wendy as a diversion, I'll probably leave Colleen. So if you want our family to stay together, leave it be."

"But she knows!"

"She won't say anything. She'll tell me 'til she's blue in the face how to live my life and what I'm doing wrong, but when it comes to the serious stuff, she won't say a word. Every time I've tried to talk to her about our marriage, she changes the subject. So I gave up. Yeah, I'm doing bad. That's all I have left. I'm actually kinda relieved she knows."

Maddie's shoulders sagged. She knew Colleen always avoided serious discussions like everyone in the family, so Bobby was probably right.

"I promise I'll be more careful," he said, plugging in the drill. "I didn't expect you and Colleen to be standing outside when Wendy left. I'll find another place to meet her. That's all I'm promising."

Maddie walked out and stood in the yard. Avoid the whole ugly issue or confront it? She knocked on Colleen's door, then let herself in when no one answered. The house was dim, lit only by the hallway light. Dozens of glittering troll eyes gave her the creeps.

"You mean I don't have to take a bath tonight?" Q asked from the back.

"Not if you go right to bed."

"What's wrong, Mom? Are you on the sad meter now?"

"The what?"

"Sad meter, from one to ten."

"I'm fine. Now go to bed."

"All right. G'night, Mom."

When Colleen closed Q's door a few minutes later, she looked surprised to see Maddie standing there. Her face was still pale, but her slanted eyes hardened. "What do you want?"

"To talk."

"Well, I don't want to talk to you."

Colleen walked into her bedroom, also filled with trolls. Maddie followed, closing the door behind her. Colleen spun around. "This is my domain. I don't have to be nice to you over here. And I want you to go."

Maddie could see how hard she was holding on to her

anger so she wouldn't shatter. She remembered seeing that look during dinner a few nights before, when Maddie had the urge to ask if she was all right. She hadn't been all right. She sensed her marriage falling apart.

Maddie was tired of ignoring things. She was tired of fighting with her sister. And so she did something she couldn't remember ever doing. She hugged her.

"Baby, what are you doing?" Colleen's strained voice asked.

It felt strange, especially since Maddie only came up to Colleen's chin. But she remembered how wonderful it had felt when Chase held her and wondered how long it had been since someone had held Colleen.

Colleen made a feeble attempt to push Maddie away. "Baby, stop it. This is silly. It's . . ." Then Colleen put her arms around her and started crying. "I don't want to lose him, but I don't know how to make it better. Oh, God, it hurts, it hurts . . ."

Maddie just held on and let her cry. After a while she led Colleen to the bed and let her keep crying as they sat together. When her tears subsided, Maddie slid off the bed and headed to the door.

"Maddie?"

She turned around at the door, a soft smile on her face at Colleen's use of her real name. "Yes?"

"Thanks."

Maddie closed the door and found Q sitting outside his door looking lost. She led him to the dark living room.

"What's wrong with Mom?" he asked.

"She's a nine on the sad meter."

"Is she mad at you?"

For once, Maddie could genuinely say, "No. Something sad happened to her today, and she needed to cry. She'll be okay. But she could probably use a hug from you now and then."

"Okay."

He still looked worried as she led him back to his room. He whispered, "How about if I give her one now?"

When Maddie nodded, he quietly opened the door and crawled into bed with Colleen. She immediately pulled him into her arms, and Maddie closed the door.

Chase had thought a lot about Maddie during the night. He hoped she wouldn't catch too much hell. If he thought his presence would have helped, he'd have gone with her. Undoubtedly, that would have been a bad idea.

He'd gotten up at dawn again and spent a few minutes on the deck looking out over the Gulf. It was still gray to the west. He saw the sailing memory again, and something new: a band of gold on his left hand. He stared at his hand searching for the telltale strip of lighter skin. If the ring had slipped off when he was floating at sea, the sun would have tanned the line. But wouldn't there still be a difference?

The warehouse door screeched when he pushed it upward, and the sound brought Barnie out of his office home.

"Morning," Chase said.

"Looks like she's ready to be turned over."

"I see a couple of spots that need some attention, but we should have those smoothed out by mid-morning." We. Him and Maddie.

"Have to go over and set it up with Carol."

"If she's still talking to you." Chase remembered how Carol wanted Barnie to fire him and how his absolute refusal touched him somehow. Hadn't anyone ever stood up for him?

Barnie wheeled out of the warehouse. "Oh, she'll talk to this guy. Just had to promise not to discuss crushed nuts again."

With a chuckle, Chase went to work sanding the rough spots, though he caught himself looking up every so often.

Maybe she'd gotten a tougher time than she imagined. Chase wasn't sure what to expect. She'd crumbled when she walked into her house, but she'd faced him down even when he'd made her cry.

Which he couldn't quite forgive himself for. *Can you ever love me more than sailing? Tell me, Chase, are you capable of loving someone?*

By ten the crane was in position, and they maneuvered the hull off the form while Chase and the marina workers pushed it toward the side of the warehouse. Then they guided the hull onto the rack they'd put in place.

"Be careful!" a woman's voice called out . . . Maddie's voice. She wore pink overalls with a yellow shirt, and the colors made her skin look vibrant. "That thing could fall and crush you."

Something inside him lifted at the sight of her. Then he realized he wasn't paying attention to the hull hovering over him and took his attention off the waif standing in the sunshine with a worried look on her face.

"Did they give you a hard time about going out on the boat?" Chase asked when the hull was in place and she'd come to his side.

"Colleen was mad, until she saw Bobby kissing Wendy, who was sneaking out of the workshop, and then we hugged, and she cried, and then Mom didn't say anything, but she put all my angels back."

Chase tried to make sense of that, but then he didn't care, because she was there and she looked at peace.

"I went to the house this morning," she said. "By myself. I didn't tell anyone, but I took some cleaning supplies and started on the floors."

Had she sat on her bed and remembered making love to Wayne? He didn't want to think about it. "And you're all right?"

A shadow of melancholy passed over her face, but she lifted a shoulder. "I'm okay."

"Thinking of moving back?"

"I'm not ready to think about that yet. I just couldn't stand to see it dusty and stale."

He wasn't sure where his smile came from—pride at how far she'd come or just the fact that she was there—but when she smiled back, he had the insane urge to pick her up and twirl her around. Which then made him think of her body plastered against his while he did it. He turned to the boat. "Better get to work."

Chase couldn't sleep the next night. The air inside the cabin was stuffy, and a restlessness ran through his veins even though it was well after midnight. All day his thoughts had been heavy, like a thundercloud waiting to erupt.

He was sure part of that heaviness was the fact that the boat was nearing completion. Which meant he was closer to heading on, to finding out who he was.

And to leaving Maddie.

He kicked the air-conditioning unit down several degrees and dropped back onto the berth. A few minutes later he rolled onto his side and tried to push those thoughts from his mind. It was inevitable, that he'd have to leave her. They'd known that from the beginning.

He eventually drifted into an uneasy sleep and dreamed of icebergs and silence and aloneness. He'd wanted to be alone, had relished it. What about his wife, probably the woman who had asked him to love her? He'd obviously committed to her. Possibly had children with her.

He kicked off the sheets and shifted on the V-berth. Moonlight spilled down through the hatch above him, but he was somewhere else: an outdoor restaurant with a roof made of palm fronds. People sat around the bar, and someone was telling a story.

He focused on the voice and realized it was his own. He was talking about a generator failing during a race and having to eat all the perishable food within a few hours' time. The woman sitting next to him made a remark about his penchant for rice with relish and hot sauce and his bare refrigerator.

The bartender brought over four shot glasses of amber liquid and a plate of lime wedges. Chase licked his lips as his dream image—or whatever it was—squeezed the lime into his mouth and tossed down the liquid.

"Hooh!" the woman beside him said, then leaned drunkenly against him.

She was a sexy blonde with long hair and high cheekbones, and he couldn't help noticing the deep cleavage of her shirt, and then she was teasing him about that, and then her mouth was on his, her tongue thrusting inside.

Chase sat up in bed. He'd felt the tequila going down his throat, the tart lime, and the salty kiss of the woman beside him. But he hadn't felt . . . involved. Maddie's kiss stirred him a thousand times more than the sexy blonde's.

He tried to bring the memory back to see if he wore the wedding ring, but it lingered at the edges of consciousness. It was her voice that haunted him. *Can you ever love me more than sailing? Tell me, Chase, are you capable of loving someone?* He rested his arms on his knees and stared at the shadows in the cabin. So his life was returning.

He could almost taste the tequila as it curled through his system. Though he'd forgotten what it was like to drink, his body hadn't. Maybe he was a weekend partier. But that didn't jibe with the guy who liked being alone in some godforsaken place with icebergs. Could he even trust these vague images?

And could he trust the feeling that he wasn't going to like who this guy was?

*　　*　　*

Three days later Maddie's mom still hadn't confronted her about going against her wishes. She was acting pretty much normal, except for the ever-present expression of betrayal. Maddie couldn't quite make herself start that conversation either or correct her when she called her "Baby."

Morning was maddeningly routine, everyone pretending life was normal. Maddie wanted to scream that nothing was normal, that it needed to be unnormal.

Escaping to her own house to clean was the best remedy to get her head together. There were too many strange vibes buzzing in the house. She tried to lose her thoughts in scrubbing floors, though she couldn't look at the sliding glass doors without thinking of Chase's harsh words followed by the most tender moment she'd ever experienced.

Ever.

She and Wayne didn't have discussions like that. They never fought. They'd had the perfect marriage. Or had they?

He'd challenged her, yes. Go parasailing, even though you're terrified. Go fast in the dark even though you don't like speed. Pretend to like it because Wayne did. Pretend to be like Wayne so you don't lose him, because who else will ever love you like that?

She dropped the sponge and fell back on her behind. Soapy water seeped into her shorts, but she didn't care. All this time she thought they'd lived such a carefree life. The truth was, she was always afraid he'd find someone he liked better. She was waiting for the balloon to pop and for him to realize he'd married a skinny nobody. He had loved her, she was sure of that. But he'd loved adventure more. He'd never gotten the hari-kari look while making love to her. Only when he was attempting something dangerous. He'd taken her with him many times, talked her into going even when she wasn't comfortable doing it.

Like the day he'd . . . left. Her mind resisted going there

like it always did. She imagined Chase forcing her to face it. Wayne could have gotten her killed. He always headed to that oyster bar, even when she was in the boat. Never once had she really thought there had been danger. Seeing that big chunk of wood in the water changed that. There *had* been danger; they'd just been blithely unaware of it.

She wrapped her finger around her big toe. *One little piggy went to market; one little piggy stayed home.*

He must have felt like he was seducing a child.

He *had* been seducing a child. He'd called her Baby just like everyone else did. Sometimes he'd tickled her until she couldn't breathe. They'd played hide-and-seek and Marco Polo in the pool. Like kids.

Forget all this. Everything was perfect and you had fun. He was happy, and he loved you. Most importantly, you were happy.

Yes, she had been happy. But she wasn't now. Because of Wayne's recklessness, he'd taken himself away from her. And because of that, she'd stopped living.

She walked to the sliding doors, where she'd stood when Chase had admitted maybe Wayne had sent him. Maybe he had sent Chase. Not an angel to heal her broken heart, but a man to help her face it.

She finished the floors and drove to the warehouse, energy growing inside her. At first she only saw Barnie working on his sails. She thought of the somber pallor that had hung over Chase the past few days. She wasn't sure what their relationship was. Friends? She suspected they'd gone past that somewhere along the way. But not lovers, since they hadn't made love. Her body stirred at the thought. A definite nine on the sex meter. All she knew—and had to remind herself—was they had no future.

How had he become such a part of her life in such a short time? She knew the lines of his jaw, the feel of his hair, and the strength of his shoulders. But she didn't know the man inside, because he didn't, either.

"He's inside the cabin," Barnie said. She climbed up onto the boat and then down into the cabin. "Oh, my gosh," she said, obviously startling Chase out of his thoughts by the way he jumped. "You're nearly done in here."

He still hadn't worn any of the clothing she'd given him, but he looked good in his faded black T-shirt anyway. She could clearly see the curves of his muscles through the thin fabric. Though he gave her a slight smile, his pallor remained. "Getting there." George, a friend of Barnie's from just north of Sugar Bay, had spent a couple of days helping out.

The cabin smelled like the tung oil Chase was using. He finished up the last corner of varnishing the teak work and stood. Before she could think better of it, she slid against him and wrapped her arms around his waist. The shirt felt soft against her cheek, though the body beneath it was solid. His heartbeat picked up a notch, even though he was slow to set his brush down and put his arms around her.

"What's wrong?" he asked.

She loved his voice and the way he felt, and she was so very afraid she loved him even though she was sure she couldn't love any man besides Wayne. She looked up at him, glad to see concern override that somber expression. "If you knew who you were . . . if you were here because you wanted to be here, and we were together"—she swallowed, not sure she was saying it right—"could you love me? I'm not asking if you do love me, I know you don't, but could you? If the circumstances were different. It's a theoretical question."

He brushed her hair back from her face. "Why are you asking me this?"

"Because I was thinking about when you kissed me the other night, no, not the kiss, what you were saying about

Wayne seducing a child, me being a child, and I realized that I was afraid of losing him, of losing his interest. I mean, look at Bobby, he's obviously lost interest in Colleen. But I tried so hard, doing things I didn't want to do, going fast, taking risks, and I realized I did it because I didn't think he could possibly love me for . . . me. I mean, no other guy in town was ever interested in me before Wayne. And I'm not interested in anyone in town or falling in love again, and understand I'm not asking you *to* love me, just if you could. Love me."

Maybe this wasn't such a good idea. And now she realized the seat of her shorts was still wet, and she smelled like lemon cleanser. And if he said no, knowing how honest he could be, she'd die. Or if he said he could, but was lying, she'd die.

He held her face in his hands and ran his thumbs across her cheeks. "Maddie, thinking about loving you"—he looked into her eyes, then shook his head—"is not a good idea. I can't let myself think about that, not when . . . when I'll be leaving soon."

He moved back and grabbed his brush. He didn't like her anymore. She'd gone too far. Or maybe he'd connected with Darcy. Her old instincts kicked in, run, leave before the hurt sets in. But she couldn't, because it hurt more to think of walking away from him.

He moved his tools and the tarp to another area and continued varnishing. She grabbed a rag and worked on a nearby section. Close enough so that their arms brushed when she raised the rag. Not entirely on purpose.

"Forget I asked, okay?" she said.

He glanced at her, and she saw to her profound relief a hint of a smile. "Maddie, you're lovable."

"I am?" She knew how pitiful she sounded, but she didn't care.

"I just wasn't expecting you to run into my arms and

ask me that. And I don't want to think about loving you or anyone because of my complications."

"Not even Darcy?"

"What? Who?"

"Darcy. The blonde who was talking to you that day I came into the warehouse the first time."

It had to be a good sign that he looked genuinely perplexed. Then light dawned, and he gave her a curious look.

"Never mind," she said before he could ask. "Ancient insecurities rearing their heads."

She ran the rag along the top edge of wood beneath him. When she reached over to dip the rag into the oil, he was reaching past her to finish the strip in front of her. She blinked in surprise when their noses brushed.

And he kissed her.

It took her by surprise, the kiss and the intensity of it. She was balanced, with one hand hovering over the can of tung oil. He was braced against the side wall, a wet rag in one hand. Only their mouths connected, and yet, her whole body responded. She heard something between an exhale and a groan escape his mouth as he deepened the kiss. That was something else she loved about him, his kisses. It was an awkward kiss, and yet it was just as passionate as the one in the water, minus the feel of his body against hers and his hands on her bare behind.

He finished the kiss, coming back for another small one, and then another, before finally pulling away. "Stop asking me questions like that," he said and went back to work.

When she glanced out the porthole in front of them, she saw Barnie watching with a surprised look. She wondered if he thought that kiss was dangerous enough to warrant mentioning to her mother.

Then he smiled. He approved, no matter how dangerous it had been. And Maddie knew falling for Chase was the riskiest thing she'd ever done.

CHAPTER 13

BY THE END of the week, the boat was really beginning to look like a boat. Maddie couldn't begin to describe the feeling of joy and accomplishment when she returned from a trip to the washrooms and took it in. Joy because Chase was letting Q help him with the deck joinerwork. Accomplishment because she had had a part in bringing this boat to reality.

She ignored the ache she felt as she thought how the closer the boat got to being finished, the sooner Chase would leave. Instead she focused on the sound of their laughter, Chase and Q's. She stayed there listening to it for a few minutes. What a precious sound it was, and it filled her with life and love.

Chase glanced up and caught her with a mushy look on her face. His smile was tinged with melancholy.

Q looked up. "Aw, Uncle Maddie, do we have to go home? I wanna stay here."

"Can't, Q. I've already caused enough trouble between me and your mom."

Q's face transformed into a pout. "I don't want to be home with Mom. She doesn't talk or laugh or nothing."

Chase jumped down off the boat and held his arms out for Q, who reluctantly slid down into them. "Let's get you washed up, big guy." Chase led him to the hose just outside the warehouse.

The look of admiration Q gave Chase almost made her

heart break. The boy was in desperate need of a father figure. His own father had his head too far up his posterior region to see what he was doing to his family.

Maddie held the hose over Q's hands as he washed off the dust and sweat. She splashed some on his legs. And then, just because she wanted to wipe that gloomy look off his face, she squirted a stream of water at his nose. That elicited a squeal of surprise and a struggle for control of the hose.

Chase stepped in. "I'd better take this before you two get into real trouble." And then he let her have it.

The water was cold against her heated self and that elicited a squeal of surprise, too. When Q giggled in delight, he got another squirt. She looked at Q. "Let's get him!"

Q tried to pull the hose from below, and Maddie grabbed hold of Chase's hands and tried to pry it loose. Their fingers slid against each other and a geyser of water sprayed upward to soak all of them. She and Chase were in a dance for control, though she had to admit she wasn't putting up much of a struggle, not when she couldn't stop laughing. He bent the nozzle and sent a shot of water down her shirt. Her nipples tightened instantly under the onslaught, but she didn't think too much about it, or the fact that she wasn't wearing a bra, because she was too busy aiming the nozzle toward his collar. She ended up sending a stream all down the front of him, which had the same effect on him as it had on her.

Q giggled at her victory, and Chase narrowed his eyes playfully. Hands clutched together over the nozzle, arm to arm and knee to knee, they twirled round and round. She'd gain an advantage and lean the water his way, then he'd shift their balance and it would spill her way.

And then they realized that in their dance, they'd coiled the hose around their legs. They both tumbled to the pine-needle-strewn ground tangled in the green hose and each other. He twisted as they fell so she landed on top of him. She might have relished the feel of his hard body beneath hers, but Q ran over and jumped on top of them. Chase squirted him, and it started all over again. Chase's arm rubbed against her left breast as he and Q fought, and she wondered if he knew it and felt the electric sizzle with each brush.

Probably not, she concluded as the two boys continued to struggle and laugh. She joined in, getting both of them with one shot. Then they turned on her, and she got really soaked.

"Maddie?"

The voice didn't belong with the fun and laughter, and she pulled her attention to Colleen watching them with disbelief and betrayal. Maddie untangled herself and scrambled to her feet. She'd never seen her sister look so lost or disheveled. Q started to walk over, too, but Chase distracted him with another stream of water so the women could talk.

"Sorry to interrupt your fun," Colleen said, surveying Maddie's wet self. Her gaze bounced back to Maddie's chest. "Gawd, Baby."

The cold water—or Chase, if she dared to admit it— had definitely had a visual effect on her. She crossed her arms over her chest. "What's going on?"

"I . . . I was going to talk to Bobby about . . . well, about ways we could patch things up. I couldn't think about anything else, so I went home early. And . . ."

Maddie put her hand on Colleen's shoulder. "You don't have to say it."

"I started to open the workshop door, but it was locked. And then I heard voices. So I came here." She took a ragged breath. "I want to move back home tonight. Will you help me?"

"Are you sure that's what you want to do?"

Colleen's eyes hardened. "Afraid I'll take your place as

the object of pity and attention around the house?"

She pushed past her sister's harsh words. "Have you tried talking to Bobby?"

"What good would it do? He knows I know, and he's still out there . . . doing it."

"Talk to him before you topple everyone's world, including Q's. You've got to confront him about this. He doesn't think you will, and that's why he's still . . . doing it. You can't put your marriage back together again until he stops seeing her."

"Just help me pack and move my things over to Mom and Dad's. Don't lecture me. Don't become the authority on marriage. I know you had a happy marriage, but I can't let Bobby run wild. And we don't have his family's money to help us make our bills or buy us a house. Will you just help me this one time?"

Maddie glanced back to make sure Q wasn't within listening distance. He and Chase were wrapping up the hose. Chase glanced at her, but she couldn't look into those eyes and think. She turned back to Colleen. "Aren't you even going to fight for your marriage?" It scared her to see Colleen look so beaten. She'd pushed her way around her family for so long, but she wasn't fighting for what was important.

"I . . ." Colleen looked up and away. "I don't know how to fight."

"No, I guess you wouldn't." When her sister was about to get indignant at that comment, Maddie explained. "Have you noticed that we never talk about issues in our family? At even the merest hint of confrontation, Mom closes the subject and ignores it. Dad lets her talk all over him. They don't listen. None of us do. I didn't realize it either, not until . . ."

She glanced toward Chase again. "Just recently. Heck, Mom won't even talk to me about my seeing Chase even though she forbade it. And maybe you do that with Q and Bobby, too. Think about it. Have you asked Q if he wants to be called Q? Have you talked to him about the teasing? I didn't think so. And what about Bobby's dream of opening his own shop? Have you sat down and worked out all the ramifications? So what if you put off getting the pool for a few more years? You have mine to use. He told me he doesn't feel like a man around you, because you keep him on a short leash."

Colleen swallowed hard. "He told you that? He told *you* that?"

"The first time I caught him. It was only a couple of days before you caught him. He hates living in a cave with the trolls."

"Gnomes."

"Are you listening to me? You stifle him, and that's why he's . . . doing what he's doing."

"Are you going to help me move or just stay here and play with that man all day?" She took in Maddie's dripping appearance. "Dumb question. That's all you've ever done, play."

She started to leave, but Maddie grabbed her arm. "Don't do this to Q. Try to work things out before he knows there's a problem."

"We can't hide problems from our children. As much as we want to protect them from the truth, sometimes it's better if they know it so everyone can move on with their lives. You should talk to Mom about that sometime." Then she turned and left.

"Q, we gotta go," Maddie said, heading to her cooler.

"Want some towels?" Chase asked.

She shook her head. Getting her car's upholstery wet was the least of her problems. Even Q seemed to sense this was a serious matter; he grabbed his backpack and didn't argue.

"Everything okay?" Chase asked. She got caught up in his eyes and in the longing to spend time with him while she still had him around. His black shirt was plastered to his body. *Don't think about him, Maddie.* As if she could stop.

When Maddie had walked into the living room the next morning, she experienced a bizarre moment of juxtaposition. Colleen was sitting on the couch in her pajamas, and Mom was talking to her in soothing tones. Is that how she'd looked over the last year, dead in the eyes, all slumped over, with Mom coddling her? She made herself face the answer: yes.

Since Chase had arrived in Sugar Bay, she'd been able to step back from her life and view it as an outsider. She didn't like what she saw. A twenty-six-year-old woman who'd never grown up. Who expected everyone else to make things better. Who wore youthful clothing and played kiddy games, and maybe related to Q better than anyone else.

Then she pictured herself working alongside Chase on the boat, accomplishing something. She saw herself kissing him and feeling her body come alive in a very grown-up way. Could she leave that safe, childish part of herself behind? Could she become a woman with Chase? Even as her body stirred at the thought, she couldn't let herself think about it when he'd be leaving soon.

When she saw Chase later that morning, she watched him work for a few minutes before he saw her. He even looked sexy wearing a breathing mask. He was a hard worker, intent on his task and precise with his movements. He was sanding the surface of the hull, and fine dust was flying everywhere.

Wayne probably wouldn't have worn the mask and goggles. He never wore restraints or safety equipment. Hated seat belts.

Chase was finally wearing one of Wayne's shirts, a blue and white striped one he'd left unbuttoned. He wore those low-slung white pants again that rode just under his hip-bones.

He glanced up and smiled, and she hoped he hadn't noticed her gawking at him. He cut the sander as she approached, pushing up his goggles and pulling down the mask. "Hi ya, Maddie."

"Hey." Why couldn't she stop smiling whenever she first saw him? Maybe because she'd wanted to come back here and be with him last night so bad, she'd ached with it.

"How'd it go last night?"

She lifted one shoulder. "As well as can be expected when your sister moves her son and her fifty trolls back home."

"Are they going to try to patch it back together?"

"Thank you. That's what I think they should do, but Bobby just let her go without a fight. She's moping around doing a fair imitation of Maddie pre-Chase." She blinked when she realized what she'd said. "Before you came along, I just sat around on the couch all day."

He ran a dry rag across the area he'd just sanded. "Aw, Maddie, I didn't do anything."

She nearly jumped when the boat creaked. "Is someone in the cabin?"

"Some guy named Ron, doing the electrical work. And, believe it or not, Barnie. He woke up about the time I was going to quit, saying he was tired of being an invalid. And he was real tired of watching the boat come together without being part of it. So we managed—and it wasn't a pretty sight—to get him onboard. He's been in there ever since. We worked on the flooring and hatches until about three. He was just starting the plumbing when I left."

"You're going to be done soon," she said, hating the tightness in her voice when she'd meant to sound perfectly casual.

He tweaked her chin. "Thanks for your help. Someday I'll pay you for your time."

"Don't . . . don't pay me. Just come back and visit."

He tried to smile, but it faltered. "You may not like who I am. You might not want me to visit."

"Of course I will." She didn't like the darkness in his eyes. Had he remembered more? "Give me some sandpaper and tell me what I need to do."

He set her to work on the stern, but before she could scrape one inch, he slipped one of those paper masks over her head and a pair of goggles over her eyes. That simple gesture nearly brought her to tears. She was used to being taken care of by her family, but that a man would think to protect her from resin dust touched her deeply. She leaned up and kissed him on the cheek, through the fabric. He brushed her hair back from her face and went back to his spot.

When they ran out of varnish later in the day, Maddie volunteered to get more. The first thing she noticed when she returned was her mom's car in the parking lot. She walked around the side of the warehouse, and her mom's voice stopped her.

"She's been acting strange ever since you came to town. Defying her family by coming here, talking back to me. She's just not herself lately."

"Maddie might—"

"Return to normal if you push her away. She's even asking us to call her Maddie, which is near impossible when we've been calling her Baby her whole life."

Maddie was going to announce her presence, but the pride in Chase's voice stopped her again.

"She asked you to call her Maddie? Good for her."

"Not good for her. She's been grieving for a year, and all of a sudden she's acting different. It can't be good. I'm afraid she's gone . . . unbalanced."

"She isn't unbalanced," he said with conviction. "She's growing up. Your daughter is a woman." Those words shivered through Maddie. "Look at this boat. Maddie did this. She sanded this section, she laid the fiberglass and the C-Flex. She helped make this boat a reality. She works hard, even though she refuses to take any payment. Look what she's accomplished. Your little girl did this. Imagine what else she's capable of."

Maddie was sure that was the most anyone had ever gotten to say in a conversation with her mother. She leaned against the side of the warehouse and closed her eyes, letting his pride soak in.

"Baby wouldn't get dirty doing this kind of work."

"Ask Barnie. She's been here every day sweating and working just like me." His voice got a little lower, and Maddie had to strain to hear. "You—and as far as I can tell, other people in this town—want to keep her a helpless girl. I think it's time you asked yourself why. Your daughter is an incredible woman, and you don't even know it."

Maddie squeezed her arms around herself at those words.

"You have no right to talk to me like that."

"I'm Maddie's friend and I want what's best for her. Don't you?"

"All I'm asking is that you put some distance between you and her until you leave. You are still leaving, aren't you?" Chase must have nodded, because she went on. "I'm afraid she's gotten . . . attached to you. When you leave, you're going to break her heart. She's been through enough, and I don't want her hurt. Again."

"Maybe I'm going to be hurt, too. Did you ever think about that?"

Maddie held her breath at those words. Did he mean them? They must have taken her mom aback, too, because it took her a few seconds to reply.

"I only care about my daughter. And if you care about her, you'll stop this useless relationship."

A few minutes of silence passed, and then she heard the sound of work being resumed. It was only after several more minutes that Maddie stepped around the corner. She decided to pretend she hadn't heard the conversation and see if he mentioned it—or followed her mom's directive.

He was standing on their makeshift scaffolding, boards held up by big plastic buckets. He looked up at her. "I suppose you heard all that?"

So much for pretending. "Okay, I heard it." He helped her up to the scaffolding, not letting go until she had her balance. "No one ever stood up for me like that before. In fact, no one in my life—including Wayne—ever stood up to my mom period." She met his gaze, realizing something else. "No one has ever been . . . proud of me. Not that I've accomplished a lot in my life, but that's because nobody ever expected anything of me. So I lived my life never committing to anything besides my family and my marriage. I only started helping you with the boat so I'd have an excuse to be around you. To, you know, give you the opportunity to see that you were my angel. I know, you're not. But then I started enjoying the work. Seeing this go from rough materials to a finished product. Sanding something smooth, varnishing the wood. It felt good. Thanks."

He tilted his head. "Why are you thanking me? You did it yourself."

"But you gave me the impetus."

She wanted to kiss him, because kissing him felt so good and she wanted to get that feeling in as much as she could before he left, but she heard the office door open and Barnie hobbled out on crutches. Even though Barnie had seen her and Chase kissing, it was a different story altogether to do it in front of him.

"After every nap, seems the boat's getting closer and closer to being done. Looks like it'll be delivered on time after all. Good job, Chase. Maddie."

She beamed.

"We're a good team," Chase said, flashing her a smile.

A team. That's what Wayne had always called the two of them. But now she could see they weren't a team at all. She had simply gone along with his wishes. She'd been his Baby in every sense of the word. And now she was nobody's baby.

"Ever since Wayne left, I've been afraid of doing anything the least bit risky," Maddie said the next evening. The peacefulness of the Gulf and the sunset opposed the turmoil she felt as she sat on the edge of the picnic table next to Chase. "But every time I'm with you, I feel like I'm risking some part of myself. Does that make sense?"

"Yeah," he answered without even thinking.

She'd made them dinner, the first whole meal she'd cooked since moving back to her parents' house. It was only meatloaf and buttered noodles, no culinary achievement. But an achievement for her.

"How long before the boat's finished?"

"A few more days if Barnie keeps helping. He and George are working on it now."

"Then you'll leave." She could already feel the ache inside at the prospect. He only nodded. "Because you have a life somewhere out there." He nodded again, staring at his left hand. "Have you remembered more?"

"A bit."

She found herself touching his arm. "You know who you are?"

"No, not enough to put it together yet." She didn't like the seriousness on his face or the fact that he wasn't looking at her. "I might be married."

Her fingers tightened against his bare arm, but she forced them to let go. "Married?"

"I saw a wedding ring on my finger. And . . . a woman."

She didn't know why she felt jealous, not when she had no future with Chase. "Do you . . . love her?"

She wished she could identify what she saw in his dark eyes. "I don't feel anything."

She ran her thumb down his finger. "But you don't have a line."

"I was out in the sun for days. I know, there should be a difference, but maybe it doesn't work that way if you've had too much sun." She was still holding on to his hand when he turned to her. "Sometimes I don't want to know who I am. Maybe I party too much. Maybe I can't . . ."

"What?"

"Maybe I'm not a nice person."

"Then don't remember any more. Stay here and be the Chase you know now." She hated the hope that shot through her at the prospect. Especially since he was already shaking his head.

"I have to face who I was—am. If I have a wife, and maybe kids, I need to face up to those responsibilities. I probably have debts and obligations. I can't just turn my back on them."

"See, that proves you are a good person. You're respon-sible." She wished he wasn't. But then, she'd lived a responsibility-free life herself, and look where it had gotten her.

"Maybe." He clearly wasn't convinced. He dipped his head into his hands. "I feel like an empty shell, Maddie.

No past, no future. No reference for anything in the world. What I'm like now, I may not be when it comes back. I have a duffel bag with hand-me-downs, which I'm grateful for, don't get me wrong. But I'm a nobody, nowhere." After a few moments, he looked at her. "All I have is . . . you. And a vague sense that I don't deserve you."

She kissed him then, taking his face in her hands the way he did to her. Her gaze was locked to his as their mouths touched. "You'll always have me, no matter what."

"You can't say that, Maddie. You don't know who I am."

"I don't care who you are," she whispered. *I love you anyway*. The words echoed through her mind, though she held them in, thank God. But the impact of them made her drop her hands and move away. "You're a great kisser." She'd wanted to say something, but that wasn't exactly on the list of comforting phrases. "Is that something you remembered? Or have you been practicing since losing your memory?"

He rubbed his eyes and laughed softly, and she regretted asking him. She didn't want to hear about the women he'd met on his journey. *Dumb question, Maddie. Really dumb.*

"As lonely as I've gotten, I decided not to get involved with anyone." He looked at her, probably thinking how he'd broken that vow. "I haven't practiced anything with anyone." His gaze dropped momentarily to her mouth. "Maybe kissing is an instinctual thing. It all came back that night in the water. I didn't think about it, it just . . . happened. I suppose making love would be the same."

She blinked at those words that sent fire spiraling through her. "Making love?"

He gave her a rather sheepish smile. "I know what it is, but I don't remember ever doing it."

"You mean you're like . . . a virgin?"

He ran his fingers back through his hair. "Guess so."

That thought intrigued her right down to her toes. Being the first woman to touch him, to be touched by him. *Don't think about it,* she told herself, but it was too late. The thought was there, planted in the center of her body, and lower yet. It made her feel like more of a woman, being the teacher, the knowledgeable one. "So I know more about sex than you do?"

"Probably."

She chewed the tip of her finger. "But if that night in the water is any indication, I think you'll pick it right up again."

"I knew what I wanted."

He wanted her. Or at least for those moments he did. When he met her eyes, there was a current of understanding between them.

"Maddie, I'm not going to pretend I don't want you. I could tell you it's because it's been . . . well, for me, forever since I've made love with a woman. But I can't lie to you. I want you, Maddie. Just you. The best thing was your mother coming to look for you that night, because I might have laid you down on this picnic table and stripped off what little you had on and made love to you right here." She tingled at his words. "But that would have been a big mistake. For you. And for me. I don't think you're ready for that kind of . . . interaction. You've still got issues to work out with your husband. Like admitting he's dead, for one thing, instead of saying he left, as though he'll be back."

He gestured to the wedding ring she still wore. "When you're ready to move on, it should be with a guy who can commit to you. Not some guy who's going to leave." He took her hand in his, fiddling with her fingers as he spoke. "You've probably only been with one man in your life." She nodded. "Make the second guy one you marry."

She tightened her hold on his hand. "What if I don't want to?"

Those words hung in the air, and she watched several emotions cross his face. "Don't say that, Maddie. The best thing we could do is walk away now."

She searched his eyes, remembering his words to her mother. "You're going to hurt when you leave?"

His mouth quirked. "Maybe."

She didn't give herself time to think about the consequences. She climbed onto his lap, her legs on either side of him and arms around his neck. "Kiss me again."

"Maddie, didn't you hear me? This isn't a good idea."

"Growing up, I was never allowed to take any risks. Then I married Wayne, and we took risks all the time, but I didn't know it. When he . . . left, I went back to being that sheltered child. This is a risk I want to take, knowing what the consequences will be. Because when you kiss me, I feel like a woman for the first time in my life. And I want to feel that again. At least one more time."

She could see the moment he relented. "Aren't you worried about people seeing you like this?"

She doubted they would be seen. The Australian pines partially blocked them. "I might be a ruined woman."

"Definitely."

"You talk as though there are men who would be interested in me. As though there is one man in town who piques my interest a tenth of what you do. I guess I'm willing to risk it. I'll pay the consequences tomorrow." Those consequences being adding another soul-searing kiss to memories to mourn over when he left.

"You're something else, you know that?"

"I'm not sure. Is that a good thing?"

"It is with you."

"Then I'm only something else with you."

They came together at the same moment, sitting in a

similar way as they had in the water. She relished being a woman with him, of feeling sensuality rushing through her veins and the parts of her body she'd long forgotten about. With Chase, it was different. He didn't tickle her, or play "this little piggy . . ." with her toes, or lathe her face with his tongue without warning.

She wanted a man.

She didn't want to compare the two of them, but they were so different. They made her feel so different, from a girl to a woman.

Now that Chase was hard, he pressed against her feminine area and sent more of that intoxicating passion through her blood.

"I love . . ." she whispered, then realized she'd said it aloud. "Kissing you," she finished.

"Mm, I'm going to miss kissing you." He opened her mouth again and plunged his tongue deep inside.

She tilted her head sideways and inhaled softly. Forgetting to breathe while kissing Chase was easy to do. But she also loved the way he smelled this close up, like the soap he'd washed with, or maybe the shampoo. He tasted like Dr. Pepper.

She had the irrepressible urge to sigh aloud. So she did. She sounded way too dreamy and lost. His own breathing was coming heavier, but she wanted him to sigh, too. She rolled her tongue all the way around his with slow, sure strokes. That did the trick. His arms tightened around her, and he let out a soft moan.

If they kissed like this, imagine, just imagine what they could do . . . in other situations. She giggled, right in the middle of their kiss. Just a soft giggle, not enough to break the kiss. But when she did it again, he backed away with a cute, questioning look on his face.

"What are you laughing about?"

She leaned forward and pressed her forehead to his.

"When we kiss, I feel this tickle in my stomach, and it makes me laugh."

He stroked the side of her face. "Maddie, you're too much."

"Mm," she said as the last of her giggle came out. "Or maybe you're my angel after all. Not in a Heavenly way," she added when he gave her a skeptical look. "But, like you said, maybe Wayne did send you here not to heal me, but to help me heal myself."

He brushed her hair back from her face. "That would make you your own angel."

"You can't be your own angel." She forced herself to get off his lap, because it felt too good sitting there. "Maybe . . . there's just you and me. For now, for these moments." She remained standing in front of him.

"For now," he repeated, that serious look in his eyes again.

"Maybe you'll come back someday."

"Don't wait for me like you waited for that angel. I may not be back."

She tried really hard not to pout. "But you promised you wouldn't forget me."

"I won't." He reached out and touched her cheek. "But I don't know what's waiting for me when I get back to my life."

"Like a wife." She waited when his nod wasn't convincing. "There's something else, isn't there? Something you're not telling me."

He rubbed his nose and said, "You know everything."

"Tell me."

"Maddie, I . . ." He searched her eyes. "I was fighting with someone before I fell off the boat."

Her heart squeezed at the thought of someone hurting him. "Did you just remember this?"

"No."

"Then how . . ."

"When I was pulled out of the ocean, it looked like someone had scratched me. So when the clues lead me home, I'm not going to know who I was fighting. If I don't get any memories from that day, I'm walking into my life blindfolded."

"Someone pushed you off the boat?"

"I don't think so. Maybe I was trying to push them off."

"Why didn't you tell me?"

He shrugged. "I didn't want to worry you."

"Were you never going to tell me?"

"Probably not."

She pushed away and started throwing the dishes from dinner into her cooler. "You talk a good game, telling Mom how strong I am. But you don't believe it, do you?"

He jumped down from the table. "Yes I do. But you're still fragile in some ways. You're not invincible, Maddie."

She'd grabbed up the cooler and faced him. "You're right. I'm not invincible. Maybe when you leave, I'll go back to being Baby again. It's not a bad place to be."

She felt like an abandoned child, alone without her security blanket. All those independent, womanly feelings had fled. Because she didn't know what to say, she turned and left.

And even when she was sitting on the couch with the moping Colleen, and her family all around her, Maddie still felt all alone.

Maddie wasn't one to be easily scared off, Chase realized when she showed up for work Monday morning. But her bravery came and went, not that he could blame her. She wasn't going to go from being "Baby" to being Maddie-the-woman overnight. At least she was dressed more like a woman in jean shorts and a blue shirt without lace or cartoon adornments.

When she took in the boat, her mouth tightened to a line. Another notch on the sad meter. "Wow, you've gotten a lot done." And she wasn't happy about it. He didn't want to think about it being because that meant he'd be leaving soon.

"Thought you weren't coming back," was all he'd commit to.

She lifted one shoulder in a shrug. "I thought about not coming back. How much easier it'd be, you know, to just let go." She met his eyes, and he didn't see any indication of easier in them. "All it took was one day of being Baby again to convince me I can't go back. Now I have to figure out who Maddie is."

"It'll be a fun journey."

"Like finding out who Chase is?"

He felt his face darken, but said, "Right." Then he busied himself with tightening the gudgeons that held the rudder in place. The returning memories were vague and elusive. Each one flashed in and out of his mind, leaving behind more questions than answers. None of them fit together, but they painted a picture of a man he didn't like. The last one was the most disturbing.

He'd been fighting with someone on the deck of a boat. He couldn't see who he was fighting, but he'd heard a woman scream.

"I said I was sorry," Maddie was saying when he focused back in. "For stomping off Saturday night. I'm confused about things. I prayed about it in church yesterday. Mom seemed happier, probably because I was acting normal, or at least normal in her mind. And I didn't come here."

"It's all right." He focused on his task, but he could see her shoulders slump at his aloofness. He wanted to remain that way, but he couldn't. "So, we're still friends?"

Her mouth quirked. "Sure. Just friends."

She'd laid some extra emphasis on the 'just'; it was relief he felt, not disappointment.

"Want to go for a test-drive Tuesday?"

She took in the boat. "On this?"

"What else?"

"It's . . . going to be ready then?"

"Just about. Barnie's working on the cabinets now. The engine's been delivered. Tomorrow we'll pull her out of the warehouse and step the mast. Once the spars and standing rigging are in place, she'll be ready. Since you helped make this happen, you should come along."

She glanced toward the bay and shook her head. "I'll watch."

"Don't tell me you're afraid to go."

She lifted one shoulder in the way that was so Maddie. "It could sink. Make sure to take life vests. What if something malfunctions, and it blows up? I saw that in a movie once. The mast could fall down and—"

"Okay already. You don't have to go."

"That's it? You're not going to give me a hard time? No prodding, or calling me a baby?"

"Nope." He knew, or at least he hoped, she'd do it herself.

"Really." She ran her hands across the surface of the boat along the divide between blue and white. "I haven't been on a boat since Wayne left. Other than the *Dinky,* of course. Too many bad memories."

"Considering everything you've gone through, it's understandable that you wouldn't want to set foot on a real boat."

"It is understandable. If you'd watched your husband . . . get into an accident right there in that bay, you'd feel the same."

He kept his focus on what he was doing and not her. "I'm sure."

"You're patronizing me, aren't you?"

"Not at all. If you're uncomfortable doing something, you shouldn't do it."

"Since when are you so nice to me? The Chase I know would be taunting me, telling me it's time to get on the boat and get over my fears. Telling me that being afraid of everything isn't living at all. That . . ." Her eyes narrowed. "How did you do that?"

He gave her an innocent look. "Do what?"

"Get me to say all that. Get me to say what you should be saying."

He mirrored her one-shouldered shrug. "I don't know what you're talking about."

"I'm going with you. I put a lot of work into this boat, I'm entitled."

"Fine."

"Give me something to do before I go crazy." She pointed at him. "And don't tell me I don't have far to go."

He couldn't help but smile, even though he didn't feel much like smiling in general. She was the one who was making him crazy.

CHAPTER 14

WHEN MADDIE RAN through the cold rain and into the warehouse Tuesday morning, she was shocked to see the boat missing. The big metal building looked empty and forlorn without the boat in some stage of creation. Even the sails weren't lying in heaps near the back.

"They put it in the bay last night," Barnie's voice said. She looked around until she spotted him hobbling on his crutches toward her from the back corner. "And a beautiful sight it was as it touched down into the water . . . and didn't sink." He rubbed his bristly chin and chuckled. "Aw, Maddie, don't look so dejected. You knew it had to come. Hell, you helped it come faster."

"I'm not dejected. Life will be a lot simpler when he's gone." She glanced outside and saw the new sailboat docked near *The Barnacle*. It was rocking in the choppy water. "I'm supposed to go with him on the test run."

"Nobody's running today. Squalls predicted out there, lots of rain. Weather bought you another day. Chase's just making sure everything's tight."

"Maybe I'll see if he needs any help."

"Maddie, wait."

She didn't like the somber look on Barnie's face. "What's wrong? Did we mess something up? You said it didn't sink."

He glanced out to the boat where Chase briefly came into view. "Found out who he is."

She thought her heart imploded at those words, then that she must be hearing things. "What?"

"Come here."

The office was dusty, and the desk cluttered with invoices and orders. On one side he'd set up a bunk that was a heap of sheets and pillows. King of clutter, Mom called him.

"No toe space," he said. "All the hidden storage you get in a boat, don't have it here."

She nodded, remembering Chase discussing it with him when they were constructing the cabin walls. "You said you knew who he was."

"Don't rush this guy, now. Learned since crushing the nuts and bumming up the leg, nothing happens fast anymore." He maneuvered to the desk and lowered himself to the chair, leaving his leg outstretched. The computer came to life. "Got to know Chase over these past few weeks. More so in the last week putting in the late hours. Know there were times when he was ready to turn in, and it *was* late, mind you. He'd go right back at it. Good worker, honest about his time. Lucky to find him."

"He found you, remember?"

"S'pose he did. Now, then . . ." He focused on the computer, squinting at the small screen.

She heard the modem start dialing. "The Internet?"

"Yup. Took note of the dates and places he mentioned. He'd checked libraries for newspaper films, but he never had access to the Internet. Maybe didn't even think about it." He gave her a triumphant look. "But this guy did."

Maddie crouched down beside Barnie, anticipation humming through her veins. "He's been worried about being a bad person. He thinks he might be married."

He lifted his eyebrow, but gave nothing away as he pulled up an article from a Florida sailing publication. "He'd been looking too far in the past. Took a few days of poking around in archives. The Miami press ran a couple of stories about it, but when nothing new came up, it kinda faded away. Especially with all the stuff goes on over there. In any case, he might not want to know."

She looked at Barnie. "You haven't told him?"

"Nope. Figured you could do that."

Maddie's knees went weak, and she gripped the edge of the desk. "Who is he?"

"Chase Augustine."

Maddie took a breath. So far nothing bad. Not a name she'd seen on the FBI's "Most Wanted" poster. "Is he married?"

"Divorced, no kids. Father owns an aerospace parts company in Miami. Brother Patrick runs it."

"And Chase?" She couldn't see him at a desk.

"Races sailboats. Is rather good at it, too. Found some older articles about his fully crewed sailboat named *Skidbladnir*—whatever that means—which his father, who's interviewed in the article, claims full credit for. Augustine Aero sponsored it. And our friend is more of a risk-taker than Wayne ever thought of being."

She hoped that was the bad part, and it was bad. "But he's been pretty careful of . . . me. I haven't seen him take any risks."

He tapped the screen. "This is who he was. Who he might go back to being."

And it didn't matter because she wouldn't see him after tomorrow or maybe the next day. "You said he was a risk-taker."

"The difference between Chase and Wayne is that Chase took careful risks. That is to say, he wasn't reckless. But if there was a problem with something at the top of the mast, say, he had no compunction about climbing up there to fix it, no matter the weather. That's what his former crewmates said, anyway. His ex-wife was quoted as saying he was married to the sea, probably the reason for the demise of their marriage. 'He would have liked being lost at sea,' she said. 'He would have liked the nobility and mystery of it.' Whenever Chase raced, he finished in the top five. And listen to this." Maddie braced for the worst. "That son-of-a-b—sorry, that lucky dog sailed in the 1998/1999 BOC Challenge. Well, now it's just called the Around Alone."

"Which is?" That didn't sound too bad.

"It's a race around the world. Alone."

"No crew?"

Barnie had a gleam in his eyes. "Nobody. Dreamed about doing it, but this guy's too old for that kind of thing now. You're gone for eight months, and unless you're sinking or in dire straits, you're in it alone."

She shivered, thinking of accidents and stormy weather. "The icebergs. He remembered seeing icebergs and feeling as though he were on the edge of the world."

"Sailing across the Southern Ocean, he would be. If you hurt yourself, have equipment failure, or even get dismasted, you're on your own. Even if you're capsized or sinking, help's hours away, usually days. Men die out there, never to be found." He patted his faded shirt. "Gets the ticker going just thinking about it. That's risk-taking, not that goofing around Wayne did. Chase might be one of the best sailors around—and it seems he was—but out there on the ocean, a lot is out of your control."

Chase was almost a casualty. "But all that's not too bad. There's more, isn't there?"

"There's more."

She waited for a moment, then finally asked, "What?," on an agitated breath.

"Maybe this is dumping too much on you at once."

"Dump, Barnie! Spill the beans."

"When they found Chase's boat—his personal sailboat,

Chase the Wind, floating around on autopilot, no one was aboard. But a woman's body was found tangled up in the keel."

Chase stared at the blustery Gulf and felt something rise inside him. He was the one who'd told Barnie it wasn't a good idea to take the boat out today, but something irresistible called to him. He could see waves crashing up over the sides of a deck, in his mind.

It was coming back to him, his life, his past. Going out in the storm might be the trigger he needed to put it all together. A gust of wet air slammed into him. He shouldn't be taking the boat out in this weather, not on its test run. But he knew he and the boat could handle it. His fingers curled and uncurled as they imagined the challenge. The excitement. The fear. He readied the dock lines and started to board.

"Chase!"

Maddie's voice sounded distorted through the wind and rain. He didn't need her right now. He felt ugly and on edge.

She was wearing an oversized yellow raincoat, and all he could see was a little of her face. "I need to talk to you," she said as she neared the boat. "What are you doing? I thought you weren't taking the boat out."

"I changed my mind."

"Are you nuts? Look at it out there!"

Waves tumbled over one another outside the boundary of the bay, which was choppy in its own right. They called to him like the curling finger of a beautiful woman.

The beautiful woman in front of him looked worried. "Chase, I need to tell you something."

"We'll talk later. I need to do this, Maddie. I can't explain it."

She said something that sounded like, "I can," but it got

warbled in the wind. Another gust of rain swept through, and then she started to climb aboard. "I'm coming with you. You said I could."

"That was yesterday when I didn't know the weather would be this bad."

"Well, it's not stopping you, so I'm coming, too."

He stood in her way, balancing on the edge of the deck. "No you're not."

She looked cold and wet, and all he wanted to do was take her down into the cabin and warm her up. In a just-friends way, of course.

"You said I should take some risks."

"I meant as in opening your heart and loving someone." The look she gave him nearly melted his reserve. *Not me, Maddie.* "It's too dangerous for you to come. You don't know how to sail." He let the aft line go.

She searched his face, worry creasing her brow. "You've got the hari-kari look on your face."

"The what look?"

"Hari-kari. It's the same look Wayne used to wear when he was about to get crazy."

"The difference is," he said, neatly stepping her onto the dock before hopping back on the boat and pushing away, "I'm not taking you with me."

She was stomping her foot and yelling, but luckily he couldn't hear her.

Once he got out to the bay, he turned into the wind. The Gulf was chopped up in the storm that was supposed to have only drenched them this morning. Conditions had changed overnight, with a low-pressure cold front pushing the storm to the east. He couldn't see one other boat anywhere. This was crazy, but he couldn't deny the drive deep inside him. On the other side of this ride was his past.

In some inexplicable way, he felt the air pressure dropping. Waves broke over the deck and soaked him. From the moment the wind had taken hold, Chase was in his element. He belonged here in this chaos, thrived on it. Wind gusts were at least thirty-five knots, and the farther from shore he got, the harder it got. The boat dropped into one trough after another, knocking him and the boat about.

He had no safety harness. That thought spiked through him, followed by a faraway echo of his own voice, both familiar and foreign: *What the hell were you thinking, Tom? Always, always clip your harness to the safety jack line!*

And then another man's voice: *I didn't think it was that bad up here. And it's easier to move around without one.*

Easier to get your ass knocked out of the boat, too! Get it on!

Chase wanted to go with the conversation and the memory, but he had to focus on his own situation. No way could he turn around now. It was coming back, he could feel it. Kissing Maddie had started the pieces, and sailing into the storm was going to bring the rest.

His thin slicker didn't begin to keep the warm water from soaking him. A wave pitched the boat sideways, but she picked herself up. Only to be lifted to another crest and dropped back into another trough. *Too fast,* an internal voice said. *Slow her down.* He dragged himself across the deck, getting slammed into the mast by another wave. What he wanted was to go faster, but he knew the boat's limits and knew this wasn't the boat to risk.

After what seemed like hours, he reefed in the mainsail, but the boat was still thrusting through the water. The boat crested and dropped again. Memories flashed through his mind as he put a second reef into the main. Nothing specific, just scenes of fighting a storm worse than this. The near certainty of dying, the regret and honor of it.

Dying at sea is an honorable thing.

Someone else's voice echoed and faded.

He'd already furled the genoa. Now he tried to bank on

the storm jib. An instinctual voice guided him. He made his way forward, only to have a wave pick up the boat and slam it onto her beam ends. The mast dipped into the waves, and Chase went into the water. He hadn't even had a chance to take a breath before water engulfed him.

His hands clamped onto the safety jacks on the deck. He was jerked back as the boat righted herself. His heart was pounding, and his body ached where he'd landed on the deck. He lived for this stuff.

He worked his way forward again and set the storm jib. Between the rain and low, heavy skies, he couldn't make out the horizon at all. It was all gray and bleak. Everything about it felt right and familiar. After a third reef in the mainsail, the boat was under control again. A condition, Chase knew, that could be temporary at best.

He thought about setting the autopilot, but he wanted to control the boat. In a moment of calm, he snugged the wheel brake and slipped down the companionway to get a pair of gloves he'd stowed there earlier. Down in the cabin, the pounding of the waves was lessened, but no less threatening. He might as well have been in a barrel racing over Niagara Falls. Which seemed an appropriate analogy when the boat pitched again.

He climbed back onto the deck and grabbed hold of the wheel, releasing the brake. The gloves helped his grip, though they weren't the appropriate ones to use for sailing. Kitchen rubber gloves, he remembered. Combined with leather outer gloves, that was the best combination.

Adrenaline surged through him as yet another piece locked into place. Just tiny pieces, though. He'd have to spend a week out here at this rate to remember everything. But it wasn't rock and roll he heard, or country music as he dashed through the waves. In all the music he'd searched for cues, he hadn't thought about classical. But there it was, a soundtrack to the wind and rain and adrenaline, Mozart or maybe Mahler.

He worked the boat upwind, adjusting as needed. He let out a triumphant scream. This was his life. Now he just needed the rest of it.

Another jagged piece came with suddenness. The struggle he'd remembered before, and the woman's scream. He held on tight when the boat crested and dropped. Held on to the wheel and the memory. His insides froze, and some part of him wanted to push it away. He could feel the shock and violence that accompanied the memory.

He could hear rain pelting the deck and sails, angry screams. He was struggling with something. No, someone. The boat pitched, sending them across the deck and against the cockpit. But he couldn't see whom he was fighting. Then he saw the woman staggering backward and hitting her head against a winch.

His own boat pitched sideways, throwing him out of the memory. He was too stunned to respond right away. All he could think about was the woman he'd pushed to the deck. What had happened to her?

The boat again righted itself, and Chase looked westward. *Keep going, run, don't face any more.*

Even as he thought it, he was already turning the boat back to shore. Whoever he was . . . whatever he'd done, he had to face it. He'd been running his whole life. That was the last key to himself that came as he lowered the mainsail completely.

Dim lights shone through the rain from the shoreline a while later. He wasn't sure how far he'd gone. All he knew was he'd been gone for almost four hours. Maddie had probably alerted Barnie to his crazy trip. No doubt he'd lost the man's respect even if the boat hadn't sustained any damage. It was even possible that the police could be waiting for him. He took a moment to go down below and check for both damage and leaks. The boat had held up well, though everything not stowed had been strewn around the cabin.

His heart was still pounding, though he wasn't sure if it was from the trip or his revelation. He'd hit a woman, that's all he could think about.

The waves abated as he neared the bay. Gusts still swept in, bringing hard sheets of rain. He took down the storm jib and powered into the bay. At first he saw no one, which relieved him. He'd still tell Barnie what he'd done, if he didn't know. But dealing with the police, especially in light of his recent memory, wasn't going to make anything easier. He had to find out the whole story before he could involve them.

Then he saw Maddie. At first she was a yellow blur. She was standing next to his boat, and she was alone. Huddled into herself, all he could see of her face were those enormous doe eyes full of anxiety. He hoped she hadn't stood there the whole time.

He didn't want to see her, and yet, the sight of her waiting for him filled him with relief and something he couldn't identify. He was evil, and she was his redemption. Not that he deserved redemption, or even her. He was worse than her husband.

And he wanted her more than anything else, even though it wasn't fair to have her. She took the lines he threw and tied them down when he pulled up next to the dock. He fully expected to hear how irresponsible he'd been, especially after lecturing her about Wayne's recklessness. He expected, and deserved, her anger for worrying her.

So it didn't surprise him when she did start screaming at him. "I thought you were trying to kill yourself! I've been listening to the radio in *The Barnacle*. The storm has been building all morning, and they've been repeating for three hours and forty-two minutes that no boats should go out today. I thought you were never going to come back, and they'd find the wreckage of the boat and not you! Men are sometimes lost at sea, you know!"

What did surprise him, when he jumped onto the dock, was the way she threw herself into his arms. "I never worried about Wayne, because I never knew he was taking chances. But, oh, God, I worried about you. When you disappeared into the storm, I couldn't breathe, it hurt so bad."

All he could do was hold her. He closed his eyes and squeezed her so hard, he could feel her ribs. He felt the ache inside, too. She wasn't his to love, but he couldn't stop himself from kissing her, from running his hands over her face. He wanted her, and he couldn't have her, but he couldn't think about any of that now.

"Let's get out of the rain," he said in a hoarse voice.

He helped her onto *The Barnacle* and down the companionway. The boat rocked in the choppy water, and the plangent sound of the rain echoed through the cabin. The moment they'd gotten their footing, he stripped the yellow coat off her. She tugged his slicker, then tore off his T-shirt. They couldn't get their clothes off fast enough, but they couldn't stop kissing, either. He didn't deserve her, but he couldn't stop himself from having her. At least for right now, for these precious moments.

Maddie was engulfed by emotions as turbulent as the weather outside. A sleepless night and then four hours of worrying had frayed her nerves. But now he was here, alive and safe, and half-naked in his cabin. She didn't want to think about the consequences, or what she knew. He was still her Chase. And for one time, she wanted give in to the explosive feelings they'd kept tamped for too long.

He peeled off her shirt, damp even beneath the raincoat. His eyes took her in as though he'd just found a sunken treasure. His face was flushed, his mouth slack, pupils big and dark.

"God, you're beautiful, Maddie."

Am not, she wanted to say, but her tongue wouldn't work. As though he couldn't hold back anymore, he pulled her close and devoured her neck and shoulder. She rocked her head back and absorbed the feel of his mouth sliding across her cool skin. He cupped her breasts in his hands, and ran his tongue over them. She sucked in a breath and arched back as his mouth loved her breasts and then went lower across her stomach.

He worked on the top button of her jeans, pushed them down. His hot breath went right through her panties, and then he pulled them down. Being naked with Chase was as natural as kissing him. But she wanted him naked, too. She ran her hands over his shoulders and across his chest. She leaned forward and kissed one of his nipples, delighting in making it harden. He tightened his hands on her shoulders and let out a soft growl, and she gave the other one attention. He watched her with wonder as she found the top edge of his jeans and tried to unbutton them. Finally she had to look down and slide the button through the hole. He was straining against the dense, wet material. Getting his jeans off wasn't smooth, but he finally kicked them away. His briefs had gone with them, or maybe he hadn't been wearing any.

She inhaled softly when she saw him naked and gorgeous. She stepped back to admire him, to take him in so she'd always remember the splendor of his body. His skin was cool and damp, but he looked hot and steamy. He was looking at her the same way, taking her in as though she were the most beautiful thing he'd ever seen.

His eyes were dark with heat, as liquid as molten gold. As though he couldn't stand to be away from her, even a few inches, he pulled her forward and kissed her again. Her body slammed into his, and she could feel the hot length of him pressing against her stomach. He cradled her face, kissing, pulling back, then kissing again.

The intensity of his eyes burned to the core of her. "Baby, it's time to grow up."

She looked into his eyes. "I'm ready."

"I can't make any promises," he whispered between kisses, as though he couldn't bear to part with her even for those words.

"I know," she whispered back, knowing too well.

He reached back and shuffled through where he kept the books he'd been reading. She had seen the books, classics, but not the single condom package. "Where'd you get that?"

"Long story."

He backed her toward the V-berth cabin. He laid her gently back onto the bed, taking her in with his eyes and his hands.

"You're beautiful, Maddie. You really are," he added when he saw the doubt in her eyes.

Not just empty words, his touch said. His eyes said. She pulled him down and kissed him hard. No one had ever called her beautiful, no one. She held tight to him, wishing she could hold him forever.

His hands were unsteady, running across her body as though it were the first time he'd ever touched a woman. In his mind, that was true. His sense of wonder touched her beyond belief. She and Wayne had been each other's first lovers, and their first lovemaking had been marked with awkwardness.

Chase wasn't awkward or hesitant. Just awed. As his thumbs circled her breasts, he took in the tremble of her body in reaction. He spread his fingers and ran them across her stomach, making goose bumps rise in their path.

"What do you like?" he asked.

"Just touch me. Anywhere. Everywhere."

So he did, gauging her reaction as his hands caressed her inner thighs, the curve of her behind, and then that private place. His touch spiraled right through her. She felt it explode inside her, and her body convulsed as it washed over her. Her face was flushed when she finally raised her head to look at him. He'd been watching her, of course, marveling in her reaction.

"Good?" he asked.

She wanted to show him how good. She pushed him down on the bed. His chest was smooth. As soon as her fingers touched him, his breath hitched. She now watched in wonder at his reaction to her touch, every intake of air, every twitch of muscle. She felt just as aroused as when he'd touched her. His whole body convulsed when she wrapped her fingers around him and stroked. It had been too long since she'd felt this intimate part of a man's body. She experienced with him every tremor that rippled through him until he grabbed hold of her hand and stilled her. He kissed the back of her hand once he'd removed it, then reached over where he'd left the condom and unwrapped it. She helped to slide it down his length.

She lay back on the bed, wanting to maximize the feel of his body against hers. He ran the tips of his fingers across her skin, which had long ago lost its chill. Then he maneuvered over her, all the while concentrating on what he was doing. She wrapped her legs around his waist and her arms around his neck.

He eased in, sliding against her wetness. Her fingers tightened over his shoulders as he gently filled her, and then he took a staggering breath and kissed her as he moved inside her. She closed her eyes and lost herself in the feeling of being alive again, more alive than she'd ever felt. She was a woman in his arms, not a giggly teenager in a woman's body. He was tense, his muscles rock hard.

"How could I have forgotten this?" he whispered in a strained voice.

Drowning in the sensations that built inside her, she tightened her hold on him, feeling him thrust forward in a single convulsion that shook his body. She caught up with him, letting herself go with the rush of heat and pressure.

They held on to each other as though each were a lifesaver in a turbulent ocean. She could hear him catching his breath, reminding her to breathe at all. He shifted to her side and held her close on the small bed.

"I wish I never had to let you go," he said close to her ear.

She turned to face him, seeing pain in his eyes. He reached up and brushed damp hair from her face.

"I was thinking the same thing," she said. She was also thinking that maybe she wouldn't tell him who he was. Would he stay here? Be content never knowing? No, she knew him that well. Chase was going to leave anyway, and he needed to be armed with the truth before he did.

But she wasn't ready to lose him altogether or think about that other Chase Augustine who might be a murderer. She snuggled against him and closed her eyes. She wanted to hold on to as many moments as she could without the ugly truth standing between them—that she'd made love with him while withholding dangerous information.

⌒◦ CHAPTER 15

MADDIE DOZED FOR a while, all the worry and then the release of lovemaking finally catching up to her. She lay in Chase's arms, feeling his body heat envelop her in peace. It felt so good to be held in sleep by a man. It seemed unreal, lying there with him, breathing in the scent of wood, salty air, and a slightly musty odor.

She regretfully floated back to consciousness, vaguely aware of a dull ache inside her. Her heart was jammed up in her throat because of what she had to tell him. She sighed and shifted, staring up at the hatch that revealed the patter of rain. He opened his eyes and looked at her. His smile mirrored the melancholy haze surrounding her.

Her arms involuntarily tightened over his chest. She couldn't stand the suspense any longer. "Chase?"

"You all right?" he asked. He had no idea how all wrong she was.

She swallowed what felt like a wad of cotton in her throat. "I know who you are."

He sat up so fast, she jumped back on the bed. "What are you talking about?"

She'd wanted to be holding onto him when she told him the news, but clinging suddenly didn't seem like a good idea. She pulled up a pillow and hugged it to her chest. "Barnie did some looking on the Internet. And he . . . found you."

As though he sensed the news wasn't good, his body

stiffened, and his eyes darkened. "What did you find out?"

She took a deep breath. "Your name is Chase Augustine. You race sailboats for a living. You disappeared under mysterious circumstances off the coast of Miami, where you live. They found your boat, but no one on it."

"What else?"

"You're not married. Divorced," she added when he looked as though he were going to ask her about the ring. "You're very good at what you do. Respected. Recently you started getting into around-the-world alone racing. Maybe that's where the icebergs came in."

"And?"

"And . . ." She looked away for a moment, then back at him. "When they found your boat . . . there was a woman's body caught up in the keel." He put his hands over his face. "Barnie couldn't find anything past the initial announcement, like who she was and if she was involved with you or had been on your boat. She might have been just floating out there." She started to touch him, but he stood and pulled on his jeans.

"When did you find out?" he asked.

"Before I came out this morning."

His movements became jerky as his anger rose. "Dammit, why didn't you tell me then?"

"I tried! There was no stopping you."

"Then how about before we fell into bed together? Wasn't that a good time to tell me I'm a murderer?"

"You don't know if you're a murderer. It was probably an accident. Or—" She stopped at the tense resignation in his face. "You remembered, too?"

He jerked on his shirt. "Not all of it. I hit a woman. We were on a boat, and I was struggling with her. It's not clear, but she's screaming, and then I see her falling and hitting her head. It has to be the same woman."

Maddie lunged for her clothes as he walked forward.

"You're not a murderer. You're probably not remembering it right."

. He stopped abruptly and she bumped into him. He steadied her, but dropped his hands. "How could you sleep with me knowing I'd killed someone?"

"Because I don't believe you did." She tugged on his arm as he started up the companionway. "No one has to know. Barnie won't tell. You can stay here, start a new life."

He took her wrists in his hands. "Grow up, Baby. I can't walk away from something like that. And if I hit her, who's to say I wouldn't hit you?" Pain flashed across his face, but he stuffed it away. "Or worse."

"Where are you going?" she shouted after him as he stepped into the rainy evening without his slicker.

"To talk to Barnie."

Then he was gone. And only then did she realize he'd called her Baby. She dropped down onto the floor in the galley and started to cry.

When Maddie had gathered herself into some semblance of a normal person, she dragged herself home. Something was niggling at her, but she couldn't find the spare energy to figure out what it was. She'd walked past the warehouse in the rain, wondering what the two men were doing, wishing she could be there for Chase. But he wouldn't let her, because she'd done wrong withholding the information until after they'd made love.

She'd pretended not to feel well, fought off Mom's offer of comfort, and went to bed. Only she couldn't get to sleep. She kept replaying everything that had happened that day. Chase was right to be angry. She'd withheld devastating information so she could make love with him. Maybe she was as selfish as Colleen had been saying for years. All her life the world had revolved around her. She couldn't stop that in a day.

Chase was going to leave. She knew that, and it would probably be the next day. He'd promised not to leave without saying goodbye, and the Chase she knew was honest and responsible. Still, restlessness ran through her body as she weighed what to do. She looked at the clock: three in the morning. She had to figure out how to help Chase, how to let him go. If she could let him go.

She sat up in bed. Who should be the purveyors of wisdom but her parents? Maybe Dad would know who to call. It had been a long time since she'd climbed into bed with them—since the month after Wayne's accident. Undoubtedly she'd wake them up, but she was going to call in one last selfish favor.

She tapped on the door, then pushed it open. The nightlight in the bathroom guided her to their big bed, and Maddie slid in. She found Mom, but no Dad.

Mom jerked awake. "Hmph?"

"Mom, it's me, Maddie. I need to talk to you and Dad about something."

"Go back to bed!" she whispered frantically.

Then Maddie heard a grunt from the other side of the room. She slid across the bed and turned on the light.

"Baby, no!" Mom said, but it was too late.

Dad blinked awake from his place . . . on the couch. "Whaz going on?"

"Damn," Mom said. "I mean, darn." She grabbed for her glasses.

Maddie looked from one to the other. "What's going on?" Her chest was already squeezing tight. "Did you and Dad have a fight?"

Mom scrubbed her hand through her tangled red curls. "Oh, Baby, we didn't want you to know."

"Know what?"

"Your father and I are . . . separated."

Maddie put her hand across her throat, more of those cotton balls returning to clog it up. "S . . . separated? Since when?"

"Last year," Dad said, coming over to sit next to Maddie in his wrinkled pajamas.

"But . . . why? How?"

"Your mom and I—"

"Decided we weren't happy together anymore," Mom finished. "It's nothing like Bobby and Colleen, I mean, nobody's cheating or nothing. We just grew apart."

Maddie took in the couch with a pillow and blanket draped over it. "You've been sleeping like this since last year?"

"Well, that first month when you came in, Dad had to pretend he'd just come back from the bathroom. We shared the bed for a bit until we felt you weren't going to come in crying anymore."

"You've been doing this since then?" She could hardly put the pieces together in her mind. "Pretending?"

Mom nodded. "We'd decided to get divorced, honey— don't wince when I say that word—just before Wayne went away. We thought it was a good time, you and Wayne all settled in and hopefully having kids soon. Then the awful thing happened, and we couldn't dump that on you, too. You needed a stable family around you. It wasn't hard. We haven't had to think about dividing things up, all that messy stuff."

"You stayed together for me?"

Dad put his hand on Maddie's knee. "Yep. We love you that much."

Then she remembered something Colleen had said about Maddie not knowing the sacrifices their parents had made for her. "Colleen knows, doesn't she?"

"I'd just told her, figuring to break it to the strong one

first. We were going to tell you that weekend, and then . . . well, you know."

Maddie stood. She couldn't get her mind around it all. Her parents, separated. Pretending to be together for her. Living a lie. Colleen knowing.

"Baby, we'll just keep on keeping on for you. You're living here now, and it makes it easier us being together."

She stumbled out of the room. She didn't even realize she'd put on her clothes and shoes until they were on. Mom was in the hallway when Maddie emerged from her room.

"Let's talk about this, Baby."

"Maddie," she said.

"What?"

"My name is Maddie. I'm not Baby anymore. Never again."

She didn't know where she was going, she just drove through the damp night. The headlights reflected off the wet surface of the road, and the tires squished in the puddles. Sugar Bay was tucked in its collective bed unaware of the turmoil surrounding her.

When she pulled up in front of the warehouse, she told herself it was to see if Barnie was awake. There was no use lying, though. She needed to talk to Chase.

All she could hear was the occasional squeak of a boat and water dripping into the bay. She walked along the wet dock to *The Barnacle*. It was dark and silent, of course, but it felt darker and more silent than ever. The companionway hatch was closed, boards fitting together to form a seal.

"Chase? Chase, it's Maddie."

She heard a door close nearby. She strained to see through the darkness. Her heart jumped when she saw a figure walking out of the warehouse. Somehow she knew, her heart already saturated with ache and betrayal, that it was Chase. And he was leaving.

She nearly lost her footing on the slick spot on the ramp.

He was walking around the side of the warehouse, away from her and the boat. In blue jeans and a black shirt, he blended into the night. As she turned the corner, the orange light from the street lamp cast him in a glow. She didn't think about what she was going to do when she caught up to him.

Jumping on his back wasn't on the list, but she did it anyway. With a curse, he lurched forward, dropping something to the damp ground before spinning around. She held on, her arms locked around his shoulders.

"You were going to sneak out of here without saying goodbye, weren't you?"

"Jeez, Maddie, you scared the hell out of me. Let me go."

He hadn't denied it, and she took out the pain that stabbed through her on him. She tightened her hold and bit his neck.

With another curse, he twisted around to shake her loose. They both went hurtling to the ground, and she landed on top of him.

She grabbed two fistfuls of his hair. "You promised you wouldn't leave without saying goodbye!"

"Dammit, Maddie, stop being an animal!" He grabbed her wrists, and she fought him for control. "That was before I knew who I was."

They wrestled as they talked, breathless in their fight. "A promise is a promise!"

He finally managed to pin her to the ground beneath him. His knees held her legs in place, and his hands pushed her wrists against the cool, wet grass. She could feel it prickling through her shirt.

"You are such a coward!" she spat at him when he lowered his face to hers. "Sneaking off in the middle of the night like the dog you are."

"Fine, I'm a coward and a dog." He sounded far too

calm, even though he was still breathing heavily. He released her wrists only to snag her hands with his, intertwining their fingers.

"Now you're beginning to sound like me pre-Chase. So you admit you were sneaking off?"

His fingers tightened. "I admit it. Now, if I let you up, are you going to stop freaking out?"

She tried to free herself, remembering her and Wayne's tickling matches. "Yeah, sure." Just as he eased off, she twisted him around and rolled him to the ground. He started to get up, then dropped back.

"Maddie, you're acting crazy. You know I could shove you off without even trying, don't you?"

All right, so Wayne was smaller than Chase. "So you could. What would that prove?"

"Only that I'm crazy for not doing it."

For a moment, the thick clouds scudding across the sky cleared, and moonlight shone across his face. No matter that he was a dog and a coward, he was gorgeous in the silvery glow. She was sitting on his lower stomach, and their hands were still linked.

"I'm sorry for leaving without saying goodbye," he said at last. "Barnie showed me the articles. Maddie, a woman probably died because of me. I have to face whatever I did. I packed up, settled with Barnie, and . . . thought about going to see you. But I don't know where you live."

"Barnie could have told you."

He let out a sigh. "Yeah, he could have. I didn't want to face you again, all right. If that makes me a coward, then it does."

She wanted to give him a hard time, but instead she leaned down and kissed him. "That was for admitting it," she said, though it was really just because she wanted to.

"Don't kiss me, Maddie," he said, even though he'd responded. "I don't deserve it."

"You don't. But only because you're a dog for leaving without saying goodbye."

"Goodbye."

She hated the finality of that word.

"Now let me up. This grass is making me itch."

Reluctantly she loosened her hands from his and climbed off. He jumped to his feet as though he suspected she might change her mind. He brushed off the grass, then realized she was watching him.

"I'm sorry, all right? I didn't know what to say to you, not after what you told me, and *when* you told me."

"Did you even leave me a note?"

He shook his head.

She walked up close. "Do you remember who you are now? Has it come back?"

He rocked his shoulder back and forth. "Not much more than a few flashes. Damn, I think you threw my shoulder out of joint."

"You deserved it. More than you deserved my kiss."

"And what the hell are you doing sneaking around in the middle of the night anyway?"

"My parents are separated and they've been pretending to be together for me, and—that's not important now. What *is* important is me catching you sneaking away."

"I said I was sorry." He brushed the back of his hand against her cheek. "Forget about me, Maddie. I've got a mess to sort out when I get back . . . home. You need to get on with your life, meet a nice guy and get married."

"Maybe I *will* forget about you."

The regret that shadowed his face was at odds with his firm, "Good. Come here and give me a hug goodbye." He yanked her hard against him and squeezed her tight, then pushed her away. "Have a nice life, Maddie." He grabbed up his bag and headed off into the night.

Just like that.

She was shaking all over, watching him disappear into the darkness. His footsteps faded away, and he was gone. She hated him. That was that, she just hated him, because he'd betrayed her trust and broken her heart. So she'd go on, then. She stomped to her car and headed home. To her dismay, the lights were on. Worse, everyone except Q was sitting in the living room.

"What's going on?" she asked, a knot forming in her stomach. Had something horrible happened?

"We should ask you that," Colleen said, taking in the bits of grass littering her body. Maddie smoothed her hair back in hopes of dislodging anything tangled in it.

"I needed time to think."

"And of course, this becomes about you again," Colleen said. "Poor Baby knows the truth."

"I am not Baby anymore. In fact, I give the title to you. Seems to fit now." She turned to her parents. "Then you can stay together for her."

"We were only doing it for your own good. So you'd be happy," Mom called as Maddie headed to her room.

She was beginning to wonder if they'd done it for themselves, so they wouldn't have to face the ugliness of divorce. But she wasn't prepared to delve into that. So she threw out another zinger. "I'm moving back to my house."

Mom pulled her housecoat tighter and sat down on Maddie's bed. "Because of this?"

"Because of this." She gestured to the angels that had been replaced for the second time. "And because I'm ready." She slipped out of her damp clothes and changed into white pants and a brown knit top.

Mom dabbed at her eyes with the corner of her coat. "After all we've done for you . . . why would you live by yourself when you can be with your family?"

"I know you've done a lot for me. And I know it doesn't make sense, me living there alone, but . . ." She blinked, realizing she was falling into the same trap she'd been in her whole life. "Mom, I'm twenty-six years old. Let me grow up."

She pulled out a suitcase and started throwing clothes into it.

"What are you doing?"

What *was* she doing? "I'm going to Miami with Chase," she heard herself say.

She hugged her mother, then headed out of the room.

"You can't stop being my Baby!" Mom protested, following her. "It's against the laws of nature."

At the door, Maddie turned to face her family. "Mom, Dad, if you want to get a divorce . . . well, do it. Colleen, you don't have that choice. You have a little boy to think about. You can make it work if you try. And stop using me as an excuse to get your way. Let Bobby open his shop, and so what if you have to put the pool off for a few more years. Better yet, I'll buy you the damned pool. Wayne's insurance company paid me plenty . . . when he died. He died, you know. He didn't go away and he won't be back." She looked at the gold band on her finger. Then with a deep breath, she took it off and handed it to her mom. "I love you all. Bye."

As she slipped into the night, she heard Colleen say, "She's gone crazy, hasn't she?"

Yes, she had. And it was about damn time.

CHAPTER 16

IT SEEMED LIKE forever since Chase had hitchhiked. Sugar Bay had seeped into his blood and made him feel at home. All right, it wasn't Sugar Bay, it was Maddie who'd seeped into his blood.

He wished she didn't know anything about his real past. He hoped she would forget about him. Now he knew why he'd opted for the coward's way out. Walking away from Maddie was harder than he ever imagined.

He'd reached the highway and now walked along the edge. There wasn't a car in sight. He probably had a couple of hours of walking before any hope of catching a ride. To his right the shoulder dropped off to a ditch and then black woods. Creatures whined and clicked as though enticing him into the darkness. Too late. He was already there.

A sailboat racer. He kept running the concept through his head, hoping more would come now that he knew the truth. Like in the movies, where everything fell into place at once. It remained frustratingly elusive.

A murderer. The pieces didn't quite fit, but all the facts were there.

He had a father, a brother. And an ex-wife. No mention of his mother. He'd probably been one of those guys who was so driven, he'd neglected everyone in his life. He could live with that part.

He heard a car coming up behind him. Only four in the morning. What kind of people were out at this hour, anyway? He didn't trust getting another ride like the one he'd caught in the wee hours in Georgia. The moment the car was in motion again, the guy said, "The spaceship is a-coming in twelve hours, but I guess I can do one last deed on this earth before I become immortal. Do ya wanna come with us?" For three hours he heard about the paradise to be found on a plane of existence between death and re-birth—a place called "Deep Purple."

Chase kept on walking instead of turning his thumb out. Besides, it was too dark for anyone to see him.

The car slowed down anyway. Scary. Maybe they'd go away if he didn't look at them.

"Get in!"

Real scary, considering it sounded just like Maddie. He turned to find her teal Sunbird cruising alongside him with its window down.

"Go home! I do not want you going to Miami with me."

"Hah! You're rubbing your nose."

He leaned closer to the passenger window, barely able to see her face in the glow of the dashboard lights. "I'm not lying, and I'm not dragging you into my problems. Besides, sounds like your family needs you right now."

"Them need me? That's a laugh."

"Maddie, are you still that naïve? I could be a murderer."

"Do you actually remember shoving her?"

"Close enough."

"If you had anything to do with her death, it was an accident. Now get in."

His fingers tensed on the top of the door. "Do you think I strangled her accidentally, too?" He was glad to see that shoot some fear into her eyes. "Didn't Barnie tell you that part? One of the articles said her windpipe had been crushed. Is that enough for you?"

That stopped her for a moment. She put her hand to her

throat. "Damn him for not telling me, and damn you for thinking that's going to scare me away."

"Don't be stupid. Go home."

He started walking again. She gunned the gas and roared past him. Good, he'd pissed her off. She turned around up ahead and started back.

Aimed right at him.

He stood there for as long as any sane man might, then dove off the shoulder when she didn't let up. She careened past him, hit her brakes, and turned around again.

"Are you *nuts*?" he screamed when she pulled up serenely next to him once he'd gathered his duffel bag and his wits.

"Why yes, I am. Get in the car or become road kill, your choice. Simple as that."

She looked serious. He was sure she wasn't, but then again, she had clearly gone over the edge of nuttiness. He got in the car, slamming the door in retribution. Now he had more grass and dew to add to the results of her previous assault. The woman was a menace.

"Good choice." And she calmly headed down the highway.

He was still having trouble catching his breath, but he screamed, "You are freaking mad! What the hell were you trying to prove back there?"

"That you need me."

"Yeah, and I need to get run over, too."

She gave him a sweet smile. "I wasn't going to run you over. Well, unless you still refused to get in the car. But I'd have given you a few chances."

He rubbed his forehead. "What are you doing, Maddie?"

"You're the one who told me to grow up and stop expecting others to fix my problems. So I'm taking your advice."

"You're blaming me for your crazy behavior?"

"I'm giving you credit. Do you realize how you've changed my life? God, when I think how I was just a few weeks ago. Remember when I first came to the boat, and you ran me off?"

He leaned his head back and closed his eyes. "Sweet memories. I've created a monster."

"Just call me Maddiestein." Her giggle pulled his attention to her.

She looked stronger than he'd ever seen her, and sexier. A credit to his own madness that he could even think that about the woman who'd nearly flattened him. Instead of the baggy clothes she usually wore, the autumn-colored top fit close to her skin.

"I've never been to Miami. Do you know how to get there?" she asked.

"Have you ever left Sugar Bay?"

"Couple of times, with Wayne. He died, you know."

He was getting flashbacks from the spaceship dude. "Yeah, I know."

"And so do I."

"You look happy about it, too. You're really starting to scare me, Maddie."

She gave him a look as though he were the one who'd lost his mind. "You accused me of not being able to admit that he died. Now I can say it. Do you know what you've done to me?"

"I'm afraid to ask."

"You've brought me back to life in a way I can't even describe. I have never felt like this before. Strong. Independent. It's like a drug, or maybe a few bottles of wine since I've never done drugs, but it's incredible, intoxicating."

"You didn't happen to have that wine, say, recently, did you? That would explain a lot."

" 'Course not. I wouldn't be driving. I'm sure you were

right, too, about Wayne having sent you." He figured those words would come back to haunt him. "All these years," she continued, "my whole life, I've been living like a baby, letting everyone tell me what to do and what to be. Even when I thought I was happy with Wayne, and I was for the most part, I wasn't really living. I told my family I was moving back to my house. I still have to work on that one. You should have seen the look on their faces when I said I was going with you!" The words were pouring out of her, as though someone had pulled a plug.

He'd pulled the plug, he realized. From that first day, and every day he'd spent with her, he'd nudged her into growing and becoming independent. He *had* created a monster!

When she'd told him about her parents being separated but not really separated, and how her sister was now the baby of the house, when she'd expended all that energy, she finally fell silent.

Maybe this wasn't so out of character for her after all. She had no problem fighting for something—or mostly someone—she believed in. And this time, that person happened to be him.

After a moment she looked over at him. "Chase? I'm sorry about almost running you over. I knew you wouldn't let me come with you any other way."

"You were right about that."

"I won't do it again."

He found himself laughing at the absurdity of that statement. "That's good to know."

"You're not going to change once you get back to your life, are you?"

He glanced over at the softness of her voice. "I don't know what's going to happen. All I know is I have a life, and a woman's death to figure out, a death I had something to do with. I have no future and nothing to offer you."

Her fingers tightened on the steering wheel. "I'm not doing this because I think we have a future. Don't get the wrong idea about my coming with you."

"Good." He actually sighed in relief.

"I'm only doing it because I love you."

Those words punched him in the stomach.

"I don't love you like . . . loving you," Maddie explained when too much silence had passed. "Not like I want to marry you love you."

He shot her a chagrined look. "Maddie, you don't love me. You've made me your cause. Now don't argue with me about this." Then he realized she wasn't. She was actually listening to him, and for some reason, that bothered him. He'd expected her to argue the point, to say those words that couldn't be true, yet moved him anyway.

"I hadn't intended to run you down."

"Ah, that's comforting." He slouched down in his seat, face leaning against his hand.

"I mean, it never occurred to me until you refused to get in the car. I was thinking, 'Why is everyone fighting me all of a sudden? What's changed?' Then I realized it: I changed. I wasn't that whiny Maddie who backs down from every fight, who gives in even when she doesn't want to. And that was all because of you."

"So you decided to run me over out of gratitude?"

"In a weird way, yes. No, listen. You were trying to push me away for my own good. I wasn't going to let you face Miami alone. We're friends, right? Because it wouldn't be smart to be anything more."

"More than you know."

She paused, then said, "Friends look out for each other. You helped me, and now I'm going to help you."

"Even if it kills me."

She gave him a big smile. "Right."

*   *   *

Chase drove into Miami five hours later. Maddie had obviously spent all her energy trying to assault him because she'd slept for the last two hours. She looked small and fragile curled up against the door with her cheek pressed against her hand. A hand, he noticed, that bore no wedding ring. He caught himself glancing over much too often. The woman had him in knots, and he didn't know what to do about it.

Nothing, that's what. He was a man incapable of offering her a future, and more importantly, of loving her. He was a murderer, for God's sake.

He hit the brakes when a black Porsche pulled out in front of him. Maddie fell forward, and he reached out instinctively to hold her back. Just the feel of her body against his hand sent a jolt through him.

"Sorry about that," he said.

Still dazed, she slipped the shoulder harness of her seat belt back into place and looked around. "We're in Miami."

"Home," he said, though he felt nothing. "Let's stop for gas and food."

Armed with full stomachs, and directions to Allister Augustine's residence, they headed across Biscayne Bay toward Miami Beach.

Maddie gawked at the mansions. "You're rich."

"And here I've been saving pennies for a haircut." His hair had long been on his nerves, hanging in his face.

"It's right up there," she said, pointing at two large columns flanking a driveway.

He pulled in and paused, looking at the ostentatious mansion that sat on Biscayne Bay: finely manicured lawn, more columns at the grand entrance, and an entrance that spanned the height of both stories of the house.

"Remember it?" she asked, not looking at the house but at him.

He shook his head, though he kept studying it. Something should come back. It may as well have been any other mansion along the road, and that made him wonder if he had the right address. The phone book had only listed an *A. Augustine*. He had to start somewhere.

"So, where are you on the nervous meter?" she asked as he pulled ahead.

"I'll tell you later," he said, sharing a grin that eased the anxiety a notch. "If this is the right address, my father probably won't even be here, not if he runs a company. But it's better than showing up there, with all those people around to recognize me."

Chase had long ago decided to keep a low profile until he had a handle on his former life. Hopefully all of it, including the events of that night on the boat. He needed to know what kind of person he was, and if he was capable of murder.

They pulled around the circular drive and parked in front of the house. He combed his hair, as though that would make any difference. He'd been missing for months. Neat hair wasn't going to lessen the impact of his arrival.

He looked up at the grand, ornate wood doors. Hell, yes, he was nervous. He had no idea what to expect.

A thin Hispanic man opened the door. His pleasant, but puzzled expression dripped away to shock. He stuttered for a moment, then said, "Señor *Chase?*"

Chase almost wanted to hug the man. It was the first time he'd seen recognition in someone's eyes. Along with the shocked surprise mingled apprehension, so Chase just said, "*Sí.* I'm looking for my father."

It took the man a few more seconds of staring before he nodded and backed inside. Chase and Maddie followed into a grand foyer with a view straight through the formal living room to the bay.

Chase figured he knew the guy who led them up a curving staircase, but nothing clicked. He thought the guy was going to phone his father, but the man led them to a door near the end of the hallway and hesitated. He seemed to study Chase as though making sure he was really there. Then he knocked.

"Señor Augustine?"

"I told you not to disturb me, Eduardo," an authoritative voice barked from the other side.

"You're going to want to be disturbed, sir." He opened the door.

Allister Augustine sat at an immense glass and chrome desk with an air of power and dignity. He was in his fifties, with silver hair and clean features. His gaze went to Eduardo first, shadowed with frustration, then to Maddie, and finally, to Chase. Disbelief colored his blue eyes, as though he were facing a ghost. Chase held his breath, waiting for the man's reaction.

"Ch-Chase? Is that you?"

Chase nodded. Again, he felt nothing. There wasn't a hint of similarity in their features.

Allister took a few steps forward and placed his hands on Chase's shoulders. "You came back," he whispered. "You're alive."

He nodded, unable to move his hands to touch his father back. Then Allister pulled him hard against him.

"I thought you were dead. You've been gone so long. We had to assume . . ." He backed away. "What took you so long to come back?"

"I didn't—don't know who I am."

At Allister's puzzled expression, Maddie added, "He lost his memory."

"He what?" He looked at Chase. "You what?"

"I lost my memory. I don't know who I am."

Allister studied Chase's eyes, perhaps searching for a glimmer of recognition. He let out a soft breath. "Why?

How? I don't understand how this could happen. Are you all right . . . otherwise?"

"Fine for a guy who has no past."

Allister glanced up at Eduardo who was watching from the doorway. "Bring us something to drink. Are you hungry?"

"We're fine," Chase said when he saw Maddie shaking her head.

"Leave us then," Allister said to Eduardo. "And tell no one he's come back."

"But—"

"No one."

Once the door had closed, Allister gestured for them to sit on the couch and fumbled with a carved wood box, extracting a cigarette.

"This is Maddie Schaeffer, by the way." Chase gave her an apologetic look for forgetting to introduce her, but she waved it off.

Maddie and Allister awkwardly shook hands over the coffee table.

"I want to know everything," Allister said to Chase.

Chase told his story, though he didn't tell him everything. "Can you tell me how I ended up out there?"

Again, Allister studied him. "You really don't remember?"

"No."

Allister opened one of the cabinet doors and pulled out a leather-bound scrapbook. Chase took in the details of the high-ceilinged office. Understated, masculine, overlooking the bay and a large yacht behind the mansion. Pictures on the wall drew Chase over. Many were of Allister with other men, important-looking men. There was one of a sailboat with the name *Augustine Aero* painted along the side. Another was a beautiful brown-haired woman posed with two boys. He felt a melancholy twinge.

"Your mother," Allister said, coming up behind him. His fingers worked the unlit cigarette. "You and Patrick."

His brother. Nothing stirred when he studied Patrick, who took after his father in looks. He had light hair and skin, patrician features. Chase was younger, but not by much. He looked tan and dark in contrast. He took after his mother.

"You don't remember her?" Allister asked, studying Chase's expression.

"No." Shame and frustration bombarded him at not remembering his own family. That black pit that held his memories hostage released nothing.

Allister set the scrapbook on the glass coffee table in front of the couch. Chase sat next to Maddie, and Allister sat across from them on a chair, his back straight. He watched Chase's expression as he opened the book, searching for a flicker of recognition perhaps.

"How much do you know about yourself?" Allister asked. He fiddled with the cigarette, then put it in his mouth. He still hadn't lit it yet.

"That I'm divorced, that I raced sailboats, and I guess I'm pretty good at it. And that . . . I'm considered missing at sea."

His father couldn't meet his eyes. "After an intensive search, the Coast Guard had to give up. I paid boats to keep searching long after. We searched, Chase. But eventually . . ."

"It's all right. I would have given up, too."

Allister's visible anxiety only lessened a bit. "So, you harbor no ill feelings toward me?"

"I don't even know you, other than that you're my father."

"Will it return? Your memory, I mean?"

"It might. Or it might not."

"Maybe it's better if it doesn't. It would mean a fresh start. How many people get that chance?"

Chase's chest tightened. "Why would I want one?" When Allister didn't answer, Chase asked, "Tell me about Chase Augustine. Who was he?"

Chase wished Maddie weren't there to hear this. What kind of person had he been? Was he someone worthy of the love she thought she felt for him? Probably not.

"You may know about Augustine Aero. I founded it when I was in my twenties, when you and Patrick were just babies. I envisioned it being the consummate family company with you and your brother taking on responsibility." Allister continued to fondle the unlit cigarette, running it beneath his nose and inhaling. "Doctor said I had to quit," he explained when he realized they were both watching him. "Nothing serious yet, but the stress was killing me." He stuck it in his mouth and talked around it. "Anyway, Patrick did as he was supposed to. He's always been like that, no fight in the boy. Hard worker, not a doubt about that. Still hasn't gotten the hang of it yet. After your . . . accident, and with my chest pains, I decided to give Patrick the reins. Well," he added, gesturing to the piles of paperwork on his massive desk, "most of them. Promoted him to president." Allister studied Chase and again asked, "You really don't remember any of this?"

Chase shook his head.

Allister took the cigarette out of his mouth and stared at it. "You, on the other hand, were the fighter. Your mother used to say Patrick was the angel, and you were the hellion. At least until I reminded her that Patrick took after me and you took after her."

"My mother . . . where is she?" He felt a flicker of pressure in his chest. Why hadn't she been called?

Allister lowered his chin into his hand. "Ella died when you were five. We were on a sailing vacation, on our way back from Bermuda. It was calm, perfectly calm that evening. You and Patrick were downstairs asleep, thank God. It was late, probably past midnight. A rogue wave came out of nowhere. Well, that's what a rogue wave is, I guess. Comes out of nowhere, maybe from shifts in the earth or some weather system far out to sea."

When Allister paused, Chase could see the pain etched in his face. He wanted to tell him not to go on if it hurt that much, but he had to know. "What happened?"

"The wave was probably forty feet high. It was a severe knockdown, with the mast going under. She was knocked out of the boat. I tried to grab for her, but she fell out of my reach. I never saw her again. Nobody did. It was just like the way you disappeared without a trace. Another victim of the Bermuda Triangle." He stuck the cigarette into his mouth and bit down so hard, it broke.

Chase felt a fist in his gut at the loss of a mother he couldn't remember. And probably had little memory of anyway. He looked at the woman who shared his features and knew she was the reason he felt melancholy whenever he looked out at sea.

"We survived. It wasn't easy, three of us not knowing a thing about running a house. The business was young then and didn't afford us the luxury of someone like Eduardo. I thought you'd never want to get on a boat again. That's how Patrick felt for a long time. But you started getting into sailing when you were eight. You raced the kids—"

"Pirate racing," Chase said without even thinking. "Treasure ships, pirate ships and neutrals. We had to capture flags."

Allister's face went white. "You remember?"

"Sometimes I get a . . . knowing. Usually it's nothing helpful, nothing specific enough to trigger the rest." He'd obviously thrown his father off. Allister sat there in silence for a few minutes, until Chase said, "Go on."

"If you can remember things like that, will the rest come, too?"

"From what I've read, every case is different. There are no guarantees."

"I think losing your mother at sea was what drove you to sailing. We never talked it about." Allister grabbed another cigarette from the oak box on his desk. He went through a ritual, passing it beneath his nose and across his lips. He directed this to Maddie: "He was always the adventurous, volatile one. He did what he damn well pleased. Had no interest in the company, though he did make a show of working there for a while. I fired him when I thought his resentment might blow up the place."

Chase didn't want to hear about that kind of anger. "Do I have a temper?"

"Sometimes, particularly when you drank."

Chase stiffened. They were getting closer to what happened that awful day.

But Allister went on with the past. "I won't say our relationship was cozy, never was. I raised my sons to be ambitious, hardworking, dedicated. You were, but not for the company that provided so well for you. We didn't talk much, you and I, while you were off living out of a duffel bag, going from one regatta to another. You told me it was the college of life and sailing. You had to put in your dues and learn. You always were the risk-taker in the family."

Chase exchanged a chagrined look with Maddie. *So I'm worse than your husband,* he said with his eyes.

Allister started turning pages in the scrapbook. "It's all in here. Your victories in the SORC, your death-defying feats climbing up the mast during a storm to untangle the jammed halyard during Cowes Week, and how the boat capsized anyway in a race that's claimed even the bravest sailors."

"What does *Skidbladnir* mean?" Maddie asked, seeing the name of the boat in the picture.

"It's a Scandinavian myth, a collapsible ship with favoring winds." Chase blinked, realizing, just as Maddie did, that he'd known without even thinking about it.

Each article was neatly cut and mounted in the book. Some of the headlines were grim, lives lost during a storm, boats sunk or damaged. As the dates moved forward, his name was mentioned more often, the whiz kid from Miami as captain of this boat or that one, coming in third, second, and sometimes first in major campaigns.

"No matter how many arguments we had, how many long-distance phone calls we ended by slamming down the phone, I still kept up with your activities."

"At least he knew you were proud of him in some ways," Maddie said.

"No, he didn't. I never told him I had this."

Chase met his father's gaze, but he didn't know what to say to an admission he knew was major. "You gave me a watch."

Allister nodded. "Out of guilt, I'm afraid. You knew it, too. If you hadn't liked the watch so much, you probably wouldn't have worn it."

The man sitting across from him may as well have been a stranger, though they'd obviously had a volatile past. Chase returned to the book and found an article about the boat with *Augustine Aero* painted on the side.

"That's when I decided to stop fighting you. You were determined to make your way as a sailor, though I know you hated our dissension. I hated it, too. So we compromised. I sponsored your first boat. It wasn't entirely unselfish. The company got exposure. It was the only way to make you a company man."

That smacked of manipulation, not much different from Maddie's family's manipulations.

"For a while, anyway," Allister added. "After losing the bid to challenge for the America's Cup—"

"I sailed in the America's Cup Regatta?" Chase asked, astonished.

"Yes, but not very well. Not your fault. You had a run of bad luck, equipment failures, crew failures. You didn't tolerate incompetence. So you got it in your head that you wanted to sail in a solo race."

"The Around Alone."

"You remember?" Allister asked.

"Read about it in an article." He traded a look with Maddie. It bothered him that they'd become close enough to read each other's expressions. She was thinking about the iceberg memory, and he was telling her he didn't want Allister to know how much he remembered.

"You always were a bit of a loner. I thought it might be because you'd lost your mother at such a young age, that maybe it impaired your ability to relate to people. Especially women."

He raised his eyebrows at that, but before he could ask what it meant, Maddie said, "He relates very well to women."

Allister took them in with an iron gaze, and Chase changed the subject. "Augustine Aero didn't sponsor this boat."

"I offered, but you refused. You wanted to do it on your own. And so you did."

He'd come in second overall in Class II, first in Leg Three. He felt a surge of pride, but only in a peripheral way. He couldn't remember the victory of that first-place win, or of completing the 27,000-nautical-mile race. It was as though he were proud of someone else's accomplishment.

But his mind wouldn't let him stray too far from his

father's previous comment. "When you say I don't relate to women well, you don't mean—"

Allister jerked his head back. "You're not gay. I wouldn't have tolerated that."

He slid a gaze to Maddie. He definitely liked women, or at least this one. "I was married. And divorced."

"You married Lila when you were both nineteen. Her father owned one of the sailboats you crewed on. You were married for a year and a half." He grew silent for a moment. He lit the cigarette, inhaled the smoke and snuffed it out. "She cried the hardest at your funeral."

Those words struck him in the gut. "I had a funeral."

"You're not officially considered dead, but your friends . . . we needed closure."

"I understand." But he couldn't explain the eerie feeling that people had gone to his funeral, had cried for him. "I'm sorry I put you through that."

He'd put them through more than just the funeral, though. Allister looked grim, and Chase knew it was time to hear what had happened.

"I leased out your apartment. We—Patrick and I—discovered you were different than we thought. You liked classical music and the kind of books they make you read in English class. You never let on."

Chase felt at last some connection to his former self. "What about my sailboat?"

"*Chase the Wind* is still impounded."

This was it, where the ugly truth came out.

"You can stay here, of course," his father said, still avoiding the issue. "In fact, this is the wisest place to stay."

"That might not be a good idea, considering . . ." Time to face it.

The door burst open and a man about Chase's age charged in. His light skin was fused with red, his blond hair nearly standing on end with rage. He took in Chase, then Maddie, then back to Chase.

"Now, Patrick . . ." Allister soothed.

"I stopped by with some papers . . . the way Eduardo was acting, I knew something was up." He threw his sunglasses and the papers on the table and stalked closer.

"Sit down, Patrick." Allister's voice was calm but authoritative.

Patrick gathered his rage for a moment, then lunged at Chase. "You son of a bitch! You killed her!" Patrick's lanky weight landed on Chase and his big hands went around his throat. "I wanted you to be dead!"

CHAPTER 17

"I WANTED . . . YOU to be . . . dead!" When Patrick yelled the words again, they were broken up by his sobs.

Maddie had already been on the defense, but Chase waved her and his father away and struggled to get out from beneath him. Patrick staggered back, his face still crimson. Chase stood to face him and whatever he had to say.

"Who did I kill?" He briefly met Allister's agonized expression.

Patrick ran his hand across his damp face. "The woman I was going to marry."

Chase dropped back down on the couch, his legs unable to hold him. He didn't know what to say. *Sorry* was pitifully inadequate.

"He doesn't remember anything," Allister said, pulling Patrick back into a chair.

Though Patrick jerked away, he complied. But the venom hadn't left his blue eyes. "He's a damned liar."

"Why do you think it took him so long to come back to us?"

"Because he's a coward! He thought he could run away and hide from what he'd done. Maybe he ran out of money." His gaze raked over Chase's faded clothes and long hair. "So he came to get daddy to bail him out again."

Chase was beginning to hate himself more and more. He couldn't even meet Maddie's gaze.

"This is different," Allister said, taking out another cigarette. "He's not a kid taking out people's boats without their permission. Or getting into a drunken fight."

Another mention of drinking.

"No, it's murder this time."

"Tell me what happened," Chase said, an ache growing in his chest.

"You were screwing around with the woman I loved," Patrick spat out, rapidly sliding his hand back through his hair. "And then you killed her!"

"It was an accident," Allister said in that decisive way.

"You're telling me he strangled her by accident?" Patrick started to get to his feet, but one look from Allister quelled him. Still, he gripped the arms of the chair. "No matter what he's done, you'll always defend him. I've put in twelve-hour days at the factory since I was sixteen, and what do I mean to you? Zip. Zero. Nada. He plays and calls it work and he was your damned hero." He glared at the sailing picture on the wall, then the scrapbook on the table. His voice went menacingly low. "Well, he's not a hero anymore."

Chase surged to his feet. "Tell me what happened, dammit. That's why I came back, to make it right."

"You'll never make it right," Patrick said. "You—"

"I'll tell him." Allister silenced Patrick with his low voice. "You're being a hothead."

In the initial scuffle, Allister had dropped his last cigarette on the blue carpet and Patrick's foot had crushed it. Maddie tugged on the back of Chase's jeans, urging him to sit down. She grabbed his hand as soon as he did. He stared at their linked hands, knowing that whatever she heard now was going to send her home.

That's the way it had to be.

Allister put another cigarette in his mouth. "Only you know—or knew what happened. The night before you disappeared, you were at Salty's—"

"As usual," Patrick added, jerking his hand back through his hair several times again.

Chase met their eyes. "Was I an alcoholic?"

"Yes," Patrick said without hesitation.

"No," Allister said, punching that one word with power. "You just drank too much on occasion."

It was getting worse. He tried to pull his hand free from Maddie's, but she held on tight. "Did I drink when I sailed?"

"Probably," Patrick said.

"You weren't stupid." Allister sucked on the cigarette, then exhaled as though it were lit. "But you had a habit of hanging out at Salty's too often with your friends, doing tequila shots like they were candy."

Chase summoned that bar memory, knocking back tequila with the sexy blonde.

"You told your friends you weren't up to catching a cab home, so you were going to crash on your boat. The next morning you and the boat were gone."

Patrick said, "You took her—"

"Enough," Allister said. The ache in Chase's chest increased as the story progressed. He already knew the end; he needed to know what had happened in between.

"The next day your yacht was spotted several miles off the coast. The autopilot was running, but there was no one aboard. The Coast Guard towed it in. There wasn't a clue as to what had happened to you. When they reached the dock, they saw her."

A sob ripped through Patrick, but it didn't lessen the hatred in his eyes. He looked at odds, dress shirt and tie with his contorted expression.

"Her body," Allister said in a dulled voice, "had been caught on the keel. You had one of those fancy designs fashioned after the boat you sailed in the Cup regatta. The autopsy revealed she'd hit her head, but that wasn't what killed her. She'd been strangled."

Patrick surged to his feet, his muscles corded. "And now you're faking amnesia in some lame attempt to get away with it. Well, it's not going to work. The police have all they need to convict you. Not only was it your boat, but your friends placed you at the scene. You're going to pay no matter what your story is."

Chase came to his feet, too. His brother was an inch taller, and Chase knew he'd held that inch over Chase's head for years. "I'm back to face the consequences."

"That'll be a first," Patrick said on a bitter laugh. "It was bad enough that you were screwing her behind my back. Why did you have to kill her?"

"That's what I need to find out," Chase said. Maddie squeezed his hand, but he still couldn't face her.

"Maybe you put some moves on her she didn't like that night. She fought you, and you . . . strangled her."

Those words chilled Chase's heart. His memory of fighting with someone, then seeing her fall. "Were we having an affair?" he asked. "Do you know that for sure?"

"Why else would she be on that boat with you? I should have suspected it earlier. Every Tuesday she'd go off to her adult ed class. Later I found out she was still going even though they were on break."

"Why would I get involved with your woman?"

"Because you could. You step on people without thinking of the consequences. You don't even like brunettes, but you still went for Julie."

Brunettes. So Julie wasn't the sexy woman in his flash of memory. Chase finally looked over at Maddie, hoping to see disgust in her eyes. At the same time, hoping he wouldn't. Her hazel eyes shone bright with faith.

Jeez, was she naïve.

"I'm going to turn myself in, but I need time to figure out what happened. I need . . . to find myself first before I face charges for a crime I don't remember committing."

Both men said, "No," at the same time.

"You go to the police *now*," Patrick said.

Allister quelled him with a look. "He doesn't go to the police at all. As far as anyone is concerned, Chase is dead. He's come back to face his crime, and that's what counts. His crime being that he was seeing Julie. The evidence is circumstantial."

"Let the police decide that," Patrick said.

"The police won't have all the information to process. Chase is the only one who knows what happened. With the evidence to hand, he'll go down for first-degree murder. It won't be a fair trial, he has no defense. I make all decisions regarding my family. Chase already has lost his life, punishment enough."

"What are you suggesting?" Chase asked, watching Patrick seethe in his chair.

"You stay missing. We get you another identity. The long hair is good, but your face and voice are too distinctive to allow you to remain in Miami. Unfortunately, it will be a, pardon the pun, dead giveaway if you return to sport sailing. Too many people know you. I'll give you access to a bank account in the Caymans. You used to talk about bumming, as you put it, around the islands when you were a teenager. You can do that for a while if you wish. It's the only solution."

"Bull!" Patrick said, once again surging to his feet. "You can't keep covering for him. That's why he's in this predicament."

Allister put the cigarette in his mouth. The paper was crinkled from handling. "I know you loved Julie, but she was cheating on you. With your own brother. Why demand justice for her death now and cause your family and the business to undergo scandal and scrutiny? Isn't it enough that he has to give up his family, his identity, and the ability to do what he loves?"

Patrick narrowed his eyes at Chase. "No."

"I said I'd face the charges."

Patrick started to head out. "And you'll do it now."

"He will not," Allister said in a voice that became menacing. "You will tell no one about his arrival here. You'll accept that justice has been served and continue to oversee Augustine Aero as president. Everything will go on as normal."

Chase could see tension ripple through Patrick's body. He looked at Chase, then at their father, and the venomous hatred never dimmed. "I understand." Then he walked out.

"You've always had bad blood between you. Competitive, both of you. And so different. He never made it a secret that he resented being the only son dedicated to the company." Allister stood. "Now, then. I've got some calls to make, since I know nothing about securing a new identity. Fortunately, I haven't lived in Miami all my life without making some connections."

Chase stood, bringing Maddie up with him since she was still gripping his hand. "I can't run away from this."

Allister stopped looking through his Rolodex. "I'll say the same thing to you as I did to Patrick. Do you want to bring shame to the family and the business when it's not necessary? Not to mention bringing shame to yourself. You're a mystery now. The respected sailor lost at sea, a woman's body found with the boat. Go public, and you'll be a thug and a murderer. With you gone, they couldn't do much. It's just another unsolved murder. If you go to them, you're going to bring upheaval to us all. You're still paying a big price."

Chase fisted his hand at his chest. "But I need to know what happened."

"Here's what probably happened: maybe you were seeing Julie, but she was a manipulative woman. She had an agenda in seeing you, though we'll never know what it was.

Maybe you found out, and your temper got the best of you. A crime of passion they call it. You certainly didn't mean to kill her. You have to believe that of yourself. Let it go, Chase. Let me do this for you. For once, accept that I know best." Allister returned to his Rolodex.

Chase headed to the door. "Where's Salty's?"

"You can't leave this house, not until everything's in order."

"I'm going to Salty's, and if you don't tell me where it is, I'll have to ask around."

Allister gave him a disappointed look that Chase was sure he'd seen many times. "Do you want to get caught? You're a murder suspect."

"I'll stay low-key . . ." He grabbed up Patrick's mirrored sunglasses. "But I need time to think."

"It's at the Harborview Marina. You will come right back."

"Later."

He'd been a coward with Maddie, but he had to believe he wasn't one in character. That's what he had to find out.

Maddie was having a hard time sorting through everything as they walked back out into the sunshine. She was scared for Chase, for what he faced. Scared to find out everything they'd just heard was true.

Chase got in on the driver's side and pulled out a map. A muscle in his jaw ticked.

She pointed at the marina. "Right there."

He shoved the map to the back seat and took a deep breath as he stared at the house. "Welcome to my dysfunctional family. Not that I can blame Patrick for hating me. Not only for killing her, but for sleeping with her."

"We don't know that. Even Patrick said you don't like brunettes."

"That's pretty flimsy evidence, Maddie."

"I'm trying to believe in you here. Work with me."

"You just need to leave. Go back home and sort out your own family problems."

"And give up on you? Forget it."

He took hold of her hand and stared at it for a moment. "I appreciate your standing by me, but I don't deserve it. Or you. I killed Julie. It doesn't matter if I don't remember. All the evidence is there."

"Are you going to run?"

She wasn't sure what he heard in her voice, but it got his attention.

"Is that what you think I should do?" he asked.

"Yes. I know it's wrong, but your dad's right. Without your memory, you're a dead man. I'm sure you didn't mean to kill Julie. You don't know the whole story. So come back to Sugar Bay. Start a new life there." She wanted to add *with me*, but they were friends, nothing more.

"Didn't you even hear what they were saying about me? I party too much, am apparently irresponsible, and all I cared about was sailing. I couldn't even keep a marriage together for more than a year and a half. Why would you want me in your life, especially if I was coward enough to run away?"

"Because you're not that Chase anymore."

"Yes, I am, Maddie. I haven't changed just because I don't remember. Eventually I'll return to being Chase Augustine, the jerk they were talking about in there. I already have a hunger for sailing. That hasn't changed, and neither has the craving for alcohol."

She couldn't contain her surprise at that.

"That's right, I've been wanting a drink since being on the ship. I haven't taken one yet, but the hunger's still there. So is my inability to . . ."

"What?"

He paused, then let out a breath. "So is all the rest of

the old Chase Augustine, and in time, it'll return."

"But—"

"Let me finish. If I got angry enough to kill a woman once, who says it won't happen again? The best thing you can do is get your little butt back home. Jeez, I've already corrupted you. You're willing to harbor a criminal. I'm not dragging you down with me. And"—he put his finger over her mouth as she was about to protest—"you don't love me. Get that through that pretty head of yours. You don't. You think your husband sent me to help you, but all I did was tell you like it was. I'm glad you grew because of me, I really am. You're going to—" he took a breath—"get on with your life, meet a guy, fall in love, the works." Sounding a bit too much like his father, he said, "You're going to drop me off at the marina and go home. Or do you want me to call your family and have them fly in so one of them can drive with you? I'd rather you not drive by yourself anyway."

He started to get out of the car, presumably to make that call, but she pulled on his shirt sleeve. "Don't you see you're just proving that whoever you are deep inside, you are a responsible, caring person? I'm not going to let you tell me what to do with my life. Okay, maybe it was wrong to suggest running away from the charges. It was a panic reaction. Like . . . telling you I love you. But I'm staying with you until this gets resolved. Because I can't go back there and live my life without knowing what happened to you. Because we're friends." The stubbornness in her expression faded. "We are friends, right?"

The word *no* faltered on his tongue. They were more than friends, but less than lovers.

She said, "People have been there for me, stood by my side, worried about me my whole life. For the first time, I have someone to stand by and worry about. You keep telling me to grow up. Standing by a friend in need, no matter how bad it gets, is part of growing up, isn't it?"

He heard himself say, "Yes."

"Don't you want a friend?" she whispered, moving closer.

At that moment, he wanted more than a friend. He wanted to hear that she loved him again, more sure this time, and he wanted to draw strength again from holding her naked body in his arms. "Yes," he said, sealing his fate.

Chase didn't want to think about what Maddie was coming to mean to him. What he had to focus on was finding out everything he could about his former self and getting to a comfortable place where he could deal with what he'd done. What he had to remember was he didn't deserve her. And he was not going to drag her down with him, even if she was determined to be dragged.

The marina itself brought no memories, either. He slid on the sunglasses and hoped no one recognized him. Or maybe he did want someone to recognize him. Then the decision would be made.

"This is nothing like my place," Maddie said, taking in the size of the marina. It was twice as large building-wise, with three times as many slips. Rows and rows of them, one after the other, reaching out to the open ocean and crammed with boats. Most of the boats were bigger than even the biggest boat at Sugar Bay.

Salty's looked just the way Chase remembered it. It was open to the air, overlooking a portion of the docks and the gas pumps. Ceiling fans lazily swirled the hot, humid air. The bar stools were battered, the floor's wooden planks had years of grime in the creases, and the booth tables were rimmed with frayed lengths of rope. It didn't bring back any more memories, but he had the sudden, overwhelming urge for a drink. He pulled Maddie over to one of the booths at the end.

There weren't many people there, only a couple of guys who looked as weathered as the rest of the place. When he looked across the table at Maddie, she was staring at the tabletop. Dozens of pictures were scattered under a yellowed layer of shellac. He scanned them, too, searching for familiar faces, like the ones he'd seen in the flash of memory. It didn't take him long to find one of himself, raising a shot glass to whoever took the picture.

"Your hair is short," she said, pointing to another one of him laughing it up at one of the booths.

He sensed somebody standing next to the table and looked up. It was the face he'd been searching for, the sexy blonde, and she was staring at him with a mixture of shock and hope. She slid into the booth next to Maddie, without looking at anything but him.

"Oh, my God, Chase, is that you?"

Her name tag read *Lila*. The woman who'd kissed him in the memory, who still had long hair and bright green eyes and a chest that peeked seductively out of her cropped top.

It was no use denying it, not to the woman who'd once shared his bed. "Yeah, it's me."

Her eyes watered, and she reached over and lifted his shades. "It's you, it's really you." She made a choking sound, jumped out of her seat and leaped onto his lap. He'd never been hugged so hard. "You're back!" She kissed him right on the mouth. "I told them you couldn't die, that you were the sailor who'd live forever." She touched his face. "But . . . how?"

Maddie's expression gave nothing away. He wanted to shift Lila onto the seat next to him, but that seemed rude considering she'd once been his wife. "I was picked up by a ship, spent two months at sea, then a few months finding my way back here."

"Why didn't you call me? I would have come for you, you know that."

"No, I didn't. When I fell out of the boat, I hit my head. I don't remember much about who I am." He ran his fingers back through his hair. "I'm trying to put the pieces back together."

"You don't know who I am?" That motivated her to slide off his lap, though she remained next to him.

"The only thing I remember was being here one night, us doing shots at that bar. You leaning over and kissing me."

He saw Maddie flinch. She looked so different compared to Lila, who was taller, lusher, and richly tanned. But Maddie didn't lose any of her own brilliance for Lila's shine.

"I guess that was back when we were married," he said.

Lila laughed, but her expression was one of study. "You really don't remember me?"

"No. Sorry."

"We've been throwing back shots at that bar, and kissing, since I was old enough to do either. Just because we weren't married anymore didn't mean we stopped . . ." She glanced at Maddie. "Well, you know . . . being friends."

"This is Maddie," he said. "She brought me here. She's helped me put some things together." He was going to say they were friends, but in light of Lila's interpretation of that relationship, decided not to.

Lila smiled at Maddie, but her eyes were summing her up. "That was nice of you." She turned back to Chase. "Do you know about—"

He nodded. "I don't remember much about that, either. Maybe you can help me."

"Anything," she said with conviction. Apparently they'd had a good divorce.

"You're saying that we . . .". He gestured, unable to say the words in front of Maddie. "You and I."

"Well, you know . . . you don't know. On and off, yeah. I mean, I've had relationships here and there, and of course, not then. But yeah, you and me . . ." She smiled.

"How about just before I disappeared?"

Lila's hands fisted on the table. "I don't believe you were seeing Julie, if that's what you're asking."

"That's what I'm asking."

She reached up and touched his hair. "I haven't seen your hair this long since we were teenagers." She forced her hands back down to the table. "Sorry, I can't stop touching you. I can't believe you're here." She glanced at Maddie, then back at him. "You didn't even like Julie. I mean, well, you know, you flirted with everyone as a rule, harmless flirting. Maybe you did that with her once in a while, but you didn't mean it."

Because Maddie was looking a little lost over there by herself, he reached out and took her hand. "I'm trying to figure out what happened that night so I can decide what to do. I'd appreciate it if you didn't tell anyone I'm here."

"Hey, Lila!" one of the men at the bar said. "Where's my beer already?"

"Be right back," she said, sliding out of the booth.

Chase realized he was fiddling with Maddie's fingers, looking at them and not her.

"She's beautiful," Maddie said.

"She's okay."

"You must have loved her a lot."

"I don't know. I don't remember her other than a brief memory."

Lila returned a minute later, sliding back in beside him. "You probably need one of these," she said, bearing a small tray with shots and limes.

"No, I don't." He pushed the tray away.

"No shots?" She offered one to Maddie, who politely refused.

"Well, I do." She knocked one back with the grace of one who'd done it a thousand times. "Where are you staying, and please don't tell me it's with your father?"

"I don't know. He wants us to stay with him, but—"

"And what Allister wants, he thinks he can get. You're staying at my place. Both of you. It's not big, but we can figure out the sleeping arrangements later."

Sleeping arrangements. That was going to be interesting. "I don't want to put you out—" he said, knowing Maddie wouldn't like this.

"Come on, Chase, I love you. You may not remember me, but there's no way you're not letting me help you. If you're not comfortable at my place"—this she directed to Maddie—"I'll arrange to have my father's boat put into the water. You used to crew for him on that boat. He's in Europe for a month, so he won't know about it."

Chase asked, "Why would you help me like this? It's beginning to look like I'm a murderer."

"Because despite the evidence, I don't believe you'd kill anyone, at least not intentionally."

She pulled her keys out of her pocket and slipped one off the ring. "You probably don't have your key anymore. You know where my place is . . . you don't, do you?" She gave him directions to a little apartment complex around the corner. "Make yourselves comfortable. Your friend here looks as tired as a piña colada sitting at a long-abandoned table." She gave Maddie a warm smile. "I've got to get back to work. If you don't want to be recognized, you'd better scram. You have—well, you know . . . *had* too many friends here."

He gave Lila a quick peck on the cheek as he followed her out of the booth. "Thanks."

He felt guilty for doing that, especially when he saw Maddie's expression. It wasn't happy.

"I'll bring some pizza around four when I get off the lunch shift." Lila gave Chase another hard hug, then went to greet a new customer.

Chase gave Maddie a chagrined look. "It's better than staying at my father's house."

"It's fine."

She'd shrunk into herself, walking beside him with her arms crossed in front of her. He wanted to kiss her until she felt secure again, but he couldn't do that. It wasn't fair to make her secure when security was as elusive as a stiff breeze in a becalmed sea.

CHAPTER 18

"YOU WERE A lousy husband," Lila said a few hours later over pepperoni pizza. "A great friend, wonderful sailor . . . terrific lover. Lousy husband." She got up and returned with a bottle of relish. "Still put this on everything?"

He scooped some out and spread it over his pizza. "Yep."

Maddie watched Lila watching Chase. There were times when she'd felt jealous over Wayne, like at the Schaeffers' Christmas party when Darcy got drunk and flirted with him. But this was different. First, Maddie had no claim to Chase. No history with him other than their several weeks and one wonderful night of lovemaking before everything split apart. Her one consolation was that Lila wasn't Darcy, not in terms of open flirting. Lila was just as pretty, maybe even prettier. And she had more claim on Chase than Maddie ever would. The other consolation was that Chase couldn't remember being with Lila. Yet.

"I didn't . . . hit you or anything, did I?" Chase asked Lila.

"You had a temper as hot as a fire-eater shot, but you didn't go around hitting people. When you exploded, it was verbally. Once in a while you'd get into a snarl at Salty's. But you never ever hit a woman."

The apartment was small, or maybe cozy was a better word. Furniture second-hand, carpet faded, but Lila had style. Warm lighting, lots of throw pillows, and flower arrangements added a nice touch. What she didn't have was a dining table, so they ate around her coffee table.

"Why'd we split?" Chase asked after washing down a bite of pizza with Dr. Pepper. That was a new preference apparently.

She slugged back Amstel Light right out of the bottle. "Difference of opinion. I wanted a husband who was around, and you wanted to be out on a boat."

"Sorry about that," he said.

"I got over it. Like I said, we got along better after our divorce. I didn't sit around waiting and worrying about you. When you blew into town, you knew where I was."

Chase rubbed his face. "Sounds romantic."

"It worked."

Maddie could see them together, Lila's light hair contrasting Chase's dark hair, making them a striking couple.

"So"—this Lila directed to Maddie—"where do you, well, you know, fit into all this?"

Maddie swallowed her bite of crust. "I'm helping him . . . put the pieces together."

"We're friends," Chase clarified, and Maddie wondered just what he meant after hearing Lila's interpretation of same. "She thinks she's my guardian angel." He winked at her, private joke, just the two of them.

Then she realized that, with Lila at his side, he didn't need her anymore. He had an ally, someone who could help him with his past, something Maddie certainly couldn't do.

She was beginning to feel a little lost and off balance. She wasn't sure where she belonged anymore. The white line on her ring finger was her last link to Wayne. She had no such link to Chase. As Lila talked about their past, Maddie felt more and more disconnected from him. Especially when Lila touched his collarbone and asked, "Where is your cross?"

"What cross?"

"You always wear a gold cross on a chain, especially when you go sailing. You nearly missed the start of a race because you left it in your room and had someone go back to get it. Hold on a minute." When she returned, she held a cross dangling from a chain. "This is the one you bought me for Christmas. You need it more than I do."

She knelt down in front of him. Her arms went around his neck as she fiddled, interminably, trying to connect the clasp. Their noses were almost touching, gazes meeting.

Maddie wanted to scream out, *I found him! I brought him here! He's mine.* Luckily she couldn't even swallow, much less scream. Chase took hold of Lila's wrists and gently removed them from around his neck, then stood.

Maddie stood, too. "Lila, can I use your phone to make a long-distance call? I'll leave some money for it."

"Sure. Phone's over there. Why don't we give her some privacy? Come on, I'll show you some pictures." She took his hand and led him to the bedroom.

The sound of her mom's voice nearly broke Maddie down into sobs of insecurity and frustration, but she swallowed them. "Hi, Mom."

"Baby! It's Baby," she said away from the phone.

"She wants to be called Maddie," Colleen said in the background.

"How are you, honey? Are you okay? Do you have enough money?"

Maddie stared at the open door, though she couldn't see into the bedroom. "I'm okay."

"Well, you don't sound okay. Here, Tom, you tell her to get home."

Her dad got on the line. "You do whatever—"

"Your mom tells you," Mom cut in.

The sound of Lila's laughter and then Chase's low laugh made Maddie shiver. She turned back to the kitchen, her fingers tightening on the phone.

"Maddie, we need you at home," Mom said. "We're all off-kilter without you."

Colleen said, "I need to ask you about things, like how it was with you and Wayne."

More laughter drifted from the bedroom. Maddie tried hard to focus on the call. Her family did need her. It didn't make sense, not when she'd been so dependent on them all her life. The smartest thing she could do was say goodbye to Chase and drive back—on her own—to Sugar Bay. The safe thing to do. The thing Baby would have done.

"I can't come back right now," she said in a near-whisper. "I know you don't understand, and frankly, neither do I. But I can't leave until things are resolved here. I gotta go. Love you all."

She hung up before they could talk her into coming back. The bedroom door loomed ahead, and she pushed herself to take each heavy step toward it. If they were co-zied up together, or worse, kissing, she'd break in two. The couch looked safe, just sit on the couch for a while, let them come out in their own time. She started to veer off, but another round of soft laughter pushed her onward. She took a deep breath and forced herself to walk to the door.

Chase was lying on his back, holding up a stack of pictures. Lila was sitting on the far corner sifting through several photo packages.

He sat up and made room for her next to him, and her heart returned to life again. "How's your family? They freaking out?"

She lifted one shoulder. "Pretty much." She was going to tell him he'd been right about them needing her, but not in front of Lila. She sat down next to him, wanting to sink against him in relief that he hadn't been reliving memories with Lila in a physical sense.

It wasn't good to be this insecure about a man she couldn't have.

"She has pictures of me going back years," he said, handing her a stack of photos.

Maddie didn't want to look at pictures of the old Chase with the short hair and hari-kari look, who partied too much and hung with crowds she could never hope to fit into. Lila was in many of them, including, of course, shots of their informal wedding. Some of the pictures were at the start or finish line of some race. Dozens of boats clustered around the sailboats as they headed out. One picture was of Chase holding some plate in victory.

Lila held up a picture. "This is Julie."

Chase took it, and Maddie knew he was trying to put this woman with the one he'd seen in his flash of memory. She leaned closer to see the picture. Julie had thick, dark hair and a lush figure she liked to show off with clothes that were much too tight, or at least that was Maddie's impression of her.

"This was at your father's birthday party last year. Does she look familiar?"

Chase shook his head.

"She'd had too much to drink that night. You and her got into an argument. She felt Patrick was unappreciated, and you were taking advantage of his hard work by playing all the time."

"Doesn't sound like a woman I'd be involved with," he said with a trace of hope.

"By the end of the night she was crying and apologizing all over you."

He set the picture down, and Maddie could see his pain at believing he'd killed her.

They talked for a couple more hours. Chase would get caught up in some story about himself as Lila told it, but he never forgot that Maddie was sitting beside him. He always included her with a smile or a word.

Finally Lila said, "You both look exhausted. I'll make up the sofa bed."

An awkward silence followed once it was made. Where would Chase sleep? Two beds, two women. Lila walked over and gave Chase a hug and a quick kiss on the mouth. In a low voice she said, "You usually sleep in my room. But I know . . . things are different now."

He stepped out of her embrace and looked at Maddie. "Yeah, they are."

She touched his face, then turned away. Maddie saw Lila's hurt look as she retreated to her room, but she was too swamped in relief to worry much about it. She used the bathroom first, changing into blue pajamas covered in sheep. She made a face at her reflection, wishing she had something more . . . sophisticated to wear. She let out a breath. She had miles to go before she even approached sophistication.

While Chase showered, she filled a glass of water and set it on the end table. The mattress was lumpy and dipped toward the middle. Would he really sleep here with her? She remembered the time they'd spent in each other's arms.

When he came out wearing an old pair of sweatpants, bare chest damp, she had to clear her throat and try to forget she'd touched that body.

He looked at the bed, then at her. "Do you think this is a good idea?"

"Better than your sleeping with her," Maddie shot out, then regretted it. "Besides," she added in a strained voice, "where else would you sleep?"

It annoyed her that he looked around at the options, which were basically nil. "I just don't want to compromise your honor."

"Too late," she said, trying her best at a coy smile.

He leaned close and wrinkled his nose at her. "Well, that's not going to happen again, is it?"

"Definitely not," she said, finding her voice going soft at his proximity.

"We have to keep this on a strictly friends-only basis until we know what we're into here." Even his voice sounded more velvety than usual.

"Strictly," she said, her gaze locked onto his.

He broke eye contact long enough to take in her face, lingering on her mouth before dragging his gaze back to her eyes. He was so close now, she had to tilt her head back to see him.

"Even a quick kiss like this"—he demonstrated, touching his mouth briefly to hers—"is a bad idea."

She slid her hands around the back of his neck. "A really bad idea."

"And a real kiss would be out of the question." But it wasn't out of the question when he captured her mouth with his, coaxing her mouth open and tasting her with a swipe of his tongue.

So much for resolve, she thought, letting her weight pull her onto the bed and taking him with her. He felt hot and sinful, and she couldn't quite resolve herself to back away. Besides, she had nowhere to go.

"Oh, sorry," a voice nearby said, breaking them apart. Lila looked both embarrassed and chagrined. She wore a silk nightshirt that showed off her long legs. "I was just, well, you know . . ." She nearly tripped in her haste to get inside the bathroom.

Chase dropped back onto the bed, his hand over his face. "Maddie, you're making me so crazy."

"Did I spoil things for you and Lila?"

He lifted his hand enough to give her a look of consternation. "The only woman here that I want more than I should is you. Now go to sleep and stop making me kiss you."

She lay down beside him. "Say that again. I liked the sound of it."

"Stop making me kiss you."

"No, the other part."

"Now go to sleep."

The next morning Lila toasted some frozen waffles. Chase watched her from his place beside the refrigerator. He had loved this woman. Without a doubt, she was sexy, probably his type. But he couldn't dredge up anything more than a detached appreciation for her looks. And of course, her hospitality.

Maddie was watching him watch Lila. The easiest way to have sent her packing was to have shared Lila's bed . . . for old time's sake. It had run through his mind when she'd offered. Yet he couldn't do it, couldn't hurt Maddie in that irrevocable way. And couldn't use Lila, either.

Maybe he *was* a coward.

Worse, all through the night he kept pulling Maddie close. That wasn't hard thanks to the dip in the mattress, but even that hadn't been close enough.

"Will your memory ever come back?" Lila asked as she handed him the last plate.

"I don't know." He wasn't going to get into the whole psychological aspect of memory repression with her. He drizzled syrup over his waffle and took it to the coffee table where Maddie was cutting into hers. "Were you with me that last night? I was supposedly drinking at Salty's before I went to the boat."

"I was working, but it was busy. You were hanging with Brian and Tombo. You three went together like tequila, lime, and salt."

"Was I the kind of guy who talked about his . . . conquests?"

"I doubt it." Lila tilted her head, letting her long hair

flow over her shoulder. "Isn't it strange to ask other people about who you are?"

"Very. Can Tombo and Brian be trusted? With knowing I'm here, I mean."

"I . . . I think so. They've been pretty scarce since your accident. Haven't been to Salty's as much. Tombo's been disappearing for a few days at a time without telling anyone. He might be into some trouble, but that's nothing new. Brian's . . . well, he's Brian. Oh, you don't know Brian, do you? He's loaded, or at least his family is. His father owns a chain of yacht brokerages, and Brian's getting into the business."

"You sure you want to alert them to your presence?" Maddie asked, tucking her legs beneath her. She was wearing pedal pushers with colored polka dots and somehow, on her, they worked.

"They were your best friends," Lila said. "You got together every Tuesday and Saturday—and every other minute you could grab—to go over sailing strategies."

Both Chase and Maddie lifted their heads. "Tuesday nights?" they said in unison.

"Yeah, why?"

"Julie met her lover on Tuesday nights," Chase said, color deepening his face. "And if I was with my friends—"

"You weren't with her," Maddie finished.

"I've got to find out how late we stayed together. And how late Julie stayed out. Call them."

Lila didn't seem convinced, but she called and left messages with both men to meet at her place later that evening.

Chase took the phone book down from the shelf and dialed a number. Then he asked for Patrick. "I'm going to find out what's between me and my brother."

It was a credit that the SWAT team wasn't waiting at Patrick's apartment. He let Chase in, though his expression was murderous. That was why Chase had insisted on meeting Patrick without Maddie, in case another physical attack ensued.

Even though it was only ten o'clock in the morning, Patrick poured himself a scotch, then held the decanter out to Chase. "Oh, that's right, you're a tequila drinker."

"I'm a Dr. Pepper drinker now."

The apartment was spacious with skylights and pale colors. It overlooked the waterway that sparkled in the sunshine.

Patrick brought the crystal decanter to the table and sat down. "All right, so talk. And don't think you're going to come here and make things right between us. Things will never be right."

"I'm not denying that I was on the boat with Julie that night, or even that I . . . caused her death. I'll do whatever it takes to rectify the situation in your eyes."

"You're going to run."

"I'm not going to run. But before I turn myself in, I need to . . . understand."

"I could kill you, you know."

Chase blinked, not expecting that response. "What?"

"I could kill you. Hell, you're already dead. Nobody would know."

Chase eyed the scotch and wondered how long Patrick had been drinking. "Dad would know. Eduardo. Lila." He didn't want to bring Maddie in on this. "You're not going to kill me."

Patrick narrowed his eyes. "How do you know? Supposedly you don't remember anything. Maybe killing runs in the family."

"Just do me a favor and don't kill me until I understand what happened." Patrick's hands were shaking, though Chase doubted with rage. He looked at his brother, studied his refined features, hands without calluses, skin without a tan. Like Maddie and her sister, he and Patrick were nothing alike. Chase kneaded the bridge of his nose. "We weren't close."

Patrick laughed bitterly. "All you cared about was sailing. I got stuck being the son Dad could be proud of. Only he was never proud of me, either."

"He is, I'm sure. He just doesn't know how to show it." When Patrick didn't buy that, Chase continued. "All right, so we weren't close. I think we've established that." It bothered him that the man sitting across from him was his blood brother, yet they seemed more like enemies. "But we didn't hate each other, did we?"

Patrick ran his hand back through his hair several times in that nervous habit. "I hated you sometimes. I resented your freedom. But if you're asking was there real hatred between us, the answer is no. We lived our own lives."

"So I wouldn't have, say, tried to steal Julie away from you out of spite?"

"No, you were just being your usual selfish self." His words slurred a little. "You wanted her, and it didn't matter that she belonged to me."

"Did I . . . steal other men's girlfriends, too?"

Patrick obviously wanted to say yes, but he reluctantly said, "No. Just mine."

Selfish he could live with. Reckless even. But the kind of man who would steal his brother's love . . . that he couldn't live with. "Don't I go for blondes?"

"Usually."

"You said her night classes were on break."

Patrick's thin mouth became a line. "She hadn't been to one in the two months before she died. Because she was meeting you."

Chase felt the hatred in those words. "How long was she at her supposed class?"

"All evening. If we weren't spending the night together, she always called me at eleven to say good night."

"That doesn't sound like a woman who's cheating."

"Well, I didn't think so, either."

"Lila tells me that I met with Brian and Tombo every Tuesday and Saturday."

"That's what you told her. A cover story, I'm sure."

Chase let out a long breath. He couldn't prove anything there until he talked to Tombo and Brian. "Tell me this, Patrick. I know I was involved with Lila. Even though I can't remember our relationship at all, when I look at her, I'm attracted to her. I saw a picture of Julie last night. No attraction. Not my type at all." Of course, Maddie wasn't his type, either, but he was definitely attracted to her. "So if I wasn't out to steal her for the sake of stealing her, and I wasn't attracted to her, why was she on my sailboat that night? Can you think of any reason?"

He banged his glass down on the table. "I don't know why she was on that boat with you! You think I haven't asked myself that same question? There is no other reason than sex. She wasn't that big into sailing, and even if she was, she wouldn't be going out alone with you. At night." He pushed the glass away. "I've got to get back to work. Some of us have responsibility around here." He glared at Chase. "Some of us aren't wanted for murder."

"Patrick . . ." Chase didn't know what to say, but his brother had already stormed out of the apartment. There was no way to make amends with him. Between their history and Julie, they were lost as brothers.

He walked around for a moment, looking at the many pictures of Julie throughout the room. In one she proudly flashed a rock of a diamond engagement ring. In another, she sipped champagne on someone's yacht. It ripped him apart that he'd had something to do with her death, that he'd taken her away from Patrick. He had to know why.

Tropical foliage shaded the parking area as Chase walked to Maddie's car. He heard a sound behind him, and before he could turn around, something covered his face. His struggles were no match for the brute force that lifted him off the ground and shoved him into a dark place. He heard a trunk lid slam shut, and then felt motion as the car pulled out of the lot.

CHAPTER 19

"YOU LOOK TOTALLY out of place sitting at that bar," Lila said to Maddie.

"Then give me a beer or something." While Chase was talking with his brother, Maddie had been investigating, which was a whole lot better than sitting around watching Jerry Springer.

"So what is it that you're doing exactly?"

Maddie tapped her little notepad. "Gathering character witnesses. It's the only way to convince him he's a good person. So far"—she consulted her list—"he's gotten some pretty good remarks. Many 'excellent sailor.' One 'narrow-minded,' one 'slave driver when it comes to sailing.' Several 'decent guy,' 'honest,' 'fair.' No one really believes he killed Julie, though they have a hard time refuting the evidence."

Lila surveyed her with a smile. "How long you known Chase?"

"Not long. Hard to believe," she said more to herself.

Lila set a frosty beer mug in front of Maddie. "And you're in love with him."

"Pretty much" wasn't on her list of replies, but that's what came out. "I know he's got a life here, with you, and his sailing. I couldn't begin to fit into that life. But the Chase I know . . . he's different. Not as driven, except to find the truth about his past. Not selfish at all. In fact, I'm the selfish one. I want him to never remember any of this and go back to Sugar Bay with me."

Lila gave her a warm smile. "He cares about you. I can tell by the way he looks at you, the way he makes sure you're not left out of the conversation. He used to be that way with me, too." Her smile fizzled, and she turned to help another customer. Maddie couldn't really dredge up much sympathy, not in her selfish state.

Sure, he cared about her. Like a friend. Well, mostly, she added, thinking of last night. Okay, she was in love with him, but love would only complicate matters. So why had they been so drawn to each other the night before?

When Lila returned, Maddie asked, "I know this is a personal question, but it's for my character research. Do you think Chase is capable of really loving someone?"

Lila gave that some thought. "I think he loved me, but he loved sailing and freedom more. That's why we're better off being just friends. No expectations, no promises."

A knot formed in Maddie's stomach. Call her selfish, but she'd never handle being second in Chase's life. All right, so there was nothing wrong with being just friends with Chase. Was there?

Her beer went warm as she asked customers who filtered in and out for lunch about Chase. What she found was that the people who had sailed with him—and there were a few—respected him, but thought he drove them too hard. Those who didn't really know him thought he was a hotshot with an attitude.

Lila said, "That's because if you didn't sail, he didn't have much to say to you. Not that he thought any less of you; he simply didn't waste his time with anyone who didn't share his passion." Like Wayne, Maddie thought. Lila dumped out Maddie's full beer mug. "If you want to know who Chase was, watch him."

"What do you mean?"

"There was an interview on one of the local news channels after he competed in the Cup. Naturally I taped it. You'll see a tape marked 'Chase' in the right side of my entertainment center."

"Thanks. Maybe I'll head back to the apartment. Chase ought to be back by now."

But when she returned, Chase wasn't there.

Chase was right there in front of Maddie, almost within reaching distance. He was sprawled comfortably in a chair, wearing faded jeans and a green shirt that had probably seen many a windblown day. His hair was much shorter. Maddie scooted closer to the television and turned up the volume as the interview proceeded.

"So you'd consider yourself a professional sailboat racer, then?" the woman across from him said.

"Not professional. That word's got a negative connotation when it comes to sailing. But yes, sailing supports me."

"In the style to which you've become accustomed?" the woman said with a laugh.

Chase chuckled, too, and even through the tinny speakers of the old television, the sound shivered down Maddie's spine. "Oh, yeah, holing up in some rusty cottage in Australia or England preparing for a race, trying to scrounge up a new sail or someone to donate time to fix a generator. Living out of a bag. Real luxury." His smile had the same effect. "And I wouldn't have it any other way."

"But your father owns a million-dollar aerospace company. Couldn't you—"

"I want to make it on my own. That's the appeal of solo racing, and why I'm pursuing that next. Not to say that up until the time I leave the starting line there's no one else working with me. I have a team that works their asses off behind the scenes, even for a solo race. Building and designing the boat, getting sponsors, researching the race course, helping with the thousands of details."

It was strange watching a different Chase than she knew. Definitely him, but only the outside.

The woman consulted her notes. "You have a reputation for having a sixth sense when it comes to wind shifts. Someone even called you a sailing god."

He laughed. "I'm just a sailor. The sixth sense, a gift from God. I never mix them up."

"Let's get to know a bit about you personally. If you had three wishes, what would they be?"

He gave her a wary look, but gave his answer some thought. "I want to be the top racing champion. Right now I'm good, but not good enough. I wish that when I die, it's while sailing, doing something heroic and daring, nothing stupid like not harnessing myself in rough weather. And third, that I die an old salt with lots of stories to tell."

"What would people be most surprised to know about you?"

"People either think I've got a death wish—those who don't race—or that I'm fearless. Neither is true. I don't want to die, like most people, but I know the risk is there for the choices I've made in my life. The part that scares me about dying? To not sail anymore, for eternity, shakes me to my core. But the fear isn't so debilitating that I would stop, because that's what makes life worth living."

"Has there ever been a time when you thought you were going to die out there?"

"Plenty of times. But you don't really think about it while it's happening. You're too busy trying to stay alive, fixing whatever's gone wrong, or sometimes just holding on. Later you have time to realize just how close you got. Dying is always a factor. No matter how big your ego is, Mother Nature will remind you how insignificant you are. In the end, she always wins."

"And one last question, Mr. Augustine. What do you

have to say to all the single women out there who have daydreams of becoming that one woman in your life?"

"Never fall for a man who's married to the sea. I've already met the woman I wanted to spend my life with, but the sea is a wicked enchantress who grabs a man and doesn't let go. It's hard to compete with the glory, danger, and adrenaline, and it's hard to expect any woman to sit home alone and worry about becoming a widow."

"Thank you, Mr. Augustine."

Maddie hit the pause button and touched his face on the screen. This was the real Chase Augustine, not the man she'd fallen for. She wouldn't have fallen for this Chase, probably wouldn't have ever met him. Would he return to this Chase?

Lila called to check in, and Maddie told her he still hadn't returned.

"Probably got caught up in something," she said. "He did it all the time, got involved and forgot to call home. When he does get back, tell him my dad's boat, *Shades of Heaven,* is in slip 142. And don't forget Tombo and Brian are supposed to be coming by my place later. I didn't tell them about Chase, and I have to work late. Should I cancel?"

"No, let them come. He'll be back by then."

Maddie nibbled on some crackers and cheese and waited. Flipped through *People* magazine and waited. Chewed her nails and waited.

Finally she found Patrick's number and called.

"Did Chase meet with you this morning?"

"Yeah, why?" That last word was laced with suspicion.

"Because he hasn't come back."

First silence, and then, "That son of a bitch ran."

"He wouldn't do that."

"How well do you know my brother?"

"Not well," she had to admit. "But I know—"

"No way is he going to give up sailing and go to prison. A guy who goes where he damn well pleases, travels all over the world, has the freedom to do what he wants . . . I should have called the police yesterday. And I would have if it weren't for my father's subtle threats. Now he's gone."

"He's not gone. He has my car."

"So? You think he's going to let a little moral issue like car theft get in the way of his freedom? He's a murderer, lady. He's not going to think twice about taking your car."

She remembered Patrick's murderous rage the day before. "How do I know you didn't do something to him? You met this morning, and no one's heard from him since."

His chuckle was low and bitter. "I wish I had the guts. What I do know is he's going to pay for what he did." He hung up.

She didn't have time to contemplate whether Patrick's rage could turn murderous. A knock sounded on the door.

Two men stood on the stoop, and they both double-checked the number on the door when they saw Maddie.

"Tombo and Brian?" she asked.

"I'm Brian," the dark-haired one said. He wore perfectly creased chinos and a green polo shirt with the collar flipped up. "Where's Lila?"

"She's working. I'm Maddie Schaeffer. Come in."

They slowly walked in. She gave them the story she'd concocted. "I'm a reporter for the *Herald*. I'm doing a story on Chase Augustine."

They both stopped. Brian said, "We're not talking to a reporter. He was our friend."

"I don't believe he had anything to do with that woman's death," she said as they turned toward the door. "Julie wasn't even his type."

"She was a slut," the man who must be Tombo said. He was tall, on the gangly side, and wore the rumpled look well. A current passed between the two men, and Tombo said, "She was, and you know it."

Brian was less convinced of Maddie's story, though she wasn't sure which part. "Actually, this is a project I'm undertaking on my own. The paper isn't interested in an old story. I was intrigued, especially since Chase can't defend himself." She had to remember to speak of him in the past tense. "I've been reading up on his life, and it doesn't add up. Do you think he was seeing Julie?"

"No," Brian said. "I . . . dated her for a while." He glanced at Tombo, then back at Maddie. "But if you print that, I'll deny it and sue you for defamation."

"Sit down." She brought two beers. "This is all off the record." She had to keep herself from jumping right in and asking about Tuesday nights. "Was she a slut?"

Brian shook his head. "Not in a sleeping-with-everyone sense. In a only-dating-guys-with-money sense."

Tombo said, "Soon as she found out Brian's trust fund limited what he got, she was out of there." He drank as though he'd been thirsty for days.

Brian said, "She didn't hide her aspirations. She liked money. She'd grown up poor and was determined to make something of herself. By marrying into it. She got a job at the marina; that's how I met her. Then she started making friends and partying with the crowd."

Maddie asked, "Did she cheat when she was seeing you?"

"Not that I know of."

Tombo said, "She was a user. Of people, I mean, not drugs. She deserved to die."

"Don't say that to a reporter," Brian said. "She prints that, and you'll be a suspect, too."

She hadn't thought of anyone else being involved. "Do you think someone else was on that boat besides Julie and Chase? Could someone have set him up?"

They exchanged glances again, wired together it seemed. "No way to prove if there was," Brian said.

Maddie covered her unease by reaching for a cracker. "What about fingerprints?"

"They checked the boat, but that didn't help. A lot of people went out with Chase. Including me and Tombo. We were working on a campaign with him."

She blinked. "He was going into politics?"

"Not that kind of campaign," Tombo said, grabbing up a handful of the crackers and washing it down with a slug of beer. "A sailing campaign. We were working on tactical strategies and sponsors since Chase wasn't taking money from his daddy. We had to admire him for that." He glanced over at Brian. "Okay, I admired him for that. Having to scrape money together regularly makes me appreciate guys who come from money but do the same."

"Look, I can't help it if I get twenty grand a month," Brian said, "I knew you held it against me." He focused on Maddie again. "Anyway, we met every Tuesday night and Saturday and worked on the particulars. Chase liked to conduct his meetings under sail."

Maddie's chest eased a bit. "Tuesday nights."

"If we weren't participating in regattas, we practiced maneuvers and tactics four or five times a week," Tombo said, helping himself to more crackers. "We'd been doing it for years. Until . . ."

"Yeah, until that," Brian said. "So there were a lot of people on *Chase the Wind* over time. We did rogue sailing weekends, no deodorant, no chicks, no beer—he never let anyone drink while the boat was under sail—just hard sailing. Even then he pushed us like slaves; he'd forget it was supposed to be fun."

"Even if we couldn't drink," Tombo said, upending his bottle. "Can I have another one?"

She got two more beers for them. "Julie met someone

on Tuesday nights. What time did you guys meet?"

Tombo said, "From four to whenever. We sailed for a couple of hours, then retired to Salty's where we could drink."

"So you were always together on Tuesday nights?" she asked, trying not to sound as relieved as she felt.

"Mostly."

That bit of hope faded. "What do you mean, mostly?"

"Sometimes we couldn't make it on Tuesdays. Why?"

"Why couldn't you meet?" she asked.

Brian shrugged. "Sometimes Chase had something else going on. I didn't ask what it was; I'm not his girlfriend. Maybe he was hooking up with Lila."

Maddie didn't want to think about that.

"Or one of us had something going on," Tombo said. " 'Member that time I was so hungover from that birthday party, I couldn't even think of sailing the next day?"

Brian frowned. "How could I forget? Who do you think you yakked all over?"

"Can you pinpoint which Tuesdays he canceled?" Maddie interrupted.

"That was months ago," Brian said. "I can't remember. Can you?"

Tombo shook his head. "They say drinking numbs your memory. I think they're right. I can't even remember what I did last weekend."

"What about the last night . . . when it all happened?"

"We went for a sail, went over some sponsorship possibilities, that kind of thing," Brian said. "Chase was dark that night. In a mood. He'd probably had a snarl with his dad. Always tension between them. Allister likes to control his sons, and Chase wouldn't be controlled. When Chase pursued solo racing, without the company's sponsorship, it got ugly between them again. They must have had it out that day. We cut the meeting short and went to Salty's."

"And got trashed," Tombo said with a grin. "Got into this whole discussion about parental control, then the usual argument about legalizing pot. I'm for it," he said with another grin. "Chase isn't. Wasn't. Anyway, he said he was going to crash on his boat, since it was right there and all. Surprised he didn't just live on it. I would if I could afford a boat like that. That was the last time we saw him."

"And you didn't see Julie anywhere?"

"Nope, but like I said, we were pretty zoned. Nobody saw her, though. The police questioned everyone who was there that night, trying to pin down that she and Chase were having some kind of affair. Julie didn't hang out at Salty's once she started seeing Patrick. She kept herself pretty discreet when she went to the boat that night."

"Could she have been meeting someone else there?" Maddie had to find something to latch onto. Her one hope was already dashed. She looked at Brian. "You?"

"Not me." He stood and grabbed his keys. "I had nothing to do with her in the year since we split. But whoever she was seeing, he isn't saying a thing."

She stood, too. "You think it's possible she was meeting someone else there, and that person killed her?"

The two glanced at each other again. Brian said, "Why would they meet at Chase's boat? We've thought about it, believe me. Maybe . . . maybe she showed up, you know, hoping to make a move on him. Maybe she startled him, and he overreacted. Maybe he panicked and figured he'd dispose of her body, took her out there and accidentally fell overboard."

It had come to this, then, that Chase had still killed her and tried to cover it up. "You sound pretty sure he wasn't seeing her."

"He didn't go for brunettes," Tombo said.

"And no matter how much of a hard-ass Chase could be, he was honorable. To steal anyone's girl . . ." Brian shook his head. "He wouldn't have done it."

"I know," Maddie said.

Brian regarded her with curiosity. She'd probably given herself away by being so involved with her "story." Tombo didn't seem to wonder at all; he was too busy grabbing up not only his beer, but the one Brian hadn't drunk. She pretended not to notice.

Brian said, "Better yet, ask him yourself."

She felt her face flush. "What?"

"I don't believe he's dead. I think he's out there somewhere."

Tombo said, "Maybe on a deserted island with a couple of chicks."

Brian kept his eyes on her. "He was too good a sailor to die out there. And I think you know something about it."

"No, I don't," she said too quickly. "The truth is I . . . fell in love with him while reading about him, even farther back than this. And I don't believe he's dead, either. That's all I know."

Brian didn't believe her, that was evident. He nodded at Tombo and they both headed to the door. "Tell him to give us a call when he's ready."

Lila came home at two, took in the empty bed, and no doubt, the look on Maddie's face. "He still isn't back?" When Maddie shook her head, Lila dropped her purse and keys on the chair and sat down on the edge of the bed. "He's gone, isn't he?"

She shook her head, but she couldn't deny that's what the dark cloud hovering over her was implying. "He wouldn't just . . . leave me like this."

"You don't really know him. You might think you do, but you don't."

She didn't even know herself anymore. "I don't believe

he would do this. He was determined to find out what had happened and face the consequences. Would the Chase you knew have run?"

"I've been thinking about it all evening. Chase was . . . well, you know, *is* a good man. He was an honest sailor, he was fair with the people who crewed for him, even if he did ride them hard. But he won a lot, too, so they couldn't complain too much. But if he still has even the slightest love of freedom and sailing, he won't stand being locked up. Especially for something he doesn't remember doing. I know he didn't kill Julie on purpose, no matter how bad it looks. But the evidence points to first-degree murder. If I was faced with that decision, to turn myself in or run . . . I would run." She smoothed her long hair back, raw honesty on her face. "His father has money and connections. He's going to get Chase another identity. And Chase will probably hitch a ride on some boat leaving for the islands—probably already has—and disappear. He'll be one of those guys who lives out of his bag, going from boat to boat. He'll be happy, and he'll be free."

"You really think he'd do that? And leave us to wonder?"

"I don't wonder. If he's gone, that's where he is. Telling us would complicate things. It's for the best, Maddie. You're sweet to believe the best of everyone, but it doesn't always work that way."

"I'm calling Allister," Maddie said, starting to get up.

"He won't tell you anything. He's a stubborn man, more stubborn than you could ever imagine being. He's respected in this community, and he wants to keep it that way. He'll do whatever it takes to protect his and Chase's reputations. Especially now that the whole Julie thing has died in the public's mind."

Maddie narrowed her eyes. "Do you know something about this?"

"No, honestly I don't. But I watched a seventy-foot Italian sloop sail off into the night and wondered if he was on it."

"But my car is gone."

"He'll get it back to you."

Maddie sank down onto the bed. "I don't believe he'd leave without saying goodbye." *Like he did last time.*

"He always did hate goodbyes. Maybe he was too ashamed to face us. But I'd rather he be out there on a boat somewhere than sitting in jail. Wouldn't you?"

She looked at Lila, her pretty face serious and devoted. But she couldn't answer.

"You're young," Lila said. "Being idealistic is understandable at your age."

"I'm not young. I'm twenty-six."

Lila looked surprised. "I thought you were about nineteen. But you're still an idealist. In the real world, people do what they have to do to survive."

The moment the door clicked shut behind Lila the next morning, Maddie woke to a silent apartment and felt profoundly alone. The silence seemed to throb in the room, then she realized it was only the refrigerator. The smell of coffee drifted through the air, the last remnants of life other than herself. She stared at the bed again, as though somehow she could have missed him lying there, maybe covered in the sheets.

He'd left. Lila believed it, but Maddie couldn't. In the same way she knew Chase hadn't killed Julie, no matter what his memories told him, she knew he hadn't left. Wayne hadn't led him to her to have it end like this.

But as one hour stretched into two, that hope stretched thin. She wanted to be there when Chase returned, but the word *if* crept through her mind.

"He didn't leave without saying goodbye," she told herself, the spoken words somewhat fortifying. But they only lasted so long until they faded away.

She did the next best thing: she called Mom. Just the sound of her voice broke Maddie down, but she forced a smile and said, "Hi, it's Maddie."

"Are you still in Miami? Are you all right? You don't sound all right."

"I'm fine." But her voice gave her away again, cracking on the last word.

"Where's Chase?"

"I . . . don't know."

"That's it, we're coming down."

"No, I don't want you to do that."

Mom got the huffy tone in her voice. "Well, we're coming anyway."

"I just called to say hi, see how everyone was doing."

"You called because you need us. You're just too stubborn to admit it."

She curled up on the chair, hugging her knees with one arm. "I wanted to hear your voice, that's all. To know you all are okay."

"Colleen and Bobby are still separated, I've got gnomes all over the house, Q cries all the time, but no one can bring themselves to tell him what's going on, and your father and I, well, we're hanging in there because we have to."

"Because that's what you've always done."

"And we'll keep doing it. We've got to keep this family together. That includes you."

"I just need a little more time here, to sort things out." Her voice was sliding toward tears, even though she kept swallowing hard to keep them at bay.

"You're crying! Let us come to you. I don't want you driving all the way back here by yourself. We'll fly into Miami and drive back together."

The tears started coming fast now. "I can't. Not yet."

"Baby, tell me what's going on this instant."

"I'm Maddie, Mom. I'm not Baby . . ." And to prove the point, she starting out-and-out crying.

"Baby, let us make everything all right again."

It was tempting to give in and let them take care of everything. Like she always had. Families stuck together, that's what Mom always said.

"Tell us where you are. Don't you know Miami's a haven of crime?"

They took care of each other. They kept her from sinking completely into despair, kept her from facing Wayne's death, kept her from healing from it. Kept her from taking chances and making things right for herself. She gathered her ragged breath and shoved the tears from her eyes with her fist.

"I gotta go," she whispered. "I love you." She hung up before she blurted out for them to come save her.

She pushed herself out of the chair and took a deep breath. No way was she leaving Miami without finding out what happened to Chase. And she knew exactly where to start.

CHAPTER 20

"YOU CAN'T KEEP me hostage here," Chase said, pacing in front of the barred window.

Allister sat in the brocade chair in the corner of the room. "It'll only be for another day or so."

"And then what? Force me to take somebody else's identity so you can sweep me under the rug?"

Allister walked over to Chase. "You think I *want* to send you away?" Chase could see the agony on Allister's face and hated that he'd put it there. "Aren't you the least appreciative of what I'm doing for you? It's for your own good. I couldn't have you out there getting caught. You're my son. I love you. I've done everything I could for you. Let you sail when you should have been working at the company I've sacrificed to build. Sponsored your sailboat so you could enter the big races. Now I'm giving you the chance for a new life. Yet, you turn your back on me. I'd hoped you'd changed since losing your memory. That at least you'd be reasonable."

"And hide from my responsibilities? Is that what you taught me?"

Allister was thoughtful for a moment, running a cigarette beneath his nose. "Yes, I'm afraid I have. You got into trouble, and I bailed you out. But now's not the time to get moral on me, son. Save yourself the shame and criminal treatment. If you can't tolerate sparing yourself, think of your family and the company. I don't want anything to endanger the government contracts I've cultivated over the years, the ones that keep us prosperous."

"So you're encouraging me to be a coward and run."

"For all of us. You think I want you to disappear again? Do you know how hard it was when I thought I'd lost my younger son?"

"Doesn't it bother you that I killed someone?"

Allister's expression darkened, and he looked out the window. "It was an accident, a terrible accident. And Chase is going to die for it."

Chase had been in this room for a whole day now, after the two brutes who'd tossed him in the trunk had escorted him here. His fear had transformed instantly to anger when he saw the house.

"How long are you going to keep me here?"

"Until all the paperwork is in order. You'll soon be Gregory Miles. I hope that by the time everything is set, you'll have come to your senses about this being the right thing to do. No sense in wasting your life and reputation. Won't bring her back."

"And if I don't see the wisdom?"

Allister patted Chase's shoulder. "You will. You're my son, even if you don't remember all the years we've spent together. For all that I've done, I ask this one thing. In time you'll come to realize it's the only solution. Until then we'll get to know each other again."

"Who are the two guys who grabbed me?"

"My bodyguards. Trained in all the arts," he added with a warning look.

Chase already knew their force. He was still bruised from his struggles with them. He wanted to pound the wall, to tell him he'd never agree to run like a coward. But he knew it would serve him better to stay silent. "Why do you have bodyguards? You're in the aerospace industry, not drugs. Or are you?"

Allister laughed. "No, I'm not into anything illegal. I was mugged a few months ago. When a man has worked as hard as I have, and is now at the point in his life where he can enjoy the fruits of his labor, he's not about to let some senseless act take it away."

As angry as he was, Chase was still compelled to ask, "Were you hurt?"

"Broken rib was the worst of it." He smiled. "Thank you for asking."

Chase didn't point out that two bodyguards was overkill. Something else concerned him more. "I need to talk to Maddie. She'll be worried."

"I'm going to take care of that now."

"What do you mean?"

"She called yesterday, asking if I'd seen you. I told her no, but later realized it serves me better to tell her the truth. Well, part of it."

Chase's chest felt tight. "That I ran?"

"She won't worry about you, which should make you feel better. And she won't stay around, not when you're already hundreds of miles away with no intention of looking back."

Chase clenched his fists and turned to the window again. A white yacht was gliding across the smooth water, its windows reflecting the sun. He didn't want Maddie to think him a coward, but maybe it was better. Then she'd go home. How long could she keep her faith in him when it kept looking worse and worse? His stomach clenched at the thought of losing her. It was for the best.

"All right."

A knock sounded on the door, then Eduardo's voice. "Señor Augustine, Missus Schaeffer is here."

"Eduardo will escort her to her car." Allister's expression softened. "I love you, son. You'll see that I'm right."

He paused before opening the door. "Any message for her?"

"Tell her . . ." *I love her, I want her, I hate doing this to her.* "No message."

When the lock clicked back into place, Chase pressed his hands against the warm glass. Did he love her? Want her? He wasn't even sure what love felt like. All he knew was every time he thought about her, he felt warm inside. And every time he thought about not seeing her again, he felt as cold as he had in that dream with the icebergs.

This was all wrong. The way he felt about Maddie, going on the run. His father thought he was doing the right thing in protecting his son. But every time he thought about running, he saw Maddie's face and knew he couldn't do it. For Maddie he had to do the right thing. Even if she didn't know about it.

Allister pressed the keys into Maddie's hand. "I'm sorry, but he left no message. Know he's safe and happy. In the end, it's for the best."

She tried to hide the fact that her insides were caving in. No message, no goodbye. He was gone, just like that. "When did he leave?"

"Yesterday."

"Where . . ." She let the words die, because she knew he wouldn't tell her.

The man standing in the shadows behind Allister had somehow lost his neck in his quest for bulk. He was almost hidden by the tall oriental pot, but his presence was undeniable.

"Eduardo will take you to your car. I know you care about my son, but I care about him more. I did what I had to do to convince him of what was best. You'll come to realize too that Chase on the run is better than Chase in jail."

Well, hadn't she thought that? Hadn't she asked him to come back with her and pretend he didn't know about his past? But that had been running with her, not away from her.

Eduardo came to her side and led her to a black Maserati.

"He's in that house somewhere, isn't he?" she asked once they left the grounds.

Eduardo trained his gaze on the road. "No, he isn't."

"Was that beefcake in the shadows going to keep me in line if I tried to search the house?"

That at least got a grin out of him. "Perhaps." He glanced down at her. "But you even I could take."

"So I guess that blows my plan to subdue you and get Chase's whereabouts. You know where he is, don't you?"

"Gone," was all he'd commit to.

"I used to watch *Miami Vice*. I thought only drug lords had guys like that lurking around."

"Someone tried to mug him. That happens in Miami, you know."

"Yeah, a real haven of crime," she said on a sigh.

He pulled into an apartment complex with all the majesty of the mansion she'd just left.

And there her car sat, alone and abandoned. Like herself.

"Do you think Chase killed that woman?"

He started to say something, then changed his mind. "No, but it doesn't matter what I think, because the police, they will think he did. That is what counts. Goodbye, Missus Schaeffer."

She looked up at the building, presumably where Patrick lived. "Do you think Patrick could have killed her in a jealous rage, because he thought she was seeing Chase? You saw that rage two days ago."

He blinked in surprise at her accusation. "No, I do not think that. Now, go. Go home, Missus Schaeffer."

If Chase hadn't contacted her by tomorrow, she'd go. But she couldn't let go of this, not yet.

Maddie had become Julie's friend. Actually what she'd become was a pretty good liar. Julie, she'd found out, used to hang out in South Beach before she'd discovered the yachting crowd. Particularly, she loved hanging out at a place called The Dive, where scuba gear adorned the walls, along with pictures of underwater scenery and stuffed fish.

A man walked by the bar, his thong bathing suit showing off a perfectly bronzed butt.

"Julie would've loved that one," Sally said. "She was a butt girl, know what I mean? Well, you probably do."

"Yep, sure do. It's just too damned bad she isn't here to enjoy it."

The bar was situated for people-watching, along the sidewalk and across the street from the beach. But Maddie wasn't here to watch people or bronzed butts. She'd started talking to the bartender and got the attention of another woman sitting at the bar. Sally had been a friend of Julie's. Maddie had introduced herself as someone who'd known Julie through Patrick.

"Did she come back here a lot?" Maddie asked. "She used to talk about partying here."

Sally took a swig of her vivid pink drink. "She hadn't come to see me in two years." She turned to Maddie. "What kind of friend is that, anyway?"

"Not a very good one."

"Once she started dating those yachties, she got too good for us."

"What'd she think, those sailing people were better than you?"

Sally slumped lower in her seat. "I guess so. She didn't even like sailing!"

"She didn't?"

"No." Sally stirred the slush with her little umbrella and searched the sidewalk. "Said she hated going on out sailboats. She dated a guy before Patrick who was into sailing, tried to teach her how to do it. 'It's boring,' " she imitated. " 'He spent all his time climbing all over the boat doing stuff, and you have to move around or shift or duck. I want my man to be paying attention to me, not the boat.' " Sally laughed. "She always did like to be the center of attention."

"Yeah, she did." Maddie pretended to search for more thongs as Sally was doing, but her mind was working.

"And you wanna know the worst part?" Sally drained her drink and set it on the battered table with a thud. "You wanna know?"

"Yeah, I wanna know."

"She used to come to this part of town, and she wouldn't even come see me. How 'bout that?"

"Really?" Maddie took another sip of her own drink, which had melted to the consistency of Kool-Aid. "What was she doing?"

"Don't know." Sally's big green eyes looked loose in their sockets as she scanned the room. "Didn't you hear me? She never talked to me."

"Oh, right."

Maybe she'd been seeing someone else. "Was it on Tuesday nights?"

Sally shook her head, sending curls flying everywhere. "Nope."

Maddie waited, then prompted her. "So when was it?"

"Every Wednesday afternoon, for at least a couple months."

"Did you see where she went?"

"Two streets over. Least that's where I saw her car come from. But did she stop? Noooooo."

"I've got to go."

Sally grabbed her arm. "You gonna come back and visit once in a while?"

"Yeah, sure."

Maddie cruised down the street that housed everything from restaurants to cheap apartments. She thought about asking every business employee if they'd seen Julie, but that seemed impractical. Particularly since some of the businesses, and the people hanging around them, were a bit on the seamy side. Her mother would have screaming meemies if she knew Maddie was driving down this street.

She *was* brave enough to go to Augustine Aerospace to see Patrick, who wasn't pleased at all to see her. He met her in the lobby and led her outside.

"What do you want?"

"Do you know where Chase is?"

Anger flashed through his blue eyes, but he simply said, "No."

It was worth a shot. "What was Julie doing in South Beach every Wednesday?"

"What are you talking about?"

"Julie went to South Beach every Wednesday before she . . . died. Do you know what she was doing?"

His puzzlement seemed genuine. "I didn't know she was going—wait a minute. How do you know about this? What are you up to, anyway?"

"I'm trying to find out what really happened that night."

He gave her a contemptuous look. "Oh, I get it. You're trying to smear Julie's name so Chase won't look so bad. Well, everyone knows she came from the bad section of town, that she spent a lot of time in bars before working at the marina, and that she was interested in upping her way of life. What, you think I didn't know she was keen on marrying into my family for the money? Sure, I knew, and as long as she was willing to sign the prenuptial—which she was—I was fine with that. She was exciting, great in bed, and she thought I was the freaking king."

Freaking. A Chase word, Maddie thought, feeling the sudden sting of his loss. "If she thought you were the king, why would she cheat on you?"

Her words stung Patrick, who turned away for a moment. "I'm sure Chase appealed to her in a different way. Women went for that dangerous aura. They thought sailing was romantic and daring."

"But Julie didn't like sailing."

"How do you know that?"

"I talked to a friend of hers. Why would she be attracted to Chase if she didn't like sailing?"

When he didn't answer, she said, "Was Chase really like that? Would he stab you so soundly in the back?"

"Julie wasn't seeing someone else. I know what people think of her, that she was a fortune hunter. But she wasn't like that with me." He ran his fingers rapidly through his hair. "She wanted to see me succeed for both of us. She was always telling me to stand up for myself, to ask my father for more power in the company. She encouraged me when it had nothing to do with money.

"When I offered her a choice of honeymoon spots, including the Riviera, Paris, or Greece, you know where she picked? The Bahamas, a place one-fifth the cost. She never picked the most expensive thing on the menu. Far from it. I had to make her order lobster, because I knew she wanted it. She said it was too much to spend on dinner. She didn't drink anymore. That was the Julie I knew. She made a mistake with Chase, a mistake that cost her her life. But if she was going to South Beach, it wasn't to do anything illicit. It was probably to visit old friends."

Again he ran his fingers back through his hair, a gesture of his frustration, Maddie guessed. "What I do know is I hate myself for giving in to my father's wishes and letting Chase get away with murder. Julie would have been ashamed of me for backing down . . . again." His shame transformed to a hard edge. "If he didn't leave . . . or if he comes back to see you, I'm going to turn him in. Let the consequences be damned."

"Didn't think you'd still be here," Lila said when she walked in that evening with a bag of groceries.

"If he hasn't come back by tomorrow, I guess I won't have much choice but to leave."

Lila gave her a pitying look that Maddie hated. "If he hasn't come back by now . . ."

"Julie was seeing someone every Wednesday in South Beach. How can I find out who?"

"Beats me."

Maddie helped her unload the groceries, planning to leave her money for food. "If she was seeing someone else, they might have—"

"You just don't give up, do you?"

"No, I don't."

"You're grasping at straws. It doesn't change the fact that Julie was found on Chase's boat and that he was on the boat that night. Unless you can prove that someone else was on the boat, and I don't know how you could, Chase still looks guilty."

Maddie leaned against the counter, feeling logic drag her down. "But why was she on the boat? That's what we need to find out. If she wasn't seeing him . . ."

Lila was shaking her head. "Maddie, we both love Chase. We know he didn't mean to kill Julie. It was an accident. I don't blame Chase for leaving, and neither should you. I'm sure it was a hard decision. But he's gone. Let's get something to eat."

Maddie glanced at the phone.

"He's not going to call while we're gone, not after almost two days. Come on, let's go."

*   *   *

Maddie woke to another morning without Chase. *Get used to it*. First one morning, then a week, then a month . . .

Lila's long hair swung in a ponytail. "So what's the plan? More snooping around?"

Maddie sighed. "I've hit a brick wall. Even if Julie was seeing someone else—and I kind of doubt she was—it doesn't prove anything. She would have met him in South Beach, not near the sailboat. Patrick said some pretty powerful things about her, how devoted she was to him. I know, blinded by love and all that. But it doesn't add up."

"And if she was after money, Chase wasn't going to get her anywhere," Lila said. "He supported himself with his sailing, but he wasn't rolling in dough. Especially since he'd broken financial ties with Augustine Aero. His apartment is nothing fancy—of course, he was rarely there—and he lived pretty much hand-to-mouth. He liked it that way. What mattered most was *Chase the Wind*. That boat was his passion."

Something nagged at Maddie about that statement, but defeat pressed down on her. "It doesn't add up. If Julie was about to marry into money, why would she risk that by messing with Chase?" She scrubbed her hand through her hair, then realized she'd picked up Patrick's annoying habit. "Even if Chase might possibly have been interested in a brunette, Julie still wasn't his type."

"Maybe they were planning something for Patrick. For his birthday or for the wedding."

Maddie started to grab onto that theory, but shook her head. "Why would she go to Chase? They weren't even close, he and Patrick. From what I can tell, Chase and Julie didn't like each other much. Every time I think I'm getting somewhere, I'm not. Yet, giving up on him . . . well, it's impossible."

"You feel that way now, but believe me, you'll get used to the idea."

Maddie watched Lila's long, tanned legs encased in a body-hugging pair of jean shorts, taut waist, and shimmering blond hair, and thought: *That's Chase's type. Not little ole me. She's the type of woman who turns him on, and if she couldn't get him to settle down, how could I?*

"What's wrong?" Lila asked at the door.

"I think it's time to go home."

She tilted her head. "He'll be back someday. When you least expect it, he'll slide back smooth as Cuervo Gold. Come by Salty's before you take off. I'll buy you a soda."

Lila left, and Maddie turned on the television. Someone else's problems always distracted her from grim thoughts for a while. She stopped at Maury Povich. A mother who changed her sex and then stole her son's girlfriend . . . that ought to do it. She threw her things into her bag, then got into the shower. As the hot water pounded her back, she kept trying to figure out what more she could do to clear Chase.

She thought she heard a noise in the living room. Maybe Lila had forgotten something. She tried to refocus her thoughts, but she'd seen *Psycho* too many times to ignore it.

She quickly dried off, wrapped the towel around her and walked out of the bathroom. And saw someone duck down behind the bar counter in the kitchen.

CHAPTER 21

MADDIE CLUTCHED HER towel tighter, but she couldn't move. This wasn't Sugar Bay, it was Miami. A haven of crime, her mother had said. And there she was without any clothes on. She could hear someone rattling pans under the cabinet. A thief then. Maybe he wouldn't notice her standing there, frozen, wearing nothing but a towel. She glanced around for a weapon. The brass lamp could cause some damage, especially if she surprised him.

She backed toward the end table and put her hands around the base of the lamp. When she pulled it up, it snagged. The electric cord, of course. It was plugged in behind the far side of the couch. With lamp in hand, she climbed across the couch and jerked the plug free. Unfortunately she lost her balance and tumbled backward over the side of the couch and into a large basket of dried flowers. Her gaze went to the kitchen, and she settled on the backup plan: scream.

Luckily the scream stopped in her throat when the thief stood up. "Chase!"

He took in her sprawled position, concern, amusement, and annoyance on his features. "What are you doing here?"

"I'm happy to see you, too." She tried to sound sarcastic, but it hadn't come out that way.

He helped her to her feet and took the lamp from her with a raised eyebrow. "And you were going to do what with this?"

"Hit you over the head. Which I may well do anyway depending on your story."

"I thought you went home."

"That's why you came back? Because you thought I was gone?"

He looked away for a moment, but faced her again. "Yes. Well, sort of."

That did it. She started beating on him, not that she could do much damage. "You just left, without saying goodbye *again*, left me wondering what had happened to you! You sent me right back to a ten on the sad meter! I deserve better than that!"

He tried to still her, grabbing her hands, then her shoulders, and then he was kissing her. It was a hungry kiss that fused her anger into passion. He held her face in his hands, tilting her head, moving closer until their bodies touched. How could he do this to her and strip away her anger? She deserved to be angry, she thought, as he devoured her mouth. No, she deserved to be kissed like this.

Her towel slipped away, and his hands slid down her collarbone to caress her breasts. Everything was all right again, he was there with her, and it was going to be okay. He whispered her name as he kissed down her neck.

He stopped at the crook of her shoulder, pulled her close and squeezed her tight. His cheek rested against the top of her head, and she could feel his breath ruffle her hair.

"We can't . . ." he said, his chest moving against her with his deep breaths.

"No, we can't," she said, but kept kissing him because it was so damn addicting. Her senses returned and she said, "Because we're only friends. And friends don't kiss like this."

"We are just friends, right? You still don't think you love me, do you?"

"No, I don't," she said, fighting the urge to rub her nose.

He was convinced he'd done this terrible thing, she could see it in his eyes, the end.

She gripped his upper arms. "We can find the truth. You're innocent, Chase, I know you are. Just like I knew you wouldn't turn and walk away from me."

"Baby, it doesn't work that way in real life. We don't always find out what happened, and the good guy isn't always innocent. I'm the bad guy in my own story. You're naïve, and I love . . . that about you. Stay with me, and you'll lose that. I won't take you down with me."

"You called me Baby."

He stroked her cheek. "You are still Baby, in some ways."

As good as he felt holding her and touching her, she pushed him away. "You call me Baby when it's convenient to consider me a child. But I'm a woman, a fact you know well, because you helped me grow into that woman." She tried to ignore the fact that she was naked; grabbing up the towel would signify vulnerability. "Tell me what's going on. You owe me that."

He glanced down at her body, then ran his hand back through his mussed hair. He was stalling, considering what to tell her. When he sighed and met her gaze, she knew she was getting the truth. "I was kidnapped."

"What?"

"By my father."

"Is he crazy?"

"Maybe." He shook his head. "He thought he could keep me hidden away until the paperwork was done . . . for my new identity."

She couldn't help smiling. "You didn't leave me."

"I told him not to give you a message. I knew what he was going to tell you when you came to the house. I wanted you to leave, just like he did. But for different reasons."

"To protect me," she said, not smiling now. "So when you came here . . ."

"I thought it was Lila in the shower. I was looking for the key to Lila's dad's boat. She keeps her extra keys in an old pot under the cabinet. I figured I'd hide out there—from my father—until . . ."

"You ran."

"Yeah, until I run." But he made the mistake of rubbing his nose.

"And you're a freakin' liar," she said. "Look, I've been doing some investigating. Julie was up to something. Maybe it had to do with that night."

He shook his head. "And that's going to prove what?"

"I don't know," she had to admit. "But the truth is here somewhere. If we keep looking—"

He picked up the towel and handed it to her. "Why don't you get us breakfast? I'll keep looking for the keys to the boat, we'll go there, and figure things out."

"Oh, no, I'm not letting you out of my sight. Besides, Lila just bought food."

"No more frozen waffles. I won't go anywhere. I promise."

He didn't rub his nose. "If you do, I'll hunt you down like the dog you are."

"Agreed."

She didn't want to leave, but she did. She knew a place right around the corner, and it wouldn't take her but a few minutes to grab something and return.

Chase waited for Maddie to leave, then picked up the phone. He got the number from information, and her mother answered on the third ring.

"Hi, Mrs. Danbury. This is Chase, the guy—"

"Who has brainwashed our girl! She's acting crazy, she won't tell us where she is—"

"I want you to come get her. Get on a plane and get here as soon as you can."

A moment of silence followed, and then, "Why?"

"Because I'm in some trouble here. She's determined to stay with me out of some misguided sense of . . . I don't even know what. I don't want her dragged down with me."

"What'd you do, kill someone?" she asked.

"Yes."

"Holy Moses! We're on a plane. Tell us where you are."

After he hung up, he slumped over the counter. If he were selfish, he'd beg her to stay with him. For her friendship, of course, nothing else. But the only right way to keep her with him was in his dreams.

Maddie burst into the apartment like a mini-commando team. Her eyes went right to him, and relief flooded her face.

He tried to hold back a smile. "Told you I'd stay put."

"Yeah, and you lie." She set the bag on the counter. "And you never did tell me: if your father kidnapped you, how'd you escape?"

"I realized he had to have some kind of escape latch in case of fire, some way to open the bars on the windows. When I got them open, one of Dad's Power Rangers was in the backyard. Then Patrick stormed over, and he and Dad had it out—about me—and then every time I started to climb out of the second-story window, a boat would go by. I fell asleep waiting until this morning when everything was clear."

She hugged him hard, and it was all he could do not to crush her against him.

"Maddie, I didn't come back for you."

Then why had his heart rebounded like a rubber band when he saw her sprawled out in a towel? He'd convinced himself it was for the best that she was gone, then had been relieved to see her there. Yep, he was a liar.

She stepped away, smoothing down her . . . *black* shirt? "You never wear black."

"Saw it in the window yesterday, and I felt black, so I bought it."

The shadows in her big hazel eyes made him want to ask again if she still thought she loved him. He had to admit he wanted a different answer this time.

"She's beautiful," Chase said an hour later when they found *Shades of Heaven*.

"Just don't call it sexy," Maddie muttered. He shot her a look. "Don't ask," she said.

He climbed aboard, then helped her. She bumped against him and grabbed at his waist for balance, but quickly let go of him.

"Wow," Maddie said when they climbed down the steps into the cabin. "Much nicer than the one we built."

Really nice, with polished teak everywhere and all the touches of home. Plenty of head room and seating space, and even a nice-sized dining table. The boat creaked as they explored the cabin. She relished just the simple brush of their arms and the occasional locked gaze. She wanted to drink him in, the arch of his eyebrows and the lines of his face.

Instead, she pushed out the question that had been haunting her since his arrival. "If you didn't come back for me, why are you back?"

"I didn't want to be held against my will. Sounds like the paperwork's going to be ready in a day or so. New Social Security number, driver's license, bank accounts, that kind of thing."

"You're going to run?"

"It's for the best." Just what his father had told her.

"What's your name going to be?"

"John Doe."

"Really? Isn't that too obv—You're kidding, aren't you? You're not going to tell me."

"Nope." He ran his fingers along the edge of the table, in deep thought. Finally he looked up at her. "Do you think I'm a coward for not wanting to face charges?"

"I admired you for being willing to face them, but I don't want you to go to jail because I don't believe you killed Julie."

"I am a coward, Maddie, no better than any other common criminal."

"Why are you trying to convince me of that?"

"Because you're looking at me like . . . how are you looking at me?"

"Not like I love you or anything. But what if I went with you? As a friend, of course."

"No. You have a family, a life. Going on the run with me is going to strip those away from you." He pushed his hair back from his face.

"Then we've got to find out what happened." She'd told him what she'd uncovered, how his being with Julie on the boat didn't make sense.

"But you forget, sweet Maddie, that I remember fighting with her."

"No, you remember fighting someone."

"No one else was on the boat. Unless they fell off, but . . . no, forget it."

"I won't. Remember, I'm Maddiestein now."

She leaned closer, her chest pressing against his. The thought of him out there sailing from island to island tore her apart. She knew running was the wrong thing to do, but if it kept him safe, she didn't care. What bothered her most was that he'd be doing it without her.

"Are you going to leave as soon as the paperwork's ready?"

He took one of her hands in his, then the other, keeping his gaze on them. "Yeah. There's a charter that needs a crewman at one of the other marinas. They're from Seattle, so they won't recognize me. They're sailing for the islands in a day or two, and I've already signed on."

She'd never felt so helpless before . . . no, she had. When Wayne was heading toward the oyster bar. She felt the same crushing sense of disbelief and helplessness. At least Chase wasn't dying. But in a way, he was. He was becoming someone else, and as far as she was concerned, he'd be . . . dead.

He stroked her fingers, gently, as though they would easily break. When he looked up at her, the smoky haze in his eyes nearly made her heart stop.

He asked in a voice that matched his eyes, "How does it feel to love someone the way you loved Wayne?"

She didn't have to think about it; the words spilled out of her. "It's smiling the moment you wake up because he's there. It's feeling a twinge of sadness when he leaves for a while. It's feeling something indescribably warm and tender inside when you look at him. It's relishing even the briefest of touches. And it's knowing you'll do whatever you have to do to make it work." Unfortunately, she wasn't thinking about Wayne when she'd said all that.

Chase absorbed her words, opened his mouth, then closed it. While she waited breathlessly for his response, he surprised her by kissing her. His kiss was slow and sweet, like warm molasses, and she gave herself up to it. The melody for "Bittersweet Symphony" played through her mind as they moved in a dream state. He peeled off first one piece of clothing, then another. Nothing like their first time, that frenzied rush of passion; this time when they made love, it was languid and surreal. Bittersweet.

Afterward, he held her without words, squeezing her against him every so often. His leg was slung over her legs, his arms tight around her. She couldn't see his face, only the curtain of his hair and the curve of his shoulder. She wasn't sure how long they stayed like that. As far as she was concerned, it could last forever.

Forever was cut far short when the sound of voices outside brought Chase to his feet. "Damn, I fell asleep. We'd better get dressed."

"Why?"

He shoved clothes at her, then stepped into his own clothing. "I'm going to leave you behind, Maddie. Forget about you. I have to, have to forget about everything I ever was. It's the only way I can get through. I'm going to leave without saying goodbye, because I hate saying goodbye. And just to make sure you don't try one of your Maddie-stein stunts . . ."

Chase climbed up the companionway, then motioned someone to come down. She almost expected his father's beefcakes to come down and abduct her. But it was even worse.

Her family had come. And they'd brought their secret weapon.

"Uncle Maddie!" Q yelled as he jumped down the steps and threw himself into her arms. "Mom said you were off . . . bal . . . bal . . . lanced, and I didn't know what that meant, and I was scared."

Maddie squeezed him tight and buried her face in his copper curls. "I'm not off balance. Just . . ." She met Chase's grim face. "Misled."

"Honey, we were so worried about you," Mom said once she'd managed the steps. "And when Chase called and told us . . . well, he said to come right away, so we got your second cousin Peter in Tampa to fly us in his little airplane."

Chase's betrayal burned in her stomach and increased when he handed her mom her bag.

Q's face was bright with excitement. "We saw Matchbox cars, but Grandpa said they was real!"

Maddie tried to smile at him, but her face hurt. Everything hurt. So Chase wanted to send her away. Fine, she'd go. She wasn't going to force her friendship on him anymore.

"We're going to drive back with you," Mom was saying while crushing Maddie in a bear hug.

"But—"

"No buts." Mom steered her to the steps. "If we have to strong-arm you home, we will. You don't want Quigley to see that, do you?"

"It's Q, Grandma," he said, tugging on her pant leg. "And what can't I see?"

"You'll see nothing." Mom glanced at Maddie. "Right, Baby—Maddie?"

She forced herself to look at Chase again. His expression was blank. If he loved her, he'd take her with him. That's how love was, because she'd damned well go with him.

So he didn't love her. Or maybe he didn't know how to love. Then why had he asked how it felt?

She climbed up the steps.

"Thank God you didn't put up a scene," Colleen said from behind her. "The way you've been acting—"

"Off balance, I believe you said," Maddie said.

"That's how you've been acting."

"Where's Bobby?" Maddie asked.

Colleen said, "There wasn't room on the plane."

Mom said, "Let's grab a bite before we head back to Sugar Bay. Is there someplace near here?"

Maddie chose Salty's.

"This is a bar," Mom said when they walked beneath the chickee roof made of palm fronds.

"Maddie," Lila said from behind the bar, question in her eyes.

"This is my family. They've come to take me home."
She debated telling Lila about Chase being on her dad's
boat, but kept it to herself. "This is my friend Lila."

Lila nodded at them and gave Maddie an *Are you okay?*
look.

Maddie nodded a yes, an outright lie, and herded her
family to a back booth near the water. Since it was just
past lunchtime, Salty's was fairly empty. As usual, nobody
mentioned having to fly out and save Maddie from her im-
pertinence. They seemed grateful when the sandwiches
came and no one had to make lame conversation for a few
minutes. As soon as Q finished his grilled cheezer, he
skipped off to the edge of the dock to look at the fish.

"What did Chase tell you?" Maddie said, after giving up
on pretending to eat her blackened grouper sandwich. She
kept seeing that grim look on Chase's face.

Mom said, "Just that he was in trouble. Oh, and that he
was a murderer."

"He didn't kill anyone. He just told you that so you'd
come right away."

"Well, he didn't have to tell us that," Dad said. "We'd
have come anyway."

"No doubt." She surveyed her family, loving them and
annoyed with them at once. They wouldn't understand her
devastation at Chase's betrayal. They'd think he was a coward for running. She had no allies, not even Chase himself.
She looked at Colleen, eager to change the subject. "Have
you and Bobby worked things out?"

"Found all those trash magazines you read," Colleen
said to Maddie instead of answering. "I was storing some
of my gnomes in your closet, and there they were. *En-
quirer, Star . . .*"

"Reading about other people's tragedies made me feel
better when I was ignoring my life. Some woman having
an alien baby had to be worse than me losing my husband.

You can always convince yourself things aren't so bad when you read those or watch *Sally*. And we're so good at ignoring problems in our family. Does Q know what's going on with you two?"

"No, and he doesn't want to know," Colleen said. "We told him Bobby's remodeling our house, so he has to stay there."

Maddie said, "He's probably scared to death that his family's coming apart and no one's telling him anything. Either get divorced or work it out."

Colleen's shoulders stiffened. "Maddie, I don't know who you think you are—"

"I am a member of this family." She took them all in. "A family that has, including me, had their heads in the sand for much too long. I used to think it was okay to live my life for everyone else. But Chase changed everything—"

"This is all his fault," Mom said. "He's the rotten apple in the barrel."

"And thank goodness. He saved my life in more ways than one. He was the first person to treat me like an adult. Sure, he said some ugly things to me, but they were the best ugly things I've ever heard. He taught me to believe in myself. And no matter what he thinks about himself, I believe in him. He let me think he'd already gone on the run so I'd go home. Calling you here, that proves his honor, much as I hate to admit it."

Mom said, "He did say he didn't want you dragged down with him. He obviously cares a great deal about you."

Colleen said, "Maybe he is your angel."

Maddie didn't want to think about that right then. "He's a good man. He used to have a drinking problem, but he hasn't had a drink since the accident. And in fact, he never drank when he sailed, never . . . ." Her voice trailed off, and her eyes widened. "He never drank while he sailed."

"You said that," Colleen said.

"He was drunk that last night."

"And that's a good thing?" Mom asked.

"Yes! He wouldn't have sailed with her because he'd been drinking. And that son of a bitch isn't going to run! He's going to turn himself in, and he knew I'd stay if he did."

"Maddie, where are you going?" Mom asked as Maddie shoved her way out of the booth and nearly tripped on a chair to get to the bar. "I have never heard her use language like that before."

"Lila! Where's the nearest police station?"

"What's wrong?"

"I'll explain later."

Maddie ran to *Shades of Heaven* without a backward glance at her family. She lost her footing and slid down the steps to the cabin. It only took a minute to know he was gone. She turned and ran to her car.

What if she was too late?

CHAPTER 22

MADDIE PULLED OUT in front of a black car similar to Allister's. She waved an apology, then glanced back to see if Eduardo or Allister were driving. The driver didn't look familiar, so she focused on finding Chase again. She spotted him a half-block from the police station. The sun reflected off his dark hair, reminding her for a moment how it felt between her fingers. Making her forget for a moment that the determined set of his shoulders meant he was indeed going to turn himself in. She pulled up beside him. "Get in the car!"

He didn't even look at her, only tilted his head back and closed his eyes.

"Get in or I run you down!"

"In front of the police station?" he asked, nodding toward a police car pulling out of the parking lot.

"If I have to."

He leaned down into the car. "I thought you were mad at me for bringing your family here."

"I am. Now, do you get in the car or do I go to jail for running you down?"

With an aggravated sigh, he yanked open the door and dropped into the passenger seat. He'd probably been walking since she left the boat. His white cotton shirt was wrinkled, and he smelled like sun-heated male.

"I'm not going to chastise you for lying, since you think

you did it for my own good. I won't even yell at you for bringing my family here."

He watched as she drove past the police station, but said nothing.

"Everyone thinks they know what's right for me. This time I'm listening to my heart, and my heart tells me you're right for me."

He leaned against the door. "How did you know what I was going to do?"

"Your honor gave you away. A man who would go to any lengths to preserve my sense of well-being is not a man who runs away from responsibility."

"Don't give me too much credit. I really did think about taking my father's offer."

"For what, a minute?"

He shrugged. "An hour."

Their gazes met, and she couldn't help but smile. "If you won't believe in yourself, then let me believe in you."

"Maddie . . ."

"If you want to turn yourself in, fine. But I still don't believe you killed Julie—"

"Not on pur—"

"Not at all." She turned back to *Shades of Heaven*. "You never drank when you sailed."

"Okay."

"You didn't. That's what your friends said. So why, when you were drunk that night, would you have sailed with Julie?"

"Lapse of judgment?"

"That boat was your life. I don't think you would have taken the chance."

He started to argue, but shrugged instead. "Good point."

When she'd turned off the car, she grabbed two fistfuls of his shirt. "We're going to go out on the boat tonight and reenact that night, you as Chase, me as Julie."

"I don't know . . ."

"You don't have to know. You said you kept thinking something would trigger your memories. If this doesn't do it, nothing will." That she chanced him becoming the old Chase didn't matter just then.

They were nose to nose when he asked, "Why are you doing this?"

She grinned and used his line. "I'll tell you later."

He recognized his own retort. "All right. But if I remember, and I did kill her, I'm turning myself in. You can't stop me again."

"I won't."

"And you'll go home."

"Let's just take it one step at a time, shall we?"

With Chase tucked away on the boat again, Maddie went back to Salty's to find her confused family.

"We'll just take ourselves a vacation in Miami," Mom said with a lift of her chin when Maddie suggested—nicely—that they go home. "Can't stop us doing that. We'll find a hotel near here and tell you where we're staying. Just in case."

"Call and leave a message with Lila," Maddie said, and got the phone number for the bar on their way out.

"Did you know that Chase was on our table?" Dad said.

"I'm sure he was. Now, go. I have a lot to do. I'll talk to you soon."

She heard Colleen say, "I think an alien has taken over her body."

Maddie headed to *Shades of Heaven*. When she climbed onto the deck, a male voice said, "What are you doing, Maddie?"

She turned to find Patrick standing there, dressed for work, yet looking somewhat rumpled. He ran his hand back through his hair in that agitated manner.

She well remembered his threat that if he saw Chase, he'd turn him in. "Just . . . taking a look at Lila's dad's boat. Before I leave. I'm leaving. Chase is gone, so there's no need to stay if he's gone, right? Right."

His blue eyes narrowed, and he stepped aboard. "He's here, isn't he? That's why you haven't left."

"Didn't you hear me? He's gone."

"He's here." He climbed down into the cabin of the boat. Maddie held her breath and tried to figure out what to do. Trap Patrick in the cabin so he couldn't alert the police? What if he yelled? She could run to get Lila, but she didn't want to leave the two men alone for even that long. Stand there and worry? That was the number one choice.

It seemed he was down there for an hour, though Maddie knew it was probably only a few minutes. Long enough for a lot of things to happen, though Maddie stopped her thoughts after the first scenario.

When Patrick returned to the deck, he wore a mask of defeat. "Why are you so devoted to him?"

She tried not to look relieved. "Probably the same reason you're devoted to Julie."

He conceded with a twist of his mouth. "She wasn't seeing someone in South Beach."

"How do you know?"

"I cleaned out her apartment when she died, and I kept a lot of her paperwork, wallet, that kind of thing. But I hadn't looked through it until now."

Because he was afraid to find something. "And?"

"I found a charge on her credit card for a karate shop down in South Beach. I talked to the instructor. She'd been taking lessons for about two months. No sordid secret."

"She didn't tell you she was taking lessons?"

"She probably wanted to surprise me. She did that sometimes, like taking belly dancing lessons. Stop trying to find something that isn't there."

"So, what are you doing down here?"

He nodded toward the line of windows of the yacht club. "Had lunch with a friend and saw you."

"And figured I was preparing the boat for Chase."

"Exactly."

By the suspicious gleam in his eyes, she knew that he didn't buy that she wasn't. She squinted up at him in the afternoon sun. "He's already gone, thanks to your father."

Patrick ran his hand through his hair and studied the boat. "Then why are you still here?"

"I'm leaving tonight."

Perhaps he saw the loss and betrayal on her expression, because the hardness on his face slipped away. She couldn't hold up to his scrutiny any longer. She walked to Salty's and wondered where Chase was hiding. "Give me a beer," she asked Lila. "I need one."

"That beer was a bad idea," Maddie mumbled as they readied the boat that night.

"How many did you have?" Chase asked.

"Just the one. I was tense after talking to Patrick, and once I got past the first few sips, I felt better."

"Beer buzz," he said.

"Then I was afraid to come back to the boat right away in case Patrick was watching."

"You were drinking a beer while I was crammed beneath the couch cushion."

"I would have rather been under the cushion with you."

They traded a grin and climbed on the boat. As soon as it had gotten dark, Chase had come out with a cap and shades and joined Maddie at Salty's. They'd cleared taking the boat out with Lila and had something to eat at the end of one of the darkened docks.

They could hear the music and conversation going on at Salty's, but the north side of the dock was quiet. On a nearby yacht, Maddie heard the tinkle of ice against glass. Two people were sitting in the dark on the stern enjoying the warm night air.

As he moved soundlessly over the deck, she searched the shadowed nooks and crannies for signs of Patrick. He could be anywhere and she'd never see him. She breathed easier once they motored out of the marina's harbor. After they cleared the moored boats, Chase raised the sails. That's when she saw his face relax, even though he was studying the way the sails moved, adjusting here and there.

"You still have a love for sailing," she said, holding on to the huge steering wheel exactly as he'd instructed.

"Just being out here makes me feel . . . whole."

She sighed, though he couldn't hear it. He was destined to be a sailor, and there was nothing she could do about it. Barnie had told her that sailing never leaves a man, nor does his love for the sea. He'd stopped sailing after a near-fatal accident, but he'd continued to live on his boat.

She looked ahead as they sailed into the darkness. Chase climbed across the deck to the stern and stood behind her. His arms around her made everything in the world okay, at least for a few minutes.

"It's different than being out on a motorboat," she said. "So quiet."

"Nothing in the world like it."

He stayed with her like that, the front of his body pressed against her backside, his hands on the wheel. Similar to the way Wayne held her when he'd sped across the dark Gulf. And yet, so different, because she wasn't petrified and pretending to enjoy herself.

"Ready?" he asked at last.

"I guess." Okay, maybe she was petrified, but for a different reason.

"Don't look so grim. This was your idea."

"I know. And your memories are going to free you, I know it."

But he still didn't let go for a few more minutes. Lila had said he wasn't much of a hugger, and yet, Chase had held her several times like this. She'd also said that Chase was a pretty good kisser, quick and intense. With Maddie, he was slow and intense, turning kissing into lovemaking. And he wasn't just pretty good, he was fantastic, which could only be because she and Chase were meant to kiss.

When they parted so he could set the autopilot, cool air swept up her back and made her acutely aware of his absence.

"There's not much wind tonight," she said.

"Tropical storm's sucked most of it down south."

"Storm?"

He chuckled. "Don't worry, it's not coming here tonight." His humor quickly faded when he said, "All right. Let's do it."

He searched the deck for the right placement. "I was here. No, here. I can remember seeing the chainplate over there." He turned, checked his memory, then turned again. His hair whipped around his face in the wind. "Now I know why I kept my hair short."

"I like it long." The lights on deck cast him in elegant shadows, carving out his features. "But I guess it's not practical for sailing."

He lifted his head and concentrated on something she couldn't see. Then he jumped up to adjust the jib before returning to his position. "What I remember is fighting with someone here." He lifted his arms in a fight stance, acting out the maneuvers. Maddie walked closer now, ready for her role as Julie.

"Me?"

"I don't know. I can't see who I'm fighting, but the person's strong."

"She *was* taking karate lessons. Which makes me wonder why she didn't fight you better. Unless she pushed you overboard."

"But I remember her falling."

Maddie moved up in front of him. "Let's say you *were* fighting me. How were you holding me? What were we doing?"

He fit his hands over her forearms and shifted her to the side. His eyes were closed as he tried to put the pieces together. "It was raining."

"You remember?"

"I can see rain, swells moving the boat. Julie was here, maybe." He moved her to the right. "I was struggling with her here, and then all of a sudden I was going overboard."

"How'd you go overboard? Did someone push you?"

"Don't know." His face was a study in concentration. "It's all kind of jumbled together."

"Go back to when you saw her fall. Where?" Maddie readied herself to portray the fall.

He studied the deck. "Right there."

She laid herself out. "Here?"

"Yeah, exactly."

Not a comfortable position to say the least. "And where were you?"

"Came from here." Chase studied his position again. "I could see the lines there."

"But how could you push her from over there?"

He worked through the sequence of events. "I told you, it's all jumbled together."

She got to her feet. "Someone else was here, Chase. That's the only explanation. *You weren't sailing the boat.* You never sailed when you were drunk, you came onboard to crash, and someone took the boat out. If Julie didn't know how to sail, she was with someone who did. Patrick?"

He was still measuring out distances in his mind.

Her eyes narrowed. "What perfect justice to frame you."

As the boat moved over a gentle swell, something thumped inside the cabin. Chase watched the tinted door of the companionway, then mouthed, "Somebody's down there."

"Patrick," she whispered, moving into his arms. "He was here earlier."

"And he's heard everything we've said. We don't want him to think we suspect him. Just in case . . ." Maddie knew he was remembering Patrick's murderous rage at their first meeting.

Chase moved away and said in a normal voice, "Maddie, I remember. I can see who it was. It's not Patrick."

Patrick watched *Shades of Heaven* sail into the night. Keeping an eye on Maddie was a good idea. He knew she was lying. For some reason, she'd made Chase her cause, and she'd do anything to protect the son of a bitch. He knew that kind of blind devotion well.

Luckily he wasn't that blind where his brother was concerned. Chase had stabbed him in the back, then killed Julie. Not that he'd intended to murder her. He wasn't a killer. When Chase had asked if there was enough hatred between them to inspire Chase to steal Julie away from him, it made him think. No, there hadn't been. In fact, most of the animosity between them was on Patrick's side. But he couldn't refute the evidence, both that Chase had killed Julie and that he was going on the run. Someone had to pay for her murder.

He headed toward his Mercedes. As he turned the corner, he bumped into Lila.

"Patrick? What a surprise seeing you here."

"Great, another Chase groupie. Excuse me."

She'd protested his innocence at Chase's funeral, which Patrick had been ordered to attend. And for nothing, since he wasn't even dead. Well, he wasn't going to get away with murder anymore.

"Wait a minute!" Lila ran to catch up to him. "What are you doing here?"

In the distant lights from the parking lot, Lila looked as beautiful as she had the first time he'd seen her at a picnic. Then her father had brought Chase over, and that was that.

"Afraid I'm going to turn your former husband in? You can't keep covering for him, Lila. How many times was he there for you when you needed him?" This wasn't what he wanted to say to her. She wasn't the issue here, Chase was. Turning Chase in.

The shadow of pain flashed over her features, but instead of retaliating, she reached for his arm. Just the feel of her touch diffused his anger. "Patrick, I wanted to tell you how sorry I was about . . . what happened. At the funeral, I wanted to come over, but you looked at me like you hated me. What did you just call me? A Chase groupie?"

"Isn't it true?" He hated the thickness in his voice and the way he couldn't break free from her hold.

"I'll always love Chase, if that's what you mean. I know you two have had your differences—" As he was going to say something, she put her finger over his mouth. She smelled like gin and lime. "But I want you to listen to me. Your hatred is coloring everything, which is understandable. Listen to your heart, not your head." She placed her hand over his heart, and he could feel her heat right through his shirt. "Chase wouldn't do anything to hurt you. If I thought that, I'd let you call the police right now. If you can't believe him, will you believe me? He's not running. He's trying to find the truth. I think that's what you want, too."

"Yes, that's what I want."

She tugged on his arm. "Please, Patrick? Can we talk?"

CHAPTER 23

MADDIE AND CHASE watched the companionway door slowly open. The silver hair wasn't what she'd expected, nor was Allister's grim face.

"So you know then," he said, climbing out of the companionway.

Her mind scrambled as she put his words together. "You?"

It was as though all his strength had been drained with those four words. Allister dropped to the deck with a sigh. "It was an accident, Chase, you have to believe that. I didn't mean to . . . kill her."

Chase dropped down next to him, though Maddie suspected it was probably because his legs wouldn't hold him. "What are you talking about?"

Maddie sat down next to Chase and took hold of his hand.

Allister took out a cigarette and stuck it in his mouth. He searched for a lighter but found none. "You don't remember what happened?"

Chase shook his head. "We heard someone down below and thought it was Patrick. I didn't want him to know we suspected him, so I pretended to think it was someone else."

"And made me think you'd remembered. If only I'd stayed below . . ." Allister said in defeat. "Let me explain before you make any judgments. One of my bodyguards was about to pick you up on the way to the police." He still gave his son a reprimanding look. "Which would have complicated matters. Then Maddie cut him off and got to you first. At least she talked some sense into you. My boy kept an eye on you, because I didn't want you going to the police again. He reported that Maddie was readying this boat. And I thought, what if you go out on the boat and remember what really happened? It's something I've been afraid of since you returned. So I came aboard before you returned and hid in the aft berth."

Chase squeezed her hand. "Why?"

"Why did I kill her? Or why did I let you take the blame for it?"

"That's a good start."

"You think I'm a terrible person, but you don't know everything. Julie came on to me like a dog in heat. I turned her away at first. I would never hurt my sons. Never. But it had been a long time since . . . well, since a woman had come on to me like that. She said all the right things. I thought, once, and that would be it. But then it became a regular thing, every Tuesday night."

Maddie watched Chase's expression. For a moment, there was relief that he hadn't done this terrible thing. But his father had, and that was almost as bad.

"Why my boat?" Chase asked in a dead voice.

"Her idea. She said she loved sailing, and Patrick wouldn't take her out on a sailboat. You're the only one in the family with a sailboat."

"She hated sailing!" Maddie interjected.

"Her intention wasn't to go sailing with me. It was to kill me."

She had to grab a breath after that statement. She heard Chase inhale deeply as well. The boat glided through the night, and for a moment, the only sound was waves splashing against the hull.

"That can't be true," Chase said.

"Preposterous, isn't it? We'd gone out once before, and she was antsy to go again. I'm not that good with a sailboat anymore, but I can manage one if properly persuaded. She was very persuasive. Manipulative, I believe I told you. It was cloudy that night, but that didn't seem to matter to her. So we took your boat out. Obviously we didn't know you were below. We got a few miles out, dropped the sails, and she laid out a picnic on the aft deck. I'm not a big wine drinker, but she insisted I have a glass. I didn't like the taste of it, but there she was begging me to loosen up and drink with her. I didn't want to drink because the last time I'd had a few drinks . . ." His face reddened. "Nothing happened. I couldn't face that failure again, so I dumped out some of the wine when she wasn't looking. Whatever she put in the wine still got to me."

"She drugged it?" Maddie asked.

"I'm sure she did. Later, she wanted to dance. It started to rain, but she didn't care. I didn't want to seem like an old fuddy-duddy, so I went along instead of insisting we go below."

Maddie could relate to that.

"The boat took a big swell, gliding over it and dropping suddenly. That's when she kicked me, one of those fancy kicks you see in Jackie Chan movies. I wasn't expecting it, and she nearly sent me overboard. I was feeling sluggish, not reacting well. I dropped down to my knees."

"The karate lessons," Maddie said.

Chase brushed his hair back from his face. "But why kill you?"

"Her devotion to Patrick. He must have told her I held him back, because she started yelling how I'd stifled him, how he'd never get anywhere under my thumb. It was then I could see how much she loved him. She had no interest in me, other than to get rid of me. Then Patrick would be in charge of Augustine Aero and inherit my money."

"Was Patrick involved?" Chase asked, then added, "If this is even true."

"She denied he was, said I had him too beaten to even talk back to me, much less kill me. Said she was strong enough for both of them."

"So Julie tried to kick you overboard . . ." Chase said.

"I fought her, of course. She thought I'd consumed more of the wine than I did. But my reactions were still slow. We struggled, though she had some vicious kicks."

"And broke your rib," Chase said.

"Yeah, she did that. You have to understand I was in shock, but I was holding my own. That's when you came up on deck. I could see it in your eyes, that you were drunk and you thought I was hurting her. She played it up, pleading for you to help her, said I was raping her. Your face transformed from disbelief to rage, and you rushed me. I couldn't get the words out fast enough, the truth, before we were the ones struggling. I shoved her, hoping to send her over the side, but she fell on the deck.

"She hit her head, but it only dazed her. She got to her feet, and then I couldn't see her. But I knew she was now in control. I imagine she thought it was the perfect opportunity: get rid of both of us so Patrick would inherit everything. If she was resigned to murder one person, another wasn't going to make much of a difference. So as you pulled me to my feet, she shoved you over the side. You didn't have a chance. You weren't expecting it and you were drunk. I tried to grab for you . . ."

Allister's face had gone white as he remembered, sinking back into moments that were obviously terrifying. His trembling hands gestured as he spoke, as though he were still trying to grab Chase. "But I couldn't. It started raining. I tried to turn the boat around and look for you, but Julie came at me again. She started calling me names, especially when she saw the blood on her forehead. She said I was overbearing because I was impotent. She said I was old and useless. Again, she knew just what to say. The next thing I knew, I had my hands around her throat. I don't know how it even happened. Maybe the boat tilted, and she lost her balance. My fingers were locked around her throat, not even attached to me, not listening to my mind telling them to let go.

"She scratched and kicked, it was all slow motion. And then it was over. I staggered back, thinking she was only passed out, and tried to find you. I looked, Chase. But I lost my bearings, and it was dark, so dark, and I couldn't hear even if you had called out." He wiped his face, now covered in a damp sheen of sweat. "I kept circling, but I had no idea where you'd gone in. An hour went by, me circling, not seeing anything. I shined the spotlight around, but . . . nothing. I had to assume you were gone. That you'd drowned."

"No wonder you looked like you saw a ghost when I walked into your office."

Allister reached out to Chase, taking his face in his hands. "I was happy, so happy you were alive. But I didn't know what you remembered."

Chase removed himself from his father's grip. "How did Julie end up in the water?"

"Once I realized—thought—you were dead, I turned back to Julie. She was still lying there. When I felt for a pulse, I realized . . . I'd killed her. But who was going to believe me? I felt like an impotent old man. I couldn't save you. And she was going to win anyway."

"What about the tainted wine?" Maddie asked. "Wouldn't that be proof?"

"All spilled and washed away by then. What I couldn't figure out is how she intended to get the boat back after I was dead. Something else that made me look suspicious."

Maddie snapped her finger. "Brian taught her! Sally said

her former boyfriend taught her some sailing, though she didn't like it. Maybe it was enough to get her back to the harbor." Both men looked impressed, and she shrugged. "I've been doing a lot of snooping."

Allister laughed humorlessly. "She had it all figured out, I'm sure. I worked damned hard to get where I am. Many years sacrificing for you boys. I've earned my respect. I was cutting back at the factory, enjoying life more. I had recently realized how much money I had amassed. Enough to enjoy every day of my life to the fullest. I'd buried myself in work ever since your mother died, and now I had the chance to grab onto life again. I couldn't face losing everything, including Patrick. He'd think I killed her, too. He'd leave, and I'd have nothing."

"Why the bodyguards?" Chase asked.

"I didn't know if Patrick was involved. In case he was, I had to protect myself. At least until I felt comfortable."

"So you dumped her overboard," Chase said.

"Yes. My plan was to get rid of her body—no one knew I'd been seeing her, and I was sure she hadn't told anyone. I brought the boat back with the running lights off, aiming for the abandoned marine yard. I set the autopilot to send the boat back out to sea and jumped off. I figured they'd find your boat, maybe find her body, but they wouldn't be together. But it didn't work that way. She got caught in that fancy keel of yours."

"And you let them think I had something to do with it," Chase said.

Allister's face colored in shame. "My choices were, give up everything and go to jail for killing a woman or . . . let you take the blame. You were gone, or so I thought. And they couldn't prove anything, so it was only a suspicion that you were involved. I hated doing it, believe me. All my life I've protected you, fixed things. For once you can help me. This was the right way. Preserve Patrick—if he didn't know what she was up to—keep him in the family, and keep my own freedom and respect."

"Then I came back," Chase said, his mouth a firm line.

"And I'm glad you did."

"So glad that you tried to get rid of me again."

"It's the best way, don't you see? For all of us. I can't lose all I've worked so hard for. I'll lose Patrick . . . I'll lose everything. But if you disappear, you live free and so do I. Augustine Aerospace continues to flourish."

Maddie tried to read Chase's expression, a maelstrom of betrayal, uncertainty, and confusion. Her voice was tight when she asked, "You still want him to run? For a crime he didn't commit?"

"It's too late to tell the truth now."

Chase said, "What if I go to the police and tell them what happened?"

Allister's expression hardened. "You could do that. I'm not going to hold you hostage for the rest of your life. But think about this: the reason the police have a warrant out for your arrest on suspicion of murder is because your two friends placed you on *Chase the Wind*. They placed you at the scene of the crime. It's enough to possibly convict you of murder. No one can place me on that boat, and Eduardo has already given me an alibi for that evening."

Maddie said, "Someone had to have seen you with Julie. I know Miami's a big place, but someone saw you two together."

"We were very discreet. And we'd only been meeting for a short time, not long enough for anyone to catch on. No one saw us together." He paused for a moment, his face freezing, before quickly saying, "No one. So it becomes your word against mine. You who are a hothead and have a history of getting into trouble. Your being missing for months doesn't help your case, either. Your amnesia will be considered a ploy. They have enough proof to put you in jail without bond, and you'll have plenty of time to think about the choice you made. I won't be able to help you."

"You son of a bitch!"

Maddie saw a firsthand display of the famous Chase temper when he lunged for Allister. He didn't fight his son; all he did was try to defend himself against Chase's fists.

"Chase, stop!" Maddie screamed, pulling on his shoulder. "Killing him isn't going to help."

When he saw the fear on her face, he jerked away from her and Allister. His face was plum red with rage, his breathing labored. "You can't do this to me."

"I'm sorry," Allister said, gingerly coming to his feet. "But it comes down to either saving you or saving myself, my company and my first son." His breathing was heavy, too. "If you take my offer of a new identity, you can save yourself, too. We can even change your appearance with plastic surgery so you can resume racing. We can make it work out, Chase. You'll have money, freedom, and respect. We all will."

She felt tangled up inside. Allister's pause gave her reason to think that maybe someone *had* seen them together once. If she could find that person . . .

Allister said, "Imagine a life free from responsibility, free from financial worries. A life free."

Chase had been weighing the options and the facts, and he wasn't very optimistic by the look on his face. He'd made his decision. Taking his father's deal was the only sane choice. Maddie could understand that. But to lose him forever . . .

Chase didn't look at either of them. He adjusted the sails and turned the boat back to shore. His face was set in stone, his eyes empty as he searched the horizon.

She wanted to say hateful things to Allister, but none of that would make a difference. He too had made his decision, and in fact, didn't see that what he was making Chase

do was that much of a hardship. Chase would still have his
freedom and sailing, the two things he valued most. "How
long will it take?" she asked Allister. "Getting his identity
and all?"

He didn't meet her eyes at first. "The paperwork is supposed to be delivered in a couple of days. The bank account
is already set up. I've secured a sailboat he can use until
he finds one that suits him. It's for the best, don't you see?"

He wanted her to see. She only shook her head and
looked away. The night air had chilled, or maybe that was
her heart that had dropped several degrees. Chase climbed
to the bow and straightened a kinked line. There was only
one way to free him from this blackmail: find that someone
who had seen Allister and Julie.

"Maddie, I see that determined look on your face. After
tomorrow, Chase will be gone. Forever. You need to be
gone, too."

She turned to see an even more determined look on his
face. "And if I'm not?"

"Don't mess with me, little girl," he said in a low voice.
"I don't want to hurt you, but I won't let you ruin my
plans."

She turned away from him and stared into the darkness.
It was either that or pound on his chest and wail that this
wasn't fair, wasn't any more fair than Wayne dying. But
she wasn't giving up. And that only left one option: proving
Allister had been with Julie.

Chase asked for a few minutes alone with Maddie when
they returned to the marina and secured the boat. He took
her hand and walked her toward one of the small metal
buildings she figured were used for storage.

Before she could say anything once they'd stopped in
the shadows, he said, "I'm sorry I made love with you,
Maddie."

It felt as though he'd punched her in the stomach. "Sorry? Why?"

"Because it makes it harder to say . . . goodbye." He touched her face. "I was being selfish, wanting one last time with you." He looked into the darkness. "I didn't want to run, but now running is my only choice."

"I'm not sorry we made love, Chase. And you don't have to apologize for your decision. But you do have another choice. You could . . . take me with you."

"No, I couldn't. You have a life and a family in Sugar Bay, and I'm not going to let you give that up for me."

"Then move there with me," she whispered, wishing she could see his face.

"Eventually someone will recognize me. I can't take that chance, not when you'll be caught in the crossfire. I thought about it all the way back here, and there's no way out. We're going to say goodbye right here, Maddie. Then I want you to go home."

"But you hate goodbyes." She could hear the tears in her voice, could feel his reaction to them.

"I know." He tightened his hold on her.

"Let's go to the police and take our chances."

"I'm afraid my father's right about what those chances will be. I'm not willing to risk it. I'll be fine, don't worry about me."

"Will you write? Call?"

He was shaking his head. "Forget about me and go on with your life."

"Meet a man, fall in love, have kids," she said for him.

He held her face in his hands, running his thumbs across her cheeks. "Exactly."

"But what if we can find someone who saw your father with Julie?"

"That was months ago. If someone saw them together, they would have come forward by now when her face was in the news. Maddie, don't get yourself hurt by looking around for something you can't find. Remember, my father did kill a woman. I'm afraid if you anger him enough, he might hurt you, too."

She curled her arms around him, holding him as hard as she could. "Let me stay with you until you leave then."

He pushed her away. "We have to let this go now, understand? I'm going to think about you and that guy you're going to fall in love with. You're going to think about me going from port to port, taking love where I can. We're going to go on because we have to. Because we have no choice."

"You'd say anything to get rid of me."

"Only because I love you." At her shocked expression, he quickly added, "Not . . . that kind of love."

She felt her face flush at those words. "Then how do you love me?"

"I'll tell you later."

Like a friend. She released the breath she'd been holding. "You never did tell me what that Portuguese expression meant. The one you called me."

He smiled, or at least she thought he smiled. "*Muida gira*. It means, you're in between the busty broads and the ones who don't rate a second glance. It means cute gal, the kind you want to snuggle up with and never let go. Go home and don't make me worry that you're into trouble." His kiss was hard and quick, and then he stepped back.

"Chase."

He'd started to turn around, but stopped.

"Will you really be happy never loving anyone? I mean *that* kind of loving someone."

"Yeah." She would have believed the resolute darkness in his eyes if he hadn't rubbed his nose. "Bye, Maddie. Have a good life."

He was gone before the panic could even set in, melting

into the shadows behind the small building. Her first instinct was to run after him, but what else could she say? Her second instinct was to call her family. Then she imagined the chaos they'd contribute and how they'd insist on dragging her out of there. She needed some time alone, time to try to imagine her life without Chase, to imagine him with a woman in every port. She walked back to *Shades of Heaven,* climbed down into the cabin, and curled up into a ball on the fore berth.

"Isn't it time to come home with us?" Mom asked when Maddie stopped in where they were having breakfast near the marina the next morning. "We can't afford to stay around here much longer anyway. This town's expensive."

Maddie watched Q pick the tiny pieces of potato out of his corned beef hash. "Look, you guys head on home. Chase needs my help for another day or two. I'll be fine to drive back by myself. It's only about five hours, and it'll give me time to think. I'll call you every hour if that'll make you feel better."

Her mother surprised her. "Don't stop every hour, it'll just make the trip last longer. Take Bobby's cell phone. He's been calling Colleen every few hours, checking on things."

At the mention of his dad's name, Q asked if he could be excused to play an arcade game.

Colleen said, "He says it's weird us not being around."

Maddie asked, "Do you think it's just that he misses you?"

" 'Course he misses his son. Bobby comes over every night to tuck him in."

"Speak of the devil," Mom said when the cell phone chirped.

Colleen answered, then said, "I don't know. I think we're coming back today. Yeah, we'll be careful. No, you don't have to come down here . . . unless you . . . want to."

Maddie could hear Bobby say, "Do you want me to?"

"If you want to."

Maddie grabbed the phone. "Bobby, do you still love Colleen? Answer the question. It's real simple."

She held it to Colleen's ear, but could hear him say, " 'Course I do."

"Colleen, do you still love Bobby?"

"This is ridic—"

"Just answer the question!" The few people in the restaurant turned around, but Maddie leaned forward, donning her best imitation of Colleen's vulture face.

"Yes."

"Bobby, tell her what you need out of this marriage."

He started to protest, but said, "I want to open my own business."

Colleen stiffened, and Maddie said, "What about the gnomes?"

"Yeah, I hate 'em. Maybe you could . . . you know, keep 'em in one room or something."

"Colleen, what do you need? Remember, I'm buying you a pool."

"Maddie, you can't . . ." Colleen frowned at Maddie's vulture look, then said into the phone, "I want you around more. And I want you to stop seeing Wendy."

"There, that wasn't so hard. Bobby puts in his notice, ditches Wendy because now that he can pursue his own dreams, he feels like the man around the house again. He promises he won't work late, and he'll leave time for you and Q. Colleen, you ditch the gnomes, or at least find them their own space. Stop nagging Bobby like he's a kid. Let him wear dirty underwear once in a while. Move back home, give this a try, stop pretending to remodel. . . ." She rolled her eyes. "And if it doesn't work, get a damned divorce and stop dragging it out."

Colleen grabbed the phone. "I don't want a divorce."

Bobby said, "Me, neither."

"Then make it work. Real simple," Maddie said as Colleen walked out of the restaurant, phone in her hand. Full of piss and vinegar, she turned to her parents. "And you two . . . I never thought I'd say this to you, but if you're not happy with each other anymore, get divorced. Same advice applies. Dad wants to open his own business too, he hates your coffee, and you never let him say anything. Dad, you never stick up for yourself. Either be happy together or split, but for God's sake, don't stay together for me."

Mom actually reached out and touched Dad's hand. "We didn't want to do the ugly D-word. It's easier just to co-exist."

"But why? Believe me, now I know about stifling myself for someone else's sake. I've been doing it for all of you my whole life. Letting you baby me, being the weakling. Don't get me wrong, I wanted it that way. It was the only way I knew."

"Well, your dad called me an overbearing mother last night, and I guess . . . well, he's right. A little, maybe."

"Go on," Dad said.

"When you and Colleen move back to your houses, we could . . . work on things. Starting with regular coffee."

Maddie smiled for the first time in what felt like years. "Kewl."

"How long are you going to stay here?" Mom asked Maddie. "I know you're a grown-up and all, but Miami isn't the safest place to be."

"And what about this guy murdering someone?" her dad asked. "We can't just ignore that."

Sure, now they were going to stop ignoring things, just when she wanted them to ignore that one little thing. "Chase didn't hurt anyone. He just told you that to get you here."

Mom asked, "So what's going to happen with you and him?"

"Nothing," Maddie said with forced finality. She pushed away from the table. "I've got to go. I'll call you soon."

"We'd better get going before that storm hits," Mom said, tossing her napkin on her plate.

"Storm?"

"Haven't you heard? There's a storm out there. Looks like it's going to move in tonight, pretty nasty."

Maddie vaguely recalled Chase mentioning a storm the night before. Lila confirmed the storm's threat a half hour later when Maddie stopped at Salty's. Walls of heavy plastic shielded the interior.

Lila was pulling down bottle after bottle from the shelves above. "We're closing early because of the storm. They expected it to stay on a northerly track, but something weatherly happened and nudged it closer to us. We're actually under a hurricane watch right now, though they're saying we're only going to get winds of forty-five, gusting to sixty in places, and a lot of rain. I guess it's moving in pretty fast now."

That explained the flurry of activity as boat owners tied down their boats and accessories.

"Don't worry, Maddie. We're not going to get blown away."

"That's not what I'm worried about." At Lila's puzzled expression, Maddie said, "I'll tell you later," and that made her think of Chase, and that made her start to race out of Salty's before she lost any more time. Her only consolation was that Chase probably wouldn't leave until the storm blew over. Well, hopefully not.

Lila called out, "Why don't we do pizza tonight?"

"All right. I'll see you later."

When Maddie walked outside, a gust of wind blew sand into her eyes. She blinked, covering her face with her hand.

Palm fronds sounded like rain as they shimmered and crackled. The sky was mostly blue, though banks of clouds skidded across the sky at an alarming pace.

A little bit of wind wasn't going to stop her. She'd gotten the picture of Julie from Lila and took advantage of the many boaters being at the marina by asking them if they'd seen her around the marina any Tuesday night. Unfortunately they were all rushed and distracted by their preparations to do more than take a cursory glance and shake their heads.

Her next strategy was to talk to people who knew Allister. She thought about Eduardo, but knew he wouldn't recant his alibi. Too loyal. What about Patrick? Shouldn't he know the truth? And if he did know, maybe he'd be inclined to help her. Maddie remembered his hostility toward her. She was going to have to deal with that porcupine carefully.

Even a hurricane seemed inconsequential compared to everything else going on. Ducking her head, she tore into the rain again. No one was around, now that the storm was moving in. Boats were dark, and the sky was a froth of gray clouds. Wires clanged against masts in an eerie back beat.

It amazed her that the glint of gold caught Maddie's eye as she stepped aboard *Shades of Heaven*. She almost ignored it for the dry cabin, but heck, she was already as wet as she was going to be. The gold, it turned out, was Chase's cross, given to him by Lila. It must have broken off when Chase and his father tussled on the deck. She tucked it into her pocket and climbed down into the cabin. A sheet of heavier rain swept across the deck just as she pulled the hatch door closed. The boat rocked, then shifted. She held on to the table for a moment until it settled into a steadier movement. Rain drummed against the outside of the boat, reverberating throughout the cabin.

Maybe meeting Patrick here hadn't been such a good idea after all. She hadn't counted on the rain moving in quite this early. What if he changed his mind because of it? She couldn't leave now, in case he did show. She pressed her hands together and closed her eyes. He had to show. The storm was expected to pass through the area tonight, and Chase would probably leave in the morning. She looked through the tinted glass cover, but the rain obliterated her view. She'd told Patrick to come down to the cabin, so he'd probably burst through that door any second.

She hoped.

Ten minutes later she also hoped she wasn't going to get sick. Throwing up on Patrick wasn't on her list of ways to engender his help. Meeting him on the boat was definitely not a good idea, not with it rocking and moving, rocking and moving, back and forth . . . She clamped her hand over her mouth and concentrated on something else.

Another twenty minutes passed, and she wondered how long she should wait until deciding she'd been stood up. The sound of the rain had changed. Not changed, exactly, but added a new element, a rushing sound like a waterfall. The water was getting rougher. The storm was obviously getting worse, and maybe that's why Patrick hadn't shown up. The boat constantly shifted now, rolling so hard, she had to grab on to the table. She used it to guide her to the steps. Rain beat an ominous tattoo on the tinted plastic of the hatch door.

Only two things would get her to open that hatch. One was Patrick's arrival. The other was the complete lack of lights at the marina. Beyond the rain-soaked plastic was a darkness that made no sense unless the electricity had gone out. She readied herself to get drenched again, sliding into the bulky jacket hanging in the closet. Wind and rain stung, forcing her to close her eyes against it. She covered her face and blindly climbed out. The boat rocked and sent her sprawling across the cockpit. She tried to face away from the rain, but it seemed to come from all directions. The wind was gusting hard enough to press her against the side of the cockpit.

Her heart picked up a beat. Something was wrong. The boat was moving. Not just rolling and tilting, but moving. But that was impossible. The sails weren't up, and she couldn't hear an engine. Or could she? She forced herself to take a breath and open her eyes.

The electricity hadn't gone out; muted light glowed in the distance. *In the distance?* No, it had to be the rain distorting her senses. She crawled to the edge of the deck, holding on to the safety lines. The furious ocean sped past them.

They were moving.

She and the boat, bouncing against a confused mass of waves, all by themselves. She let out a scream of disbelief and terror.

CHAPTER 24

"I HAVEN'T SAILED in this kind of weather in years!" a man's voice said from behind her.

Maddie swiveled around to find Allister raising one of the smaller sails, the storm jib she thought. He'd bypassed the hari-kari look and gone straight to crazy. "Nothing like riding into the storm to clear a man's mind and remind him his problems aren't that bad after all."

The rain may as well have turned to icy sleet. "What are you doing? There's a hurricane out there!" she screamed over the wind.

He started pulling his way toward her, using wires and lines to keep his balance. "It's not going to become a hurricane until it moves north tomorrow."

She looked behind them, seeing the telltale foam from an unseen engine. Even now she could barely hear it.

Allister jumped down into the cockpit area. "Ah, the beauty of a quiet genset." He cut the engine.

She scrambled away from him, her feet sliding on the deck, fingers numb as she kept holding on to whatever she could find. Unfortunately there wasn't much room to go anywhere. "Stay away from me!"

"Maddie, where are you going to go? Overboard, if you're not careful."

As if to make his point, the boat heeled over as a wave hit it broadside. She lost her hold and fell. Obviously more used to being on a boat under sail, Allister kept his balance. And grabbed her.

She tried to struggle, but he'd taken her by surprise. That combined with the paralyzing fear that she had been about to go overboard sapped her strength. Thunder rocketed through the darkness. She was sure she'd been dropped straight into hell. The seas roiled and foamed all around them, spitting up spindrift like a thousand mad dogs.

"Why are you doing this?" she asked as he maneuvered them to the cockpit.

He looked mad in the cast of the running lights. His silver hair was plastered to his face, and his eyes were eerily peaceful. "You were going to talk to Patrick. I knew what you were going to tell him, and I couldn't take the chance."

She tried not to notice the mixture of pain and resignation on his face. "Patrick knew? About you and Julie?"

His hold lessened slightly, but not enough to elicit hope of escape. "He didn't know I was seeing her, no. But he saw her at the estate one morning. He'd stopped by unexpectedly and caught us together. Luckily she'd only just arrived and pretended she'd been looking for him. He didn't suspect a thing. And he wouldn't, unless you told him your story. Patrick told me you'd called him and wanted to meet here. I told him you were still desperately trying to concoct some alibi for Chase, and that he not waste his time talking to you. Patrick always does what I say."

He seemed calm, holding on to her arm with one hand, the wheel with the other.

"Are you . . . going to kill me?"

"I'm not a murderer, not intentionally. But I'm too close to saving everything to have you throw it off. Tomorrow Chase will leave, you'll be gone, and Patrick will continue to drive Augustine Aero into the future. Nothing will change. It's for the best, don't you see?"

Before she could disagree with him, his hand slid up around her throat. "I'm sorry," he said as his fingers tightened.

She kicked and struggled, but she was no match for his strength. She tried to speak, to plead or reason, but she could barely breathe. He was looking right at her, his face still that mask of regret and resignation. All she could do was look into his eyes and hope the sight of her dying haunted his dreams. Black spots danced in front of her, obliterating Allister's face.

She felt her knees give way, and she tumbled to the cockpit floor in a lifeless heap. Except that she wasn't lifeless. *I'm still thinking. Can I think if I'm dead? Can I be coughing and gasping for breath if I'm dead?*

When she'd gathered in enough air to think rationally again, she looked up at Allister. He was staring at hands still poised in a choking position. The boat tilted, and he staggered toward her. Even while he grabbed on to the edge of the cockpit, he still couldn't tear his gaze away from his hands.

"I can't do it," he said in a voice that barely overrode the sound of the seas around them. "I *am* impotent. Even with so much at stake, I can't do it." Then he looked at her, this time with only resignation in his eyes. Resignation at his failure.

"Because"—she coughed, trying to clear the burning from her throat—"you're not a murderer. You killed Julie in self-defense. That doesn't make you a murderer. And they'll believe you. The police, Patrick . . . they'll believe you."

"What kind of father am I, to let his own son take the blame for something he did? To sleep with his other son's fiancée? You see, no matter what, everything is lost. I am a coward."

Maddie pulled herself to her feet. "Then do something about it! You can still make this right."

He stared past her, a blank look in his eyes. Maddie couldn't see much beyond the confines of the boat for the blinding rain. Land was lost to them, and the wind pushed them faster and farther from hope. Allister spit out water and wiped the rain out of his eyes. He set the autopilot and said, "Go down below."

She slipped and scrambled to the hatch, then climbed inside. Turning to quickly shut it behind her, Allister pushed in behind her, oblivious to her efforts. The relative calm and quiet inside the cabin made her ears ring. She was shivering, as much from being there as from being soaked. But she wasn't ready to give up yet. She started flipping switches to turn on the radio equipment, then saw mounted above the navigation station something that looked like a cellular phone. While he relatched the door, she grabbed for the device. As she frantically searched for the proper buttons, she realized it wasn't a phone at all.

"Give me that." Allister grabbed it from her. "You're not going to give anyone our position, so you don't need the GPS." He opened one of the portholes and threw it out, then took a seat at the navigation table.

Someone spoke over the VHF, giving coordinates in a staticky voice. Allister reached in the folds of his raincoat desperately searching for something. She didn't know what to expect from him now. He finally dug out a pack of cigarettes, lit one and inhaled as though it were his last breath.

"We can still make this all right," Maddie said. "Call for help."

"Yes, it will be all right." Those were the right words, but they sounded dead as they came out of his mouth. He took another deep drag from his cigarette, making Maddie cough. "There's something noble about dying at sea. That's what counts, you know. Nobility. Integrity. Even when Chase disappeared under questionable circumstances, people still regarded him with respect. Fighting a losing battle with Mother Nature is cleansing. It's the only way I can redeem myself. Then I won't have to face that look of betrayal on Chase's face again. Or on Patrick's."

"You're serious," she said through a tightened throat made scratchy by smoke. "About dying out here."

The waves pounded against the boat like a thousand angry mobsters. *We want Maddiestein! Send her out to us!* She blinked, eradicating the voices in her head. *Stay calm,* she told herself, though her stomach wasn't listening. *This isn't happening.* "Okay, call me selfish, but what about me? If you die in a shroud of nobility and mystery, then I die, too."

"I'm sorry."

She was paralyzed by fear and isolation. Worse, she knew next to nothing about sailing, other than the few tidbits Barnie had told her over the years. She shoved her numb hands into her pockets and felt Chase's gold cross. She squeezed it in her palm and prayed, *Help me, God.*

The waves lifted the boat, then dropped it with gut-shattering thuds. They both held on to the wooden handrails above them. Dread mounted, building pressure inside her. Fear rippled across his expression. He had to change his mind. Being pummeled to death wasn't really a good way to die. Or drowning. She swallowed hard just before being thrown against the ladder.

Her stomach lurched as the boat lifted, then dropped into the trough of a wave. They were being hit on all sides; at least it felt that way. Rocked and bumped and crushed under wave after wave. When the boat lifted up even higher than before—she counted the seconds—and then dropped to the side, it sounded as though half the ocean had dumped down onto them. Another wave slammed into their starboard side, pushing the boat over so hard, everything inside, including Maddie and Allister, went flying. She was sure the boat was going to roll completely over. Her body hit the side of the navigation table, and she landed on top of Allister. Part of her brain suggested trying to overpower him, but her aching body reminded her that she probably weighed about half as much as he did.

Books, charts, and other debris showered them. And then for a moment everything went quiet. At least as quiet as it had been, considering the thrashing waves outside. Something round was digging into her hip, and she reached around to dislodge it as he pulled himself out of the heap of books and found his cigarette pack.

She was lying on the VHF radio mike. The cord coiled down from the radio's mounting. Her heart was now firmly lodged in her throat.

Slowly, very slowly, the boat creaked as it righted itself. She held on tight as gravity tried to throw her away from the side of the cabin wall. She pressed the mike to her back.

When she'd gotten used to the relative calm compared to the knockdown, the boat was slammed to its side again. Allister had just gotten himself back into his seat at the table when it hit. He was thrown over the table this time, and Maddie tumbled into a heap beneath the table. She quickly crawled back out again, positioning herself with the mike behind her. She just needed a chance, a few seconds. But with Allister right there, how would she ever hail a mayday? As soon as she uttered anything, he'd snatch it from her and do God-knows-what in retaliation. Sticking her up on deck would be worse than getting beaten up by the waves down here. And besides, she had no idea where they were.

"This is incredible!" he shouted triumphantly, once again retrieving his cigarette and sucking in a breath of it.

"The power, the energy. Now I know why Chase loves risking his life for glory." His eyes were luminescent, and then he was jarred by the boat as it righted itself again.

No sooner had it righted itself when another wave knocked it down again. This time, water gushed in around the hatch. As the boat righted itself again, water poured from the deckhead and drenched them and the navigational table.

"Allister Augustine, wouldn't you like to experience it again?" she asked, watching the sea water drip down over the VHF radio mounted on the wall. "Another time, months from now? If we die out here, you won't be able to. You didn't murder Julie on purpose. Don't you think the police will believe you? Isn't it better that Patrick know she was trying to kill you, and that you had to defend yourself rather than him thinking Chase is a murderer? Rather than him knowing his father is dead and that he took an innocent woman with him? You'll have both Julie's and Maddie Schaeffer's deaths on your head."

"Your death will not be on my head. I took the boat out, and you happened to be on it. There was nothing I could do about it."

Chase was haunted by memories of the moment he realized his father wasn't going to tell the police the truth. *It's for the best* his father's voice echoed, louder than the sound of the rain beating against the window. *The best . . .*

He understood Allister's position, he really did. He had everything to lose. And as Allister explained, Chase had little to lose, especially since he'd already lost his memory—and his identity.

Yet, he couldn't explain the aching loss he felt whenever he thought of Maddie, though hadn't he known he couldn't love her the way she deserved? He felt an aching loss . . . like how she'd described loving someone.

He was back in the room he'd been held hostage in, though this time he wasn't locked in. Until the storm passed, he had no place to go. He didn't want to drag Lila into his problems.

He drifted into an uneasy sleep, dreams of being in a dark maze, then being locked away in a room. Someone was hammering on the window calling, *Chase, wake up!* A dark-haired man with teddy-bear features stood outside the window. *Maddie's in trouble!*

Chase jolted up and stared at the window. Rivers of rain washed down the glass, but no one was out there. Then again, no one *could* be standing out there, because it was two stories up. And now that Chase thought about it, the guy had looked dry. And familiar. Chills sprang up on his body when he recognized the man's face. It was the same guy who'd directed him to Sugar Bay. Wayne Schaeffer.

Chase stumbled down the stairs and found the nearest phone. Lila answered on the third ring. "Where's Maddie?"

"Chase, where are you?"

"My father's house. I need to talk to Maddie."

"She's not here. I don't know what's going on, but she's gone, *Shades of Heaven* is gone, she was going to meet Patrick at the boat, and I don't know what to do!"

"Slow down! What do you mean, she was meeting Patrick?"

"She was going to meet him at the boat."

None of this made sense, especially if Maddie was supposed to be getting ready to leave. "I'll call him."

"Wait! He's . . . here."

It was making less sense by the second.

"Chase?" Patrick said. "Maddie called me earlier and asked me to meet her at *Shades of Heaven*. I mentioned it to Dad, and he said she was still trying to find a loophole to clear you, and I should ignore her. I was going to, but then I thought that maybe you were on the boat, too, so I showed up at the docks. The boat was gone. So I . . . came here."

Chase didn't even bother to hang up, not that he could take a breath for the tightness in his chest. He raced upstairs to his father's wing of the house, but found it empty. Allister had let the bodyguards go that evening before he'd left the house to attend to some matter. Chase started looking through the drawers in his bedroom suite, tossing everything onto the plush carpet. His next stop was the kitchen with its banks of cabinets and drawers. Who else would know where the keys to his yacht were?

"Chase!"

Chase was startled by Patrick's voice bouncing off the marble in the foyer. He nearly skidded across that marble when he raced to the foyer. "What are you doing here?"

"Sounded like there was trouble. I told Lila to stay put in case Maddie called and headed right over. What's going on?"

The boat was gone, the boat was gone. It kept running through Chase's head, that and Wayne's words about Maddie being in trouble. "I need to get on Allister's yacht. Where does he keep the keys?"

Patrick led Chase to the wood-paneled study. He opened the bottom drawer of the built-in bookcase, rifled through assorted pens and keys, and pulled out the keys to the yacht.

"But you can't—" Patrick's words were lost as Chase raced to the back doors and ran through the wind-driven rain to the dock.

Xanadu was lashed tightly to the dock and decked out with bumpers. Chase unlocked the door and walked into the navigation station, following by a heavily breathing Patrick. The yacht was dark, and Chase flipped the array of switches to turn on the lights and equipment.

Channel sixteen was already in use. A woman's voice came through as though from a distance.

"You didn't murder Julie on purpose. Don't you think the police will believe you? Isn't it better that Patrick know she was trying to kill you, and that you had to defend yourself rather than him thinking Chase is a murderer? Rather than him knowing his father is dead and that he took an innocent woman with him? You'll have both Julie's and Maddie Schaeffer's deaths on your head."

"Your death will not be on my head. I took the boat out, and you happened to be on it. There was nothing I could do about it."

His heart nearly exploded at the sound of her voice. "Maddie! And Allister. She's getting him to confess to Julie's murder." But his father's words sent a cold chill down his spine. "He means for them to die out there." Then he heard a crash.

Patrick's face was drenched with rain and colored with confusion. "What the hell is going on, Chase? What do you mean, Dad confessing to Julie's murder?"

Chase grabbed the mike. "Dad, it's Chase. Come in. We need to talk. Over."

Just hearing Chase's voice sent a jolt of warmth through Maddie's chilled body. Unfortunately she couldn't answer because Allister now had the mike. It took everything inside her not to lunge forward and try to wrestle it out of his hands. And thus probably get herself hurt. For now, she had to sit tight and hope his calm, as well as the storm's, would continue.

Not that it was exactly calm out there, but at least the boat hadn't been knocked down in the last several minutes.

"Talk to him," she said in a soft voice.

He stared at the mike clutched in his hand. "I . . . can't."

Another voice, not Chase's, came over the speaker: "People conversing on channel sixteen, this is the U.S. Coast Guard Miami, Florida. We need your position and a description of the vessel. Are you in immediate danger?"

"This is Chase Augustine, Coast Guard. Please stand by. Dad," he said more urgently this time. "We can work this out. Bring the boat back. Everyone knows the truth, but we can work this out. Give us your position. Respond, over."

Allister shot her a hateful look, though Maddie sank in relief that at least Chase would be cleared of Julie's murder. If nothing else came of this, he was free. If nothing else . . . if she died out there.

The boat shook under the constant barrage of waves, and she felt them get lifted up, then dropped again.

"You had the button pressed," he said.

"Yes. So it's over. Now you can be a hero and face the consequences. That's the only way to make it right. *That's* true nobility, not dying out here." She gestured to the boat. "And taking me with you."

Allister turned off the radio just as the Coast Guard officer started talking again.

She pulled herself to her feet. "Show your sons that real men take responsibility for their mistakes. And no matter what, Patrick deserves to know his fiancée was a murderer. Didn't you raise them to respect the truth?"

"I'd rather die out here than face them."

"But why? You have years to make things right with them. Didn't you teach them forgiveness?"

"I taught them how to be good men. Then I let them down."

She knelt at his feet. "We can't die out here. Do you understand me? We can't die!" She grabbed for the mike, but he pushed her back. She lost her balance and fell to the floor.

"It's for the best. A noble death. It's for the best." And he kicked in the radio.

"No!" She threw herself at him, taking advantage of his one-legged stance. The boat had different ideas, though, and they both went tumbling across the cabin. More water poured in from the hatch. It wasn't going to hold much longer. The pressure of the water was making the boat creak and groan.

Allister had taken the brunt of the fall, smacking his head into one of the short walls. He was dazed, blinking to orient himself. Lying next to him was a metal box that looked like a toolbox. She picked it up, closed her eyes, and knocked him in the head with it. The sound of metal against bone made her shudder, and she opened her eyes to see what she'd done. He was out of this world.

She hadn't escaped that last tumble injury-free herself, she realized as she limped back to the navigation table. The radio was cracked and wires hung out. She had to fix it, somehow. She looked through the toolbox, then started going through the cubby holes and drawers looking for pliers. She found something even better: a portable VHF radio.

"Chase!" she yelled into it after fumbling with the dials.

"Maddie, thank God. Are you all right?"

She would have relished the sound of his voice, but she was thrown against the side of the cabin again. "It's pretty rough out here," she managed a moment later.

"I'll bet. Where's my father?"

She glanced over at him. "He's out of the way for now."

"Can you tell me your position? There's a GPS—"

"Gone." She picked up one of the soggy pieces of paper. "And the charts are ruined."

"Why don't you give me some good news?"

"I get seasick."

"Oh, Maddie." He laughed sympathetically. "I've been on another radio with the Coast Guard. They know the situation. They need you to count slowly to five and back again so they can get a fix on your LOS—line of position. They're working on getting an FBI agent in to handle the situation, so hang in there."

She didn't understand, but she counted to five and back anyway.

"Okay, listen to me. The Coast Guard's only going to get a general position on you. They're going to send a cutter out to locate you, but they can't do anything until they have the proper authority onboard because its a hostage situation. And it's going to take some time to find you in this storm anyway. What we need to do is stabilize the boat. Are any of the sails up?"

"A small one. The storm jib, I think."

"You know something about sailing."

She could hear the pride in his voice. "That's about it, though."

"All right, has the boat been knocked down?"

"A few times. Water's coming in from around the hatch."

"Damn. All right, I need you to start the engine. I don't know how much fuel's in the tank, but you need to keep the boat turned into the storm to keep it from getting knocked down again. I don't think you can afford to go through it again. If the autopilot's on, you'll need to turn it off. The engine may not last long. Every time the boat gets lifted out of the water, the engine's going to whine, and eventually it'll burn out. But we've got to take that chance." He told her how to turn on the engine. "You're going to have to go up on deck."

"Are you nuts?" she screamed.

"Look for a life jacket in the cabinet by the companionway. There should be a line with a clip. As soon as you get on deck, clip yourself to the lifeline. You won't get thrown overboard. Then you need to head into the storm. If that doesn't stabilize the boat, we've got a couple of other options, like lashing the tiller or showing less jib."

Maddie looked up the steps and saw the waves pounding

against the hatch. "Are you sure you can't just come save me?"

"I wish to God I could, but not without knowing where you are. I'm afraid you're going to have to save yourself. Hey, remember: you're Maddiestein. You can do anything. Besides . . ." His voice sounded a bit choked. "You can't die out there. I love you."

"You do? Like a friend, or . . . ?"

"Remember when you described how loving Wayne felt? That's how I feel about you."

"Really?"

"Yeah, really."

"That's great, because I wasn't talking about how I felt about Wayne. I was talking about you!"

"Maddie . . ." He cleared his throat. "Let's get you out of there so we can discuss this further. Now get up on deck!"

Fear and love welled up in her throat. Fear of dying wasn't the worst; fear of never seeing Chase again was. She set the radio down and grabbed the life jacket out of the closet. She changed jackets, then climbed the steps and prepared to enter hell again. Because if he loved her, she sure as heck couldn't die now.

As soon as she'd clipped herself to the lifeline, the boat lurched and snapped the line tight. She waited for it to break and send her flying into the foamy water, but it held. With a silent prayer of thanks, she grabbed hold of the wheel. *Into the storm,* she thought, surveying what she could see around her. Which wasn't much. The rain blended with the sea which blended in with the black sky. She leaned over the side and watched the waves coming in from the south, turned off the auto pilot, and turned the boat into them.

She could feel every bruise she'd gotten as she stepped back down into the cabin. Knowing Chase was down there, in a way, kept her going. "It's still rocking pretty bad," she said, not mentioning that her stomach was doing the same.

"Okay, let's work on the storm jib. If it's not helping, let's take it down."

"How do I do that?"

He gave her instructions, and she climbed up the ladder and brought the small sail down. It seemed to take hours as she struggled against the wind. Her fingers were numb, but luckily her brain was nimble as she went through Chase's instructions. The naked mast rocked and shook its standing rigging when she was done. She readjusted the wheel brake and went below.

And couldn't find the radio.

The sound of the storm was louder inside the cabin. Trying not to imagine a huge gash in the side of the boat, she turned to find that the porthole above Allister was open again. And he was awake.

"We'll never make it," he said in that dull voice.

Disbelief swamped her. *"You threw the radio out the window?"*

"It's for the best."

She grabbed him by the shirt. "Then you get us out of here! You know how to sail."

"It's too late."

He wasn't going to help.

"Fine, I'll do it myself."

He tried to grab for her, though his motions were slowed. She took advantage of that and hit him over the head with the box again. He slumped back.

"I've become a violent woman," she said, but fear quickly replaced her anger and shock. Without any communication, how was she going to get this boat back into harbor?

She wasn't, not into the harbor they'd sailed from. Right now she'd take any harbor, any land. The storm was heading north, so what she needed to do was sail the boat into the storm and head toward Florida's coast. Which meant staying up on deck holding on to that wheel. Staying down here wallowing in self-pity sure wasn't going to accomplish anything.

She climbed back up and managed her way back to the wheel. The compass was covered in spray, but she wiped it quickly enough to get a reading. She could barely see through the rain, but she squinted and kept her eyes on the vast gray wall in front of her. As long as the compass maintained an easterly heading, she'd be all right.

It felt like hours, and maybe it was. Every time they lifted up on a wave, the propeller whined. Then the sound was drowned out when the boat dropped again. The boat fought her, but she fought back, and at last the wind and waves started easing up. The rain was a steady, but light flow.

She pried her fingers off the metal tubing of the wheel. The pressure in her chest eased, too. It was still dark, but the boat was beginning to stabilize. She jammed her numb fingers into her pockets and felt the gold cross again. The edges bit into her palm as she squeezed it and thanked God for getting her through the storm. Now all she had to worry about was getting back to land.

And to Chase.

She wanted to believe they'd have a future now that he was cleared of Julie's death. But if sailing was in his blood, she couldn't compete with the mistress of the sea. She pushed aside thoughts of the future and relished the way her body melted in anticipation of being with him again. She had mastered the sea, and she was ready to master her future.

Right after she threw up.

CHAPTER 25

ANOTHER HOUR HAD passed, or Maddie guessed it was an hour. Her watch face was obliterated with steam. She had gone below once to find something warm to put on. She climbed back down into the cabin, not sure what to expect. Allister was sprawled unconscious amid a pile of books and other clutter. She jerked some of the wires out of the radio and tied his hands behind him.

She'd found some old shirts below one of the berths and gratefully changed into three of them before putting on the life jacket again. It was still dark outside, and a rugged wind reminded her that she hadn't completely escaped the storm's reaches. Bands of rain swept through every so often.

When she saw the light in the distance, she was sure it was her imagination. It was coming from the north, bouncing up and down on the seas. Her eyes felt as big as the compass as she watched it come closer. That's all she could do. There was no light to flash, no voice loud enough to penetrate the wind and distance. As it neared, she could make out the red and green lights on the right and left sides.

Please let it be the Coast Guard, she thought as a large yacht came into view. No, too fancy for the Coast Guard. Then she saw a man racing along the front bow yelling something she couldn't hear. But it didn't matter, because her heart had already responded.

"Chase!"

It was too rough yet to tie the boats together. He threw her a line once the boats were lined up and told her to secure it on her end. Then he maneuvered along the rope hand over hand. When he climbed aboard, she threw herself against him so hard, she nearly pushed him back over the side.

"Whoa!" He pulled her hard against him and didn't let go for a long time. He said her name over and over, as though he didn't think he'd ever get a chance to say it to her again.

After the rush of feeling him lessened, she managed to ask, "How'd you know I was out here?"

"First tell me where Allister is."

"Down below," she answered, but she never let go of Chase. "He was pretty out of it last time I went down."

"You're cold." He cradled her face and smiled. "But you're okay, you're really okay."

"And you're here. Guess you're my guardian angel after all."

He shook his head. "You are your own guardian angel, Maddie."

"That's silly."

"Think about it. All those changes you attributed to me . . . you made them. You changed. Nothing I could have said or done would have changed you. Wayne did send me here, but all I did was open your eyes a little. You did the rest."

She suddenly felt light and free inside. "You sound so sure Wayne sent you."

He smiled. "I wasn't sure the guy who sent me to Sugar Bay was Wayne. But when he woke me up tonight and told me you were in trouble, I knew."

A chill washed over her. "Wayne woke you up?"

"In a dream. It was definitely him, the guy in the picture you showed me."

"You're serious?"

"How do you think I found you? I realized that if Wayne had sent me to you to begin with, and if he'd woken me up, then surely, if I believed, he'd lead me to you. And he did."

"There's something else you haven't told me."

"I'll tell you later." He didn't conceal his secret smile. He touched a tender spot on her cheek. "Did my father do this?"

She touched it, too, realizing it must be a bruise. "No, the boat did it. I've probably got an impressive collection of them all over my body."

"Well, we'll just have to see about those," he murmured, kissing her gently.

A horn shattered the moment, bringing her attention back to the fancy yacht circling them. She was surprised to see Patrick leaning out of the doorway. "Coast Guard's on their way," he yelled. "Probably be another two hours."

"What did Patrick say about all this? How did he get involved?" she asked.

Chase squeezed her tighter against him. "I'll tell you all that later. Right now I just want to hold you and enjoy the silence."

She guessed that meant she couldn't ask him about him loving her, and if he could love her more than sailing. He squeezed her tighter and made a soft, satisfied sound. That would have to do for now.

An hour later the seas had calmed enough to lash the sailboat to the yacht. Chase helped Patrick get aboard.

Patrick looked at the hatch door. "I want to see him."

It was the first time Maddie had seen his handsome face without the animosity. Now it was creased with pain. "I'm sorry," was all she could think of to say.

Chase hadn't gone down to see Allister. He told Maddie

he didn't want to leave her alone, even for a minute. But she suspected he just didn't know what to say to the man who had tried to steal his life.

Patrick climbed down into the cabin. He returned a few minutes later, his face white with stress and grief.

"He's still pretty out of it. He keeps mumbling about the nobility of dying at sea."

"Do you know . . . everything?" Maddie asked.

Patrick nodded. "I heard the confession. Chase explained the rest during the ride here. I can't believe it." He looked at Maddie, then at Chase, running his hand repeatedly through his hair. "I'm sorry I didn't believe you. I . . . jumped to conclusions because I wanted to believe the worst of you."

"It's all right. We haven't had the greatest relationship."

Patrick laughed. "No, we haven't. Maybe we can get a fresh start. Since it looks like I'm going to be making most of the financial decisions for a while, maybe I could finance one of your sailing campaigns."

Maddie couldn't help but stiffen. If Chase went through anything like what she'd gone through out there, she never wanted him on a sailboat again, at least not racing around the world, and not alone. But she had no right to say anything, so she bit her lip.

Chase shook Patrick's hand. "I appreciate that." Maddie had started to drift away, and he pulled her back. "But since I can't remember much about campaigning, or racing, I'd better not go that route."

"Are you sure?" Patrick asked, taking the words out of Maddie's mouth.

"Positive."

"Really?"

"Really."

Patrick apparently couldn't believe his landmark gesture was being turned down.

"Do you want to come back to the company? I guess I'm wondering what you're going to do with your life."

"Take it one step at a time. I'll be in touch. He's my father, too, and I'll stand by you during the trial."

Patrick's expression softened. "I appreciate that."

Chase gave Maddie a gentle squeeze against him. "Would you mind keeping an eye on things on this boat? I want to get Maddie aboard *Xanadu* so she can lie down until the Coast Guard arrives."

"Yeah, sure."

Chase helped her get aboard the luxury yacht. Through the tinted glass she could see what looked like a living room. Heaven was a black velvet couch.

She didn't like all these vague references to the future, but she was too much of a coward to ask him what his plans were.

"Patrick couldn't believe you didn't want to accept his offer," she said as he guided her to that full-sized couch.

He chuckled. "Yeah, he was always one for repeating a question over and over again. 'Really? Are you sure?' Comes from years of Dad questioning our decisions."

Maddie halted, pulling him to a stop since their arms were linked around each other. "Wait a minute. What do you mean he was always like that? You don't remember—you *do* remember!" She could tell by the glint in his eyes.

He rocked his hand. "Some of it came back while I was talking to you on the radio, scared to death I'd lost you out there when you didn't answer. More came during the ride here."

"Is that why you were so quiet this past hour?"

"I was thinking about a lot of things, mostly how good it felt to have you back in my arms. That you were the only one who believed in me, including myself. But yeah, that, too."

She turned to face him, her chest feeling like a helium

balloon was being filled inside it. "You told Patrick you still didn't remember."

He lifted his shoulder in the same way she did. "I still need time to think about his and my relationship before I tell him. Maybe we can put the rivalry in the background first."

"And what about you?"

He brushed damp strands of her hair back behind her ears. "I still need to figure out who I am. I'm not used to having an identity yet."

"I know what you mean. Since I met you, I've changed so much. But . . . what are you going to do now? And don't you dare say you'll tell me later."

His laugh was soft and low. He moved closer and cradled her face in his hands. "We're going to find each other. Find out who we are together. All I know is I want you in my life, my *miuda gira*. And if I'm lucky enough that you feel the same, we'll take it from there."

"I guess you're lucky enough."

"Maybe we can start a charter business in Sugar Bay, day trips out to the Gulf. Bring in some tourists."

She took his hand and led him toward the couch. "Let's just start with tonight, okay?"

Anything is possible when it's true love . . .

Second Time Around

Tina Wainscott

When a tragic accident ends Jennie Carmichael's life, her last thoughts were that she never told her boss, private eye Sam Magee, how much she loved him. After all, how could attractive Sam care for his painfully shy, wheelchair-bound assistant? But then a miracle happens. Jennie awakens to find she has been given a second chance . . . until she realizes she's returned to life in the body of Maxine Lizbon—Sam's detested ex-wife who was murdered. Now Maxine's killer is stalking Jennie. And Sam, the one man who can help the most, is the one who least wants to—unless Jennie can show him the love he's always yearned for . . .

"Wainscott has a talent for making unusual situations believable . . . Bravo!" —*Rendezvous*

"A fabulous romantic suspense drama that melts readers' hearts . . . *Second Time Around* is worth reading the first time around, the second time around, and the nth time around." —*Affaire de Coeur*

"Highly satisfying . . . a well-written, romantic, feel-good must read." —*Gothic Journal*

2TA 10/00